ANGUISHED PASSION

"Zoe?" Simon repeated, because the look in her eyes had no warmth; it was a sad, introspective look. "I love you." He tried to take her in his arms, but now her eyes reflected something new and volatile as if she were nearly terrified. She pushed his hands aside and rose to her feet, taking up a white petticoat to shield herself.

"No." She half-gasped, half-groaned the word. She stood a foot or two from him and this vision of her was indelibly printed on Simon's mind. "Simon, don't say that! I don't want you to love me! I don't want to love anyone!"

Now he too scrambled to his feet. A harsh fear tugged at him as he went to her.

"You can't say that! You can't mean it. Not after this. Zoe, you can't lie to me. I know what you felt."

"I'm not denying what I felt. But I know it for exactly what it is. It's a trap. A physical passion that will give me nothing but regrets. I won't be caught in it. I won't!"

SYLVIE SOMMERFIELD

WINTER SEASONS

LEISURE BOOKS **NEW YORK CITY**

*To the loving memory
of my wife,
Sylvie F. Sommerfield*

—John Sommerfield

A LEISURE BOOK®

December 1996

Published by

Dorchester Publishing Co., Inc.
276 Fifth Avenue
New York, NY 10001

Printed in the United States of America.

Prologue

Trudy Marsh grew up in a small Ohio town, trying to obey her mother's injunction to be a lady, which proved the worst possible preparation for the life she was to lead. She was raised in a family that worried too much about what the stiffly religious folk around them thought, and worried too little about the effect that strict conformity would have on Trudy. She turned into a dull, but pretty girl.

In 1856 Trudy was married off to a prudish, cold-hearted, older man who promptly got her with child and then continued to make her life a living hell.

Trudy held her thoughts and her dreams within when she followed the hearse that carried her wretched husband to his grave. But for her and her child, Zoe, life only became more unbearable. The difficulties of a woman alone, raising a child, were monumental, and if Trudy panicked occasionally, it was understandable.

Then Roger Carrigan came into her life like the roll of thunder and lightning. He was tall and handsome. His hair was thick and gold, and his green eyes flashed a fire whose danger Trudy would not recognize until it was too late. He was attracted by Trudy's shy breeding and pale charm, and her face filled with awe of him. He smiled the smile of one who knew his power. She was his for the taking . . . and he took her.

It took another two years, and a son, before she realized what a drastic mistake she had made. But by then she was inexorably caught.

The marriage was ill-fated from the start. There was a violence that filled Roger. He followed only his own dream, without care for those who did not share his vision.

He was unable to compromise or listen to logic, or to thoughts that did not conform to his private philosophy. Before Trudy had given birth to her second child, Zachary, Roger had made the decision to uproot them. They moved again and yet again before the third child—a sweet, shy little girl they named Martha—made room for the fourth, Eli.

Trudy lacked the strength to stand up to Roger, or to his children . . . or to life. Everything was too much for her. When Zoe was thirteen, Roger came home to tell them that he had decided to uproot the family again. He would take them to Colorado. Silver had been discovered there.

When Trudy found out that they were going out to a country of rugged peaks, barren gulches, drunken brawls, and casual death, she simply stopped struggling.

It was a country few women could cope with. For it was a man's world without law and order and without gentleness. It was savage and dramatic and thrilling, but not to Trudy. She would come to hate the wild, untamed land. Her frail spirit needed security, and order. Roger Carrigan had given her neither of these things, only more children.

And so they moved toward another town and another battle they had little chance of winning: a tired, pregnant woman with no spirit left, a thirteen-year-old girl who tried her best to mother her smaller brothers and sister, and a fire-breathing fanatic who cared little for their comfort. Zoe had just begun to learn to hate Roger Carrigan.

Chapter One

1870, Colorado

Simon Tremaine, at sixteen, was already developing into the large sinewy man he would become. He was lean and hard, used to working from sunup to sunset. He wore a well-washed and well-worn shirt that had once been blue, with the sleeves rolled to just above his elbows. It stretched across his back as his arms extended full length to control the horses that drew the wagon containing his family's possessions.

He took some pride in his task; for it was a man's job to guide the huge wagon and the four horses that drew it. He also took pride that his father entrusted the job to him, even though it was against his mother's wishes.

He loved both his parents, but in completely dissimilar ways. He hated disloyal thoughts, but the older he grew the more he wondered about what had drawn his parents together. They were so dissimilar that it continually amazed him.

His father was a large man, a gentle, quiet man. Jessie Tremaine possessed a kind of inner peace that kept him level no matter what situations arose. He spoke little, but when he did, it was after considered thought.

From him Simon inherited his height, a thick shock of pale blond hair, which badly needed to be cut, and the tendency to keep his thoughts to himself. From Irene Tremaine he acquired a pair of smoky gray eyes and a smile that could melt the hardest heart.

Irene was a woman of iron will and possessed a tongue that could flay an adversary. She had been a teacher, and

9

neither she nor Jessie had ever allowed Simon to question how or why they had married, nor why they were on they way to Colorado with the rest of the wealth-seekers.

She had been adamant about Simon learning to read and write. Simon had developed a love for books, although his mother had only brought along one trunkful. He had read them all over and over again. She promised there would be many more once they were settled.

Somehow Simon knew his mother was used to the things money could buy. It showed in the way she corrected his manners and struggled to teach him . . . sometimes against his will.

The long rows of wagons jolted to a halt. Since the sun had risen the wagon train had moved westward across an expanse of plain toward the mountains just ahead. Now it drew to a stop. They would rest the train here tonight and cross the last rugged peak in the morning. It would be a long and tedious affair, but wealth lay beyond the last pass.

Slowly evening fires were lit, and the sounds of laughter and murmured conversations filled the air.

Simon sat beside their fire while his mother ladled large helpings of thick stew for him and his father. He was about to eat when a slender form passed nearby. Zoe Carrigan. He felt the same unwelcome surge of pity every time he saw her, or her brothers and sister. His pity extended to her mother, who seemed a lifeless ghost of a woman. But he knew he'd never reveal this emotion to Zoe, who would only spit back defiance.

Simon wondered why he cared what happened to Zoe Carrigan. Maybe it was because he admired Zoe's resilience and courage. Her stepfather was certainly not one to be admired or respected. No matter how Simon battled his feelings, he continued to worry about her.

He knew her stepfather whipped her often. Yet he sensed that Zoe was somehow beyond Roger's reach. She always seemed to be searching for something Simon couldn't understand; she seemed to hunger for something just beyond her reach.

In a way Zoe's vulnerability touched him. He didn't

know why he wanted to reach out to her. He only knew he did.

Early the next morning Zoe sat on the front seat of the wagon, waiting along with everyone else for the excitement of crossing over the last pass.

She was a slender girl of thirteen with long graceful legs, and a body that was just beginning to bud into womanhood. Her hair was a riotous auburn, but it was her eyes that drew attention. They were filled with distrust and suspicion, but when Simon looked into their depths he was always shaken by the experience. They were gold . . . a tarnished Renaissance gold, and they sparked with a defiance that kept everyone at bay.

Zoe, at the moment, was poised like a bird on a limb, ready to fly. Roger was just finishing the harnessing, and Zoe wanted to scream for him to hurry and be gone. She hated his presence with a passion that often shocked her. He spun about, his attention suddenly on her.

"What're you doin' out of the wagon? Didn't I tell ya to take care of your ma? Zach can drive when the time comes."

"I was just lookin'. I'll get back in . . . Pa." She hated calling him Pa, but her mother insisted. She also hated the way he looked at her. Her dresses were always a size or two too small, for she had to wear them until she absolutely couldn't, and only then could she pass them down to her sister, who wore them until they disintegrated. The dress she wore now was tight across her chest, revealing the gently rounded breasts that at first had pleased her, but now, under Roger's gaze, somehow made her feel shame.

It annoyed Roger that he could never quite intimidate Zoe, that her eyes always met his directly . . . sometimes accusingly. He meant to break her before he was finished and turn her into a docile, obedient daughter.

"Well, I don't want you runnin' around with all these men about. I ain't raisin' you to be no whore like that Cara Jardeen. Don't think I ain't seen you talkin' to her."

Zoe knew that in any confrontation with Roger, she would be the loser, and she wanted desperately to see her

one and only friend. Zach had promised to start the
wagon off so Zoe could enjoy a moment's freedom. She
wanted to walk and talk with Cara.

There was an unnamed ache in Zoe that rose and tore
at her with a wild and savage hunger. She had had it for
a long time now, but she did not know what it was. All
she knew was that she had it.

What this treasure she sought was, she didn't know.
What she wanted didn't go into words easily. It was a dark
thing that moved before her, getting between her and the
light. A fire inside that had the effect of darkness. It was
so deep and so powerful that soon it had to be recognized.

From some distance away Simon watched the confrontation between Zoe and her stepfather. He made a mental
wager on how long Zoe was going to stay put as she had
been told to do. It would be only moments after her stepfather was gone before she would be climbing down from
the wagon.

Whether she liked it or not, Simon was going to speak
to her about her stubbornness. She was asking for trouble. He knew exactly where she was going, just as he knew
her innocence. He almost had to laugh. Zoe was innocent,
but he wasn't. His sharp good looks had already brought
him a few tastes of the pleasures to be found in Stelle's
wagon of soiled doves. If his mother got any inkling of
his nocturnal excursions, there would be hell to pay.

How was anyone supposed to explain to a child like Zoe
why she should stay away from Cara? Again pity filled
him. He knew Zoe was living a life of silent desperation,
but he didn't know what to do about it. Simon was old
enough to want to change the wrongs he saw and young
enough that he didn't know how.

He was irritated with himself. He wasn't Zoe's guard-
ian; he wasn't her brother. He had no business meddling
in her or her family's affairs. He had enough uses for his
energy without getting involved with a child who seemed
to be deliberately heading down a road filled with trouble.

Finally he sighed in disgust. He shouldn't interfere . . .
but he knew he would at the first opportunity. Just as he
knew Zoe would look at him with those strange gold eyes
and discount all his warnings. Zoe had planted her feet

on a road, and it would take no less than an earthquake to move her.

Satisfied that he had cowed Zoe, Roger rode his horse away from his wagon. Now was her chance. She slid down and ran toward the forbidden last wagon, while Zach started their wagon off behind the others.

When Zoe got to the back of the last wagon she called out to Cara, who stuck her head out from behind the canvas cover.

"Zoe! If your pa sees you here, you're going to be in trouble."

"I don't care, and he ain't my pa."

"Wait, I'll come out and walk with you. That way if he goes by the wagons he might not notice us."

Zoe was pleased at this. She and Cara had become a strange pair of friends. Cara was only seventeen. Much older than Zoe's thirteen, yet young in heart. A delicate-looking girl with blond hair and blue eyes that had once been as wide and innocent as Zoe's were now. They were no longer so. She was not exactly unhappy with her life, but she was not happy either. She had lost so many dreams and seen too much along the way.

She often looked at Zoe with an understanding pity in her eyes. She knew what led girls to the position she herself was in, and she knew Zoe was on the road already. She'd seen Roger watch Zoe when she wasn't aware, and she understood the look far better than Zoe ever could.

Simon watched as the wagons moved forward. Then, amid the dust and the cluster of people, he saw Zoe and Cara walking together. Didn't she realize that walking to the top of the pass with a prostitute was like waving a red cape before an already enraged bull?

He couldn't figure out why Zoe kept asking for trouble. She knew her stepfather for the brutal and fanatical man he was. Why didn't Zoe obey him, when obeying him would have made life so much easier? Why did she insist on contradicting every word he said? What was it Zoe was looking for that made her so headstrong and independent? He might have admired those qualities in someone else, but in this situation they scared him to death. Zoe would never bend, but he was sure Roger Carrigan meant to break her.

It was fall, and frost had singed the country. Reds and golds warred with blazes of green and rust, leaving the landscape ablaze with vivid pageantry.

As Zoe and Cara moved along amid all the other walkers, Roger caught sight of them from a distance. He stared in disbelief.

"Zoe Carrigan!" His booming voice drew everyone's attention. Zoe cringed. For one precious moment she had laughed and been happy.

Roger watched her face grow pale, and felt a strange measure of elation and satisfaction. This time he would back Zoe down and master her. He strode toward the two girls and grasped Zoe by the arm, jerking her roughly a few feet away from Cara, who was glaring at him with a dark and knowledgeable frown.

"What's wrong with you?" Cara asked. "Zoe wasn't doing anything wrong." Cara had long ago lost her fear of men . . . and any respect she'd ever had as well.

"Who are you to say what is right or wrong for decent folk?" Roger glared at her.

Cara's eyes met Roger's, and there he saw a cold knowledge. It succeeded in making him even angrier. Women were supposed to be docile, pliable, submissive. Cara was none of these, and she was not in his power.

The air was filled with tension. Simon stood with clenched fists, wanting to come between Zoe and Roger somehow and knowing the only effect he might have would be to make Roger believe something worse about Zoe. Hell, she was just a kid, and her old man was already accusing her of ugly things. What was he going to do as Zoe grew older?

There was a whispered murmur through the crowd, and Simon clenched his jaw until his teeth hurt. He could almost feel Zoe's shame as she cringed from the hate-filled words her stepfather threw at her.

Somehow he had to find a place where he could talk to Zoe alone, and make her understand that she was not to blame. That she was only doing what most girls her age would do. Roger Carrigan was the one who was wrong.

Zoe was so young . . . so . . . so vulnerable.

"You stay away from my daughter," Roger sputtered to Cara, but his eyes no longer met hers.

"Zoe's my friend, and I'm hers."

The fire in Roger's eyes blazed higher. He knew for a certainty that if he pushed Cara any further, words would be said against which he had no defense. He knew she was aware of the frailities in him that he was unsuccessfully battling.

Zoe was still struggling in Roger's grasp. She also knew there was no one who could help her. She struggled, and tears streaked down through the dirt on her cheeks, tears of helpless fury, not of pain. She was beyond pain; she was a seething bundle of rage.

Simon watched them, and was shocked at the tears that stung his eyes. Zoe's pride had been dragged in the dirt, and there was no one to help her pick up the pieces. He was just as shaken by his own emotions.

Why did he care what happened to this strange little girl? If she were his sister he would at least be able to do battle for her. But all he could do was watch the battle and guess at how it would end. Roger dragged Zoe the rest of the way up the hill to their wagon.

Zoe fought spasmodically against that relentless grasp. When they finally stood beside the wagon, he was still holding her against him. His eyes were like broiling fire as he glared down at her.

"From now until we get to town, you are forbidden to speak or go near that girl again. You do and I'll tie you up in the wagon. Do you understand me?"

"No! Why? Why can't I talk to her? I wasn't doin' nuthin' wrong."

"Don't back-talk me. You'll do as you're told."

"I hate you!" The words were out before Zoe could regain her control.

A new rage sparked in his eyes, and he struck her sharply across the face. The blow was solid enough to make her head spin and knock her to the ground. She looked up at him towering over her. Innocence could never know the depth of his emotion. A raw and brutal desire held him. She could see the blackness dance in his eyes, and knew her first real terror. She just didn't know what it was she was afraid of, but it bent her spirit like a young sapling. She bowed her head and began to cry. Anyone who knew Zoe knew that to make her cry was remarkable in itself.

Zoe realized something huge and black loomed between her and Roger Carrigan, but she couldn't understand. Her stepfather's hands were shaking, and she thought she sensed a kind of fear, and that astounded her.

He reached down and gripped her arm, dragging her to her feet.

"Now you get to the wagon. You'll be punished later when I consider what needs doin'. Until then I don't want to see your face outside that wagon. You don't obey me, it will only go harder on you later."

She didn't answer, and finally she wriggled free and raced to their wagon. Shame, disappointment, and a strange new emotion she could not understand tore at her. She wanted to cry, to scream, to lash out at someone or something, but the shadows were too vague. They vanished before her helpless fury like a dark mist.

Chapter Two

That night he used his belt on her, chastising her, curing her of an evil, he said. She stood stoically under the whipping, aware that the younger children were watching in wide-eyed fear. What he couldn't prove to her he was proving to them.

She never wept until she was curled in her blanket; then finally she slept.

But dawn was to bring a whole new fear. Something drastic had happened to her during the night. It was just before dawn when she awakened, and it was with the startling shock that she had wet the bed. She touched herself and then looked at her fingers, and a jolt of terror raced through her. She was bleeding! Oh, God, she thought, I'm going to die!

There was no one she could turn to. Her mother slept an exhausted sleep, and Roger lay beside her. The last person Zoe wanted to waken was her stepfather. Hot tears filled her eyes. She was going to die, and maybe it was because she was what Roger had said: a bad girl. Would God punish her by making her bleed to death? It filled her conscious mind that Roger's God would do just that to teach her to be obedient. She made quick pleading prayers, promising God she would be obedient always if he would just not let her die.

But mild spasmodic cramps gripped her lower abdomen and she could feel the warm flood of moisture. She had to tell someone, she had to have someone help her. Her desperate mind turned to Cara.

She eased herself from the wagon, knowing what would happen if she wakened anyone. Fear lent wings to her feet as she wrapped a blanket around herself and raced barefoot across the distance to Stelle's wagon.

Outside the wagon she swallowed heavily, then called out for Cara. She was afraid to call out too loudly. She shivered in the cold night air and pulled the blanket tighter. She could feel the tiny rivulets of blood trickle down between her thighs, and tears of shame and self-pity glazed her cheeks. She called out again, and Cara's surprised face appeared.

"Zoe! What in tarnation . . . what're you doin' out here this time of morning?" Cara whispered roughly.

"Oh, Cara, you've got to help me. I'm sick . . . I'm dying!"

"Dying? Shoot, girl, you don't look sick to me. How could you be standin' here if you was dyin'?"

"But I am. Pa gave me a whipping last night for walkin' with you. He must have broken something inside me."

"How do you know? Are you in pain?"

"Just . . . just a little . . . but . . ."

"Then how come you think you're dyin'?" Cara's voice was slightly exasperated.

"I am," Zoe moaned. "I'm bleeding." She could not hold the tears back any longer and sobbed in anguish. "I'm bleeding and I'm going to die!"

Cara already had a suspicion of what the problem was, and she felt a tug of sympathy for a little girl who had turned into a woman before she knew what childhood was about.

"Climb in here, Zoe. Me and Stelle will help you. I don't think you're dying. You just need to get cleaned up. This ain't nuthin' that don't happen to all of us."

Zoe was absolutely certain that Cara was lying to her to keep her from crying, but she climbed into the wagon while Cara wakened the other girls and Stelle. Stelle's mouth was grim when she was told what had happened and when she learned that no one had prepared Zoe for this.

They set about efficiently cleaning her up and explained to her what was happening.

When they finally convinced her she was not going to die, they told her some of the basic facts of life. Their embellishments came from experiences Zoe's mother would never have known or been able to speak about. Her frigid upbringing would have forbidden it.

During those quiet dawn hours, Zoe received a brief education. When Zoe went back to her wagon she was a different person.

Of course some of the information she had received had served to confuse her as well. She could have a baby now . . . but the process of getting one was still something of a mystery.

She walked slowly, caught in tumultuous emotions that confused her completely. She had never felt so utterly alone in her life. Despite the loneliness, it never occurred to her to go to her mother. She knew she would be cautioned to be an obedient girl, just as she knew that a multitude of excuses would be made for Roger.

With her blanket wrapped tightly about her and her head bowed, she didn't sense the darker shadow that detached itself from a nearby wagon and moved toward her.

Simon had been restless, so he had climbed out of the wagon for some air. He had seen Zoe as she left Stelle's wagon. She looked like a homeless waif. Her auburn hair had been loosened to flow about her shoulders, and her thin form seemed fragile in the long flannel nightgown. He could feel the utter desolation that emanated from her, and again, a tug of pity mingled with a self-conscious annoyance filled him. There was no reason to speak to her, but he found himself already moving away from his wagon toward her.

If he had a sister or brother, he wouldn't have wanted to see them suffering as Zoe seemed to be.

"Zoe?"

She gave a startled gasp, and in the light of pale gray dawn he saw her frightened eyes. When she recognized him, she seemed to shrink and breathe an audible sigh.

"What are you doing out here this time of night?" Simon continued. "Your pa finds out and he'll be shoutin'."

He watched her eyes grow wary and her chin jut stubbornly.

"You goin' to tell him?"

"Lord, no, Zoe!" he exclaimed in shock. "What would make you think I'd do a thing like that? I'm only tellin' you. You shouldn't make it so easy for him."

"I didn't do nothin'," she said sullenly.

"Sure you did, and you did it on purpose, just to prove he can't beat you down."

"I hate him," Zoe muttered, more to herself than to Simon.

"Most everybody on the train does. Just like they feel sorry for your ma and . . ." He stopped as her eyes flashed.

"I don't need nobody to feel sorry for me! I don't care what folks think about me, and I don't care what you think either, Simon Tremaine." There were tears in her voice that she would die before she would shed. This night had been bad enough for her without his feeling sorry for her.

"Shoot, you sure are touchy, Zoe. I don't feel sorry for you. Half the time you ask for what you get."

"Sure," she said derisively, "I just love to get whipped."

"Then why do you keep buckin' your old man?"

"He ain't—"

"I know, I know. He ain't your pa. Sometimes for a kid that's so smart you're sure dumb."

"You really think I'm smart, Simon?"

"Yeah, until you pull a dumb stunt like walkin' to the top of the hill with Cara. A girl like you don't have no place with ladies like that."

Zoe's defenses came to the fore. Stelle and Cara had befriended her when no one else would. They had walked her from childhood to womanhood. She would not betray that friendship.

"I ain't goin' to turn my back on friends. *I* don't pretend I don't know them in the day, then sneak out to their wagon at night." She looked at him accusingly. "Maybe nobody else saw you, Simon, but I did."

Simon flushed in acute embarrassment and shock. Zoe saw more than what was good for her.

"You wouldn't . . ."

"No, I wouldn't tell your ma and pa. Unless you think you should be talkin' to *my* pa."

He was shocked to think that a little girl was actually blackmailing him into keeping his silence. He felt helpless to reach her, and the helplessness made him angry.

"No wonder your pa gets so fired up at you. You sure are one aggrevatin' kid."

"I ain't no kid," Zoe began. But now her embarrassment matched his. She became silent, and again her head bent and her eyes were shielded from him. A new wave of sympathy filled him.

"Zoe," he began, "I didn't mean to hurt your feelings. I just wanted to tell you how much easier it would be for you if you just tried not to cross your pa so much. Wouldn't it be easier on you if you just stayed out of his way as much as you could?"

"You think so? You think it's easy workin' all day, singing hymns and prayin' half the night, and knowin' everybody is either laughin' or hatin' you?"

"I didn't say it was easy, but you're growin' up. One day you'll get married and get away from all this." He was surprised how much that thought bothered him.

"Married!" Zoe snorted. "The only way I'll ever get married is if a man has more money than he knows how to spend, and I'll show him where to spend it. I ain't ever gonna go hungry again, and I'm going to wear pretty clothes and have perfume of my own. Wait and see." Her tone was belligerent, as if she expected him to laugh.

But he couldn't laugh; he couldn't get a laugh past the lump in his throat.

"You don't believe me," she continued, "but wait and see. No man is going to get me into being a drudge like Ma and me are now. No, sir, if he ain't got money, then he can whistle up a stump. Money is the only thing that's important, and one day I'll have enough money to tell Roger Carrigan what a miserable man he is. I'll take Ma and my brothers and my sister away where he'll never find them, and he can just go preachin' anywhere he wants."

"Zoe, you're thinkin' wrong. You—"

"Don't tell me I'm thinkin' wrong. Look at all these people. Even . . . Pa . . . everybody's runnin' for silver. What for? 'Cause everyone wants to be rich. Well, so do I. And you can mark my words, Simon Tremaine. One day I'll be rich, one way or another. I'll be rich. Just you watch and see."

With these words she spun about and walked away from a stunned and silent Simon.

All that day, to Roger's satisfaction, Zoe was quiet and docile. He was pleased with himself. He had tamed her. He had made her understand that he knew the way and she must follow in strict obedience.

But Zoe was not tamed; she was only introspective, studying her strength and finding something new. She was not a little girl any longer.

It was into Georgetown, Colorado, that Roger Carrigan brought his family the next evening. That night was a long and brutal one as they listened to Trudy's moans of anguish while Roger's latest child struggled to be born too soon to face a cold and empty world. In the end the struggle was useless. The child died. A grave was the harbinger of the life they were beginning in Georgetown.

Chapter Three

Five Years Later

Zoe had been forced, for the past five years, to control her resentment toward her stepfather, while she attended school and worked the balance of her waking hours. Now, nearing the age of eighteen, she hated the drudgery of her life even more than she had as a girl, and she made herself promises. One day she would have the luxury of a quiet minute to herself, the chance to take a walk alone, the opportunity to sleep in a bed that belonged to her and her alone.

Her mother, after their first few months in the mining town, had begun to take in washing, which, within the next few months, fell on Zoe to handle. Her only revenge was to accept washing from Cara and others of Stelle's girls, without Roger's knowledge. It was a small satisfaction she nourished, because her hatred for him tended at times to overwhelm her. Besides that, she secreted the coins away, thinking them a doorway to freedom. Money would be her release from this prison.

Cara and Zoe did not see each other often. Mostly it was when they could slip away and walk up the high hill beyond town and sit on a huge boulder to talk. But in the town Zoe made an assortment of friends.

From the women for whom she washed, she learned many things, like cleanliness, and how to take care of her teeth and hair.

Her brother Zach, now nearing sixteen, was the only person who knew about her extra washing, but he hated his father as much as Zoe did. Zach and Roger had never

reached any point when the child could talk to the man
. . . or when the man would hear. Zoe loved Zach, but she
could see every day in his eyes the knowledge that one
day soon he would leave and never look back.

One day Zoe was fumbling for her shawl behind the
kitchen door when Zach came in.

"Where you goin'?"

"I'm takin' the girls their clothes."

"You can't carry that yourself to a . . . that kind of
house. Pa would skin you."

"I can go and come back before he knows."

"Zoe, he's goin' to whip you again if he hears about you
takin' a wash down there."

"You ain't gonna snitch."

"Me! Lord, Zoe, I ain't ever gonna tell anyone what
you're doin'. Especially him. I wouldn't tell him to close
the door if a flood was comin'. You want me to help you?"

"No. Better one of us in trouble than two. I'll be back
in time to put supper on the table. If he comes, just tell
him I'm deliverin' wash and you don't know to who."

"All right, but you be careful."

"I will." She hoisted the basket to a more comfortable
spot on her hip, opened the door, and left.

At the back door of Stelle's place she set her basket
down and knocked on the door. It was opened by Cara,
and Zoe was let in to a warm, good-smelling kitchen.

"You're frozen, girl," Cara said. "Want something warm
to drink? I got some tea."

"Yes," Zoe replied quickly. When Cara handed her the
cup, she curled her hands about its warmth and sipped
gratefully. At that moment Stelle entered the kitchen. She
saw the basket at once.

"Zoe. You sure been doing a good job on our clothes.
I'm giving you an extra dollar this time."

"No, Stelle, it's still four dollars."

"That don't include delivery. Five dollars and I won't
take no sass." She reached into her pocket, withdrew the
coins, and handed them to Zoe.

"But . . ."

"No sass." Stelle smiled. "Besides, Friday is your birthday. A girl ain't eighteen every day."

Zoe flushed and accepted the coins. Stelle and Cara were probably the only ones who would remember.

"I've got to go," she mumbled hastily, and turned to the door before anyone saw the tears in her eyes. Neither one of the women said anything because they both knew how Zoe would feel about sympathy.

When the door closed behind her, Stelle and Cara looked at each other.

"Poor kid," Stelle said.

"Maybe now," Cara said quietly, "but I think Zoe's smart. She's gonna get away from this someday."

"Yes," Stelle replied slowly. "Providing some man don't tangle her life up." Her look was all Cara needed to understand.

"Well," Cara said with a sigh, "maybe she can outrun him too. She's been doin' it so far."

"She's getting prettier by the day, and that man has a soul blacker than any man he ever hoped to save. 'Save,' " she scoffed. "He's an ugly man, that's for sure. But all his kids are just looking for a way to get away from him. Me, I hope they all make it . . . especially Zoe and that young Zach. That boy is real smart."

"She ain't even his kid, and that scares me. In his twisted mind that might justify him doing whatever he wants."

"God," Stelle breathed, "I hope not."

Zoe walked slowly home, her hand deep in her pocket, still clutching the coins Stelle had given her. She hated to go home to the darkness and the tense atmosphere of Roger's house. She hated to see the look in Roger's eyes as he followed her movements around the kitchen.

The evenings were long as she cared for the others and got them tucked safely into bed, and even longer from then until the time Roger left to attack the fleshpots in town. He would watch her constantly as she finished the last of the chores. She had no intention of preparing for bed while he was still in the house.

So she walked slowly, crossing onto the street where all the little shops were. She couldn't buy, but she liked to look at the dresses that hung there. She looked at them with the same unknowing longing that had plagued her for years.

She was so engrossed in the store window that she didn't hear anyone approach until a quiet, tentative voice spoke from behind her.

"Zoe? Zoe Carrigan?"

Chad King had been standing on the corner of Main Street with several of his friends from school. As is the way of boys of eighteen or so, they were feeling the call of their bodies without having the mental control of men.

They bragged to each other about their prowess with girls, when there was not, in reality, one moment's real experience among the five of them.

Chad was the son of one of the top supervisors at the mine, a man just a few positions down from the owner himself. He lived in a nice house on the right side of the tracks and had enough money to be able to buy what he chose.

Chad was a nice-looking boy, taller than Zoe by a head. His eyes were dark brown, nearly matching the dark brown of his hair.

"Say"—Joey Knight, one of Chad's closest friends, nudged him—"isn't that Zoe Carrigan over there? That loudmouth old man's daughter? The one who pretends he's a preacher?"

Chad's gaze followed Joey's, as did the others, and the same predatory heat lit them all.

"I've heard a lot of stories about her," Carl Stoner said, insinuation deep in his voice.

"Yeah," Joey added, "they say she likes to hang around with Stelle's parlor girls. I'll bet it won't be long until she goes with them."

"She sure is pretty," Brad Ryan agreed with an ugly laugh. "And if she really wants to learn to be a parlor house girl, I don't see why we shouldn't be the ones to help her with her education."

This brought an appreciative and excited laugh to the entire group.

"I couldn't agree with you more," Joey said. "We have an obligation to help her."

"Come on, you guys," Chad said, "you know people just like to talk 'cause they hate her father. Maybe Zoe ain't really like that."

"Then again," Joey said wickedly, "maybe she is. It would sure be interesting to find out."

"Well, there ain't no way to do that," Chad said.

"Sure there is." Brad laughed. "It only takes one of us to get her to agree one time. Then we can all share the fun."

"You sure do talk stupid sometimes, Brad." Chad's voice was cold. "You can't just grab a girl off the street. And wouldn't her old man howl if someone tried."

"You know, you're not too smart, Chad." Brad laughed again. "There's a lot of ways to get a pretty girl like her alone. Then"—he shrugged with a grin—"you can just let nature take its course. I have a hunch she'd be more than willing."

"What ways?"

"Well . . . one of us could invite her to the dance on Friday."

"Sure," Chad said derisively, "can't you just see one of us walking in with her? We'd be laughed out the door."

"Now who says you have to go to the dance . . . at least not right away."

"What?"

"Invite her, pick her up, and take a nice little ride in the country. We'll meet you somewhere and we'll have a real party. I'll bring a bottle and I'll bet Zoe can show us all some fun." Joey smiled.

"And her old man will never know the difference," Brad said.

"I'll bet Zoe's waitin' for someone she can have some real fun with. Hanging around those parlor girls must have given her some pretty hot ideas by now. Hell, she's probably like a bitch in heat, just waitin' for the right chance," Joey added.

The vision his words brought released an erotic sensation that swirled through Chad. Suppose Zoe was as they said. He licked his dry lips, imagining Zoe naked in his arms, giving him freely what he usually dreamed about.

The other four could see the heat growing in Chad, along with the acceptance of their plan. After much denial, argument, and pressure, Chad was the one chosen to entice Zoe to their planned rendezvous.

He inhaled deeply, crossed the street, and spoke her name.

Zoe spun about, unsure of whom she might have to do battle with, but well prepared to do it. She came face-to-face with a boy who was known around Georgetown as one of the catches of the year.

Chad was a little nervous, but Zoe didn't know that his nervousness was caused by the fact that he still wasn't too sure he wanted to do what he was about to do. He came from a well-to-do family, socially accepted by all the better people. And he really didn't want his name connected with Roger Carrigan's daughter. His parents would kill him. But the sensual visions refused to be dismissed. His parents would never have to know, and if it worked out . . . Lord, Zoe would be there all the time to use as a release for his youthful desires. He gazed at her, his imagination rampant. Her burnished hair caught the glow of the sun, and her willowly body, as she walked, stirred the restless desire to a conflagration.

"Hello, Chad." Her voice was warm and friendly.

"What are you doin'?"

"Delivering wash. I'm just going home. I only stopped to look at that dress in the window. Isn't it nice?" She returned her attention momentarily to the window. Still he watched her. What did he care about the dress?

"Yeah, real pretty. Zoe, I wanted to ask you something."

She returned her attention to him. "Ask me something? What?"

Just looking into her eyes caused his body to react in a way that startled him. The palms of his hands were sweaty and he unconsciously rubbed them on his thighs. "There's going to be a dance on Friday."

"Yes, I know. It's the same day as my birthday."

"Well . . . ah . . . I was wondering." He inhaled deeply. "I was wondering if you'd like to go with me? If I come early I can show you my father's new carriage. We could even take a nice ride out in the country for a while . . . before the dance, I mean."

Zoe stood in stunned silence. No one had ever asked her to go anywhere. Could it be possible that for once in her life she was being accepted? Could she find friends beside Cara and Stelle at last? The thought brought a spark of excitement to her eyes that entranced Chad.

"I'd be pleased to go with you, Chad."

"Good," he replied, wanting to conclude their conversation before he was observed. "I'll come for you around seven o'clock."

"That'll be fine." Her heart sang as she watched him walk away. She couldn't wait to tell Cara. But a moment later reality struck. She did not have one dress fine enough to wear to a dance. A choking kind of distress filled her. She had five dollars in her pocket. She needed to go home and count the small tin of coins she had hidden so very carefully.

But it was long after the rest of the family had gone to sleep when she gathered enough courage to slip from her bed, kneel beside it, and draw her small tin can from its hiding place. She took the meager number of coins from the tin can one by one so they would not clink together. She added the five dollars that she had just gotten from Stelle, but no matter how she counted them, it wasn't much. Surely not enough to buy the beautiful dress she'd seen in the window and a pair of shoes to match.

Tomorrow she would go and see just what her few coins would buy. She still had nearly a week to try to scrape together enough. She had to have this chance, this one night.

Fifty dollars . . . Doubts began to batter her courage, but still she clung tenaciously. She had so few joys in life, she couldn't let this chance slip away.

Once the door closed behind Roger the next day, she rushed to get the others off to school. She carried a tray of food to her mother, then hastily grabbed a shawl and rushed toward town.

The clerk in the shop was a polite young man who recognized her.

"Hello, Zoe."

"Hello, Henry. How are you today?"

"Just fine. You sure look pretty today."

"Thanks." Zoe presented one of her rare beautiful smiles.

"You need something, Zoe?"

"Yes, please. How much is that dress in the window? The deep blue one with the lace."

"That one," he said, "is a very good choice. If you want the gloves and the shoes and shawl to match, well . . ." To her delight, he named a sum that she could just afford. "Shall I take it down and wrap it for you?" His voice was cultured and soft, but his eyes and the half smile he wore told Zoe as no spoken words could that he was certain she couldn't buy it.

Zoe smiled the first real smile of satisfaction she'd ever felt. "Yes, I'd like you to wrap it for me, please, and I'll pick out shoes and gloves as well."

Now his smile was warmer, and he looked at her with a look that pleased her. When she took the bundles and left, she was feeling nearly euphoric.

For two days she went about her daily work in a kind of haze. Her face was expressionless and her eyes seemed larger than ever. Roger felt as if he had finally forced Zoe into her proper place. She was docile and made no objection to lengthy prayers at table and before bed.

She rose the third day and began to prepare breakfast. Tonight . . . tonight.

Chapter Four

Zoe had never felt so exuberant or such happiness as she waited out the rest of the day. She had hidden the dress well, not daring even to look at it again. What if it were only a dream? But finally evening came.

Her mother, who was confined to her bed now, was so heavily dosed with laudanum that she would never know if Zoe went out or not.

As on most Fridays and Saturdays, Zach, Martha, and Eli would be forced to go with their father as he stood on street corners and shouted his personal version of the word of God. If she did not find a way out of it, so would Zoe. She had already told Zach her plans with the surety that he would keep her confidences.

Suddenly, Roger walked inside the house and closed the door behind him.

The atmosphere changed, as it always did the minute he came in. Eli put the only toy he had, a small, hand-carved wooden soldier, away in his pocket. Zach seemed to withdraw into himself, and Martha also grew silent. They all waited to see how Roger was going to act.

The table had already been set, so Roger washed at the sink and they all found their seats. He bowed his head and began the blessing.

Zoe could not seem to keep her gaze from drifting to her stepfather. He ate with the slow methodical manner he always used. Food meant little to him, and he was not careful to keep enough on the table to nourish his children.

Tonight, Zoe could hardly swallow down bite after bite. With agonizing slowness the meal came to an end, and

Zoe and Martha began to clear the table and wash the dishes.

"Pa?" Zoe said tentatively. Roger grunted a noncommittal response. "Can I please stay home tonight? Ma is real restless. I might have to give her some more medicine." Her voice died as he turned a piercing gaze on her. She felt as if her heart might stop, and her mouth went dry. She clenched her hands in the folds of her skirt, but kept her eyes on him in an innocent look . . . she hoped.

"All right," he said gruffly, "just for tonight."

Zoe breathed a sigh of relief so deep it hurt. She struggled against impatience and for control.

Just before they left, a very nervous Zach leaned close to his sister. "I wish you hadn't had to lie. I'm scared for you, Zoe, but I really want you to have fun."

"Everything will be all right," she whispered back.

Then they finally left. Zoe turned and rested her back against the closed rough wooden door. Finally! Finally she had the house to herself. The dream began now.

Slowly she undressed, feeling vitally alive for the first time. Naked, she stood in the lamp glow and it turned her sleek, curved, young body to ivory. She soaped her firm body with its length of limb and small high breasts.

She had no way of knowing the eyes that watched her through a crack in the back wall of the kitchen were filled with the torment of illicit lust.

Roger Carrigan licked dry lips as he watched. He had sensed something was happening, and had sent the three children to a neighbor. He knew what it was. His conscience did battle with the need he refused to recognize. In his mind he fought a terrible battle. All that was good in him fought the demon he refused to recognize.

Still, he could not tear his eyes away from the golden beauty washed in the hazy lamplight. Only when Zoe had put on her best petticoat, and had lifted the lovely mist of blue silk over her head and let it slide down her body, did Roger know how he intended to stop her.

He had to punish her. He had to wash his own unrecognized guilt clean in her punishment. He moved from the wall and walked around to the front porch.

Zoe heard a step on the porch, and realized she had

been so absorbed in her finery that she had not realized Chad had arrived. She took up her shawl and draped it about her shoulders. She had no intention of keeping him waiting. The sooner they were away from the house, the safer it would be for the both of them.

She half ran to the door and flung it wide with the exuberance of youth and anticipation . . . and came face-to-face with Roger Carrigan.

They stood looking at each other for a long time, each held by the enormity of the emotions that swirled about them. He wore his old coat; his head was bare, and his hair windblown. Suddenly the always smoldering embers in his eyes burst into flame, and his searing gaze swept over her.

Zoe took a step back, instinctively crossing her hands before her protectively. Step by step she moved away. There was a gleam in his eyes that struck terror to the depths of her. She could only sense the reason for those slowly clenching hands. He followed her across the doorstep and into the room until he had her backed against the farthest wall.

Zoe never took her eyes from him. She could feel her back against the wall, and knew there was no way to escape the retribution those blazing eyes promised.

"Little whore." The voice was raspy and harsh and as she stood frozen, he reached out a huge sinewy hand. A strong, callused hand used to the rough, hard work of the mine. She knew he was going to destroy the dress . . . the beautiful dress . . . and anguish tore at her. The only beautiful thing she had ever owned and he meant to destroy it. She couldn't bear the pain. She was frightened, more than frightened. His eyes were filled with more than her inexperienced mind would ever understand.

"I'll take it off, Pa . . . I'll take it off." Her voice broke on a harsh sob.

"No." His voice seemed to come from a distance. "I'll take it off. I warned you, Zoe . . . now I see I have to make you understand."

Discipline was in his mind, but not in his heart. He was losing control before the haze of red lust that filled him. His hand fastened on the dress and Zoe tried to protect this most valuable of possessions. The dress she had so laboriously saved coin after coin for.

The sound of tearing fabric brought a wrenching cry from her. She fought, but he was stronger, and in minutes the dress lay in fragments about her. She stood only in her thin petticoat.

It was over, she thought. He would most likely whip her, but it didn't matter anymore. Then she looked up into his eyes and realized it was far from over.

His heated gaze was locked on her rigid body, revealed more than concealed by the scrap of silk.

He reached out, gripped her wrist in a hold she could never hope to break, and jerked her forward until she collided against him. She could feel a pulsing heat emanating from his body as they were pressed so intimately to each other.

Then suddenly she felt his arms close about her. His breath was hot as his hard and demanding mouth descended on hers.

His hands were pulling at the silk, caressing her body, drawing her even tighter against him. Paralyzed by the sudden attack, Zoe could not think. Then fear began to well up inside her like a black cloud.

With all the desperation of a trapped wild animal, she began to battle. Roger had lost hold on all reason, and his being was overcome with the hunger he'd battled for so long.

They writhed and jerked in unison as if in a macabre kind of dance, their blended shadows leaping against the walls of the kitchen.

She knew she had to get away, she had to run, or he would possess her in a way that would destroy both her spirit and her soul.

A roaring filled her ears. Something within her screamed silently as if her innocence was breaking along with her heart. She could stand it no longer. Blindly her hands sought a weapon, any weapon. Then her fingers closed on a sharp knife Martha had carelessly forgotten to put away.

She jerked away from him, but he clung to one wrist. Then she raised the knife between them.

"Let me go! Let me go or I will kill you!"

"Zoe," he panted, "let me . . . I must . . ." He was gasping, his eyes wild.

She pushed the knife toward him and with her jaw clenched to keep from screaming, she spoke again. "Let me go!"

Roger blinked, as if a veil had suddenly been lifted. If, in his own agony, he recognized hers, it was many years too late. Their eyes held for what seemed like an eternity. He saw the grief and the tears, and worst of all . . . he saw the hatred, and it was the hatred that loosened his hold.

She backed away from him, with the hate glowing in her eyes, and he stood, unable to stop her. The hate was so tangible Roger could feel the force of it like a wall.

When she was several feet away from him, Zoe turned and ran from the house. She ran, numbed by what had happened. Where could she go? She could not go back! She could not live in the same house with him . . . feel the heat of his eyes on her and know . . . and know that one day he might succeed.

She struggled to protect the remnants of her pride. But she knew shame followed and she had to outrun it. She began to move faster and faster. She was blinded now by tears as she ran. She had no idea where she was going. She only knew she had to put as much distance between her and the shame as she could. Each step, each breath, was accompanied by a promise. She would never be shamed like that again . . . never!

Zoe raced away from the horror, and the eyes of the man who had broken her pride. She didn't know where she was going; in fact the tears that blinded her made her surroundings invisible. She was just as unaware of the wide-eyed stares of the people she passed. She could not go home! She would never go home again!

Her feet sloshed in the half-frozen snow. Her extremities, feet, hands, nose, were the first to warn her that no matter what her misery, she could not remain out in this cold much longer. A sob caught in her throat.

There was no place to go in Georgetown where he couldn't find her. He would drag her home, and who would stop him? She had to have someplace to hide. But where? She sucked in an ice-cold breath that seared her lungs.

Zoe was running again, but now she knew where she was going. Defiance filled her. Many times in the past she had tapped on Cara's window and they had spent stolen minutes talking. Now she was desperate, scared that Cara might not be there. There was a dim light from within. She tapped and when no answer came, she tapped again, louder and more frantic. When the window slid open, Cara gaped in shock. But it didn't take her long to realize what had happened. Obviously the boy who'd taken Zoe to the dance had gotten carried away. She wondered if Zoe was just scared . . . or hurt.

She helped Zoe to climb in the window, and urged her into a nearby chair. Zoe sat on the edge of the chair, clutching her hands together in her lap.

"What's going on, Zoe?" Cara demanded. "That boy got a little too fast for you?"

In a rush Zoe began to talk, and Cara heard a story that made her eyes go cold and her face grim. It was something she had dreaded for years.

For an instant, she was seeing another girl with a too-ripe body and a too-amiable smile who had had no one to care for her.

"You wait here, Zoe. I have an idea. I want to talk to Stelle for a minute." She went out, closing the door carefully after her.

Zoe sat there, lacing and unlacing her fingers. She lost all track of time. Then Cara returned with Stelle, who recognized Zoe's condition at a glance and gave no-nonsense advice.

"We got to get you away from here as fast as we can. The next train will leave tomorrow night," Stelle said.

"You know that . . . her pa does too," Cara cautioned.

"I suppose," Stelle admitted. "Sure as God made little green apples, he'll be there."

"What am I going to do?"

"There has to be another way," Cara said thoughtfully. "Maybe . . . maybe there is." She looked at Zoe. "I think you'd better get a little rest if you can."

"What are you going to do?" Zoe asked.

"I'm gonna go with you."

"Oh, Cara," Zoe sighed. Cara could see she was near collapse. She found some clothes and thrust them at Zoe. "Dress . . . right now!" Her voice held authority, and Zoe blankly obeyed.

The sun was barely over the horizon when Zoe walked to the window to look out on Georgetown on what she hoped would be her last day there. The few tears she cried were for her mother, her sister, and her brothers. But after a few minutes she wiped away the tears. She could not look back or her heart would break, and she could not go back or Roger Carrigan would break her. She could only look ahead. She would not allow the pain inside again. She built a wall of ice around her heart.

She knew now what it took to survive in the world: allow no one near enough to hurt you . . . and find a way to make a very great deal of money, because money was the only protection anyone had. At eighteen she was saying good-bye to all she had known. She knew what she was running from, but had little idea of what she might be running to.

The train was on its way to Aspen. As the engine grunted and puffed, readying itself for the stiff climb ahead, Cara and Zoe breathed their first sighs of relief. By boarding the train at the next stop down the line, they had eluded Roger Carrigan.

Resentment and hatred flowed in Zoe's veins, and she was both dulled and supported by their drugging effect. On the carriage ride through the streets of Aspen, she dimly heard Cara's chatter. She sensed it was only an attempt to draw her out of her brooding.

"We're going to enjoy living here, Zoe. You'll see. It's so much better than Georgetown."

Zoe was still drugged by her own emotions when they reached the small hotel that would be their temporary dwelling. When they were taken to their rooms, Zoe was awed by more luxury than she had ever seen in her young, eventless life.

There was a thick Brussels carpet, gilt picture frames, mantle figurines, and doilies on the chair backs.

The first night both Zoe and Cara slept twelve hours. Then they were prepared to face the new town and their new future. The following afternoon, they began to make plans.

"Cara, will you find another job in a parlor house?"

"No. I've had enough."

"But I thought you girls had fun, Cara. You were the only girl I knew who laughed most of the time." Zoe found it hard to explain the importance of that laughter.

"Well, sure, you have to laugh in that business. You think a man wants to drink . . . or sleep with a girl who moans and cries all the time?" She laughed briefly. "He can get that at home."

"I thought . . . well, you always seemed . . . you said . . ."

"Shoot, nobody runs down their job to an outsider. But I don't want to see you get hurt."

"But I thought all the girls sort of . . . took care of each other."

"It's not like that, Zoe. Listen to me. It's a rough business. In the end, you're by yourself . . . alone and lonely. Sooner or later you lose your looks and the men turn their faces away. Then it's drink . . . disease, or an alley suicide."

"Then what about us, Cara? How are we going to end up? How are you going to survive?"

The question was the last thing Cara expected. Wasn't it just like this crazy girl? Here she was worrying about Zoe, while Zoe was scared to death about what was to become of *her*.

"Me?" Cara's chin set determinedly. "I'll get along. I'm different from you. You're the thunder-and-lightning kind that always flies high once they learn to fly. Me, I've got a good head for business, and I saved every coin I could just for when this day came. I'm going to find some kind of business to start."

"What about Stelle? You said she was coming to Aspen too eventually. When she gets here, she'll want you to work for her again."

"Stelle and I are friends. Like you and me. When she comes here she'll have her place, but if I've made my decision . . . well, she'll pretend not to recognize me. She'll give me a chance. What I do with that chance is up to me."

"You said you had a good head for business, Cara. What if we started something together? I know I don't have any money to put in, but I can work hard. Maybe together we could do something for us both."

"What kind of business? There's only one I really know, and you don't need to work hard at that one. I'm not sure yet what I can do."

The enormity of the step they had just taken rushed over Zoe. She tried to think of a way out, but there didn't seem to be one at the moment.

"Tell you what," Cara said. "We have some money and we have time. For tonight, let's just go out to a really nice restaurant and enjoy ourselves."

Zoe agreed, and for the balance of the afternoon, like any two excited young girls, they spent the time deciding what they would wear.

Finally, Zoe decided on one of Cara's amber lansdown dresses, which draped low off her shoulders and surrounded her full high bosom like the chalice of a flower. She carried a fragile fan in her hand, and realized she had never felt quite so pretty as she did now under Cara's encouraging words.

Cara watched Zoe move about the room. She was an actress, a force without even knowing she was one. Look at her, Cara thought, with her great big golden eyes, bedroom eyes if ever I saw any, combined with that uppity, don't-touch-me look.

They walked down the huge stairway and went to the hotel's dining room, where they were catered to by the maitre d' as if they were princesses. Cara laughed to herself in the sheer joy of being treated like a lady for the first time.

After they had ordered, Cara opened the discussion about what sort of business they could start. Zoe's response shook her equilibrium. Zoe had begun to think, and Zoe had ideas of her own.

"The business isn't the most important thing. First, I'm going to make a new identity for myself."

"But, Zoe, how . . ."

"That's another thing. My name."

"Your name? I don't understand."

"I'm going to wipe the past away, and the first thing is to change my name. Zoe Carrigan died in Georgetown. I intend to make my life what I want it to be and not what other people want to make it. Help me, Cara. We have to start with new names."

Cara was stunned in to momentary silence. She was twenty-two and Zoe was eighteen, but suddenly she felt as if Zoe were the older one.

Up to this point she had been leader and Zoe had been the innocent follower. Now the reins had subtly changed hands, and Cara could do little more than watch in a kind of breathless surprise.

"I'm thinking of a name," Zoe said. "It has to be kind of special and one that won't cause anyone to mistake me for what I was. What about Sarina for you?"

"Sarina," Cara repeated inanely.

"Sarina . . . ah! Sarina Falcon. Sounds great, doesn't it! We'll christen us both. Tonight we'll be born."

"Sarina Falcon. I kind of like that. What name have you chosen for yourself?"

"Laura . . . Miss Laura Champion."

"God, Zoe . . . I mean, Laura. When you get the bit in your teeth you really run with it."

"If we're going to do it, Sarina, we have to do it right. Tonight we'll make up a whole new past. One we can both be proud of."

"What if—"

"No what-ifs. We cut our past away and start all new." As the waiter passed she called to him.

"Bring us some champagne," she ordered.

When it came they raised their glasses and made a soft clink as they touched.

"To the future we want. We'll make it happen. To Sarina Falcon and Laura Champion."

They drank to the birth of two women who planned to reach for the stars.

Chapter Five

The word about Zoe's humiliation spread like wildfire through a gossip-hungry town. That, and the fact that her stepfather had gone on a maniacal rampage, was the first news Simon heard the next morning.

He couldn't believe it when his mother told him about it at breakfast, but when he and his father walked toward the mine to begin the day's work, they could hear confirmation of the gossip from every direction, for it was one of the most interesting things to happen in Georgetown's humdrum history.

Simon felt a deep pity for Zoe when the entirety of the story was told, and was surprised to find his father agreeing with him.

"Wonder where that poor kid has run off to?" Jessie said. "Course, I expect any place would be better than where she was. That is a plumb angry and vengeful man."

"He's just plain mean. What could Zoe have done to deserve such treatment? She's stubborn, but that don't give him the right to do a thing like that."

"That breed of man don't need a real reason for what he does. Somehow he got the idea he's the right hand of God, and that's a feeling of power that shouldn't be given to any man, much less a man as weak and hard-hearted as Roger Carrigan."

"I don't think Zoe had any kin anywhere to run to. She must be scared and hiding."

"She'll have to come back and face him sometime. There ain't no way a girl as young and pretty as she is can make her own way . . . unless . . ."

"No, Pa. Just 'cause Zoe was nice and spoke to Stelle

41

and her girls don't make her one of them. Zoe isn't that kind."

"Then she'll have to come back, or he'll find her and most likely make it worse on her."

"God, Pa, somebody ought to do something."

"Simon, nobody can interfere in a man's family."

"But . . ."

"There aren't any buts, boy. That man is a hard, vengeful fanatic. He'll bring the law down on anybody who gets in his way. The law says you can't get between a man and his family. It's none of our business." Simon was silent for some time. Then Jessie spoke again. "You do understand me, don't you, boy?"

"Yeah. But understanding don't mean I have to like it."

"No, it don't. I just don't want you doing anything to make the problem bigger. You've got enough trouble in your life without hunting for it. You best keep your mouth shut about Zoe or you might have the old man down on you anyway, accusing you of helping her or hiding her."

"He don't want to get down on me. I'm not a little girl he can push around."

"You don't need any trouble," Jessie reiterated.

"I'm not looking for it, but I'm not running from it. Zoe was a friend."

"Stay out of his way."

"You know he's always preaching around the mines. It's pretty hard to stay out of his way."

"You know what I mean." Simon was silent. "Simon?"

"Yeah, I know what you mean. I'm not goin' out of my way to cause trouble."

"Good. Your mother would be right distressed should you tangle with that self-appointed preacher."

"I suppose." Simon felt a sense of loss. Though both he and Zoe had too many hours of work and too little time to waste in the pleasure of long conversations, she had become an important person in his life, and he felt as if in some way he had failed her.

He had defended her more times than she would ever know about, and at one time had fought Robbie Matthews for saying some pointedly unkind things about Zoe and her family.

He'd watched her blossom slowly, and lately he had felt a kind of shyness around her because suddenly she was not just plain Zoe. She had become a beauty, but he'd never told her of his changing feelings. He'd sensed that Zoe needed a friend more than she needed a relationship that could only bring her new grief.

Her face lingered in his mind, and he worried about where she could be. How far could an eighteen-year-old girl go with no family, no money, and no friends? He would have helped her by giving her money, at least . . . if he knew where to find her.

He remembered the last time he had seen Zoe and talked to her. It was only a week or so ago, yet it might be the last memory Simon would have of her, so he drew on it.

Zoe had been lugging the inevitable basket of clothes when he caught up with her on his way home from work.

He called out her name and trotted toward her when he saw her ahead of him, watched her turn, recognize him, then smile.

"Hi, Simon."

"Hi." He stopped beside her, regaining his breath. "Where ya goin'?"

"Takin' Mrs. Forrest's clothes to her."

"Want me to carry them for you?"

"From the way you look, you just got off work. You've got to be tired. Besides"—she laughed softly—"you sure are dirty."

He liked her laugh. Zoe laughed rarely, and it pleased him that she reserved many of her rare smiles for him. He, better than anyone else, knew Zoe had very little to smile about.

"All right, I'll just walk with you," he said.

He watched her glance quickly around, and knew where her fears lay.

"He's not around, Zoe. He's down at the mine giving the usual sermon."

Her cheeks flushed, but she turned to resume her walk and he fell into step beside her.

"How's your mother?" he asked.

"She can't get out of bed much anymore," Zoe said with

cold finality. "She's been real sick since she lost the last baby. It's hard for her to do much."

"So you do all the work. I see you lugging baskets of wash all the time. Besides everybody else's laundry, you have to do all your ma's work and take care of the kids. You ought to have someone to help."

"I'll hire a maid first chance I get," she said with a laugh, "or maybe when Pa gets rich . . . or hits a strike . . . or some dumb congregation gives him a church so's he can tell everyone how they're going to hell for thinkin' and breathin' and livin'."

"You can't hate God or the church because of your pa, Zoe."

"God ain't done much for me lately to thank Him for, and I don't see any of the good respectable people from any church coming to help Ma when she needs it."

"It's mostly cause your pa drives everyone away."

"If they was really the good folks they say they are, they wouldn't pay him no mind. They'd help her."

"Yeah . . . I suppose."

"I don't mind the work," she said firmly. "I got my own plans. I can take care of myself . . . and Zach and the kids too for as long as I have to. One day . . ." She stopped as if suddenly aware she was saying too much. She trusted no one. As close friends as they were, it seemed she didn't trust him completely either.

"I think you do more work than any other girl I know. You can do anything. You ought to make some miner a real good wife."

She spun on him, her eyes filled with more anger than he had ever seen there before. It brought him to an abrupt halt before her.

"I ain't ever goin' to marry any of the men who grub in these mines. I ain't ever goin' to be like my mother, so don't think that I am. You're still feeling sorry for me, Simon. Well, don't. I'm doing just fine, and I'll keep doing just fine 'cause I know where I'm going and what I want to do. There ain't no man who can promise me anything to get me to marry him and bury myself in nothing but hard work and having kids until I die young and worn out."

There was a violence, a coldness in her eyes that still had the power to startle him. Her vehemence was a force he could hardly deny.

"I'm sorry, Zoe. I didn't mean to rile you up like that. I only thought . . ."

"Well, don't think like that. I'm not like you, or anybody else you know. I'm not going to settle for what life wants to give me. I'm going to reach out and grab what I want."

"Not like me?" He was puzzled and a little hurt.

"I'm sorry, but . . . yes, not like you."

"I don't understand."

She sighed, and was quiet for a few moments. Then she turned to him again and her voice was gentle, almost as if she were talking to one of her younger brothers. "Is this what you want, Simon? To dig in the ground for a handful of silver just to live on? Do you want to live under some rich man's thumb all your life? Do you want to live in this dirty godforsaken town the rest of your life? You think about that sometime. Me . . . I think about it all the time . . . all the time."

That was the last time he'd seen her, but the words she'd said would never leave his mind. He wondered if Zoe was taking the first step toward a dream she'd had for a long time. He broke the silence again.

"Pa?"

"Yeah, Simon?"

"You ever think of doin' something besides working in these mines makin' someone else rich?"

They walked several feet before Jessie answered. "I guess I have." This surprised Simon, but he remained quiet. "I always had a feel for building things. Fact is, I was a good carpenter, and I laid out a couple nice-looking homes before . . . but that don't count now. I'm here, and if we're lucky one day maybe we can strike it rich on our own."

Simon would have liked to have asked a lot more questions, but his father closed the discussion firmly when he pointed toward the mine entrance.

"There he is, still wavin' his fist in God's face and threatening everyone with eternal damnation."

Ahead a small group of men were gathered around Roger, more awed at his performance than impressed by his words and his threats. For the first time he actually looked pathetic to Simon.

"The damn old fool," Jessie muttered. "If he'd put as much fire into working, his family wouldn't be starving to death. I heard his boy Zach was in trouble in school again. They're thinking of tossing him out."

"I wouldn't be surprised," Simon replied. "Those kids are goin' to run as far and as fast as they can. He's going to be one lonely old man. I think Zach's staying around because of his mother. She's real sickly. Zoe's leaving is gonna be hard on her. Course it's going to be pretty hard on Zach too. That kid thinks Zoe is just about all he's got. If he's wild now, with Zoe gone he's going to be worse."

As they grew closer to Roger, his fury-filled eyes fell on them. He said nothing to either man, but Simon could feel the heat of his gaze. He clenched his teeth grimly and returned the look coldly. If Roger wanted to accuse Simon of helping Zoe, he'd have to come right out and say it.

Still Roger said nothing. As Simon passed, he could feel the other man's gaze following him, and he felt distinctly uncomfortable.

Weeks passed and the gossip died to a whisper, but as long as Roger remained a thorn in Georgetown's side, Zoe's scandal would never be allowed to die completely. When anyone mentioned Roger Carrigan, Zoe's name usually surfaced in the conversation, and they mentioned Roger's name a lot.

But as the gossip died down, Simon's longing for Zoe did not. He expected to see her face among the crowds of people, to see her slight form with the large basket balanced on her hip. To see her burnished hair from a distance, and her quick, shy smile that faded all too quickly. He wondered where she was and how she was, and if he would ever see her again.

He wished a million times over that he had let her know he wanted to be more than a friend to her. Maybe then, when she needed help she would have come to him. He felt guilty that she had not. And he felt a kind of lonesomeness and longing for something he could not fathom. He wondered if he was the only one who truly missed Zoe. But he had forgotten Zach.

That night, that terrible night that Zoe had run away, Zach had been forced to bed with no answers. His mother's weak tears, his father's raging had meant little compared to his fear for Zoe. The next day he was told by an infuriated Roger that Zoe would be found and punished.

He had prayed harder than he ever had pretended to pray before that Zoe wouldn't be found, yet he wanted her back with painful desperation. He just wanted to know Zoe was safe. But as the days went on, he was not to find even that bit of satisfaction. Zoe had disappeared into thin air, and his life seemed bleak and empty.

Roger forbade the children to mention her name. Zach managed for several days, but finally could bear it no longer.

"Pa," he said at a silent supper table. "Anyone find Zoe? Will she be coming back?"

Roger's face had gone white with anger, and he glared at his son. Zach stood up slowly and faced Roger, bearing the penetrating gaze of those eyes in hopes of hearing one word about Zoe.

"I told you never to mention that ungrateful slut's name in this God-fearing house again. She has gone to be a harlot and will walk the path to Hell alone."

Zach gulped back both his tears and his fears. "Zoe ain't no slut." He managed those words before Roger struck him hard enough to fling him back in his chair.

"You'll never mention her name again, do you hear! Never!"

"Yes, sir," he mumbled. But the embers of hatred that had smoldered so many years burst into a conflagration that filled Zach. He was silent during the rest of the meal, then quickly escaped the house.

The air was cold and Zach's coat was thin, but he didn't care. In fact, the heat of his inner tumult left him unconscious of the cold. He never meant to go home again, no matter what he had to do. What he wanted was to find

Zoe, but he had no way of knowing where she might have gone.

Despite experiences that made him older than his sixteen years, Zach was still a child in many ways. A lonely, unhappy child with no place to go to find the warmth he desperately needed. Tears swelled within him, but he would not cry. Zoe had once told him how little good it did to cry.

With his hands stuffed deep in the pockets of his ragged jacket, and his head bent against the chill, he did not see the large form until he collided with it. Actually he bounced off Simon's solid frame. He was lifted to his feet before he could recognize whom he had run into, but Simon recognized him almost at once.

"Zach, what are you doing down here this time of night?"

Zach looked around, and was totally flustered to find where he'd drifted. He looked up at Simon, but remained stubbornly silent.

He needed to say nothing to Simon. Simon recognized grief when he saw it. He also knew what Zach must be running from. Unfortunately, there was no place for a boy Zach's age to run to. Simon knew it, and he was sure Zach knew it too.

"Look, kid, you've got to go home. You can't get into anything but trouble on the streets at night."

"I ain't goin' home."

"Zach, look . . ."

"I ain't, so just go on and do what you was doin' and leave me alone." His words were defiant, as was his stance. But the fear and pain in his eyes were all too real.

"I can't do that," Simon replied, but he felt helpless.

"I didn't ask for no help. I can take care of myself."

"You sound like . . ."

Zoe's name hung between them, and at that moment Simon was certain of what was really grieving Zach. Just as he knew that, like Zoe, Zach would accept no sympathy.

Simon chewed his lip thoughtfully. He'd been on his way to visit one of Stelle's girls, and that was no place to take a kid like Zach . . . unless . . . He considered just how mad Stelle would be if he brought Zach to her for a hot meal and some stronger words of advice than he knew how to give. Stelle was a woman, and it seemed to him she was the kind of woman who would know how to handle Zach and a very sensitive situation.

"Come on, kid. I know a place you can rest and get warm for a while before you decide what you're going to do."

"I ain't goin' home." Zach's defiant voice sounded more alarmed than he wanted it to.

"Did I say I was taking you home?" Simon said, aggravated at his own helplessness. "I just said I know a place where you can get warm and rest awhile. Don't be a mule. Come on."

He walked away, hoping Zach would follow him. He was relieved when he heard the footsteps behind.

He went to Stelle's back door, hoping she wouldn't be too mad, or at least that she would give him time to explain. He knocked, and when her cook Josiah opened the door, he looked at Simon in surprise.

"Why didn't you just come to the front like you always do?"

Simon flushed, and stepped a little aside so Josiah could see Zach.

"Josiah, go get Stelle. She's the only one I know that can handle this."

Josiah nodded without question. He knew who Zach was, and was pretty sure what was happening. He let them into the warmth of the kitchen, closed the door, and went to fetch Stelle.

Zach's eyes were wide. He'd never seen a kitchen as nice as this one, or felt one so warm. He inhaled deeply, realizing that warmth had a scent all its own. He could hear music and laughter and contained, with effort, the curiosity that ate at him. Both he and Simon stood in silence. There was nothing Zach wanted to say and nothing that Simon could say.

When Stelle entered the kitchen, both Simon and Zach were surprised to see she was smiling. This pleased Simon because he still wasn't sure how he would have faced her anger.

"You're Zoe's kid brother," she began.

"I ain't no kid, and I don't know why he brought me here." Zach jerked his thumb toward Simon.

"Mostly because you were freezing out there, you ungrateful pup," Simon replied angrily.

"It don't matter, Simon," Stelle said. "He's here and that's good. I've been trying to figure out a way to get word to you. Zoe said—"

"You know where Zoe is?" Zach asked hopefully.

"Not really, kid. I only know she took a train out of here."

"Zoe didn't have no money for no train," Zach said belligerently. He was sure she was lying to him.

"Look, kid, she took a train and she's gone."

Zach gulped heavily, and his heart seemed to be squeezed by a large fist. He refused to cry, but he felt a little like he was dying.

"Sit down and I'll have Josiah dish you up a bowl of the soup we had for supper."

Simon could see Zach wanted to protest, but his hunger got in the way of his pride. Stelle shouted for Josiah, and at her orders he brought a large bowl of hearty soup that Zach did immediate justice to.

When he finished wiping the bowl clean with the last of three thick slices of bread, there was renewed color in his cheeks. Stelle and Simon remained silent until he finished. Stelle was the first to speak.

"Zoe left word for you."

"For me?"

"Yeah. There's something she wanted you to have."

"What?"

"She left some money for me to give you. She said to tell you you're not to tell anyone you've got it, and you're to keep it for yourself. She wanted it that way, and you'd better see it is that way. Your old man finds it and you can kiss it good-bye."

"Money for me? How did Zoe get money? Why didn't she take it with her?"

"Now how do I know that?" Stelle said. "You're just to have it." She reached in the low neckline of her dress and withdrew a sheaf of bills. She handed it to a still-shocked

Zach. Of course, she figured, he could not leave Georgetown; he was much too young. But at least he'd have
money to get some good food now and again, providing
he wasn't careless or dumb enough to let Roger find out.
She knew that if Zoe had had any money, she would have
left it for her brother.

Zach listened carefully, but his mind was forming plans
of his own that might have startled both Stelle and Simon.

"I better go," Zach said carefully.

"Good idea," Simon said. "If you want I'll walk back
with you."

"You don't need to. I know the way home by myself."

"All right, all right. So go on home."

Zach nodded. Then he looked up at Stelle with eyes that
harbored more bitterness than Stelle had imagined a
child could feel. This boy had not been a child for a long,
long time. Then Zach turned and walked out into the
night.

Stelle and Simon looked at each other; then Stelle
shook her head and sighed deeply. "There's nothing else
anyone can do."

"I know."

"How come you brought him here?"

"I don't know. He was cold and he looked so hungry
and so . . ." Simon shrugged. "I guess since you were a
friend of Zoe's . . . since Cara was a friend of Zoe's, I
thought you might be able to do something."

"Just what in Sam hill did you expect me to do, Simon?"

"I thought you could tell him where Zoe is."

"Tell him . . . or tell you?"

"Where Zoe went isn't any concern of mine. There's
nothing I can do about it. Besides . . . she never even said
good-bye. So it looks like she didn't care."

"It matters a lot that she didn't say good-bye, Simon?"
Her question was gently asked.

"Maybe . . . a little. I thought we were friends."

"She was scared and she ran."

"She could have said . . ."

"She could have said nothing! Look, there isn't anything wrong with caring. And there isn't anything wrong
with you feeling what you were feeling. It's just a shame

that you never told Zoe that you cared as much as you did."

"I couldn't help her," Simon said helplessly.

"Nobody could have helped Zoe. She's the kind that makes her own way. But you might have made it easier."

"I just wish . . ."

"Wishing is for babies. You have to stop wishing and grab hold of life, or one day you look around and find out life is passing you by."

Her words struck Simon hard because he had sensed that his father had let life pass him by.

"I gotta go," he muttered.

"Simon . . . I didn't mean to say anything to hurt you. But a man has to make life bend the way he wants it . . . or it bends him."

Simon nodded and walked out of the kitchen. This was one night he didn't choose to stay to sample the pleasures of Stelle's parlor house.

Simon found there was an immense difference between realizing how life had trapped him and knowing what to do about it. He also faced the fact that in many ways Zoe had more courage than he did.

It made matters worse when he heard Roger was searching for Zach. It seemed no one had seen him since the night Stelle had told him about Zoe's gift. Perhaps it had seemed to the boy that she had reached out to touch him. There was no doubt in Simon's mind that Zach had gone to try to find her.

Six months after that Zoe's mother, Trudy, died. It seemed she just lay back and closed her eyes. All her will and all her strength were gone. Martha and Eli were temporarily taken by sympathetic, well-meaning neighbors, none of whom harbored an ounce of compassion for Roger.

Simon was one of the few who went to Trudy's funeral. It was not out of respect for Roger or even for Trudy; it was a way to show how he felt about Zoe. Maybe she would never know, but he would, and that would have to be enough.

There were few people at the funeral. In fact, it was

embarrassingly difficult to find pallbearers, so Simon offered his help. Roger didn't thank him. It seemed for the first time reality had struck Roger. He was silent throughout the funeral, standing bareheaded, the wind whipping his dark ragged coat about him, and his eyes fixed on the rough wood casket as it was slowly lowered.

Simon meant to speak to him. He had no idea what he could say, for it was hard to put sympathy in his voice when he, along with all the others, knew Roger was the one responsible for Trudy's life ending at the age of thirty-six. But Roger gave no one a chance. When the funeral ended he bent down, picked up a handful of dirt, and dropped it onto the casket. The rattling thump was all that broke the silence, except for the wind. Then Roger turned and walked away. No condolences followed him, only dark accusing eyes.

Roger enclosed himself in his shack, and wasn't seen or heard from for days. But no one came to offer solace. In fact, the people of Georgetown were doing their best to forget him.

Simon pushed Roger from his mind also. As far as he was concerned, Roger was responsible for all the tragedies that had befallen his family, and he deserved whatever suffering he was going through. Simon had problems of his own.

The situation in his own home was deteriorating and he just didn't know why. What had been a slight tension between his parents was slowly growing stronger. Unspoken words and emotions seemed to hang between them like a thickening cloud. During the next year his father seemed to become gentler, more reserved, and quieter, while his mother seemed to be growing colder, stiffer, less tolerant. To Simon it seemed she was somehow prodding his father. Toward what, he didn't know.

Nothing specific was ever said, but it seemed to Simon as if his mother was always expecting something, something it seemed his father could not provide.

The atmosphere made him tense and kept his nerves on edge. He took every opportunity to escape it. Perhaps that was how he got caught up in fighting for the rights of the miners. It was a subtle, insidious thing, and Simon could not even pinpoint exactly where it got started.

He would linger before and after each shift, sit with groups of men that gathered, and listen to them talk. The conversations always returned to the poor working conditions, poor safety procedures, and very poor pay for the dangerous work they did.

The young are easily caught up in idealistic causes, and Simon was not immune. He had injustices in his own life he could not fight against, so he relished a cause he could do battle for.

He came out of the mine one night, tired and dirty and disinclined to go home. He felt the need of a strong drink. Without realizing it, he had been gravitating to one saloon or the other after work for the past year and a half. He was nearly twenty-four, and he could handle as much two-fisted drinking as the next man.

He walked into the saloon and found a table occupied by several men who, like himself, had just come from the mine tunnels.

"What's going on, boys?" he inquired of the general crowd.

"Been another accident over at the Comstock. Two miners killed and no one to give a dime to care for their families," Gus Barnes, a seasoned miner, growled.

The men around them stirred and muttered under their breaths. There was trouble brewing.

"Seems to me a man ought to be able to leave something for his family should he get himself killed," another man interjected.

"Hell, we don't get a wage to live on, let alone have anything to save," another argued.

"Appears to me that's wrong too. Those rich bastards live safe and warm and have all the comforts while we slave below for near to nothing," Gus added.

Simon remained quiet. These men were older than he, and wiser. They also had families and he didn't. But he listened and recognized the truth behind their words. If he should die, his father would still be there to take care of his mother. But if his father should die . . . The thought was almost frightening. If his father were not around, his mother would either starve or work as a drudge for someone else the rest of her life.

What of the families that had small children? He knew there was no law to stop the mine owners from putting boys as young as nine . . . even eight . . . to work in the dark holes of the mines.

"Somebody ought to do something!" He spoke the words without thinking, and he spoke them loud enough that it brought the entire table to silence. All eyes turned to him. It shook his courage, but he did his best to return their looks straightforwardly, as if what he said were actually possible.

"Just what do you think ought to be done, boy?" Barnes said. "I suppose we ought to go up to the supervisor and tell him to ask the owners kindly if they'd give us a living wage for a change . . . maybe build a hospital, or maybe just get a doctor? Maybe we might ask 'em kindly if they'd make the mines safe enough so's a man could count on seeing the next day once he went down. Who's going up to say all that, boy . . . you?"

There was a ripple of bitter laughter around the table, but Simon's face remained grim.

"Maybe it would work if we all stood together. That way we could just tell them none of us will work if they don't do something."

"You talking a union, Simon?" Barnes asked. "That's a good way to find yourself dead one day."

"Nobody's been killed around here."

"That's because nobody's been causing any trouble. You go up there saying things like that and you just might be the first."

"But if somebody doesn't say something or do something, it's never going to get better."

"Simon, those owners would start a war and kill half the men in this town if they even heard a rumor about a union. You best keep your thoughts to yourself. You're still young yet, and you don't have a family. Most of the men would laugh at you if you started shouting for a union. Best just keep your mouth shut, boy, if you know what's good for you."

Simon was silent, but his mind was spinning with a

whole new group of thoughts. What if the men did stand together? What if they demanded fair treatment or just refused to work? If the men stood together . . .

He had a couple of drinks, then left to go home. He wanted time to consider the ideas that were sprouting in his fertile mind. As he left, he was completely unaware that all the eyes that followed him were not friendly. One pair had watched and heard everything that was said. Several minutes after Simon left, that man rose too and left the saloon.

Once the thought had ingrained itself in Simon's mind, he could not seem to rid himself of it. He lay awake at night thinking of ways this idea could be made a success.

He began to listen closely to the miners, and to observe the squalid conditions of their lives more closely. The closer he watched, the more his dormant anger began to surface.

Something within him recognized that this was the battle he'd been meant to fight. Still, young as he was, he realized that Barnes had not cautioned him for nothing. He would have to be very careful that the plans that were forming in his mind were not revealed.

About a year after he'd begun listening and observing, the word seeped out to his father, who became angry at Simon for the first time in his life.

"What the hell do you think you're doing? You've endangered your life, not to mention mine and your mother's. If word of this gets back to the owners, you'll find more problems than you bargained on."

"I haven't done anything, and they can't stop me from talking to the men."

"Can't they? Simon, for God's sake, what are you trying to prove?"

"That this kind of living is wrong! That these miners shouldn't have to sacrifice their lives so that a few owners can live in luxury. These people need to eat! They need a hospital and a doctor! God, Pa, kids are dying all the time! Somebody ought to stand up and do something!"

"Why you? Why the hell do you think this is your fight? Don't interfere in this. All you can do is get hurt."

"I can't back away, Pa. These mines need a union now. Before one more family can starve, before one more kid can die, and before one more man gets killed down there for want of a little safety. Somebody's got to fight, Pa!"

He could say no more, and he knew he had not changed his father's mind. He sighed deeply, then turned and walked out of the house.

Over the following two years he worked slowly and carefully, talking to men one at a time, planting seeds he hoped would sprout into a full-fledged revolt.

Then one night he stood on his porch for a moment of peace, and looked up at the star-studded sky. He'd spent an exhausting day, and the calm night was soothing. He was a different man now. He had a goal to work for. He would go on with the fight no matter what anyone said, and one day he would unite these men and help them destroy the oppression they lived under.

To clear his mind and clarify his plans, he decided to go for a walk. The night was clear and cool and he walked slowly, letting his mind wrestle with these new and complicated ideas.

He never knew that he was followed, and he never sensed the blow that was coming until the lights of the town exploded before him.

He was knocked unconscious after the first blow, but that did not satisfy the three men who had attacked him. They had their orders.

Slowly and methodically he was beaten, until they were sure the lesson they were teaching would be fully understood.

Then he was carried through the dark alleys to the train depot. His bruised and bloody body was unceremoniously dumped in a railroad car and the door slid shut.

A half hour later the train left Georgetown, carrying with it an unconscious and half-dead Simon Tremaine.

Chapter Six

The first thing that rattled through Simon's semiconscious mind was pain. It burned through his entire body, and his head pounded with it. He was lying face-down on a rough wood floor, and he tried to move. But even the first slight movement brought another wave of pain that drew a low groan from his bruised, swollen lips.

He lay still, trying to get his sluggish mind to identify where he was and what had happened. Slowly the memory came, and with it came anger. A kind of anger he had never tasted before.

His father had been right, at least about this. Someone had known exactly what he was doing. He had touched someone's vulnerable spot. He stirred and tried to get to his hands and knees, but the constant rolling of the train and his lack of control over the pain that washed over him made it impossible. He sagged back to the floor with a breathless gasp as nausea struck.

It took every ounce of strength he had to roll over so he was lying on his back. Through a hazy wave of pain he looked around him. The car was empty now, but obviously it had been a cattle car, for the stench added to his misery.

He had no way of knowing how long he'd been out. He could tell by the weak rays of sunlight coming through the sideboards of the rail car that it was day. It had been early evening the last he remembered. But had he been out for hours or days? His body attested to the fact that whoever had done this had done a right good job of it.

For a panic-stricken minute he wondered if bones had been broken. It was horrible to think that he might not be able to move to get help when the dizziness and nausea faded. A broken leg . . . or arm . . . or worse might find him dead before anyone knew he was in the car at all.

This brought up the next question. He worried about how far away from Georgetown he was, and how long he'd been gone. But worse was the thought of how far the train was going before it stopped.

No matter. At the moment he couldn't move. Every attempt renewed the pain, until the rail car faded behind a red haze.

Trying to control the misery, he forced his mind to think of something else, and the most satisfying thing he could think of was finding the men who had done this to him and methodically beating them to death.

Logic then took hold. It would never satisfy him to get the ones who had beaten him. After all, they'd most likely been paid to do it. No, it was better to get the one who'd paid them.

He was weak, and the dizziness and hazy red veil grew stronger, until he could not fight it anymore. He never knew when the fever took over and he slipped into unconsciousness again, and delirium filled his mind with wispy visions.

It was sound that brought him up from the darkness again, but different sounds, strange sounds. His eyelids were heavy, and he opened them slowly, trying to focus. Everything was a blur. Then a voice came from somewhere nearby.

"Ah . . . so you're finally coming around. Good."

Simon blinked and again tried to focus. Finally with intense effort, things began to form in solid shapes. Then he was surprised again. It looked to him like he was in someone's bedroom.

"Where . . ." he began, but his voice was hoarse and raspy. His throat was dry. He swallowed and tried again. But the second attempt was as useless as the first, and the man bent closer to him.

"Save your voice, son. Here . . . drink this."

Simon felt the man's hand slip behind his head to lift it, then felt the touch of cool water against his dry lips. He tried to drink quickly.

"Whoa, boy. Take it easy. Too much is only going to make you sick. Drink slowly. There's plenty more where this came from."

Simon drank a few swallows, and the glass was taken away and his head laid gently back on the pillow.

The water seemed to revive him, and he concentrated again on trying to focus his eyes on the man who stood by the bed.

He wasn't a big man. Still, Simon got the impression of a man of stature and he didn't know why. The stranger had an almost frail appearance until one looked closely at his face. There was strength there. The face was long and slightly narrow, with a wide thin mouth and a pronounced jaw that promised obstinacy. Clear blue eyes were deep-set beneath heavy eyebrows and a wide forehead. His hair, just a fringe around a bald pate, was snowy white.

He wore a baggy pair of pants, and his suspenders hung off his shoulders about his hips. The long underwear top he wore had seen better days, but it was clean.

Simon gathered his strength again, and the words now came easier.

"Where am I?"

"In my bed for the time being." The old man chuckled at his own wit.

"I mean . . . where? What city? How did I get here?"

"You mean you don't even have an idea what city you're in?"

"Last time I remember anything I was taking a walk in Georgetown."

"Georgetown! You're quite a ways from home if Georgetown's home. You're in Boulder. I'm Augustus McCree . . . folks call me Gus. It was my son who brought you here more dead than alive."

"How long have I been here?"

"Nigh onto a week, and if you come from Georgetown you've been sick a lot longer than that. You're skinny as a rail and weak as a cat, so you better lie still for a while. Pete will be home directly, and he can tell you more about how you got here, since he's the one come draggin' you home."

"A week," Simon groaned. His parents must think him dead. "I have to get up."

"Sure." Gus chuckled again. "Condition you're in, if you can make it out of that bed you'll be lucky. Best you lie still and let us get some food down you so's you can get a little more strength back. I got some chicken broth ready for you."

"Broth." Simon smiled. "I'll need more than that if I want to get on my feet."

"In time. You put more than that in your belly first off and you won't be able to hold it."

"When does Pete get here?"

"He ought to be here before long. He's been looking in on you every day, just waitin' for you to come around. I'll go down and fetch some of that soup for you."

The old man started for the door.

"Gus?"

"Yeah?" Gus turned to face Simon.

"I'm grateful. It's not too many folks who would take in a beat-up stranger and take the time to nurse him back to health. I'm obliged to you . . . and to Pete."

"You owe Pete more than me. I just lent you my bed for a while. It ain't like it ain't been used the same way a pile of times before." Gus inhaled, and frowned as if he'd said more than he wanted to. His mouth pressed into a firm line. "Pete is one for picking up folks that are down. I reckon he took the story of the Good Samaritan too much to heart." Then Gus's voice gentled, and Simon could hear the thickness of deep affection in it. "He's a good boy, that one, and I hope it don't get him killed one day."

At this he opened the door and walked from the room, closing the door quietly behind him and leaving a very curious Simon to puzzle over his words.

He was back a short while later with a bowl of steaming soup. He sat on the edge of the bed, cooled each spoonful carefully, and fed Simon the entire bowl. Simon was grateful for the taste, and the warmth was soothing.

He tried to question Gus between spoonfuls, and realized the man was being deliberately evasive. When Gus left with the empty bowl, Simon knew no more about him and his as yet unseen son than he had before.

There was little choice but to wait and see what Pete was like and how he'd run across Simon in the first place.

Simon's whole body was one huge ache, and he was surprised that he felt so tired after he'd been lying for so long and sleeping. Yet he was exhausted. Despite the discomfort he drifted off to sleep.

Sometime later, he was wakened by the murmur of voices outside the bedroom door. He was awake at once, hoping that his rescuer had come and he could get some real answers.

The man who came in a minute later was of average height, a bit on the slender side, with a shock of bright red hair and eyes as green as grass.

He looked like someone who contained the urge to smile and laugh with difficulty. Yet there were deep grooves about his mouth, and a vague sadness emanated from him.

"Evening," he said. "It's good to see you awake."

"I take it you're Pete?"

"That I am."

"My name's Simon Tremaine and I'm grateful to you for saving my life."

"You sure were a mess. I take it you made someone real unhappy with you. They did a fine job of beating you. I'm afraid the doctor did as good a job as he could do on your face."

"My face?" Simon repeated blankly. Then a tremor of shock went through him. "Get me a mirror."

Pete nodded. There was little use in trying to hide the facts from Simon. He would be out of the bed soon enough, and would realize the beating had been worse than he now thought. Pete left the room, and returned a few minutes later with a mirror and Gus. Without a word he walked to the bed and handed Simon the mirror.

Simon's hand shook, and for a minute he didn't have the courage to look. He looked up at Gus and Pete as if he expected them to laugh and claim it was all a joke. But they didn't laugh. In fact they didn't even smile.

Slowly, with a trembling hand, Simon raised the mirror

and looked at his reflection. An irritated-looking red scar ran from his left temple down near the corner of his eye, and continued to the corner of his lower lip. Three smaller scars extended from the corner of his mouth to his jawline on the right side, and another small scar extended from his right eyebrow to the hairline above his ear.

"Good God," he breathed.

"The doctor said the red color will fade and some of the smaller scars will disappear," Pete offered. "But you'll carry a reminder for the rest of your life."

Simon was staring at himself as if he still couldn't quite believe it. They had not meant to kill him. They had done exactly what they'd intended to do—they had given him a permanent reminder that he had stepped on someone's toes.

The anger began to boil up from deep within him. It was like a black hand around his heart, squeezing out all the light and life and leaving a black throbbing organ of hatred.

For a moment he felt as if the next breath wouldn't come. He realized Pete and Gus were watching him closely.

"Simon, the scars won't be as bad as that when they're healed up," Pete said. "But there's nothing more the doctor could do. You're lucky to be alive."

Simon looked up at Pete, but Pete returned his gaze steadily. "There's more wrong, isn't there?"

"Yeah," Pete replied.

"Pete . . ." Gus began.

"He has a right to know all the truth. He has to live his life."

"What truth?"

"Your leg was banged up pretty bad. Looks like somebody meant to stomp it. You're going to carry a limp from now on, and you can consider yourself lucky the doctor didn't have to take it off. For a while it was touch and go."

"Anything else?" Simon asked bitterly. "It looks as if they took real good care of me."

"Simon, whoever it was meant to leave you with a reminder. What the hell did you do to cause something like this?" Pete smiled for the first time. "You messing around with some rich man's pretty young wife?"

"A reminder," Simon repeated. "I don't need this reminder. I don't ever intend to forget. How soon can I get out of this bed?"

"Have some unfinished business to take care of, do you?" Gus spoke quietly. He had never taken his eyes from Simon's face.

"Yes, some unfinished business," Simon said bitterly. "But I can finish it."

"You know the men who did this?"

"No, but I know why, and I know the group they belong to."

"So you're going to go flailing around and strike out at everybody in the hopes of getting the ones responsible."

"What the hell do you expect me to do? Just accept what they've done and go on my way? I can't do that. I don't think either of you could either."

"What I expect you to do is use your head and consider your future. They could do worse to you next time."

"They'd never have that opportunity," Simon said with grim coldness.

"Simon," Pete questioned, "why the hell did someone beat you like that?"

Simon looked up at Pete. He didn't know anything about these two men except they had saved his life. But if he went on to condemn the mine owners and supervisors, he might just be talking to two men who could turn out to be enemies.

"Whatever the reason," Simon replied, "I'm grateful I fell into your hands. I must have been quite a problem when you first brought me here. I owe you a lot, and I'll pay you back. The doctor alone must have been costly."

It was clear to both men that Simon meant to give them no answers at all. They could see it in his eyes.

"Don't worry about the cost. The doctor is an old friend, and he doesn't charge us that much. Pete has been in enough scrapes to keep him in business." Gus chuckled. "As for paying us back, it's enough to see you get back on your feet."

"Just how soon will that be?"

"Doc's coming around today to look you over. He can answer that question better than we can," Pete said. "Until then, you'd better get some food in you and get some rest or you'll never get back on your feet. You look real peaked."

"Yeah," Simon said tiredly. "I guess a little rest will do me good."

Simon must have slept for quite a while. When he woke up, a lamp had been lit, and he could see it was dark outside. Someone had thrown an old quilt over the sheet that had covered him.

His head felt thick, as though filled with cotton, and he knew it was from lying still so long. But when he tried to scoot himself into a sitting position, excruciating pain made him gasp.

At that moment the door opened and Pete and Gus, accompanied by another man, came in.

"How you feeling, Simon?" Gus asked.

"Like hell." Simon was almost panting from the sudden sharp pain. "My leg . . ."

"You're trying to sit up," the third man said. "It's a little too soon for that. Best you be real still or you might cause complications I won't be able to do anything about."

"This is Doctor Paul Riley," Pete said, answering Simon's unspoken question. Pete chuckled. "And you'd best do as he says, 'cause he's not above smackin' you alongside the head to keep you quiet."

"Now, Pete," the doctor said with amusement in his voice. "You know I'm not a violent man. Fact is, I abhor violence," he continued as he sat on the edge of the bed and put his black bag by his feet. "How you feeling, son?"

"I was fine until I tried to move. Doc, how bad is my leg?"

"Bad enough to make you limp the rest of your life, but not bad enough to make you a cripple if you do what I tell you."

"How long am I going to be laid up like this?"

"You're healthy and you're young, so you'll mend

quicker than most. But you'll still be in this bed another week or so. After that you can sit for a while. After a few more weeks we'll get you up and see how well you can walk."

"God! You're talking about months!" Simon protested.

"Look, you're lucky. You don't realize how badly you were beaten. You could have been bedridden for more than months. It could have been the rest of your life."

"I know you're right . . . but . . . months."

"There somebody you want us to notify?" Pete asked. "I can go down to the telegraph and send a message."

Simon was going to say a quick, relieved yes, but he stopped to consider. If his parents let the word get around that he was all right and that he was laid up here, someone might come and try to finish the job. He hated to scare his father, but he thought it might be best if he just went back when he was well enough to do it.

"No," he said cautiously, "don't bother, Pete. There's nobody I want a message sent to."

Neither Pete nor Gus said anything, but both were more than sure Simon was lying.

"You best let me look you over," Dr. Riley said. "Then, since that broth stayed down, I think it's time you began to get some more solid nourishment." He turned to Pete and Gus. "You two can go get some food for this boy. April is coming in tomorrow. He's going to need a lot of tending if he wants to get out of this bed, and April is going to do the tending for me."

Pete and Gus nodded and left, and the doctor continued with his examination. Simon studied him as he worked.

He was weathered, like old leather, his face lined and his hair crisp, thick, and white as the first snow. One look in his dark brown eyes told Simon this man had seen much and felt much. He was thin, and Simon noticed quickly that he had the slenderest, longest fingers he'd ever seen and that his hands and nails were clean.

"You been doctoring here long?" Simon asked.

"Quite a spell. I apprenticed to the old doctor when I was near your age. Took over his practice when he died. You might say I've been here near as long as the town has been."

He examined Simon's leg carefully, but at the moment Simon chose not to look at it. He'd had about all he could handle for one day. It would take a while before he could really cope with what had been done to him. Done by a few men who would resort to violence before they would try justice.

"Not many of the mining towns have a doctor," Simon said.

"I know. But there's no way for me to be in more than one place at a time. We have a reasonably good hospital here in Boulder and that's where I wanted to take you. But Gus and Pete insisted you be cared for here."

"Why?"

"I guess," the doctor replied quietly, avoiding Simon's eyes, "they felt it best that no one knew you'd been found in the condition you were in. I don't suppose you'd know the reason for that?"

"I'm a complete stranger to both of them. I suppose they were just being generous."

"Yeah . . . I suppose."

"Doc?"

"Yes?"

"How bad is my leg really going to be?"

"I don't think it's going to be as bad as I thought at first. It's beginning to heal. You'll have some scars . . . and a limp, but you'll be able to get around just fine. You won't be doing no fancy jigs, though. You just relax and let me and April take care of you."

"I don't think I need a nurse."

"Look, Gus and Pete, they have to work at the mine, and you'll be left alone. I don't want you to be alone. You're the kind who'll be trying to get up and get what he wants. I don't want you to be doing any unnecessary moving, and you have to eat."

"Who's April?"

"April's my daughter . . . my girl . . . she looks like her mother. She keeps house for me and she's right good at it." His eyes held Simon's. "April . . . she's a little . . . slow. But she's real special and she'll take good care of you. She's also as pretty as Christmas. I wouldn't want anyone to consider taking advantage of her . . . condition."

Simon flushed in angry embarrassment. "You think I'd do a think like that? I wouldn't, no matter what the situation. You, Pete, and Gus saved my life. I don't repay my debts that way."

"Just thought I'd mention it. It's not only how I'd feel, but how Gus and Pete would feel. There's a pretty special place for April in this house."

"I'll be on my best behavior."

"April will fetch and carry for you. See that you're fed and comfortable. She can change a bandage near as well as I can, and she'll know if you need me again."

"I could get spoiled like that." Simon smiled.

"It will only last until you can get out of bed. Then she'll turn into a real demon getting you moving again."

"I can't wait to meet her."

"It'll be an experience, I can promise you that. April is . . . surprising is the only word I know."

"You said she was . . . slow."

"Well, slow isn't really quite it . . . different might be a better word. She can't read and write because letters seem to get jumbled when she looks at them. She's also real innocent about life. You see, she always sees the pretty things in it."

"What's wrong with that?"

"The world isn't an innocent place, Simon. You know that as well as I. So do Pete and Gus, and most others. But April doesn't. It makes the world a dangerous place for people like her. So far she's had a lot of people to protect her."

"Maybe I'll join the group."

"I wouldn't be a bit surprised. Well, I got to get along. Mrs. Pearson is about to give her husband his fourth. Not that she needs me, but it makes old Hank feel better if I hang around." He stood up, gathered his materials, and snapped his bag shut. Then he walked to the door. There he turned to look at Simon again. "Now you just have patience with yourself, boy. I know it's hard for a young man like you to be tied to a bed, but you force that leg, you'll do yourself more harm than good."

"Don't worry. I want to get out of this bed, but I'm not going to make a cripple out of myself to do it."

"Good. I'll see you sometime later this week."

"Thanks."

Dr. Riley nodded and left the room. Shortly after he'd gone, Gus returned with a tray that held a steaming bowl of hearty stew, several thick slices of buttered bread, a hefty slice of apple pie, and a mug of very black coffee.

Simon was wakened the next morning by a stream of sunlight that filled the room with brilliance. He also awoke with a ravenous appetite. Besides that, a good bath would have made him feel a lot better. He was considering how he'd be able to bathe himself when there was a timid knock on the door.

"Come in," he called.

Simon knew to expect a girl named April. He knew that she would be his nurse for the rest of his confinement. He also knew he had been subtly warned about his treatment of her, so he expected she'd be attractive.

In fact he expected a lot of things, but the girl who opened the door and walked in was completely beyond anything he could have imagined.

She was enough to knock the breath from a man. Simon suddenly had the thought that she looked exactly the way one would envision an angel.

Her hair was the same color as the first morning sunshine, pale shimmering gold. Held by a green ribbon, it hung to her waist. Her eyes were so blue they were very nearly purple. Her skin was smooth and softly brushed with pink, and her mouth was the color of roses. She was small, but her body was definitely all woman. Simon was stunned into momentary silence. He could do little more than stare. She was the most beautiful thing he had ever seen. Her beauty was delicate and ethereal.

"Good morning." Her voice was as delicate as she was. "I'm April."

Simon found his voice at last, even though it was a little hoarse and unsteady. "Good morning ... April. My name's Simon. I'm sorry to put you to all this trouble."

"It's no trouble. Would you like me to bathe you first, or do you want to eat?"

At this Simon nearly choked. She was going to bathe him! Good God, that was impossible. No man could keep himself from responding to a girl who looked like April if she was giving him a bath.

"I have hot water on the stove and it will only take a little while to get it."

"Ah . . ." Simon thought rapidly. "If . . . if you just get me some, I'm sure I can do it myself."

"You need a shave too," she said thoughtfully, as if what he said hadn't really registered. Then, as if she had made her decision, she smiled a wide smile that was totally devastating. "I'll shave you first, then bathe you, and you can eat after that." At this she turned and left the room, leaving Simon rather breathless.

"Oh, Lord," Simon muttered to himself. He started searching desperately for some way out of this predicament. He was pinned to the bed, and he'd never felt so helpless in his life. Any other time the situation might have been interesting, or even funny, but at this moment he was scared to death.

He could hear her footsteps in the hallway, and a few minutes later the door opened again and April returned with several towels over her shoulder and a large basin of steaming water. She placed the basin on a stand near the bed, laid the towels beside it, and left the room again. Simon was beginning to sweat. She returned in minutes with a shaving mug, a strop, and a straight razor. She set these beside the basin.

"Look, I can shave myself," he protested as she began to slide the razor back and forth across the strop.

"Oh, I don't mind." Her smile was warm and pleasant, as if this were an unimportant occurrence. Simon was shaken by the startling innocence of this girl.

She tucked a towel about his neck, dipped the brush in the hot water, and began to stir a lather in the mug. Simon closed his eyes as she bent close to lather his face. He kept his eyes closed while she shaved him expertly. Then, she laid the razor aside and stood up.

The following half hour was one of the most nerve-wracking half hours of Simon's life. He was bathed thoroughly and very effectively by a girl who paid him no more mind than if he had been a baby in need of a bath. She had not spoken, but had concentrated on what she was doing. Finished, she gathered basin, towels, and shaving equipment, and with a smile, left him staring at the closed door.

Chapter Seven

It was at that moment that Gus came in. He had no problem reading Simon's face, and could not help laughing. "Having a rough morning, Simon?"

"I just met April," Simon replied. He had to smile painfully at Gus. "Don't you think we can make some other arrangements, Gus?"

"About being cared for? No, April is a good nurse for Doc. She'll be back to change your bandages. Just don't pay her any mind. She'll do her job efficiently."

"Don't pay her any mind! Hell, a man would have to be dead to do that." Simon tried to laugh, but the laugh faded when he saw that Gus was no longer amused. "Sorry . . . I didn't mean to say that."

"Doc tell you much about April?"

"A little. That she's kind of slow and special in some way. I can see where she would be. She looks like . . ."

"Like an angel in a woman's body." Gus sighed as he sat down in a chair beside the bed. "What she is, Simon, is a little girl in a woman's body. Somewhere along the line everything stopped for April when she was about thirteen. It was fever that affected her mind, quick and severe, and it has tortured Paul for years. You see . . . he was unable to do anything about it. Somehow it crushed him. Now . . . she's his life. She's what keeps him going. He's carefully trained her to do some tasks, and she has been so much of a help to him that she's been able to gather everyone's love about her like a shield between her and the hurts she could suffer. Many love her, even Pete, my son." Gus saw Simon's quick frown. "No, Pete would never touch her, he would never hurt her. But he longs.

72

You see, April has no way of knowing or understanding that longing. He longs, and will forever remain a brother to her . . . and a man who would kill to protect her."

Gus and Pete had supper with Simon that night, and it became a daily affair. The talk was at first superficial, but as time went by they grew more relaxed, and with the relaxation came trust.

April flitted through their daily life like a firefly—sparkling . . . elusive, yet brightening their days with her innocent sweetness. Simon found himself wanting to protect her more and more every day, like a big brother.

One night, after Simon had successfully reached the point of being able to sit up and swing his leg over the edge of the bed, Pete came in wearing a smile and carrying a bottle.

"Since you've been confined so long, I thought you might like a little nip. Sort of get you back into circulation."

"I don't think a drink or two will put me back into circulation, since I can't even stand up yet." Simon grinned. "But it will sure make that bed a little more bearable."

They had a drink or two before it came to Simon that Pete had more in mind than just a relaxed drink.

Pete sat on a chair near the bed, his foot against the bed and his chair tipped back. "Simon?"

"Yeah?"

"You're going to be up and around pretty quick now."

"Lord, I hope so."

"You're going back to Georgetown." It was not a question but a tentative statement.

Simon was silent, thinking of his still half-formed plans and his fully formed need for revenge.

"Yeah, I guess there's nothing else I can do. I can't let them just get away with what they did . . . I just can't. I have to do something."

"You're likely to walk back into the same kind of fix, and this time they might not be so gentle."

"Gentle!"

"You could be dead."

"They didn't want me dead . . . they wanted me to remember. They wanted me to stay crouched in a dark corner with my tail between my legs like a good dog."

"This time. Next time . . ." Pete shrugged.

"What are you getting at, Pete?"

"Even as mad as you are, one man is not going to make a difference."

"You're talking organization."

"We already are."

"We?"

"We're called the Knights of Labor."

"Fancy."

"Not fancy, smart. We know damn well that it's the only way."

"You trying to make this sound easy?" Simon chuckled.

"No one said the road was going to be easy. But alone, the road's impossible. I want you to listen to what we have here. If you really don't think it's a better way than going it alone . . . then, when you're well enough, we'll put you back on the train for home."

Simon looked at Pete closely. There was no doubt Pete was sincere, that he wanted Simon to be part of the group he was in. Just as there was no doubt in Simon's mind that Pete would put him back on the train as he'd said he would do.

"You willing to just look . . . and listen?" Pete asked quietly.

"When?"

"When you're able to walk out of this room."

"Where?"

"We have a meeting place not too far from here. You might be surprised at just how far we've progressed."

"I'll look and I'll listen."

"But no promises."

"No, no promises."

"You're a hard man, Simon Tremaine." Pete laughed softly as he handed the bottle back to Simon. "What do you say we get happily drunk?"

"Sounds good to me." Simon took the bottle and gulped down a hefty swallow.

*   *   *

Simon was surprised at the size of the group of grim-faced men who called themselves the Knights of Labor. They had been talking in low voices among themselves, but Simon was quick to notice that they became silent when he arrived with Pete and Gus. There was no doubt in his mind that deference to both men was being clearly shown, as well as curiosity about his own presence.

"He's all right, boys," Pete said in a voice that would carry through the crowded storage house where they were meeting. "He's one of us." Pete went on to explain who Simon was and how he had gotten where he was. There was a whisper of relieved sighs.

"Well, boys," Pete spoke again. "We've been talkin' and talkin', but there's nothing being done. We have to decide just where we're going."

"We need guns! Then we'll show them where we're going," a man from the crowd shouted.

"No!" Simon's voice echoed about them. He was afraid the use of guns would lead to a disaster. It would be hard, but passive and persistent resistance was better than armed violence. The men all grew silent, and Pete turned to him as if he expected Simon to continue.

"Look," Simon said, "most of you men are married. The highest wages you get are about two dollars and fifty cents a day. That's about seventy-five dollars a month. I figure it costs sixty-five dollars a month just to survive—thirty dollars for groceries, ten dollars rent, another ten on clothes, six on fuel, four for water, three for milk, and two for insurance so you can bury your dead. Most of you work at least twelve hours a day, and mostly you work for six or sometimes seven days a week. If anything happens to you like a serious illness or injury, you'll be forced into debt, and probably never be able to recover.

"And for those wages you face daily, sometimes hourly, the possibility of sudden and violent death. You deserve fair wages! You deserve some kind of commitment on the mine owner's part to care for your families if something does go wrong. But you can't get any of these things if you don't work united. You're too small now.

"I can see by your numbers that all the miners in Boulder aren't signed up with you. You need them all, and more. You need to unite with the miners from George-town, and Aspen, and all the other towns. You need to get them all to sign with you. Then you'll have power. Then you can call a statewide strike. Set a time and everyone will go on strike at the same time. You'll bring everything to a stop. Silver's high on the market now, and the owners can't afford for all the mines to shut down for any length of time. Then they'll talk to you . . . they'll have to."

Simon stopped talking and there was utter silence. He turned to look at Pete and Gus, who were smiling broadly. Simon caught his breath; then he smiled as well. As reluctant as he had been to get involved, he found his sense of justice had caught him again.

Then men were crowding about, trying to get the answers to the inevitable questions. How? When?

"You've caused quite a commotion, Simon," Gus said with a laugh. "Now you have to have some answers. Where do we start?"

"I'm no leader," Simon protested.

"No? After what you just said, denying that is down-right impossible."

"Look, Gus . . . your group's not strong enough."

"So we'll get stronger," one man inserted vehemently.

"Yeah!" another echoed.

"If we ain't enough, we can do like you say and get men from Georgetown and Aspen too."

"How are you going to do that?" Simon challenged him.

This quieted them all temporarily as they looked at one another for answers.

"You tell us how," Pete said quietly. He had a feeling of certainty that Simon was the man to handle the job. Whether he knew it or not, he had the manner of a born leader.

"All right," Simon said, capitulating. "You start a campaign to sign up every miner in Boulder. You send a couple of representatives to Georgetown to do the same, and a couple to Aspen. When and if you ever reach the point that you have them all signed up, you call one big, state-wide strike. Then, if someone doesn't come out from under a rock and kill you, you just might pull it off."

"Well"—Pete grinned—"if we're going to do all that, then we'd better get started planning."

"You're impossible." Simon had to grin in return. "Don't you know when you're outnumbered?"

"I might have . . . if I hadn't met you."

"This wasn't exactly in my plans, Pete."

"I know, Simon. But, in a way it can be made part of them. Start the union, and break the bastards in Georgetown who tried to get you. It's a way to revenge yourself without playing the game alone and getting killed. You can make yourself strong enough so that they can never put you on your back. It's a better way."

"All right, all right. But it might go wrong. I might get you and your father killed too, along with some other good men."

"I don't think there's a man here who's not ready to take that chance. Simon. Let's at least fight."

"Okay . . . we'll fight."

Pete clapped him on the shoulder, and they turned to face the crowd of expectant men. It was going to be a hard uphill climb, but for the first time Simon began to think of a solid plan to retaliate against the men who had hurt him and to plot his future.

Six Months Later

Simon stood up and slammed the papers he had been reading down on the table with such violence that Pete jumped.

The months of hard work had culminated in what Simon knew had been a premature move by the Knights of Labor. They had taken their demands to one of the larger mines against his better judgment. And they had gotten exactly the reply he had expected.

It was obvious that the mine owners in Boulder had heard about their demands, and realized this was different from the usual murmurs of discontent. They had also heard that a campaign to unionize miners had been extremely effective.

"Don't get so upset, Simon," Pete said soothingly, but he looked worried.

Simon grabbed up the papers he'd been reading. "Just listen to this response from the mine owner.

" 'We decline to submit to this or any illegal and inequitable interference from whatever source it may emanate.'

"Illegal! Inequitable! They are the ones who are inequitable. And listen . . .

" 'We will immediately close down all mines operated by us in this district and keep such mines closed.'

"Damn them. Now we have to move more quickly than we'd planned."

"Move how?" Pete questioned.

"We have to send out men to get the miners in the other towns signed up as soon as possible."

"That can't be done in a day."

"I know that, but it's got to be done now."

"Who's going to go?" Pete asked.

"I think it would be best if you went to Georgetown. I'd go there, but I'd draw too much attention from the wrong people. I'm pretty well known there. The mine owners know why I . . . left in such a hurry. It would be inviting trouble. I'd . . . I'd also appreciate it if you'd take a letter to my parents. It's time they know I'm still alive."

"I agree. But I know you pretty well. You're not going to lie around here and wait."

"No, I'm not. I thought I'd go on to Aspen."

"Alone?"

"There's no one else I'd want to have sticking his neck out."

"Do you really think we can get this campaign back in order?" Pete asked.

"Providing we can keep the miners from talking so much and carrying the word to the owners."

"And how do we do that?"

"By not telling anyone what we're doing or where we're going."

"Take about a day for people to miss me and Dad. Course, not too many people have been that close to you.

I expect you can leave without a lot of folks missing you much."

"I've counted on that. What kind of excuse can you make? Maybe it would be better if Gus stayed here. I wouldn't want to get him hurt. That way folks will believe you've just gone somewhere for a visit."

"Sounds good to me." Pete laughed. "But I want to stand around and hear you explain that to my father."

"Well . . . ah . . . I thought I'd leave that up to you," Simon said with a chuckle.

"And I thought you were so brave," Pete chided.

"There's bravery, my friend, and then there's just plain foolishness."

"Well, don't worry about it. I'll explain to him. When are we going to get started?"

"Best we don't both go at the same time."

"Right again."

"I'll go first. No one will miss me."

"I'll wait a few days, set something up as a reasonable excuse, then I'll get going. When do you want me back?"

Simon thought for a moment. "It will take a while to get the miners signed up. We have to work carefully."

"Absolutely. So when do you want me back?"

"What do you say to four months, whether we have them all signed up or not?"

"Four months it is."

Simon stood. "I'm going to take a walk and leave you to explain things to Gus."

Pete watched Simon leave, knowing he had a lot of things to sort out in his own mind.

Simon walked slowly, using a solid wooden cane Gus had carved for him. Inside a house he could maneuver well, but stony, uneven ground still caused him some trouble. He shoved one hand in his pocket and gave his mind freedom to drift.

He'd felt a need for action for a long time, and he had to bring himself to face the motive for it. He was afraid of being afraid. He was scared the beating had done him more than physical damage, and he had to know it wouldn't weaken his resolve when the time came to stand up for what he believed.

It was funny, but lately his thoughts had turned to Zoe Carrigan. It had been a long time since he'd seen her, yet her indomitable courage still lingered with him.

Beating or no beating, he had an idea that Zoe would never be afraid, and he wondered where that streak of courage came from, and if he could match it.

She'd stood against such odds. He wondered where she was now and what she was doing. She must be a grown woman now. She'd been eighteen when he'd last seen her. Probably she was married and had children already.

Well, he had his own future to think about and his own fears to conquer. He had to fight back somehow or he'd never be his own man again. He'd always walk in the shadow of fear, and he couldn't live like that.

He walked until he was tired, and returned home for supper. They spoke little at the meal, for there was no need.

The next day he rose early and boarded the first train that left Boulder for Aspen.

Chapter Eight

Denver, Colorado

At twenty-eight, Brent Dewitt had everything it was possible for wealth and position, and good breeding, to provide. He was tall, broad of shoulder, and gifted with lean gracefulness. He was handsome, with a Greek god's face, thick black hair, and sea-blue eyes fringed by thick dark lashes that would be the envy of any woman. He'd been raised with wealth, educated extremely well, and trained in the law, and had traveled extensively. To all outward appearances he was close to perfect, and his attendance at a gathering would set young girls' hearts aflutter. He would be a prize catch.

Brent's only fault went completely unnoticed by nearly everyone but himself. Only his father knew the biggest flaw in Brent's character.

Stephen Dewitt had always been a little stronger, a little wiser, a little more ambitious, a little more able, more decisive, and more aggressive than his son. As Brent grew, so did his knowledge that he did not quite measure up to his father's expectations. In a million subtle ways Stephen never let Brent forget it. His expectations always seemed to be a bit more than Brent could live up to.

Business deals, when placed in Brent's hands, seemed to sour, and in time his father would come to the rescue, shaming his son inch by inch, blaming Brent for the weakness this implied. Never in words. Never did Stephen say Brent was a disappointment, but Brent sensed it, and eventually it destroyed what self-esteem he possessed.

But his uncertainties were well concealed beneath layers of impeccable manners and aristocratic arrogance. Because the bitter lessons he had learned from his father were accompanied by others taught by his mother. From her came the knowledge that family name and social standing meant everything. That one truly was known by the company one kept, and that people of their social standing did not rub elbows with people beneath them.

An equally important lesson was learned in the cradle. The Dewitts had wealth, a great deal of it, and many would use Brent as a means to get hold of it. So he must be careful when choosing friends, and eventually when choosing the woman who would share his wealth with him. Somewhere along the line it was tacitly agreed that when the time came, the correct woman would be chosen for him.

That woman turned out to be Barbara Crandell, potential heir to nearly as much money as Brent would inherit, and as aristocratically superior and unbending as Brent's parents.

Tall and thin, she was a trend-setting creature from her first appearance in society. She knew when to smile, even though the smile never traveled beyond her lips. She was in total command of herself at all times, and had never surrendered to an emotion that might interfere with her goals. She had no plans to surrender to any of the "lower" emotions in her marriage either. Marriage was less of a relationship than a merger between two fortunes to create a much more formidable and powerful one.

She and Brent were paired for just about every social event, and even without the formal words from him, their ultimate union seemed to be "understood."

If, deep inside, Brent chafed against his life and his father's domination, he tried his best to keep it under control. Still, the occasion came when he decided to try to grasp an opportunity that had suddenly arisen.

Most of Stephen's wealth had come from the depths of the silver mines. He owned three that produced exceptionally well. One in Georgetown and two in Aspen.

It was a brilliant Sunday morning, but Stephen felt no pleasure from the sun, the breeze, or the song of the birds outside his window. He sat at his desk with a letter in his hand that he now read for the fourth time. His anger and muttered curses were just as vehement the fourth time as they were the first time he'd read the letter. Finally he crumpled the paper in his hand and tossed it on the desk. It was at that moment that Brent walked into the room.

"Father?"

"Confound it, Brent. Now is the worst time for me to have labor problems at the Aspen mines. I have too many difficulties brewing here to run off and see to them."

Brent caught his breath. He desperately needed something to enlarge him in his father's esteem. Like a knight, he needed to do battle for his king to gain some semblance of stature. He needed to solve some conflict to establish his own confidence in himself.

Brent admired his father, and that only made Brent's seeming failure look bigger to him. He tried to ignore the subtle voice in the depths of his being that insidiously whispered he was too weak to be what he knew his father was.

"Labor problems?" Brent asked.

"Those miners, they've been deliberately slowing down the work at the mines until the silver is just trickling out. They have demands, it seems."

"What kind of demands? Who are they to demand anyway? They should consider themselves lucky. Some of the miners in Georgetown are completely out of work."

"I don't know what they want, but Williams seems to think we should look into it. But damn it! I can't go right now. Senator Glass will be here from Washington tomorrow, and I've got to be here."

"Why don't I go?" Brent suggested quietly.

Stephen's momentary hesitation was more expressive than a million words could have been. But Brent remained stubbornly quiet. His father would not only have to refuse, he'd have to give reasons.

For a long moment Brent relentlessly held Stephen's eyes with his. Suddenly he felt an overwhelming sense of desperation, as if this might be the last chance he had to redeem himself in his father's eyes and in his own.

"Well . . . maybe you could go out there and check up on the mines," Stephen said. "I've been told there are some troublemakers trying to organize the miners into a union. If so, I want you to find out who they are and see if you can put a stop to it. If they look like they're getting up any strength, let me know. Strikes are expensive, more expensive than a troop of strikebreakers. I don't want them to know why you're there. You can, I'm sure, make some reasonable excuses for your presence. Having a fling before marriage maybe. I hear there are some very fine sporting houses in Aspen. Some even you have not frequented, and I believe at one time or another you've frequented most of the ones here and in Georgetown."

It was said with a laugh, but Brent's ear detected a slight touch of derision, and he felt guilty somehow. His father had a way of making him feel guilty of some unseen weakness just by looking at him.

"I'm sure I can go and find out what you want without causing any untoward curiosity."

"This is your inheritance in jeopardy here," Stephen said. "I'm not going to let a grubby group of mud-diggers destroy everything I've built."

"What are their demands anyway?"

"Their demands are beside the point. I won't be told how to run my mines, nor will I be forced to pay men more than they're worth."

"All right, all right. I'll just go and spend a week or two and find out what's going on."

"It isn't so much what's going on; it's who is causing it to go on. I want names. I want to know who the men are who have the temerity to come into my mines and make demands. My God, it's like coming into a man's house and defiling it."

"It might take a little digging to get all the names. Men who organize unions like to keep as much attention from themselves as possible."

"Then dig. You have unlimited expenses." Stephen looked closely at Brent. "This is not a fling, Brent. I want you to pay close attention to what you're doing. This is your future you're playing with."

"No one knows that better than I, Father, believe me," Brent said in a voice rigidly under control.

"When will you go?"

"As soon as possible."

"You must talk to Barbara tonight. I wouldn't want her to be upset if you're gone longer than you plan."

"No, of course not. I'll speak to her."

"Have you decided when you will be married?"

"No . . . not yet."

"Getting cold feet?" Stephen chuckled. "You've made a good choice."

"Have I?" Brent's smile was vague. "I don't really recall making any decisions at all."

"Brent, don't be ridiculous. Barbara is perfect for you. Look at her family, at her background. She is a prime example of what men in our position need in a wife."

Brent smiled again at the reference to "men in our position," as if it were a satisfactory business deal and his father was marrying Barbara as well as he. Of course he didn't doubt for one minute that Stephen and Barbara would get along famously. They were two of a kind.

"We'll decide on a wedding date soon enough," Brent said. "For now I'd like to concentrate on this little problem of ours."

"Make sure that by the time you come home it's a little problem that's only a little memory."

"If you'll excuse me, Father, I think I'll set about making the arrangements."

"All right. Shall we see you at dinner tonight?"

"I don't think so. I have some other plans."

"All right. We'll talk before you leave."

"There's not really much to talk about. I understand what needs to be done, and I don't want to waste any time. If I can manage it, I'll leave tomorrow."

"All right," Stephen agreed, but he watched Brent as he walked to the door and left. He wasn't too sure of the probability of Brent's success, but he wanted him to succeed at least once. Brent, as far as Stephen was concerned, spent too much time playing, drinking, and having his fling with a number of colorful women. He just didn't want Brent caught in a position he couldn't get out of. He sighed deeply, and hoped that the marriage to Barbara would set Brent on the proper path. He'd hate to rewrite his will and set men to guide his son in the future.

But one way or the other he would safeguard the fortune he'd so carefully built.

When Brent arrived in Aspen he was mildly surprised at how active the town seemed to be. His accommodations at the hotel were more than he'd expected as well, and he was pleased to find the town boasted more than one quality parlor house. Despite his father's implied disapproval, he intended to have some fun while he worked.

He knew that much of the gossip of any town found its way to a parlor house sooner or later, and the girls in the parlor houses would tell him. He knew how to ask and how to stimulate response with an unlimited bankroll.

He rose early the first morning he was in Aspen, shaved, and dressed carefully. He had registered under his own name, and was amused that it hadn't been recognized by the clerk. At this moment no one knew his mission.

He strolled about the town, getting to know it, and allowing himself to be seen as nothing but a curious passerby.

He walked, he looked, and he listened. He stopped for a casual lunch sometime later and chatted with the waiter.

"There seems to be quite a bit of activity in Aspen."

"Yes, sir. We have everything from musical theater to the best parlor houses in the state. You just passing through?"

"Well, I was, but I might be persuaded to stay awhile."

"Be worth your while."

"Any 'special places' you could recommend?"

"Sure, Aspen can offer just about anything you're looking for. For some real fine food you might try the Golden Palace. Course if you like some good plain home cooking and a pretty face, try the Silver Strike. It's plain and simple but darn good, and it's run by two of the prettiest ladies around these parts."

"Sounds like a deluxe parlor house."

"Good Lord, man, don't say that out loud. The Silver Strike is just a nice restaurant. It serves about the best food a man can have and none of it has anything to do with parlor house girls. Miss Champion and Miss Falcon are hard-working ladies. They're kind of quiet and reserved, but they serve a darn good meal."

"It sounds fine. I'll give it a try. You sound like you know Miss Champion and Miss Falcon pretty well. Do they come from Aspen?"

"Nobody knows where the ladies hail from, and no one has the nerve to go up and ask them."

"Now you really have me interested."

"They keep pretty much to themselves. Built a small house up on the crest of the hill just beyond town. They work hard and handle their money carefully. Do a lot of charity work in town too."

"Can I get someone to introduce me?"

"Ain't likely."

"No harm in a gentleman trying, is there?"

"Want a piece of advice?"

"Sure."

"These aren't parlor house girls. Like I say, they keep pretty much to themselves and don't seem to look favorably on gents misinterpreting their positions. More than one man's had his whiskers singed, and some of them have been miners with a lot of coins in their pockets. Those two are aristocrats if ever I've seen one."

"Thanks. I'll stop in and eat there."

"Well, I think the most you'll get will be one of the best meals in the state."

"We'll see." Brent was much too used to having whatever he chose to take the waiter's advice too much to heart. At least the challenge might make his time in Aspen more interesting.

Brent spent the balance of the afternoon browsing the town, looking, listening, and asking subtle questions.

He dressed carefully for dinner, intrigued by all he'd heard about the two lovely ladies who owned the Silver Strike. Of course he suspected they weren't quite the "ladies" most people thought them to be.

He walked slowly to the Silver Strike, and got his first surprise when he walked in the door. One look around told him his informant had been right. This was no parlor house.

Brent felt he had stepped from the rough mining town

of Aspen into one of the most tasteful and best-run places he'd ever seen. It was neat and clean, and the smell of well-cooked food awoke his appetite.

A waiter approached. "May I help you, sir?"

"Ah . . . yes." Brent smiled. "A good dinner, I hope. You've come highly recommended."

"Yes, sir, the best food in town. You staying or traveling on?"

"I've just gotten into town. I guess I'll be staying a couple of days."

"Well, you haven't made a mistake coming here."

Brent smiled again and looked around. The room was large, the tables circular and adequate for seating at least five or six people at each. Several smaller tables lined the perimeter of the room for couples or single diners.

Against the far wall a flight of steps went up to a balconied area. Brent's attention was drawn to it when a door at the top of the stairs opened and a woman stepped out.

She turned from the door and started down the stairs, and when she stepped into the light Brent gave a slight, audible sound. He had seen many beautiful women, but he could not remember seeing one as beautiful as this.

He watched as she descended the stairs slowly, looking around at the crowded tables. She was enough to take a man's breath away. He wanted to go on watching her, but at that moment the waiter spoke. "I have a table for you right here, sir."

"Yes . . . thank you," Brent replied, but his eyes remained on the stairs. "Who is that lovely creature?"

The waiter's eyes followed Brent's. "Ah, that's Miss Laura Champion. She is the owner of the Silver Strike . . . or rather the co-owner."

"I should like to meet her," Brent said. But he was rewarded by a frigid look.

"Miss Champion is not here to entertain, sir. This is not a parlor house. If you are looking for a woman, I suggest you find another establishment. Might I suggest Miss Pearl's. It's at the other end of town."

Brent knew he'd overstepped himself, and the last thing he wanted to do was leave.

"I hadn't meant to suggest such a thing," Brent replied quickly. "I apologize. My table?"

"Yes, sir, if you'll follow me." The waiter's attitude displayed little acceptance. Brent followed.

The table he was given was some distance from Laura Champion's. But he could still see her. He watched, trying to think of a way he could acquire an introduction to the beautiful Miss Champion.

Beneath the glow of the lights, her skin looked luminous and her burnished hair glowed like a muted flame. He ordered his food, and ate while he still contemplated avenues of approach. He was about to throw caution to the wind when a tall, handsome man entered the room.

From the way the waiter smiled and displayed some deference, Brent was sure this man was someone special. He regarded him closely. He was a tall, strongly built man with an aura of restrained power. The fact that he walked with a limp and his face bore a scar or two only seemed to add to the aura rather than detract from it. He was enveloped in a veil of mystery that intrigued even the casual onlooker. His clothes were not in the latest style and looked rather worn. If Brent were to hazard a guess, he would have labeled the stranger a miner, dressed for a night out after a week's hard labor. He had the look of a man who worked hard physically for his money.

Brent was even more impressed when the man walked across the room without the guidance of the waiter, pulled out a chair, and sat down opposite Laura Champion, who regarded him with a smile. Brent intended to watch and wait. Obviously this was no run-of-the-mill miner. He meant something to Laura Champion.

Simon had arrived in Aspen almost two months before Brent. It took very little time to find himself work, and although the work was of the lowest type, it gave him legitimacy. Finding a room to board in was difficult at first, since he wanted one some distance from town. Eventually he found one at Mrs. Broderick's boardinghouse. The room was reasonably priced, clean, and private. She provided one meal a day and asked no questions. Within a week or two he was firmly established as a laborer and had already set about the work he had come to do.

Simon, intent on his goals, did not go into the town until he'd been in Aspen nearly a month. He wanted to blend in quietly and unobtrusively. When he finally did go into town it was almost reluctantly. He'd already begun feeding ideas into his daily conversations with the miners. He sensed their unrest, just as he sensed this was the most opportune time to transform that unrest into something more formidable.

He'd gone into town on a Saturday night with a group of men he worked with. Their usual haunts were Delilah's parlor house, or Miss Pearl's.

But Simon wanted to see more of the town and since the evening was young, he decided a walk would give him a good view of the city.

He was walking slowly a short distance from the Golden Palace when he saw a woman leave a rather elite clothing store and enter a carriage.

He stopped walking and stood watching in puzzlement. She looked so familiar. Yet he wasn't certain. She was dressed so elegantly . . . it couldn't be . . . but . . .

The carriage moved past him slowly and when it was right beside him, the woman turned her head and their eyes met. Her gaze widened in fear as she recognized his face.

Zoe! It was Zoe Carrigan! He would know her anywhere, despite the obvious changes in her life. Her skin was still the same flawless cream. Her hair still shone with the brilliance of autumn leaves beneath a glowing sun. Zoe.

He was shocked into immobility, and minutes later the carriage had gone on its way.

So this was where Zoe had run that night. A multitude of questions crowded his mind. She had looked so elegant, so well dressed . . . and so afraid. He had to have answers. Even more important, he had to erase that look of fear from her face. Whatever she was doing, he would be the last to cause her harm.

His only question was how he was going to go about talking to her. He knew she'd recognized him. If she had wanted to talk to him, she would have stopped her carriage and done so.

After a few subtle questions he found out she owned the Silver Strike, so that seemed the best place to begin.

The moment he walked in the door, a waiter approached him.

"Yes, sir?"

"I was looking for someone, but I can see she's not here."

"Maybe I can help you."

Simon had no way of knowing if Zoe had changed her name or not, and he didn't want to jeopardize her position. He shook his head negatively, made a quick escape, and re-adjusted his plans. He'd find Zoe on his own.

Zoe had seen a face from her past, and it was so unexpected that the shock nearly undid her. It was Simon Tremaine, and there was no doubt in her mind that he had recognized her. The problem was, what would he do about it?

Once she had regained her control she thought back. Simon had always befriended her. Surely he would keep her secret now. But what about Cara? He had known exactly what Cara was. Would he keep that secret as well?

Her courage returned. By the time the carriage stopped in front of the house she shared with Cara, she was back in control. When she walked inside, Cara was coming down the stairs. She recognized something was wrong at once.

"Zoe, what is it? You look like you've seen a ghost."

"I have, and I'm not quite sure yet what to do about it."

"Just who is this ghost? Someone we both know?"

"Yes. You remember Simon Tremaine?"

"Simon Tremaine . . . yes, I remember him. He came to Stelle's often enough. What the devil is he doing in Aspen?"

"That's what I want to know."

"You think he'll let the cat out of the bag?"

"I don't know. One way or the other I have to find out, don't I?"

"Yes, I suppose."

"No supposes. We can't let him see you and me, put two and two together, and come up with something that could ruin what has taken us almost seven years to build."

"Lord, Zoe, I knew you shouldn't have stuck with me. I was sure one day it was going to spoil your plans. Just when that wealthy Mr. Mitchell was beginning to show interest. One word from Simon and Mitchell will never pop the question."

"Stop that, Cara. Let's not panic, and don't go blaming yourself for anything. We made ourselves a promise and we have to keep it. One way or the other we'll stick together. Remember how we worried last year when Stelle arrived to open her new parlor house in Aspen? But she's never let on that she knows either one of us."

"Stelle's different. She understands our situation. You'd have been better off if you'd never connected yourself with me. If Simon Tremaine talks to anyone about my past, you'll be tarred with the same brush, even though you've never been with a man."

"And if I'd never connected myself with you I'd still be back in Georgetown, wearing patched dresses too tight for me and fetching and carrying for my stepfather . . . or maybe it would have been worse than that." Zoe's voice was low and steady. "When I ran that night . . . who could I have run to? Don't ever tell me things like that again, Cara. We're friends and that's the way it's going to stay, Simon Tremaine or no Simon Tremaine."

"What are you going to do, Zoe?"

"I'm going to talk to him. I always could talk to Simon. He was a friend a lot like you. I don't think he'll give us away."

"Talk to him? How are you going to arrange that?"

"Knowing Simon like I do, I'll bet I won't have to arrange it. I have a feeling *he* will."

"In front of the whole town! That's not much better than blabbing. You know how gossip spreads. Folks are going to want to know who and what he is. Then they tie your names together and Mr. Rich will walk out of your life."

"I'm wondering too."

"Wondering? What?"

"Who and what he is. Why he's here. He had no problems at home as far as I know. So why is he here . . . in Aspen?"

"That is a puzzle, isn't it?"

"Ummm . . . it looks like I have as many questions to ask Simon as he has to ask me."

"Oh, Zoe, this makes me nervous. We've worked so hard to be respectable. We've built a good life. Look, you took the time to teach me to read, write, and talk decent. We have good reputations."

"We always knew the danger was there. It's money that has stood between us and the wolves, not our reputations. It's only money that will keep us from being the way we were. We'll get through this, and I'll get all the money I need. Let's not give up so easy."

"Zoe, look. We've got some money in the bank. Let's take it and get out of here. We can build a place like the Silver Strike in any town, maybe Boulder or Denver even."

"And what happens when we start somewhere else and someone else comes along? I'm not going to be run out of town because we've seen one familiar face. We have to have a little more courage than that. Like you said, Cara, we've worked too hard and made too much of ourselves. I'm not going to give it away."

Cara stood up and paced the floor for a few minutes. She and Zoe had deliberately divorced themselves from the manual labor of the restaurant as soon as possible. They had hired a very efficient man to help manage what they had so laboriously built. But Zoe kept the accounting in her own hands, and had managed it with ruthless care. Since a lady was not meant to run a business, Zoe kept her accounting work a secret, and they were respected. Meanwhile, Zoe fed the gossips stories of inherited money, genteel family ties, and sorrowful but unknown tragedies. It worked well. Zoe understood the use of rumor and how easily something was believed if it was whispered in confidence.

Zoe sat in silent contemplation. She guessed that it would not take Simon too long to inquire about her. She also knew that it would not take him too long to find out where she lived. She expected him. Her only problem was what to do about a very nervous Cara.

Another thought troubled her. Would Simon have enough sense to inquire about her without using her real name? All he had to do was link her to the name Zoe Carrigan, and someone else might begin to ask questions too.

She decided to face one problem at a time.

"Cara, I have a feeling Simon Tremaine will be at our door sometime within the next week. It won't take him long to move around town and find out what my name is."

"Zoe! How can you be so calm about it? We just won't answer the door and—"

"Cara, we're not going to do that."

"Just what are we going to do?"

"We aren't going to do anything. I'm going to talk to him alone. And there's not much point in you arguing with me. If he comes, I'm going to talk to him. I . . . I have some things I want to know too."

"About your family?" Cara said softly.

"Yes. I don't want to know about . . . him . . . but my mother . . . my brothers and sister. I'd just like to know that they didn't have to pay for what I did."

"What you did," Cara scoffed. "What you did was what he forced you to do. You had no choice but to leave. What he was doing to you was terrible." Cara walked across the room and sat down beside Zoe. "I know how you feel, Zoe. I guess I can understand why you want to talk to Simon. I'm just worried for you. What if he isn't the same man you knew before?"

"That's a chance I have to take. Cara . . . I won't run. I just won't."

Cara sighed and stood up slowly. She knew from past experience there was little sense in arguing with Zoe when she had her mind set.

"All right. I suppose you have to do it, so I'll stay out of your way. I'll go up to my room when he comes. If you want me all you need to do is call."

"Thanks, Cara."

Cara nodded and left the room. Zoe sat for a long time

thinking back over the past seven years. Back to George-town . . . back to her family. She could feel the heat of unshed tears. Tears she would never allow.

She had faced adversity too many times in her young life to allow tears to defeat her. She had her goals. She knew what she wanted and where she was going, and she didn't intend to let anything or anyone stand in her way.

She had no idea how long she sat in the dimly lamplit room. But she was aware of everything, as if all her senses were heightened.

For the next few days she waited in an almost breath-less anticipation. She had no doubt Simon would come and she was prepared for it.

A few nights later, she heard a carriage stop outside, then footsteps on the porch . . . and a solid knock on the door. She nodded to Cara, who promptly disappeared up-stairs. She rose slowly and walked to the door. Without hesitation she opened it and smiled up at the visitor.

"Hello, Simon. I've been expecting you. Come in." She moved aside to let him pass her.

Chapter Nine

Zoe closed the door and followed Simon into the room. The changes in Simon were so obvious that they held her speechless for a moment. She knew that a great deal of pain must have come with the visual changes. It was written on his face. His eyes were filled with shadows. She wondered if the changes in her were as obvious.

"It's been a long time, Simon."

"Almost seven years."

"A lot has happened in seven years. I'm surprised to see you here."

"No more surprised than I was to see you. You look beautiful, Zoe. From what I hear, you're doing really well. I couldn't be happier about that."

"Can I get you something? A drink, maybe?"

"No, thanks. I really came just to talk to you."

"Simon . . ." she began.

"Zoe, let me clear things up. I didn't come here to cause you any problems. I know you've changed your name, and I can see you've put the past behind you. Behind you is where it belongs. I wouldn't cause you any kind of grief. We were friends, remember?"

Zoe felt a sudden constriction of her breath that was a combination of relief and a feeling closely akin to pain. This was a friend—outside of Cara, maybe the only friend she had ever had. The knowledge brought tears to her eyes.

"I remember." She said the words softly, and crossed the room to stand beside him. "I have never forgotten you, Simon. You were kind to me . . . so few people were." She inhaled deeply. "But that's the past and I intend to keep it locked away."

"Our pasts are always part of us."

"Not me. There is nothing there I want . . . except . . ."

"Except?"

"My mother . . . Zach . . . the kids?"

Simon wanted to avoid her eyes and to avoid the questions, but he could do neither. Zoe deserved honesty.

"Your mother died, Zoe. After you left it seemed all her spirit was gone. When Zach ran away too . . . well, it seemed that she really didn't want to go on."

"Eli and Martha . . . what about them?" Zoe's voice was thick with the pain and grief his words caused.

"Eli and Martha were taken in by neighbors. They're well and maybe a whole lot better off. Zach has . . . just vanished."

Zoe walked away from him and stood near the window looking out through the lace curtains with unseeing eyes.

"And . . . him?" She could not bear to say Roger Carrigan's name. The hatred dripped from her words like acid.

"He was the same when I left. No, maybe worse. At least some people used to listen before. Now no one listens. He's a lonely old man. He's left alone in that old shack to fend for himself. The last time I saw him I could only see how pathetic he had become."

"Pathetic." She spun around. "You talk as if I should have sympathy for him! As if I should care."

"No, I don't mean that. I'm not thinking of him. I'm thinking of you."

"Me?"

"You carry this hatred. Hate is like a disease. It eats at you until it eats the best part of you away and leaves nothing. Sympathy is not what I'm suggesting. But maybe you should forgive him and wipe him out of your heart. That way you'll have room for other things."

"You ask too much, Simon Tremaine. How can I forgive him for killing my mother, for nearly destroying my life, for all the things he did to Zach . . . for breaking us apart so that I have no family. No, I'll never forgive him, never. There are so many things about which you know nothing."

Simon could see there was no room for argument in Zoe's mind, and he didn't want to lose her trust. "You've done well with your freedom."

She looked around her. The house was comfortable, but far from elaborate. She had always thought of it as temporary. A place to use until she could acquire what she really wanted. She had no intention of telling Simon this.

"Thank you. We like it, and it's quite adequate."

"We? You haven't gotten married, have you?"

For some reason this thought annoyed him, and he was surprised at his response. He wanted to hear her say no.

"Married!" Zoe laughed. "I haven't met a man with enough money to put a ring on my finger."

"Money, is that what it takes?"

"What else is there?"

"You might find someone to love."

"Love! Oh, Simon, don't be a fool. Do you know what love is? Love is a trap embellished with pretty words and flowers. In the end it leaves you nothing. Not even yourself. Love killed my mother and destroyed my family, and I won't make the same mistake. I know what I want and your precious ideas about love have nothing to do with it."

"Every man isn't your stepfather."

"I don't intend to try to prove that one way or another."

"What are you looking for?"

"Wealth," Zoe said bluntly. "Enough money and power so that nothing can ever touch me again. I want to travel and I want pretty clothes, silks . . . furs . . . everything. I want to be safe from the Georgetowns and the Roger Carrigans of this world."

Simon felt her bitterness and her pain, and he felt a deep sympathy. He would have liked to put his arms about her to comfort her somehow, but he knew her pride wouldn't accept it.

Zoe smiled to dismiss the subject. "And you, have you married?"

"No."

"Why not?" She chuckled. "You're a believer in love and living happily ever after."

"Maybe"—he laughed in response to ease his next words—"I decided to wait for you."

Her eyes grew chilled and her words were just as cold. "Don't, Simon. Don't ever think of me. I could never make any man happy. I can only pretend, and you are too much of a friend for that." She smiled again to cover the sudden antagonism between them. "Come for dinner tomorrow night. There's so much I want to hear about . . . you and what you've been doing."

"All right. I haven't had a lot of good meals lately."

"I'm a good cook now that I have some good food to cook. We'll be glad to have someone to talk to."

"You keep saying 'we.' I suppose you and Cara left Georgetown together and stuck together?"

"Yes. I'd say she's the best friend I have." Her voice was challenging.

"Cara Jardeen—isn't her friendship a little dangerous for the kind of plans you have? What if a wealthy suitor turns out to be one of Stelle's old customers? It would sure ruin your plans."

"Cara's a friend! She's the only reason I ever found my way out of Georgetown. She's the only one who ever stood by me no matter what. I don't intend to turn my back on her."

"What a contradiction you are, Zoe. One minute you want to cut away all your past, and the next you're protecting the one person who could ruin your future."

"You don't have to understand. There are some things you just can't throw away, and Cara's friendship is one. She would never hurt me . . . and I will never hurt her."

It struck Simon like lightning, and he gazed at Zoe in a kind of rapt wonder. He loved her. He'd known her most of her life, and now it had dawned on him that he loved her in a unique and protective kind of way. He wondered if he had always loved her and had just never recognized it. It was a strange and sobering situation, because Zoe had made it so clear she would not return his feelings.

"Well, I'll be glad to come to dinner. I hope Cara won't mind."

"Come to dinner at seven, Simon. I'm sure you and Cara will have a lot to talk about."

"I'm looking forward to it."

She walked to the door with her arm linked in his. He liked the gesture, and understood it for the offer of friendship it was. That didn't mean he wasn't aware of the new maturity in Zoe and the lush woman she had become. It gave him a twinge of jealousy to realize a woman who looked and acted like Zoe would most likely have very little trouble acquiring the rich man she wanted. But when Zoe found out that selling one's self very seldom led to happiness, Simon wondered, would the discovery break her or not? He intended to stick around. Maybe he could find a way to change her plans.

When Zoe closed the door behind Simon, she sagged against it for a moment in utter relief. Simon was the same. He wouldn't betray them.

She heard Cara's footsteps on the stairs, and straightened to turn and look up at her.

"He's gone?"

"Yes."

"Well?"

"He's the same, Cara. Kind and trusting. He won't say anything to anyone. He just wants to keep our friendship like it was."

"Simon always was one of the nicest of them. When he grew to be a man, he became a real one. I remember . . ."

"I don't want to hear your memories of Simon Tremaine, Cara."

"Well, he was some kind of a man. A woman could do a hell of a sight worse. He'd care for a woman that was his."

"He's still a miner."

"How do you know?"

"Look at him. He hasn't one dime to rub against another. And a woman that was his, as you so casually put it, would have a batch of kids and so much washing and cleaning and doing without that she'd be old before she was forty. Then he'd find his pleasure with pretty parlor girls, and she'd listen to preachers with their promises of paradise in the sky when you die. It's not for me, Cara.

I've walked that road before. I don't intend to ever walk it again."

"So what's he doing here? I thought he'd never leave Georgetown."

"I don't really know. I've asked him to come to dinner tomorrow night."

"How does he look, Zoe?"

"Different. He's been terribly hurt somehow—physically, I mean. He has a scar on his face and he walks with a limp. We'll see if he wants to talk about it. If he doesn't, we'll let it go at that. If he's going to stay in Aspen, then I want to keep him as a friend."

Cara nodded, and watched Zoe as she ascended the stairs. She had an instinctive feeling that Simon's sudden reappearance in Zoe's life meant more to Zoe than she knew, and that it was somehow going to have more effect on their lives than either of them had planned on.

Simon bought a new suit. It was as much of a surprise to him as it was to the men he worked with. When a few comments reached his ears, he defended himself with a smile.

"Gents, you're all jealous. Tonight I am going to have dinner with not one, but two very pretty ladies."

"Sure you are," one friend chided. "What I think is you bought that rig for a funeral."

"Whose funeral?"

"Yours if you're messing around with the foreman's wife the way she'd like you to."

This brought a round of laughter.

"Go ahead and laugh, but I'm having dinner with Miss . . . uh . . . Laura Champion, and her friend Miss Falcon."

"You ain't."

"I am. They're ladies who recognize a gentleman when they see him. Besides, I think they want to talk to someone who knows mining and about investing in a mine."

"That would make them mine owners," one man said. "Why should you be friends with mine owners, when you been telling us all that we have to get together and do something about these hellhole conditions we're working in?"

Simon knew the man was right. He was here for a reason and Zoe had temporarily sidetracked him. He had to support what he believed in and put Zoe second.

"You're right. I was just having a little fun."

"Then you ain't having no dinner with those two nice ladies?" A third man laughed. "I didn't think they'd have much to do with a drifter like you."

"Yeah," Simon said quietly. "You're right again."

Later, as he walked the distance to Zoe's house, he had time to think. He was in a bad position to get involved with anyone. He had things that had to be done. He'd have to handle this friendship carefully, or he was going to draw as much attention to Zoe as he was to himself, and neither of them afford the scrutiny.

Zoe seemed to have been waiting for him, because he had just approached her door when she opened it.

"Good evening, Simon. My, you look nice."

"Thanks. You look absolutely beautiful."

"Come in."

"Something smells good."

"I hope so. It's been cooking all afternoon."

"I really appreciate this, Zoe . . . or should I call you Laura?"

"Zoe to you."

They entered the large living room from the entrance hall and Simon stopped in the doorway.

"Cara." He smiled. "It's good to see you again."

"Simon . . . you have gotten older," Cara said. Then she walked to him and looked up into his eyes. "And a lot wiser, I'd say. It looks like someone tried to teach you a lesson."

"Cara!" Zoe interrupted.

"It's all right, Zoe. She's right. Only it's a lesson I have no intention of learning. Instead, I intend to do some teaching."

"Yes indeed," Cara said softly. "You have grown older."

"And hungrier." He laughed. "You have no idea how long it's been."

"Then come on and let's eat." Each of the women linked an arm through his and they walked into the dining room.

*   *   *

Simon set his wine glass down and leaned back in his chair. "And so, that's how I came to be here and that's how I got blessed with this." He patted his leg. "It's a reminder just in case I ever forget what I have to do."

"But I don't suppose you plan to forget," Zoe said quietly.

"No . . . I don't suppose."

"You see, Simon," Zoe said, "it's the same with me. We all have things we can't forget and things we have to do about them."

"You see your situation as the same as mine, Zoe?"

"Don't you?"

"No."

"Why?"

"Because . . . it's a matter of price tags. I figure I've paid my bill in advance. But . . . I think you're going to have a bill in the end too big for you to pay. It could cause you a lot of grief."

"Don't talk to me of bills or payments, Simon. If you paid once, I paid a thousand times over. Can I guess how you're going to collect your bill?"

"Sure . . . guess."

"By starting a union and proving they can't stop you by beating you up."

"Oh, Lord," Cara said with a despairing gasp.

Zoe laughed. "And I intend to marry money, and the only men with money around here are the mine owners. It looks like we're going to stand on opposing sides."

"No, Zoe." Simon smiled. "There's nothing in the world that can put us on opposite sides. I guess we'll both do what we have to do. But . . . we'll stay friends, I hope."

"I'd like that, Simon."

They spent the rest of the evening talking of Aspen and its progress and the success of the mines. Simon went into detail about the miners' difficulties, but he could see Zoe had built a wall between herself and the men she scorned. She had climbed out of poverty, and had little pity for those who did not do the same.

He found Cara's reaction to the conversation particularly interesting. Occasionally she cast Zoe a look that came very close to sympathy. It was obvious that Cara cared a great deal about Zoe and that she too seemed doubtful about the path Zoe had chosen.

Both Zoe and Cara walked him to the door when he left. He had hardly gotten to the front gate when he heard his name called. He turned to see Cara moving toward him.

"I guess it was a surprise for you to find me here."

"A little maybe. But if I remember right, it was you who always befriended Zoe. Even when she was a dirty-faced kid."

"She's my only friend, Simon, and I'm worried about her. She's a sweet girl and sure as hell she's going to get hurt."

"And there's nothing I can do about it any more than you can. You've tried, haven't you?"

"Yeah, I guess."

"Zoe is not going to listen to me any more than she is you. The only thing either of us can do is to be there if and when she needs us."

"I'll be here. It's why I came in the first place. Under that hard shell is a scared little girl."

"You know, Cara," Simon said thoughtfully, "when I knew you before . . . well, it was different. I'll admit to you that I told Zoe your past might just be the thing that would destroy her plans. I want to tell you now that I'm sorry I said or thought that. She's lucky to have a friend like you. I'd like to be one too."

"Thanks Simon." Tears sparkled in her eyes even though she smiled. She stood on tiptoe and kissed his cheek. "I won't forget that. I guess together we can keep a pretty good eye on her. Who knows . . . two to one are pretty good odds."

"Good night, Cara."

"Night."

She stood by the gate and watched him walk away. "Oh, Zoe," she whispered, "you're crazy."

Simon continued to work the mines and to organize the miners. Daily he fought to make them listen. Daily he battled their fear of the owners and their knowledge that the owners could close the mines and deprive them of everything.

Once or twice a week he would meet Zoe when she came to the restaurant to pick up the books, and they would have dinner together and fight the same battle.

They were seated together early one evening, and while Simon was talking he noticed Zoe's attention drifting. He turned and looked across the room to see a man sitting alone at a table regarding them closely. When Zoe's eyes met his, he raised his wine glass and took a sip.

Zoe bent close to Simon. "Who is he?"

"I don't know."

"He must be new in town."

"How do you know?"

"Simon." Zoe laughed. "I've made it my business to know about every wealthy bachelor in Aspen."

"Maybe he's married."

"Maybe."

"Zoe!"

"We don't know that's a fact"—she smiled again—"but it won't take me very long to find out."

"Do you know how you sound?"

"Like a very smart woman."

"Don't play games. Your hands are shaking."

"I guess you're right. I sound like I have more courage than I really have."

"Zoe, no matter how you try, you can't be so hard and self-serving."

"I can be whatever it is necessary for me to be!" She stood abruptly, angry because Simon had touched her vulnerability. "You're a friend, Simon, but stop trying to tell me how to live my life."

She left the table and went upstairs to gather the accounts to take home.

Simon sat for a long time in deep concentration. But after a while he began to be aware that the man who'd attracted Zoe's curiosity was regarding him with the same serious study. Why it should unnerve him he didn't know, but somehow he began to feel this man was going to have an effect on his life and not necessarily a good one.

* * *

Word circulated fast when the foreman at one of the Dewitt mines finally found out that the son of the owner was in town.

Zoe was fascinated when she learned who the stranger was. But her dreams of capturing wealth had never included the specifics of how to go about it. Cara was amused at Zoe's predicament.

"Now, Zoe, if you'd been one of Stelle's parlor girls, you'd know how to go after him." She laughed.

"That's hardly funny. I don't want to be his mistress, you know." Unfortunately, that was all Mr. Mitchell had had in mind, so he had been rebuffed coldly.

"Zoe, you've always said you needed money. Well, I've checked. He has all the money you could want . . . but Zoe, it's his father's, not his. I suppose Brent Dewitt will get it all one day. But right now he works for Papa. Maybe you'd better forget about this one."

"Cara, how did you find out all that stuff? He's only been in town a week."

"A week's long enough to find out anything about anyone."

"Did you know him before, Cara?" Zoe asked quietly.

For a few minutes Cara was quiet; then she nodded. "Yes," she said softly, "I did . . . a long time ago."

Zoe sat slowly down in a chair. If Brent Dewitt knew Cara . . . then he knew she had been a parlor girl. Simon had warned her of just such a situation. She swallowed what she felt was obvious defeat before she had even tried. It wasn't fair. She was not what he would surely think she was.

Cara came and knelt down beside her chair, hating the look of defeat on her friend's face. "Look, Zoe, I hate to see you tangle with any more men like Mitchell. I don't think Brent would treat you that way. I've had this crazy idea since I recognized him."

"What crazy idea?"

"Look, Brent will remember me, so there's not much point in waiting until he does."

"I don't understand."

"I'm going to let him accidentally run into me. I'll tell

him I've given up my former life, found a position with a very beautiful lady who's so kind and so lovely. But she doesn't know about my past. I'm going to throw myself on his mercy. Men just love a feeling of power. He'll feel grand about being able to be magnanimous, especially if I cry. Then, when he promises he'll never tell, I'll give in and promise to introduce him to you. I know him. He'll use what I was as a way to get to meet the sweet, innocent Laura Champion . . . and I'll let him."

"It will never work."

"No? Trust me, Zoe. I know men a lot better than you do. He'll be frothing at the mouth just to be able to meet you. I swear, you'll hear wedding bells in no time."

"You sound awfully sure of him."

"My heavens, Zoe. Are you getting cold feet?"

"I'm . . . I'm scared."

"Of what? It's what you want, isn't it?" Cara asked, suddenly wondering if she was doing the right thing, getting Brent and Zoe together.

"I don't know what I'm afraid of, and yes, it is what I want."

"Then . . . if it's what you want, just keep on being a lady with spunk like you've always been. All you need to do is be seen. Let him take it from there. You need never say a word about where you came from or who you were."

"And if it doesn't work? If he thinks . . ."

"That you were one of us? There's not a chance. He knew Stelle's girls. He never saw you there. Besides that, Zoe, you have something special. You see, you look like the lady you want to be. You can take a chance and grab what you want. He'll look at you and he'll know you're not one of us. You have that kind of an air, Zoe. You can do it." She paused.

Zoe could not quite let go of her fear. She could not stand the thought of being shamed again. To be pointed to as an outcast, as someone to be laughed at and ignored. She struggled to find the old courage.

"Zoe?"

"I hear you," her voice rasped as if her throat were constricted.

"Well?"

"All right. But if it doesn't work, things will really change for us here. You understand?"

"Yes, I understand. But it will work. Trust me."

Zoe turned to look into Cara's eyes. "I do trust you. It's me and my life that are hard to trust. I just can't see my dreams coming true."

"After what you've known, you deserve to be happy." Cara rose and looked down at Zoe. "Tonight I'll go down to the restaurant. You stay here. I can handle everything. Do you hear me, Zoe?"

"Yes." Zoe nodded, and as Cara started to walk out, called to her. "Thank you, Cara."

"You're welcome." Cara smiled and left Zoe alone with her thoughts.

Brent had seen Laura Champion just once. But he couldn't get her out of his mind. She was an extraordinarily beautiful woman. One who did not belong in a drab mining town like Aspen. He'd asked questions, and heard the sound of admiration and respect in each answer.

He spent his days at the mine office, but he spent his evenings in town. First he always went to the Silver Strike for a prolonged dinner, hoping she'd reappear.

He'd not seen the young miner either, but he'd asked more questions and heard disquieting answers. There were many rumors about him, and some of them included the elusive Laura Champion.

He walked into the restaurant just after seven one evening, and was met graciously by the head waiter, who'd already been handsomely tipped.

"Your table is ready, Mr. Dewitt."

"Thank you."

He sat, he ordered, he sipped his wine, and he waited. He expected a woman to walk down the stairs . . . but not the one who did.

Cara had come to the restaurant early because she had been told about Brent's constant presence. She stood in the room at the top of the stairs with the door cracked open just enough to let her see the table below.

She watched Brent walk in and smiled. She believed her plan would work. Dewitt was certainly the kind of man Zoe had always said she wanted. His attitude was aristocratic . . . and his family was dripping with money. She remembered how he used to throw it about in the parlor house.

Satisfied that he was comfortable and enjoying a good meal, she opened the door, stepped out into the hall, then slowly walked down the stairs.

With peripheral vision she saw him look at her . . . return his gaze to his meal . . . then abruptly lift his head and look at her again, a look of utter surprise crossing his face. Cara found a seat at a table and waited.

He rose slowly, as if he couldn't quite believe what he was seeing, and walked toward her. He stopped by her table, but Cara did not look up at him. She acted as if she was engrossed in her own thoughts.

"Cara? Cara Jardeen!"

Cara looked up slowly, letting a flicker of recognition touch her face before fear replaced it. Suddenly she looked away. This was enough to convince Brent he had the right woman. He smiled and took the seat opposite her. "Hello, Cara, it's been a long time."

Cara looked at him, knowing her timing was perfect. "Brent Dewitt . . . please keep your voice down. I don't want anyone to know . . ."

"That you're one of Stelle's special girls."

"Please." She bent toward him, her voice pleading, her wide eyes filled with an expression close to begging. "Don't call me that."

"What are you doing so far from Georgetown? I thought you were one of Stelle's favorites."

"Actually, Stelle has opened a parlor house here in Aspen, but I left her a long time ago. A girl has a right to change her life, Brent. I just didn't want to be one of Stelle's girls anymore."

"Just what do you want here in Aspen? It's filled with miners. I should think the best bet would be to open your own parlor house."

"I don't want anything to do with no more parlor houses. I have a good job here with a nice lady. She doesn't know who or what I was. I even changed my name. I like my job. She's good to me and she didn't ask me any questions about my past. So I didn't tell her. When I had enough money to be a partner here, she agreed. She's been good to me and hasn't asked questions. I can't let her know what I was."

"That doesn't sound very fair to her."

"She's kind and generous and my work is easy. I just do some of the shopping for the restaurant and help her with the accounts."

"Sounds simple, and very rewarding."

"It is. Brent . . . you won't give me away, will you? This is a real chance for me. I don't want to go back to that old life."

"You don't need to worry. By the way, what should I call you?"

"Huh?"

"What did you change your name to?"

"Oh." Cara paused for effect. "Sarina Falcon."

She watched his expression go still, without changing her expression at all. He remained quiet for some time, and Cara held her breath.

"Sarina Falcon . . . very nice. And . . . and who's the lady you work for?"

"Oh, she's really something, Brent," Cara gushed. "She's so beautiful, and she's alone in the world since her dear mama and papa died in a terrible accident. Anyway, she—"

"Cara!"

"What?"

"What's her name?"

"Oh . . . it's Laura Champion."

She knew that Brent was caught the moment she said Zoe's assumed name. His eyes glowed with anticipation, and Cara could have laughed because she could see Brent mentally licking his lips.

"Laura Champion," he said softly. "I have heard of her. In fact I have seen her here in this restaurant. I should very much like to meet Miss Champion. I'm sure you wouldn't mind introducing us."

"Oh, Lord, I couldn't do that! What if she asks me where I met you? What if it gets her started asking questions I can't answer? I can't tell her we met in Georgetown! I can't!"

"Cara," he interrupted, bringing her ragings to a halt. "You can do it. It's quite simple if you'll just stop babbling."

"But it will cause me trouble, and it might cost me my job. Brent, you wouldn't do that to me."

"Listen to me. It isn't like you to be stupid and flighty. You have nothing to be afraid of. I haven't been worth a chunk of fool's gold since I saw her here a few nights ago. I'm taken with the girl, Cara. I can't keep my mind on much else." He sound aggrieved. "I want to meet her."

"But . . ."

"No buts. You value your position with her and I value an introduction. Suppose we balance one with the other. You agree to introduce us, and I won't mention your past to her."

"But's that blackmail." Cara gasped as if this was the most horrible thing she had ever heard.

Brent told himself he was merely infatuated with the most desirable woman he had ever seen, and that he had only the usual pursuit, capture, and conquest in mind. After all, he already had a prospective bride at home.

He admitted that he was mad about Laura Champion, which was perfectly acceptable as long as his intentions remained strictly dishonorable. But he could not admit to himself to what extravagant lengths he might be willing to go to get her. Life had not equipped him to fight against his own desires. Until he had seen Laura Champion he had never wanted anything that was not his for the asking. And now he wanted her.

"What's it to be, Cara? It is certainly not too much to ask of someone who was such a close friend of mine as you were. Just introduce me. I shall take care of the rest, and you can simply vanish for the evening. Come now."

"All right," Cara said, giving her voice a resigned and somewhat despairing cast. "I guess I have no choice in the matter. But she's alone and unprotected in the world.

You wouldn't take advantage? She's . . . pure. There's never been a man in her life."

"How do you know?" His voice throbbed with excitement.

"In my line of work, believe me, I know," Cara said dryly. "Be here tomorrow at seven. I'll introduce you."

"You'll not regret it, Cara. I'll make it worth your while."

Just don't hurt her, Brent Dewitt, Cara thought. Or I'll never forgive myself for my part in all this.

Chapter Ten

Zoe had planned and schemed and sought this introduction to Brent, and now she was afraid to face him. She had told Simon very little of the truth, but even so, she could read the disapproval on his face, though he said nothing. But she didn't want barriers between her and Simon. He was the only true friend she had besides Cara. Only they knew what had led her along the path she walked.

"You don't approve of me, Simon."

"It's not that, Zoe. I care a great deal about what happens to you."

"Then why aren't you wishing me well?"

"Because I don't think you'll be happy. Tricking someone into a relationship will never work. What will you do if he finds out that you don't love him? That you just want to marry him for position and money."

"I can learn to love someone. After all, I learned to hate, didn't I? If he's kind to me, if he offers me a good life, I can learn to love him."

"I don't think love is something you learn."

"Oh, Simon, stop being so romantic. I don't think this thing you call love really exists. One learns to deal with things one day at a time. I don't expect wild passion and fairy tales. I'm sure my mother was such a dreamer, and look what it did for her. That's a trap I'll never fall into."

"It isn't the lack of love, Zoe. It's that he'll feel betrayed. That doesn't make living together a very happy affair."

"He'll never know."

"Sometimes plans don't work out the way we expect."

"Why are you trying to destroy the one chance I might have to make something of myself?"

Yes, he thought, why am I saying these things? I should wish her luck. But something deep inside him wouldn't let the words come out. He didn't want Zoe to "catch" and marry Brent Dewitt. He wanted . . . hell, he didn't want her to marry anyone.

He laughed at himself. He was the epitome of all the things Zoe wanted to leave behind her. She had never looked at him as anything but a friend, and he knew she never intended to.

He loved Zoe, but he couldn't change what he was and what he knew he most likely would always be. He had nothing to offer Zoe but himself.

Still, he felt Zoe was in for heartbreak, and all he could do was stand around and watch.

"I'm sorry, Zoe. I didn't mean to toss cold water on your dreams. I do wish you well, you know that. I just wish your plans could be achieved with more honesty."

"I promise you one thing, Simon."

"What's that?"

"I will never be dishonest again. If this does happen, I will make Brent a good wife. I'll be loyal and faithful. I'll never let him regret marrying me."

This, of course, did not make Simon feel one bit better. He struggled with the need to beg Zoe not to go through with it. He wanted to tell her he loved her, maybe had loved her from the time she was a child. He wanted to tell her she was unique and very special to him, that he admired her unquenchable spirit and her courage. But he couldn't. Zoe had her goals set, and she could not see past them. To her, Simon was a friend from the past, and it was a past she had long ago chosen to walk away from.

"I guess . . . I guess that's all you can do," he said.

"Then you will wish me luck?"

"I wish you happiness, Zoe," he replied gently. "I wish you contentment and success in finding what you want."

Zoe was still for a moment. Something about Simon made her pause. It was as if he were saying something terribly important, and for some reason she couldn't hear it. Then she smiled. "Thank you, Simon. I am grateful for your friendship, you know. You and Cara are all I have.

If . . . if Brent and I do marry . . . would you give me away?"

Simon felt a heavy constriction in his chest as if his heart were being squeezed of its lifeblood. He wanted to shout no! He wanted to tell her that he couldn't give her away. He inhaled a deep ragged breath. "I'll be honored to. But don't you think you're setting the cart before the horse?"

"I suppose."

"When do you . . . meet him?"

"Tonight."

"Just how have you arranged it?" The words were bitter on his tongue.

"Cara has invited him to the house. She just arranged a casual meeting. Once we've become acquainted I hope his interest will grow." She omitted much of what really was taking place.

"I'm sure Cara will handle it quite well," Simon said. "After all, she's quite used to clandestine affairs."

"That's not what this is!"

"No? You have to keep deluding yourself." Simon rose before Zoe could protest any further. But he could see the flush of anger on her face. Still, behind those eyes he could see the vulnerable girl. He knew she was uncertain, maybe a bit afraid, just as he knew she would see whatever she started through to the bitter end. She knew no other way. "Maybe I will wish you good luck, Zoe," Simon added before he walked away. "I have a feeling you may need all the luck you can get."

He walked away, and Zoe watched until he was gone. Her eyes glistened with tears, and she felt somehow bereft, as if she had destroyed something, and she didn't know what.

Later that night she stood before the full-length mirror in her room and examined herself. What would Brent see? What she wanted him to see? Or would he see beneath the surface and know what she was? She looked into her own eyes. Was she any better than Cara, or the rest of Stelle's girls?

Yes, with her it was different. Marriage put her in a

different category. She would be giving as much as she was getting. Finally she decided that the end justified the means.

Still, as she left her room and walked to the top of the stairs, the old, simple, naive, and frightened Zoe was just below the surface.

With each step fear tugged at her. It glazed her eyes until she could barely focus on the occupants of the room below her. When she did come to the doorway, she could only stand there. Fear sharpened the planes of her face and made her eyes enormous in her pale visage.

Brent stood up slowly. She had a vague impression that he was tall and carefully tailored. Cara still sat on the damask-covered settee, but her eyes glowed when she heard Brent's slightly muffled intake of breath. His expression was one of enraptured admiration.

"Laura, I'm glad you came down," Cara was saying. "There's someone here I want you to meet. This is Brent Dewitt from Denver."

Zoe walked toward them on legs that felt like lead, and she extended her hand.

"Good evening, Mr. Dewitt. Have I not seen you somewhere before?"

"Yes. I was dining in your restaurant. I'm afraid I could hardly take my eyes from you," he continued somewhat boyishly. Her heart slowed a little from its harsh thumping. She smiled, and Brent returned it. "But I've had a devil of a time trying to meet you. Sarina has been generous enough to invite me to your home."

"You're quite welcome, Mr. Dewitt."

"Please, would you do me the honor of calling me Brent? I hope that we can be friends." His hopes certainly match mine, Cara thought with an inward chuckle. "Sarina seems to value your friendship as highly as I do," he added.

"Sarina has been wonderful to me. I would consider any friend of hers a friend of mine as well."

"Have you known her long?"

Cara frowned. Was he going to ask difficult questions?

"Oh, I know she came from Georgetown"—Zoe smiled—"and I know she is an excellent partner. She takes care of her share of the work. She's invested in the restaurant and we make a profit. I am comfortable with that."

"Then your home was in Georgetown?" he asked, puzzled. He'd known Georgetown and Cara for a long time and no one had ever mentioned Laura Champion.

"I've . . . I've lived in several places."

He frowned a little. "I know of your parents' untimely deaths. Have you no family to share your home, or is it just your preference to have a companion?"

Alarm leapt to her eyes. This would never do.

"I haven't any family at all. I'm alone in the world."

He settled back on the settee beside her while Cara, who had risen to make room for Zoe, found herself a quiet place to observe. His shoulder touched Zoe's as he leaned back, and the panicky look in her eyes seemed like virginal terror to him. Cara, however, read it differently. It was a sudden touch of conscience and insecurity. Brent was instantly contrite. If she wasn't a novice, he thought, she certainly gave a remarkable imitation of one.

"Do you care for the theater, Laura?"

Her face lit up. "I'm afraid circumstances, and my being alone, have forbade my attending. But I would love to go." She forgot herself momentarily and added, "I have never been."

"I've tickets for the new play at the opera house tomorrow night. A box, in fact. I wonder if I may have the pleasure of escorting you to the performance. Of course," he added hastily, "your companion must accompany us as well."

"I would be very pleased." Zoe's voice was quiet and reserved and when she looked up at him, real pleasure was glowing in her eyes. He was totally lost to a flush of raw desire.

They spoke for a while of inconsequential things like the town, its progress, and other mundane matters that annoyed Brent. He would have liked to have taken Zoe to a quiet place where they could spend some time alone.

"Did you ever notice how time races when you're happy?" he asked Zoe. "But all day tomorrow I'll be pushing the clock's hands ahead."

"So will I." She smiled shyly up at him.

He bent nearer and spoke in a tone too low for Cara to hear. "And I'll be remembering you exactly as you are at this moment."

Which was not to be wondered at, for Zoe's eyes were luminous. He had invited her to the theater. He wasn't treating her like a tart; he was treating her like a lady. Nobody had ever treated her like a lady before, at least not a handsome young man. Her memories flew back to Georgetown and the brutal shame she had felt there. This was so different.

"And I'll remember you," she answered softly. He bent close to her, close enough that the delicate scent of her perfume and the nearness of her soft inviting lips made him catch his breath.

Reluctantly he stood up, taking Zoe's hand and bending over it for longer than was strictly necessary. After a look of gratitude for Cara, he said the last of several good-byes and was off.

Brent walked back to his hotel with his head in the clouds. Every gesture Zoe had made was imprinted on his memory. But he had to do battle with questions. She seemed a delicate, refined lady, yet there was something so . . . so . . . untutored about her. It was queer. How did she happen to be here? Where did she come from? The mystery of Laura Champion intrigued him. Yet he could not think of any girl in Denver, not even the promised Barbara, who could approach Laura's amazing femininity and beauty.

The next night Brent arrived promptly at seven, and pretended to be sorrowful that Cara had developed a headache and could not accompany them. He escorted Zoe to his carriage as carefully as if she were royalty.

Rapturously Zoe settled back in the corner of the carriage, which smelled of clean leather and a pleasant scent of tobacco. This was better than anything she had dreamed. Brent was richer, older, and more agreeable than the boys she had known in Georgetown. She no longer had a thundercloud of a stepfather to ruin everything. Her clothes had come straight from the best of shops, and Brent—well, Brent acted as if she was wonderful. Never had she been treated with such gentleness by a man. Of course Simon always treated her with kindness, but Simon was a friend. He knew the dark part of her life and understood. She wondered if Brent would be as understanding. Well, no matter. She never intended for him to hear one whisper about her past. Who she was and the dark shadow of Roger Carrigan were buried forever.

The brilliant lights of the opera house, the gilded boxes at either side of the velvet curtain, the swimming sea of faces, the glitter of jewels, all combined to intoxicate her.

Brent neither knew nor cared what was going on around them, or that they were the subject of much of the humming conversation before the curtain went up. If Zoe had any doubts that she looked enchanting in her gold gown, Brent quickly dispelled them.

Every time he looked at her he swayed slightly toward her, like metal drawn to a magnet.

Under his admiration she bloomed. Her cheeks were flushed and her eyes burned bright with pleasure. From her naive, excited remarks, Brent was forced to conclude that this was indeed her first visit to the theater. The knowledge made him feel oddly protective.

After the performance he hustled her out before anyone could make his way around to the back of the box seeking an introduction. He had ordered a wine supper for them, he said.

As they rode from the theater, a group of miners were gathered in the light of the street lamp. Ragged, shadowed men. She looked away quickly. It was as if the tentacles of Georgetown had reached out to touch her. But soon she forgot them in her interest in the lights, the white linen tablecloths, and sparkling silver of the elegant restaurant where he'd taken her.

Brent shone; he told amusing stories of his travels, and every glance of his sea-blue eyes paid homage to Zoe.

"Laura," he said softly, as he reached across the table to take her hand in his.

The sudden swift pressure undid her. This girl, who had been brought up near the parlor houses and who had a stark knowledge of the traffic of bodies that went on in a mining town, had never received a caress in her life, had never experienced the swift deliciousness of it. She smiled shakily.

"Oh, Laura, I know so little about you. I want to see you again. Will you share your time with me? We need to know each other."

Zoe pressed her hand upon his and smiled her most beguiling smile . . . and agreed. She would spend as much time with him as he chose. Her dreams that night were sweet.

It occurred to Zoe several weeks later that she had seen very little of Simon. But she had begun to hear about him. Whispers at first. And then rumors of a union.

Zoe was sure that Cara and Simon had become friends, that they confided in each other. In fact she felt a bit jealous and left out. She knew Simon was keeping his distance because of the situation between her and Brent.

Because Brent's father owned two of the largest mines in Aspen, and the situation at the mines was so desperate, most people in town kept their distance from Brent. Of course that meant very little to Brent, who wasn't really interested in the miners' petty problems. The foremen could keep the men working, and that kept the flow of money going to his father to keep him happy. As long as his father was happy, money would come eventually to him . . . and he spent as much as he got on Zoe.

He too had heard of Simon's meddling in miners' affairs, but he had laughed it off. One man could make no difference. Brent had long since forgotten his original purpose in coming to Aspen.

It was Cara who seemed to understand best the difficulties Simon was struggling with. They had developed a friendship based on mutual respect and a love for Zoe.

Every time Cara talked to Simon, the conversation turned to Zoe. Was she well, was she happy, did she really think the rest of her life should be spent with Brent Dewitt? It did not take Cara too long to figure out what was wrong with Simon.

"Another evening out with the illustrious Mr. Dewitt?"

Simon asked as he stretched his long legs before him. He was seated in Zoe's parlor with Cara nearby.

"You know how she is, Simon. She has a hunger for all the good things. She'd never done so many . . . exciting things before she came here. It fascinates her."

"I know . . . so does that bastard . . ."

"Just because Brent's father is some kind of a greedy old miser doesn't mean the son is. I've heard them talking—Zoe and Brent, I mean. He doesn't care about the miners one way or the other. You remember that last explosion that killed a couple of men. I guess Brent has that all taken care of. He just came here because there was the rumor of a strike. He's not your enemy, Simon. He's convinced that the situation at the mines is under control."

"That's probably what he's telling his father, Cara, but it's a long way from the truth."

"Simon, what's really eating at you? You have more than half the miners ready to stand with you."

"Half isn't good enough."

"You'll get them all in time. That's not your problem, is it?"

"Just what do you think my problem is?"

"Want the honest truth?"

"Would you say anything else?"

"You're in love with Zoe."

Simon was silent. Was it so obvious to others how he felt about Zoe? "That's a pretty far-fetched supposition, isn't it?"

"Is it? Stelle used to think you had a crush on her ever since she was a kid."

"Zoe has her plans. I don't fit into them, and I don't blame her for having them. I just wish she'd found someone besides that parasite she's so fascinated with."

"You'd have found the same faults with any man."

"Maybe . . . maybe not. Cara, he's a weak man. He's full of his class, his society, his position. If he ever finds out one piece of scandal about Zoe, he'll turn on her so fast her head will swim. She's blind to everything but his charm and his money. Doesn't she realize the money comes from his father? None of it's his."

"Why don't you tell her?"

"About him? A lot of good that will do."

"Not about him. About how you feel for her."

"I've come close to it a couple times, but she's mired so deep in the misery of the past that it's impossible to tell her things could be different for her than they were for her mother. I wish she didn't see Roger Carrigan in every man alive."

"That man left a lot of scars on her. Scars we can't even see."

"I know."

"Simon, if Brent proposes to her, she's going to accept him."

Simon stood up and walked a short distance from Cara to the window, where he drew the curtain aside to look out. He'd thought he'd heard a carriage. He had. Brent's carriage was coming up the drive.

"Simon?" Cara asked. She knew he had not misunderstood her words.

"I know, Cara." He didn't turn to look at her because he didn't want her to see the misery in his eyes. But he continued to speak. "If you think I'm going to try to do anything about it, don't. This is what Zoe wants, maybe what she needs. I won't try to stop her. In fact, she asked me to give her away. It might be the last thing I can do for her."

"You'll leave Aspen?"

"No, I can't do that yet. I have a lot of work to finish here."

"And," Cara said softly, "you think she might need you."

"I'd better get going. I'll leave through the back door if you don't mind. I'm in no mood for the elite Mr. Dewitt. Their carriage is right outside. They must be talking." He turned to face Cara. "Good night . . . and Cara?"

"What?"

"I don't think it would be very smart to tell Zoe I come here like this. She might think I'm nosing in something that's none of my business. Besides, I don't think she needs to keep explaining me to Brent Dewitt. He's too aware of me for my comfort anyway."

"I never mention when you've been here." Cara smiled.

"Even though I'd love to, just to see him turn a little green."

"You don't like him either?"

"Not . . . not really. I know he professes to care about Zoe. But there's something . . . I don't know how to describe it. Just something I don't trust. God, I wish I'd never . . ."

"Never what?"

"I guess I'm kind of responsible for a lot of this. But I felt it was what Zoe wanted, or what she needed. Now I'm not so sure."

"How can you be responsible?"

"Come on, I'll get my shawl and walk you to the back gate, and we'll talk on the back porch. I wouldn't want Zoe to know I told you this."

Outside, on the back porch, Cara explained to Simon how she had "arranged" Zoe and Brent's meeting.

"So you see, Brent thinks she's some shy half-child that was left orphaned and alone . . . and vulnerable. I suppose he's tried to seduce her into his bed by now and has been made to understand she's a 'nice' girl who won't settle for anything but marriage."

"And he'll propose."

"As sure as God made little green apples."

"And Zoe and Prince Charming will live happily ever after."

"I'd like to think that. If money is Zoe's goal, and if it will really make her happy, then she will live happily ever after."

"And us, Cara?"

"Us? I don't know about you, Simon, but Zoe and I . . . well, it's more than just friendship."

"I can understand that." He stopped and looked down into Cara's eyes. Then he rested his hands on her shoulders and smiled. "I guess you and I are kind of stuck with the same problem. We love. There's nothing we can do about it. I guess there's no way to insure the fact that those we love will love us. We have to go on the best way we can, and the best way is to go on loving."

"I guess." He bent to kiss her cheek, and she added, "I'm sorry, Simon."

"Don't be. I guess I had my opportunity to reach out and help Zoe a long time ago. Way back in Georgetown. If Brent can make her happy, then she deserves it."

"I don't believe you really mean that. I think you just hide it all behind that iron wall. Be careful, Simon. You're a man too."

His mouth was grim, but he said nothing more, and she watched him disappear in the dark.

Simon trudged through the city, heading for his room, which grew lonelier every night. Cara was right. Sometimes he could hardly contain his frustration and need. He wanted Zoe, and he knew it was useless. Brent Dewitt, Brent's father, and all the mine owners were his enemies, but he hated Brent with a separate kind of passion. It made him sweat when he thought of Zoe and Brent together. Abruptly changing direction, he went to the nearest bar and ordered a drink, which was followed by another . . . and another.

Two days later, as Brent dressed to go see Zoe, he mulled over uncomfortable thoughts. How did one tell a girl one was mad about that she was too flamboyant, too noticeable, that she attracted as much attention as an eagle in a chicken yard?

She was so beautiful, yet so strange. So . . . so violent, he thought unhappily, recalling his mother's sleek gentleness that always got its own way through devious, lady-like means. Whereas with Zoe, one felt that if one prodded her too far, she'd not hesitate to make a scene.

Yet he'd found he could not do without her. She was in his blood like a tropical fever. He wanted to scold her; he wanted to shake her, he wanted to make her over, but he never stopped wanting her.

He could not understand Zoe. If he could just find out something about her background, he believed he could uncover the mystery. But she refused to speak of it.

That evening he questioned her persistently, and Zoe promised herself to be open with him about everything else in her life from now on, but not about her past. Not about being Zoe Carrigan instead of Laura Champion. Not about her unspeakable childhood, and her stepfather stripping her dress off and trying to steal the only part of her he had not degraded already. She had to close her eyes tightly for a moment to overcome the loathing she felt for the past.

They were returning to Zoe's home, and she had invited him in for coffee and dessert. She was very certain that Brent was going to propose, and she had planned her acceptance carefully.

In the carriage he held her hand while they discussed the play, and when they arrived at her home they sat in the carriage a short while, and Brent took advantage of the secluded moment to kiss her. It was a somewhat chaste kiss and a bit disappointing to Zoe, who had expected more fervor . . . more passion. But she pushed the thought aside. Passion, to men like Brent Dewitt, came after marriage. Maybe he was only being considerate of her. She had the patience to wait for passion.

As they stepped from the carriage, the low rumble of thunder could be heard in the distance and there was the scent of rain in the air. When they arrived at the door, the first drops of rain had begun to fall.

Cara had put brewed coffee in the silver pot and left it on a low table with a very convenient note that she had been called away to sit with a very ill friend. In truth she was already sound asleep.

Brent draped his coat carefully over a chair and went to the fire. He knelt and stirred the embers into new flame, then replaced the poker, stood, and dusted his hands meticulously. Meanwhile Zoe went to the kitchen and carried in a tray laden with sandwiches, chilled fruit, and coffee cake.

They sat before the fire and ate a little, but Zoe could sense Brent's tension.

Brent felt anxious as he gathered his courage; then suddenly the tension melted like tallow when she looked at him.

He gazed at her and all his doubts faded. She was so altogether desirable, sitting there with the flames reflected in her burnished hair and her gold-brown eyes glowing.

"Laura," he said gently, "I've fallen in love with you. I

think you know that by now. I'm asking you to give consideration to marrying me."

If Zoe had expected some rush of pleasure or a sense of profound excitement, she was disappointed. Instead there seemed to be a hollowness deep inside her, and the feeling of accomplishment and satisfaction was noticeably absent, as if the scene was from a well-rehearsed play. Zoe pressed his hand in return and smiled.

"Yes, Brent, I would be very happy to become your wife."

Brent's eyes lit with pleasure. He stood, still holding her hands in his, and drew her up beside him. Then he took her in his arms.

The storm gathered and the air was breathlessly still, as if it were waiting for the tempest to strike. It was just as still a half hour later when Brent left the house, got into his carriage, and drove away.

Only then did the dark shadowed form detach itself from the blackness of the trees and walk slowly to the porch.

If the walk was erratic and unsteady, there was no one to see it. The man raised a large callused hand, curled it into a fist, and knocked.

The storm finally reached its breaking point. The knock was accompanied by a sharp crack of thunder and a bolt of lightning that brightened the area as if it were day. Then the heavy rain began to fall like a thick curtain of silver drops.

The storm began to rage like a fury. The man knocked again . . . and Zoe opened the door. Her eyes grew wide with shock.

"Simon," she gasped. She backed up one step . . . two . . . three, and he moved toward her inexorably. Then he reached out and pushed the door shut.

Chapter Eleven

The storm broke with an intensity that drowned every other sound. Yet over it Zoe seemed to be able to hear her own heart beating. She had never see Simon like this. She gathered her courage around her and took a deep breath. Simon would never hurt her.

"What is it, Simon?"

"I've been thinking," he muttered.

"And drinking, it appears. You're soaking wet and half drunk. Simon, go home and sleep it off. We can talk over what you've been thinking about tomorrow if you want." She wasn't sure just why she felt her nerves tingle.

"No . . . not tomorrow, Zoe. I'm going to tell you now. You can't marry Brent Dewitt. It's a mistake."

"I think I should make the decisions about what I want to do with my life. You're saying things you don't mean."

"I'm a little drunk, and that's not drunk enough. You asked me to give you away. Well, I'm not giving and he's not taking."

"This is ridiculous. You don't realize what you're saying." She was puzzled at his attack, and uncertain about how much of his words were prompted by drink and how much by something else.

"Don't I? I don't think I've ever meant anything more in my life. I'll stop this marriage."

She turned from him, trying to control her anger. But she was less than successful.

"Please just go home. I don't want to argue with you, and I'm not going to stand here and listen to you rave about something you have nothing to do with. I don't understand what's gotten into you."

"You've gotten into me. I thought I could just turn my back like I've always done. But this time I can't. This time . . . this time I have to do something."

Zoe's patience was reaching its limits, and her anger made her ignore a new kind of glow in Simon's eyes.

"You can't do anything! Why are you doing this? Why don't you understand? This is not your life, it's mine, and I intend to live it. I have everything I've always wanted and I'm not letting go."

"No?"

"No, and if you hadn't been drinking you wouldn't be talking like this. Now forget your sudden streak of unneeded gallantry. Stop trying to save me from whatever it is your muddled mind is conceiving. Let me alone!"

"I wish I could, Zoe," Simon said miserably. "I've just spent hours trying to wash you out of my mind. I can't."

"Simon, if you want to remain my friend, please . . . just go home and go to sleep."

"Only after you tell me that you've changed your mind. That you're not going through with this marriage."

"You must be crazy."

"Then you're still going to do it?"

"You bet your life I am." She stood defiant, and even through the slowly vanishing haze of whiskey, Simon could see she meant it. But the haze was not vanishing fast enough to bring caution with it.

"No . . . you're not." His voice was determined. "I'll stop you."

"There's no way you can do that."

"Watch me." He turned and started for the door. Zoe ran to place herself between him and the door.

"Where are you going?"

"Where I should have gone before."

"Simon?"

"After I have a long talk with Brent Dewitt, he'll take his fancy gentleman's ways back to Denver where he belongs."

Zoe's face went gray and before her eyes she could see all her plans crumbling before her. She was scared . . . really scared for the first time in a long, long time.

"Talk . . . Simon . . . you wouldn't."

"Yes. If it's the only way I can bring you to your senses." he started for the door. When he opened it the viciousness of the storm made him pause, but only for a second. Then he was striding across the porch.

Desperation lent wings to Zoe's feet. She dashed after him. She was soaked to the skin by the time she caught him at the front gate. She grabbed his arm and spun him around to face her.

"Please, Simon! At least come back inside and talk it over with me. You can't just do this. Not in your condition. You don't know what you're doing. Please, Simon."

Her pleading penetrated the haze of alcohol, and he allowed her to tug at his arm and draw him back inside with her. When she closed the door, both stood panting and soaking wet. Zoe walked back into the living room and Simon followed.

She stood in front of the fire searching desperately for words that would stop Simon from destroying her plans. She shivered with a coldness more internal than external and clasped her arms about herself.

Simon was assailed by more conflicting emotions than he could handle. Zoe looked so helpless . . . so lost, like a bedraggled kitten carried in out of the rain. And . . . he had never, through all that Zoe had suffered, seen her cry. It shattered something deep inside him. He went to her.

When Zoe lifted her eyes to his, she found she could not read his thoughts.

"Simon, you have to listen to me."

"I have listened to you. You forget how long I've been your friend."

"My friend," she repeated gently. "And you were going to go to Brent." Her voice died on a soft gasping sob. It wrenched Simon, who was already fighting a growing force Zoe was unaware of.

He reached out and wiped a tear from her cheek. Then brushed a tendril of wet hair from her forehead. An electrical current arced between them, and he became acutely aware of everything about her.

Suddenly she seemed tiny, in need of someone to stand between her and any more hurt.

Zoe caught her breath as the warmth in Simon's eyes

enveloped her. Both were held momentarily immobile as this strange drawing thing slowly sent tendrils to touch and entwine them.

Simon took another step toward her. Like an insidious liquid heat, she seemed to fill him. At that moment he wanted to kiss her more than he wanted his next breath.

Zoe stood still, not because she wanted to but because her limbs felt heavy and her breath felt labored.

Outside, the storm increased to a thunderous roar, its fury enclosing the quiet house.

Gently he cupped her face in his hands, looking down into her eyes as if he could see into her soul. Then he bent his head and kissed her.

The first kiss was a gentle brush of his lips across hers; then he kissed her forehead, her closed eyes, her cheeks. His mouth returned to hers, this time to drink deeply of the sweetness he had dreamed of for so long.

The dam within her burst and released the floodgates of a new and frightening thing. Desire, unfamiliar and overpowering, flowed through her like molten lava. Slowly her lips parted under his searching mouth as his tongue explored the sweet recesses within. She responded with a heated need that blinded her senses to everything but Simon.

For the first time Simon fought his own logic. He fought every warning his mind was busily giving him. He even ignored the truth, that after tonight, they would both have to face tomorrow.

He moved closer, until their bodies touched. One of his hands still cupped her face, while his other arm slid about her waist and pulled her to him. His mouth found hers again and again, at first lightly, sensitively. Both were unsure, and unprepared, yet neither was able to stop the avalanche of desire that burst between them.

His mouth was hard and overpowering now as she parted her lips to accept the demand of his. His tongue invaded, and she began to respond to the intensity of his almost overpowering attack. She began to search, her tongue taking turns with his to taste deeply. She slid her hand through his thick hair to draw his head still closer, and a hunger in her cried out for more. She was no longer docile or accepting, but avid in her response.

For a moment they were wild, caught in an explosive passion fueled by a hunger long dormant and restrained. Like a chained beast, it was suddenly free and beyond control.

When their lips parted they were both gasping for breath, gazing at each other in profound disbelief.

For minutes they wouldn't even remember, they stood touching as Simon held her trembling body pressed to his. He could feel the pulsing warmth of her. The softness of her body when it touched his made the heat of desire leap in him until he felt as if he were on fire.

Again their mouths met in a kiss that was filled with a sureness of purpose. They both wanted to immerse themselves in this growing awareness . . . or growing forgetfulness.

His hands slid down her back to curve around her buttocks and press her tight to him, while the kiss deepened. Her arms about his neck, she molded her body to his.

With hands that trembled from the fierce current that flowed through them, Simon reached for the buttons on her dress, working them one by one until he could push the wet material aside.

For a long time Simon knew nothing but the taste of her, and the heat of her body moving against his. The hunger he had tried to keep leashed exploded, tearing him apart.

Her hands on his back urged him on in silent but knowing invitation. Rhythmically he stroked her skin with hands so surprisingly gentle she found it almost beyond belief. He filled her senses until she shivered wordlessly, telling him of the pleasure he gave her. His caressing fingers learned the satin curves of her body as her hands were beginning to know him.

Simon had to suppress the groan of hot need that made him want to throw her to a bed and tear from her the answer to a need he wouldn't name. It made him want to cry in anguish . . . and in fierce pleasure.

Through half-closed eyes, dazed by an emotion she could not control or even recognize, Zoe watched Simon undress. It was as if both of them existed in a dream.

They sagged to the soft carpet with one will, and Zoe felt herself totally undone, as slow liquid rhythms uncoiled deep in her body.

He caressed her tenderly, tracing his fingers across her suddenly very sensitive skin. His hand moved lower, to her waist, then the curve of her hip. Then it skimmed the soft flesh of her belly, the fine enticing down, and the warm center between her thighs. She closed her eyes, and her body moved against his fingers as she whispered a sigh of encouragement.

Simon was exhilarated by the combination of whiskey and a sea of sensations as Zoe offered her mouth to his.

It began to grow, this feeling that walked the edge of violence, and neither could restrain the search for a fulfillment that each hoped would supply one breath of peace.

Zoe looked up into the smoky gray eyes that burned with passion. She saw the waiting and the strength coiled in his large muscled body. The contrasts and complexities that made up Simon both fascinated and unnerved her, for behind the granite strength, she saw pain and anguish such as she had never known. And she wanted to take his pain within her and soothe it.

His mouth caught hers at the same moment he pressed himself to the depth of her.

Deeper and deeper he penetrated, slowly and languorously, until he was immersed completely within her, feeling her surround him.

She took him inside her and her rhythms perfectly matched his. The yielding grew deeper, with ever-quickening undulations.

She arched to meet his thrusts, wrapping her legs about him. She pressed her hands in long strokes down his back to his hips, to urge him deeper.

Simon moved slowly at first, despite the need that hammered inside him. He gave her what they both wanted, holding back nothing. His motions began to grow in force and speed; then he felt the intimate pulses of her body release about him, and he could think of nothing more than the need he had held in check for so long. He arched again and again, giving himself to her as deeply as she had given herself to him.

For slow, sweet moments that did not allow the intrusion of the world and its blackness, they lay spent in each other's arms.

The storm outside seemed to have spent itself as the storm inside had done. The low rumble of receding thunder could be heard only in the distance. It was drowned by the returning sense of reality that flooded them both.

For Zoe it was startlingly painful. For Simon it was a profound feeling of acceptance. There was no doubt left in his mind about how he felt for Zoe or the choices they would make.

Zoe sat up, bending her head forward so that the thick mass of her hair shielded both her face and her tumultuous thoughts from him. Confusion reigned. She had never been so shattered or so uncertain before.

Simon sat up beside her, and for a long moment he let the silence enfold them. He looked down on her bowed head and felt a tenderness fill him. He reached out and caressed her hair.

"Zoe?"

Slowly she raised her head to look at him. There were no tears, no recriminations in her eyes. But there was a look of wariness that made him frown. Surely she knew, after what they had just shared, what he felt and that he would never just walk away from her.

But Zoe was seeing other visions. She was seeing her mother. Had her mother felt the same tremendous passion for Roger Carrigan? Was that why she had sacrificed everything, given everything to him and asked for nothing in return?

She could see visions of the same kind of future for her. Of dirty mining towns and small dirty shacks. She could see doing without everything to feed the mouths of hungry children, and being hungry herself. She could see growing old before her time and living with regrets and dreams she would never realize.

"Zoe?" Simon repeated, because the look in her eyes had no warmth; it was a sad introspective look. "I love you." He tried to take her in his arms, but now her eyes reflected something new and volatile, as if she were nearly terrified. She pushed his hands aside and rose to her feet, taking up a white petticoat to shield herself.

"No." She half gasped, half groaned the word. She stood a foot or two from him, and this vision of her was indelibly printed on Simon's mind. "Simon, don't say that! I don't want you to love me! I don't want to love anyone!"

Now he too scrambled to his feet. A harsh fear tugged at him as he went to her.

"You can't say that! You can't mean it. Not after this. Zoe, you can't lie to me, I know what you felt."

"I'm not denying what I felt. But I know it for exactly what it is. It's a trap. A physical passion that will give me nothing but regrets. I won't be caught in it. I won't!"

"Passion! Is that all it was to you?"

"That's all it is. You were drinking and we both lost control."

"For God's sake, Zoe. I'm not drunk. I think I have been in love with you since you were a child."

"You were sorry for me."

"No!"

"Yes! I could see it in your eyes. You were sorry for me then, and now you think I'm making a mistake and you want to protect me. I won't be a victim like my mother was, Simon. I won't live like that again."

"You're not—" He gazed at her in profound disbelief.

"Going to marry Brent? Yes, I am. I know you can go to him, tell him everything. But . . . if you love me as you say you do, you won't. If you tell him about me, Simon, I shall go away. I shall go so far you will never find me. I'll make a new start. I've done it before. But I will never forgive you . . . never." Her voice died on a ragged note.

With her hair in a disheveled tangle about her shoulders, her ivory skin shielded inadequately by the petticoat, and her honey-gold eyes blazing, she made a picture that held Simon spellbound. He could not believe that what she was saying could be true after what they had shared.

But Zoe's defensive stance and the determined look in her eyes told him she believed her own words. Her fear of the past and her inability to see beyond her goals of wealth and position were still powerful forces that controlled all her rational thoughts. She was not going to relent. Yet he could not let her go so easily. Desperation made him grasp for any idea he could find. He would have begged her if he'd thought it would work, but he knew Zoe too well. She was strong and relentless in her search for what she thought would make her happy. This made her blind to any answers other than her own.

"Don't you see, Zoe, that it won't work?"

"It will work."

"No!"

"Why not?"

He didn't want to hurt her, but he had no choice. He felt she might get hurt worse later.

"Because you're not in his class." She looked as if he had struck her. "Zoe, what will happen when he takes you back to Denver? What will happen when his rich aristocratic family finds out you've not got the 'background'? They'll hear it in your voice. They'll see from your actions that you don't know how to live their kind of life." Simon bent to gather his clothes and dress as he spoke.

"I've been doing fine up to now." Her voice was thick with hurt.

"Sure. You're here in Aspen, away from his family. There's no problems because he's fascinated and he wants you. Things will change, Zoe."

"Stop it, Simon. You're jealous, and I'm not going to listen to you. I want you to leave."

She was pulling on her clothes now, and the old angers were growing. He could see the same old walls again.

"Zoe," he said gently, "I love you. You have to listen to me."

"I don't have to do anything of the sort. I know what is right for me, and I'm not going to let it go because . . ."

He went to her and gripped her arms, drawing her close to him. "You can't do this!"

"Simon, this can only make it worse."

"I can't let you go."

"I'm not yours to keep or let go. I belong to no one but myself."

"Why are you so damn blind!" He shook her to punctuate each word.

She twisted from his grip and backed away from him.

"I don't want to love anybody," she panted, speaking as if the words were being torn from her. "And I don't want you to love me. I just want you to go and leave me alone. I don't want to hear all the reasons why I'll fail. This is my life, and I'm going to have it the way I want it. I'll fit. I'll learn, and Brent will be patient enough to teach me."

"You're a dreamer."

"Are you going to betray me?"

"You know I can't do that."

"Then maybe it's better we never see each other again."

"You know I can't do that either."

"What are you going to do?" The words were said softly.

"I'm going to be scared for you, Zoe. I'm going to worry about you, and I'm going to be around to make sure he doesn't hurt you. I'll wait until you come to your senses and realize you're reaching for something that exists only in your mind. You see, Zoe . . . when you get what you want, you're going to find it's hollow."

They continued to look at each other across a void that was growing larger . . . deeper and blacker. Zoe fought with all that she had to keep from going to him. She could not surrender her dreams so easily. Not even when the magic had been so real. She would find that magic with Brent. But even if she didn't, the magic was not enough to replace what she would be giving up if she walked away from Brent now.

Simon drew a deep ragged breath and released it. He had lost and he knew it. He felt miserably helpless. He'd been drunk, and he'd made a mistake. Forcing Zoe to recognize physical need was not enough. It had only succeeded in making her more afraid that she was following in her mother's footsteps. That alone was enough to terrify Zoe. What had happened between them had been shattering to his emotions. He could sense that it had been even more devastating to her. She couldn't take the chance of dropping her guard. He said nothing more. He snatched up his jacket and left, slamming the door behind him.

Outside, he stood on the porch and took several deep breaths. The storm had left a clean moist scent in the air. Any other time Simon would have taken pleasure in it, but tonight he felt nothing except a sense of despair and loss.

When the door closed behind Simon, Zoe almost sobbed in relief. She had never felt so torn. The way she trembled made her wrap her arms about herself to try to contain it.

How dare he do this to her! How dare he deliberately try to open doors she had spent so much time locking. It had been deliberate, she knew it. Why had she been so vulnerable? Why had she allowed him to reach her like that?

The memory of their passion was a taste on her lips, the feel of his hands against her skin, and the wildness that had possessed her. It was a memory she would have to rid herself of.

Simon had been a friend she had trusted. He had been her only real friend besides Cara. She couldn't lose that. She needed it. She couldn't even question why.

Zoe sagged into a chair beside the fireplace. She wanted to cry. She could feel the thickness of tears in her chest, and the sting in her eyes. But she couldn't cry. She couldn't release the hard knot of pent-up emotions.

"Zoe?" Zoe looked up to see Cara standing on the stairs, clutching her robe about her, still sleepy-eyed. "Zoe, what's wrong? I heard the door slam. Did you have some kind of fight with Brent?" Cara continued down the stairs as she spoke, and crossed the room toward Zoe. She was watching Zoe's face, and she could tell by what she read there that something deeply disturbing had happened. She knelt by Zoe's chair. "Are you all right?"

"I'm fine, Cara." Zoe's voice was flat and strained. "And it wasn't Brent who slammed the door. It was Simon."

"Simon? What was he doing here?"

"I don't know why he came." Zoe stood abruptly, avoiding Cara's eyes. "I wish he hadn't."

"Was Brent here when he came?"

"No."

Whatever had happened between Zoe and Simon, Cara knew it had reached inside Zoe and shaken her drastically. It was then she realized the condition Zoe was in. Her clothes were wrinkled and—she looked closer—wet. They were wet, and Zoe herself looked as if she'd fallen in the river. Her hair was loosened and fell about her in a tangled mass.

"Zoe, what happened tonight? You look as if you were out in that storm."

"I was."

"Why?"

"When Simon came he . . . he was half drunk. He was raving about . . . about not giving me away and how he was going to go and tell Brent all about my past. He left angry. I had to make him come back, so I ran after him."

"Simon never would have done that, not to you."

"Not sober maybe. But . . . I've never seen him like that."

"What made him change his mind?" Cara looked closely at Zoe. "Zoe . . . what did Simon say to you?"

Zoe stood and walked a few steps from Cara, and Cara sensed at once exactly what Simon had said. Still, she waited for Zoe to answer.

"He was drunk."

"What did he say?"

"Cara, he didn't know what he was saying."

"You said he was only half drunk. If he got so worked up and came here like that, he must have had something to say."

Zoe swallowed heavily, but when she turned to face Cara again she had found some control. "He said he loved me. That he didn't want . . . no, wouldn't let me marry Brent. He wants me to marry *him*. Don't look at me like that. If you think I'm going to act like a love-struck child and fall into his arms, you're crazy. There's no future there, only a copy of the past, and I've run from that past too long to let it catch me and destroy everything now."

"You never said you loved Brent . . . and you never said you didn't love Simon."

"I love no one. That's an emotion I just can't afford. It blinds you and keeps you from making the kind of decisions you should make. I have to control my life, Cara, because if I don't, I've already had a good view of how I'm going to end up." She sighed deeply. "When I was a child I was caught in a situation not of my making. I can't be blamed for the squalor I had to live in then. But I would only have my own stupidity to blame if I chose that kind of life of my own free will."

"Sometimes life has a way of choosing for us."

"No, it's a pretty weak person who lets that happen. Smart people, strong people choose their own way. Let's not argue about this. Not you and I. I intend to marry Brent Dewitt."

Zoe walked from the room and up the stairs, and after a few minutes Cara could hear the firm closing of her door.

Zoe lay awake for a long time. Despite her attempts, she could not forget what had happened between her and Simon. She could not believe her own reaction. Brent had kissed her several times, but she had never felt the violence . . . the explosive passion that she'd known with Simon. It was the emotional situation, she told herself, the storm, the fact that Simon had been drinking. It was a combination of time and place that had taken them both off guard and entangled them in a way neither would have allowed had they been in control.

For a while she hated Simon for the awakening of emotions she would rather have left dormant and unexplored. She hated the betrayal of her own body as well. But she had been overwhelmed by something she had never known before.

She would deal with it. She would put it behind her as she had put her past behind her. She would marry Brent; the dreams she had had for so long would finally be a reality. Still, it was long hours before she found sleep, and even then her dreams were nothing but confusion.

If Zoe found sleep difficult, Simon found it impossible. He spent the hours alternately hating himself for what he had done and consoling himself that he'd been right . . . Zoe was wrong. Neither approach did him much good.

Right or wrong, he was powerless to stop her. But even if she never married him, marrying a man like Brent Dewitt was a very bad mistake. He felt helpless mostly because he knew he could not forget her. He could not turn his back on her. She would need him, and he would be there to pick up the pieces if . . . or when she stumbled and fell.

Brent had gone home from Zoe's elated. He could hardly wait to put his feelings on paper and inform his family that in a few weeks he would take a wonderful and beautiful woman for a wife.

He wrote a letter to his father first, then penned another to his mother. Barbara never entered his mind. In fact, all of his thoughts were on Zoe. His family's opinion did not matter . . . at the moment. Because he felt Zoe was so special, because he was so infatuated with her, he did not allow any adverse thoughts. He did not allow his unconscious realization of their differences to surface. This marriage was what he wanted, and that was reason enough for its success.

His superior attitude would not allow him to believe that he could not "form" Zoe into what his parents would expect. He felt like Pygmalion, and the feeling was intoxicating.

The fact that Zoe would be his wife, subservient and obedient to him, was no less invigorating. He'd had many women, but there was something about the mystery of Zoe that made him ache to solve it.

He also thought of her mysterious friend, the miner. That would have to cease immediately. No scandal could be attached to the Dewitt name. And Cara! Good God! Cara would have to be put out of Zoe's life and as much distance kept between them as possible. Maybe he could give Cara enough money to make her find another town in which to settle. It would be one of the first things he would look into. Zoe might resist, but surely a girl like Cara would have enough sense to know that if her past was ever discovered it could only do Zoe harm.

Oh, well, that problem could always be solved. Girls like Cara knew quite well that money was the vital thing. She would see which side of her bread the butter was on.

With these small annoyances out of the way, he finally drifted off into a sleep filled with the most pleasant of dreams.

Chapter Twelve

Stephen Dewitt crumpled the letter in his hand and threw it so violently that Joanne Dewitt jumped in shock. His face was red from sheer fury. This was not what he'd expected. From Brent's first letter he'd hoped that Brent was finally going to prove himself. He had not planned on this.

"Stephen, please . . . maybe it's just a fling."

"A fling! A fling for a Dewitt to marry some . . . some nobody! Dishonoring our name by giving it to some cheap little fortune hunter! I won't have it! I won't have our name dragged in the mud. I won't have all my plans destroyed!"

"What are you going to do?"

"First I'm going to find out about this . . . this Laura Champion. I have not acquired a fortune for the sole purpose of letting my son squander it away."

The next day Stephen sat behind his desk and watched with satisfaction as Will McQuade, a brawny, hard-faced detective, stood waiting for orders.

"McQuade, I want you to take a little trip for me. I need you to look into the background of a woman."

"A woman? Yes, sir. Where do I find her and just how deep do you want me to dig?"

"You'll find her in Aspen and her name is Laura Champion. As to how far I want you to dig, I want to know everything about her from the day she was born. All her background . . . all of it."

"Right. All of it. I won't leave a stone unturned."

"Good. I'll handle all your expenses, whatever they are, and pay you handsomely. There's a big bonus in it for you if you can do it fast."

"When do you want me to leave?" Will asked.

"Today, if there's a train, first thing tomorrow if you can't get one till then."

"Whew, you really are anxious."

"Anxious is not the word. Angry is the word. I need this information."

"All right," Will said quietly. "I guarantee you you'll have it as fast as I can get it."

"When you get it, telegraph me. I want to know at once." As he spoke, Stephen reached into his desk drawer and withdrew an envelope that looked interestingly thick to McQuade, who took it and put it in his pocket. He would count the money later.

It was the next morning before Will could get a train. He had a lot of time to plan just how he would trace Laura Champion. He had no doubt that he would be successful. He had never failed before, and a woman was not going to be his first failure.

When McQuade had stepped down onto the train platform, he was somewhat surprised at how much the town of Aspen had grown since the last time he'd been there.

He picked up his baggage and found transportation to the closest hotel. Once settled, he went downstairs. It was time to begin work.

He knew that gossip was the very best way to begin, and the best of the stories were to be heard in bars, barbershops, and bawdy houses. But before he began to put his ear to the ground, he wanted to see just what Laura Champion looked like. He drifted around town asking subtle questions, ones that would raise no suspicion. It was the next day before a young urchin pointed her out to him as she was crossing the street.

Will watched her walk to a small dress shop and go inside. He crossed the street and lingered outside the shop, taking the time to light a cigar and acting as if he were only lazily surveying his surroundings. He was but a few feet from her when she came out of the shop.

She was pretty . . . no, she was more than pretty. McQuade was curious enough to wonder what the woman had done to Stephen Dewitt to get him so riled up. He followed her for a while. When she got into a carriage he watched her disappear, and then smiled to himself. This would be an easy job. This woman made an impression on people, and it would not be hard to retrace her steps and find out where she came from and what kind of a path she walked. Yes . . . this job was going to prove more than interesting.

In all his years with the detective agency McQuade worked for, he had never run up against a stone wall as inpenetratable as this one was proving to be. It seemed, to all intents and purposes, that Laura Champion had not existed before she'd appeared in Aspen. This alone made him more than suspicious. No one appeared out of thin air, and no one left their past behind unless there was something in it they had to keep hidden.

It didn't take him long to find out Laura Champion and Sarina Falcon owned a small but well-kept restaurant. Thinking that would be a good lead, he began to check on Sarina Falcon's past, only to find it hidden in mystery as well. Now the situation began to intrigue him.

Laura Champion may have been keeping company with Brent Dewitt, but McQuade found she had another friend as well. A young miner named Simon Tremaine. A closer look at Simon brought McQuade the knowledge that he was far more than just a miner. He was a man intent on changing the miners' situation. A rabble-rouser . . . a troublemaker. The detective made copious notes, sure that Stephen Dewitt would want to know who was really behind his problems with the mines and the miners of Aspen.

Slowly it began to occur to him that if Laura Champion and Simon Tremaine were friends here in Aspen, maybe they had been friends elsewhere. Tracing Simon Tremaine was not difficult. He had come by train from Boulder. McQuade took the train there, and in a matter of days the story of Simon Tremaine began to unfold, and the path led to Georgetown. He bought his ticket to Georgetown with a sense of certainty that he was about to find some very important answers.

Still, it took almost a week of intense investigation before McQuade could link together two names, Laura Champion . . . and Zoe Carrigan. Once he began to investigate Zoe Carrigan's past, the gossips were quite willing to talk about Roger Carrigan's daughter. Most of their willingness came from a hatred of Roger.

She was a strange girl, a withdrawn girl who preferred the company of a parlor house madam and her girls to that of the "better" element. Oh, she was pretty, they admitted, and all were more than willing to give him a description.

His notes grew. Zoe Carrigan had run away with one of the girls from Stelle's parlor house. Of course nobody knew where they had gone, but all the good citizens were quite sure it was somewhere where they could open a parlor house of their own. After all, they were two of a kind, weren't they?

It was only then that McQuade paid a visit to the hovel that Roger Carrigan called home. He found Roger seated in a rocker on his front porch. After all the stories he had heard about the wild-eyed preacher, Will was a bit surprised to find an emaciated man who looked old beyond his years. There was still the light of fanaticism in the depths of his eyes, but clearly his physical capabilities had not kept pace with his mental drive. He looked like a man who had been drained.

"Mr. Carrigan?"

"Yes . . . what do you want? Who are you?"

"My name's McQuade. I'm looking for your daughter Zoe."

If the flame in Roger's eyes had blazed any higher, McQuade would have been burnt to a cinder. Roger's jaw jutted and his teeth were clenched. "I ain't got a daughter anymore. Like a sinner from Sodom, she deserted her family to taste the life of iniquity. She tried to turn her brothers and sister against me, and because of her I'm reviled. I may have lost them, but I still stand firm in the Lord. God will wreak punishment on her! She will burn in Hell!" He half stood, one hand on the rocker arm and the other fist raised in the old gesture of fury.

Will thought he had an idea of what Zoe Carrigan had really run away from.

"She ran with her immoral, ungodly friends, and she'll accompany them through the gates of Hell to burn forever!"

"You have no idea where she is?"

"No, and I no longer care. I tried to do my duty by her, but she was wicked and willful from childhood. She was a bad seed, and she'll see a bad end."

"I see." McQuade closed his little notebook and put it in his pocket. "Would you mind if I sit on your steps and chat with you for a bit, Mr. Carrigan? It's warm out, and I'd like a minute's rest before I start back to town."

"No," Roger muttered as he eased back down in the rocker. "Sit awhile."

McQuade knew how to handle people, how to get the most information. When he left Roger Carrigan over an hour later, he had all the information he wanted. He had also seen a small picture of Zoe Carrigan, one that Roger Carrigan adamantly refused to part with.

Later that afternoon he caught the train back to Aspen. He knew the picture he had seen was of Laura Champion. But he wanted to know more about her. He'd been given orders, and when he reported to Stephen Dewitt he wanted to have everything Stephen wanted. He wanted to find out everything about Laura Champion there was to know.

He arrived in Aspen early in the evening, and returned to the hotel in the hope of a quick dinner. He was tired and tomorrow was another day. He felt it would be only a short time before he could report everything to Stephen's Dewitt's satisfaction.

Once inside the hotel he could hear music, and when he questioned the desk clerk he was somewhat surprised.

"Someone having a party?"

"Yes, sir. It's a wedding."

"Oh, really? Somebody important getting married?"

"Important?"

"Sounds like quite a celebration."

"I would say so, sir. The son of one of the biggest mine owner's is getting married."

"Oh? Who might that be?"

"Mr. Dewitt. Mr. Brent Dewitt."

"You mean Mr. Dewitt's family is here?" This surprised McQuade.

"No, sir. Now that you mention it, it is kind of funny that none of Mr. Dewitt's family has come. But then maybe he just wants to surprise them."

Will was sure he already knew the answer, but he asked the question anyway.

"Who is the lucky bride?"

"Well, in this case, sir, Mr. Dewitt is the lucky one. He's marrying a real nice girl. Pretty too. She owns a small restaurant up the street a ways."

"Her name wouldn't be Laura Champion, would it?"

"Why yes, sir." The clerk beamed. "Do you know her?"

"Yes, I do." He felt what he said was the truth. He knew Laura Champion about as well as anyone could. Most likely he knew her better than her husband did. He wondered just how much of his new wife's past Brent Dewitt really did know. He also wondered about Laura Champion. Was she the wild, wicked girl her father proclaimed? Was she an ex-parlor girl looking for a rich husband? Or was she someone else altogether?

"If you know them, sir, why don't you go on in and congratulate them. It's an open party. Since neither the bride nor the groom had family, and there were so few friends here, they decided to invite any of the hotel guests that cared to come."

"I think I'll just do that." He smiled at the clerk and turned to walk toward the celebration. He'd heard a million stories about Zoe Carrigan. He'd heard the same about Laura Champion. They conflicted with each other. Now he wanted to see if he could get close enough to her to look in her eyes and see what the truth might be, for he was pretty certain the truth lay somewhere in between.

He walked into the room. There was not a large number of people there, and the bride stood out among them. Under the chandelier her hair glowed like a live flame.

The handsome man standing beside her must be Brent Dewitt. Somehow, to McQuade's eye, they did not seem to be the typical bride and groom. When he looked closer he realized that Brent wore the typical look of any happy groom. He was smiling down at her, completely unaware as the preacher awkwardly stumbled over the words of the wedding ceremony. No, it was Laura who had a quiet look of sadness about her.

A bride who was marrying a man as rich as Brent Dewitt certainly had nothing to be sad about. He watched her for another moment, and then turned to leave. He had a telegraph to send. He was pretty certain the elder Mr. Dewitt wasn't going to be too happy about the course of events.

In the telegraph office, McQuade stared blankly at the paper, trying to figure out exactly how to word the message. There was no other way except the plain truth. It was a long involved message, but the price of sending it didn't bother him. Stephen Dewitt paid well for what he wanted. He ended the message with the fact that the Laura Champion he'd come to investigate was now Mrs. Brent Dewitt. He went back to his hotel to await whatever answer Stephen Dewitt intended to send. There was no doubt in his mind there would be one.

The warmth of the April evening couldn't penetrate the chill around Zoe's heart as she listened to the preacher's fumbling. The only two legitimate churches in Aspen had frowned on the unseemly haste of the wedding. So Brent, Zoe, and Cara had set about finding a preacher to officiate at the ceremony. In desperation they'd finally settled on an elderly man who'd assured them he was an ordained minister. It had taken Brent quite a search to find him. He had discovered that men of the cloth were rare in the rowdy town of Aspen.

Zoe only had time to think scornfully that he was a funny kind of preacher, and then Brent was bending down and kissing her hard on the mouth, and she pushed the old fellow to the back of her mind.

She was married, and somehow the thought that her goals had been accomplished made her feel shaken and a little breathless. If she was momentarily insecure and afraid, she stifled those emotions determinedly. It would work. She would make it work.

She looked around the parlor, hoping against all reason

that she would see Simon among those gathered to witness the event. She still felt the emptiness he'd left behind.

From across the room Cara saw the bride gaze around the room at the few invited guests, and knew whom she was searching for. She sensed a sadness and a kind of quiet misery in Zoe. Whatever had happened between her and Simon, it must have been very troubling, for it had left Zoe with a dark, shadowed look in her eyes.

Cara was sure it would have taken something pretty powerful to keep Simon away. It was the only time Zoe had not confided in her. She intended to find him and try to get a glimmer of truth from him. Simon had to know. She knew this just as certainly as she knew he would not have deliberately hurt Zoe. She shook her head with a puzzled frown. Simon had seemed to accept Zoe's plans. What had caused the sudden change? Well, the small celebration would soon be over and she could find him and ask.

Zoe felt her nerves begin to tingle. It was nearly time to leave the party and go to the suite Brent had arranged for them. Each time Brent lovingly called her "Laura dear," or "Laura, my sweet," she wanted to cry out that her name wasn't Laura! She wished there was more truth between them. Grimly she held on, sure that when the celebration was over and they were alone, it would be different.

Yet when Brent turned to her and told her it was time for them to leave, her throat went dry and her hands began to sweat. She knew Brent had drunk quite a bit of champagne. She could tell by the feverish glow in his eyes and the warmth of his hands when he touched her. She could feel their heat through the silk of her dress sleeve. Nonetheless, she urged him to have one last drink, hoping it might take the edge off of his fervor, and she took one herself, hoping it would calm her and make the coming night easier.

Across the room Cara watched them drink the last drink. She saw Brent take Zoe's arm and move with her across the room. Zoe's face was pale. The back-slapping, hand-pressing well-wishers did not seem to penetrate her rigid calm. Cara realized that the only emotion that filled her was pity. She had tasted too often the hollowness that came with loveless giving. When Zoe and Brent had left the room, Cara went to get her shawl. She put it around her shoulders and went out to find Simon.

Simon had found the most sheltered corner in a dark and noisy barroom as far away from the hotel as he could get . . . and as far away as possible from any well-meaning friends intent on finding him. His fierce glare soon made it clear he needed and wanted no company. He had nursed the bottle of whiskey, but as the hours passed, the bottle came closer and closer to being emptied.

Visions that could only be obliterated by total unconsciousness still danced before his eyes. Zoe standing calm and beautiful before a preacher. Zoe laughing up at Brent as they danced, holding Brent's attention completely with her mysterious honey-gold eyes. Zoe standing in the lamp glow, her skin like cream and her flaming hair hanging loose and free about her. Zoe in Brent's arms. He muttered an obscene curse and reached for the bottle. He would kill this vision if it was the last thing he ever did.

Anger was his only protection, but he found he could not focus his anger on Zoe. So he centered it on Brent. Brent, the selfish, hard-hearted mine owner. Brent, who oppressed the miners until they could barely survive. Brent and his kind, who were a destructive force that broke men with their greed. Plans of revenge were hidden behind the need to help the miners. He would see Brent in the dirt. It boiled within him, this need to bring Brent down. If Simon knew, in the back of his mind, that this would not bring Zoe any closer, he ignored it. He could not hate Zoe . . . so he hated Brent instead. And poured the drink that emptied the bottle. He drank it quickly and called for another bottle.

It was set before him and he reached for it, pausing and looking up as a shadow fell over the table. It took him several seconds to recognize who was standing before him.

"It's over." He was not asking, but making a statement of fact. He did not need Cara's nod to confirm it. He continued to reach for the bottle, opened it, poured a drink, and downed it without speaking. Ignoring the risk to her hard-won reputation, Cara sat down opposite him.

"Simon," she said softly, "Zoe was looking for you. You were supposed to give her away."

Simon laughed a hard, bitter laugh. "She didn't need me there, Cara. Zoe has everything she's ever wanted. Maybe now she'll finally be happy."

"I'm scared for her," Cara said softly. For a few seconds her words really didn't register in Simon's mind. Then he blinked and looked closely at her.

"Scared? Why? Zoe doesn't seem to be scared of anything. I guess she never was. She has what she's been chasing all her life. What do you want me to do, spoil that for her?"

"Oh, Simon!" Cara cried helplessly.

"Stop worrying, Cara. Zoe can handle it. She handled her father all those years. She'll handle Brent Dewitt and his money. You're the one who's got problems ahead."

"Problems?"

"Cara, Brent Dewitt knows who you are. I don't want to hurt you, but he knows what you were too. You don't think he'll take the chance of having the Dewitt name associated with a parlor girl, do you? You'll be the first change Brent demands of Zoe."

"I don't want to put her in that position," Cara said miserably. "Simon, that's not fair."

"What is fair?"

"Nothing, I guess." She stood up slowly. "What are you going to do?"

"I think I am going to Boulder for a while. I have a little business to take care of. And you?"

"I should leave before Brent and Zoe tell me I have to. I won't put Zoe through that. She's been through enough in her life. I hadn't thought . . ."

"That Brent would force her to make such a decision? That he would tell her who you were? You can count on it, no matter what he's promised you. He can't afford to do anything else. Where would he be if Daddy cut off the money? He's not exactly one to go down into the mines and work for a living."

"Not hardly."

"Besides, now that people know who he is, he wouldn't stand much of a chance down there."

"I suppose not." She inhaled a ragged sigh. "What a hell of a mess. Like I said before, Simon, I'm scared for her."

Simon sat back in his chair and slowly poured another drink, tossing it down before he answered. "So am I."

"Then why didn't you stop her?"

"How?"

"She said . . . she said you told her you loved her. If you did, you should have found a way to stop her."

"It's too late for any of that now. Maybe . . . a long, long time ago, I might have stopped her. But that's water under the bridge. I lost the chance, and there's nothing I can do about it now. There's nothing you can do about it either, Cara. I think . . . maybe you ought to sit down and have a drink with me. Tonight neither of us is fit company for anybody else."

Cara nodded slowly and sat back down.

Mr. and Mrs. Brent Dewitt entered their suite, and Brent closed the door behind him and turned the key. His eyes moved quickly to hers. There was something electrifyingly exciting about locking the door on the world and turning to Laura . . . his wife.

Zoe was conscious of the beating pulse in her throat as she moved away from him across the immense carpeted room before he could touch her.

She made a self-conscious ritual of hanging her lace shawl over a chair. She felt as if she were suddenly made of fine glass. That one sharp word, one insensitive word, would shatter her. She wanted to hear from his lips that he was proud of her, that he thought she was beautiful.

Still, she kept an acre of tapestry carpet between them. She couldn't understand why she could not control the way she was shaking.

She unclasped the string of pearls Brent had given her for a wedding present, and laid them on the dresser. "I saw everyone admiring my pearls. They are beautiful. Again, I thank you."

"It was you, not the pearls."

"Well, you were far and away the handsomest man in

the room," she said, putting as much conviction as she could muster into her words.

At this stage of their relationship his reserve entranced her. Living with Brent, she prayed, would be a series of surprises. He was both lordly and beseeching, reserved and impetuous, remote yet close.

"Brent . . ." she began, not sure enough of herself to initiate anything. She needed time. But Brent was moving across the room toward her, and she knew there was no more time.

He took her shoulders and instead of kissing her, warming her, leading her gently, he turned her around and began to work the hooks down the back of her gown. His hands felt dry and hot against her chilled skin.

Watching his face in the mirror, she could see his brows knit in a concentrated frown as he struggled with the hooks. He slipped the dress down off her arms and let it fall in a heap around her feet. He bent and kissed her bare shoulder.

Then he drew her into his arms and began to kiss her fiercely. She could hardly catch her breath. He drew her to the bed with him, and the breathlessness grew into something almost wild.

Brent wanted her, and he took her desire for granted. Her mind screamed for her body to respond, as she well knew it could, but it didn't. What crushed her was that Brent didn't seem to know . . . or to care if she was finding the sensual pleasure he was.

Sometime later, sated and content, Brent turned from her, drew the covers over himself, and slept. Zoe lay awake, staring into the night. She didn't cry . . . she couldn't cry. Something inside her seemed to go dry. She had chosen . . . had gotten what she had chosen. Now she would learn to live with it. Time would make things better. When they had grown more accustomed to each other it would be better. It had to be better.

The following morning Stephen Dewitt read the lengthy telegraph message not once but twice:

SUBJECT IS AN EX-PARLOR-HOUSE GIRL WHO HAS MOST LIKELY ENGAGED IN THE ACTIVI-

TIES FOR MONETARY REASONS STOP UNFOR-
TUNATELY ARRANGEMENT BETWEEN THE
TWO SUBJECTS IS NOW LEGAL AND PERMA-
NENT STOP YOUR FAMILY HAS BEEN EN-
LARGED BY ONE STOP THE ACTION TOOK
PLACE TONIGHT AND BY THE TIME YOU RE-
CEIVE THIS WILL HAVE CERTAINLY BEEN CON-
SUMMATED STOP PLEASE ADVISE AS TO ANY
MOVES YOU WANT ME TO MAKE STOP A FULL
REPORT WILL FOLLOW SOON STOP
   MCQUADE

So, his son had married, had he, without obtaining
his approval. Without consideration for his social position and his name. He had married a girl with loose
morals because his loins were overheated. Well, by God,
he was not going to let the boy get away with it. Brent
was going to pay for his irresponsible behavior; he was
going to do what his family expected him to do one way
or another.

First things first. Stephen prepared a letter for Mc-
Quade. Then he prepared an even longer letter for his
wayward and disobedient son.

Then he stood and left his office to see that the letters
were mailed.

He went out to give some strict orders to his very surprised servants, who dashed about carrying his orders
out.

That same day crates and boxes were carried out.
Joanne protested, but the protestations fell on deaf and
angry ears. Stephen was going to bring his son under control and force him to follow the path that had been laid
out for him long ago.

Stephen knew Brent in a way that he was sure Brent
didn't know himself. He knew his strengths, and he knew
his weaknesses, and he knew just how to use both.

He would convince this ambitious, greedy girl not to
interfere in the affairs of the Dewitts. He would pull the
rug right from under her feet and watch her fall with great
pleasure. Then he would show Brent exactly the kind of

girl he'd been foolhardy enough to marry. He could welcome his wayward son back later, chastised . . . and alone.

He was glad he had hired McQuade. Will McQuade was the best. When the full report came, he would have all the answers. That would be the time to put his money to work to make sure his son was returned to him no worse for wear than having a bit more experience under his belt. Stephen smiled and poured himself a congratulatory drink.

Chapter Thirteen

I've been married a week, Zoe thought. It was still hard to believe. It was also hard to believe that she and Brent were having their first argument . . . and it was over Cara.

Brent had been the one to decide they would live at the hotel in the finest suite available. He enjoyed the way the employees fawned upon him. He'd been pleased when Zoe had decided to give the house to Cara. Now he was pressuring her to give Cara the restaurant too, and to cut her ties to her friend.

"But Brent, Sarina is my best friend."

"There's much you don't know about your friend. Why don't you just give her the restaurant? You don't need the money any longer. That way she'll have a livelihood and she can afford to live by herself."

"She's lived with me since we came to Aspen."

"Well, she cannot live with us!" Brent proclaimed fiercely. "Besides, it does not look quite right for you to be in her company all the time. We have not been married long, and I don't want to share any part of you with another person. What do you think people would say?"

"Damn what people would say!"

"Laura . . . really. Come to your senses. You're a Dewitt now. We have to consider what people would say. We won't always be living in Aspen, you know." Brent cautioned himself that he must not let on that he intended to remain in Aspen until he had polished Laura's rough edges and made her acceptable to his father. He did have his reputation to consider, and Laura was . . .

"Because I'm a Dewitt, must I turn my back on my friends?"

-156-

"Speaking of friends. I won't have my wife engaging in conversation on the street, in broad daylight, with a man like Simon Tremaine. He is a troublemaker. It's scandalous, Laura, and I won't have it."

"But Simon—"

"Simon is a young, handsome man. Do you think I do not hear rumors? He is in love with you." Brent came to her and put his arms around her. "If I sound jealous, it's because I am. Being my wife will demand a lot from you when we do go back to Denver. We have a position to maintain. I don't want slander and whispers to follow us and ruin things. Besides, your . . . friend Sarina won't be able to go to Denver with us anyway."

Zoe had never faced such emotions before. Brent was professing jealousy, telling her he couldn't stand watching another man look at her. Having never been plied with sweet words and professions of love, she was susceptible to his emotional blackmail.

"All right, Brent, I won't speak to Simon again. He's gone from Aspen anyway. And . . . and I'll offer Sarina the restaurant. I'll . . . I'll try to explain . . ."

"You're very understanding, Laura. I understand how hard this is for you. But if Sarina is really your friend, she will understand your position. Your reputation is very important. As for Simon Tremaine . . . well, I don't want him around you. I don't want him looking at you. I don't want him being familiar with you. Others might think they can do the same. You're my wife . . . you're a Dewitt."

Zoe started to protest again, but she realized more protestations would only convince Brent that there was something she was hiding. She knew this was a sore point for him. Often he related incidents from his past, and Zoe knew he kept subtly bringing up such things because he had an avid need to find out about hers. Frequently when Brent looked at her, his eyes were bright with unspoken questions that he did not have the courage to ask. She could not say anything. Her childhood must be a forgotten thing.

"I count the time from the day I married you," she always told him with a smile and a fond look. "I have no childhood. I was born again on my wedding day."

Zoe could understand his possessiveness when it came to Simon, but his demand that she separate herself from Cara was painful. She had tears in her eyes when she tried to explain the situation to her friend. Cara had known from the night of Zoe's wedding that they would have to live separate lives now. Simon had been wise enough to see it clearly. But Cara knew it was painful for Zoe, and she didn't want to make the situation any worse. As far as Cara was concerned, Zoe deserved all the happiness she could find. She herself would be more than satisfied with the restaurant and the house. But she knew she would miss her friend more than she could ever put into words.

"It just proves what a good job we did on you and how classy you've become, Zoe. You don't fit in a miner's shack, or a small-town restaurant. He thinks you're too good for me now, and that's all right. It's how it should be. It's what we both worked for."

"Cara, it's not fair."

"Funny, I said something like that to someone once. He only said . . . what's fair? I guess not much is. You have to go on with your life, Zoe. I won't let you throw it all away because of me. You're going to have everything you've always wanted. Don't be a fool and let the past pull you back down into the mud. Go on . . . get all you can out of your new life."

"Cara, what are you going to do?"

"Just like you, go on with my life. Maybe if you write . . . at least I'll know what's going on with you. When is he taking you back to Denver?"

"I don't know. He keeps putting it off. He says he has to . . . enlighten me about his family's expectations, whatever that means. I guess it won't be long."

"Well, I wish you all the happiness in the world, Zoe." Cara stood and embraced her. Then Zoe turned and walked out of the house. Cara just stood there, staring after her and wanting to cry.

Zoe had left so many people behind, but none of those losses had hurt as much as this . . . except for Zach, Eli, and Martha. She felt an ache in her chest that made breathing difficult. She had to fight the urge to run back to Cara and tell her she meant continue seeing her, no matter what Brent said. But she continued on.

Later, Zoe sat on the window seat in their suite, looking out over the bustling town of Aspen. What would life in the Dewitt mansion in Denver be like? For a few minutes she was more afraid than she had ever been in her life. She had cut all the ties to the past. Now, she had only the future, and it was still buried in a mist of uncertainty.

At that moment Brent opened the door and walked in. Zoe turned toward him with a smile. But her smile faded as she gazed at Brent's ashen face and saw the letter he clutched in his hand.

Simon's trip to Boulder was successful in more ways than one. He was able to report to Pete that the four months he'd spent in Aspen had been productive ones, and he met with the leaders of the Knights of Labor. Pete had made progress in Georgetown too, and it was agreed that Simon should return to Aspen on a more permanent basis to lead the miners there.

Although he dreamed often of Zoe and the one forbidden night they had shared, he was able to reestablish his equilibrium while he was in Boulder. Focusing on his work helped distract him as long as there was distance between them, but when he saw her again . . . He shrugged the unwelcome thought away.

Simon was tired, bone weary, yet he was satisfied. He'd only been back in Aspen for a week and he'd been working a ten-hour shift at the mine. Then he had spent another three hours every night talking to a group of the miners, answering their questions, encouraging them, and doing his best to open their eyes to the miserable conditions surrounding them. They listened, because he was one of them. He worked side by side with them and understood their plight. Still, they were a little wary, even a little afraid of him. Even though he was one of them, he had less to lose than the majority of them, who had wives and children depending on their meager wages.

"It's easy for you," one miner said this very evening. "You ain't got no kids to feed. One man fights back and he finds himself spending a hell of a cold winter with no heat and no food. I gotta work."

"One man," Simon repeated. "You're right about one man's power. But it's a different story if everyone stands together. If we all stand up at the same time, the mines would be effectively crippled."

"Sure," another miner answered, "until they brought in other miners. Then we'd all be starving."

"They can't bring in other miners if everyone—every miner in Colorado—stands up at the same time. Then the mine owners would have to listen. They wouldn't have a choice."

"That ain't possible."

"Why not?"

"'Cause it ain't. Nobody can make 'em do that."

"But if it could happen, what would you do?"

The miners looked at each other, too uncertain to answer and too wary to make a commitment.

"From what I hear, you tried to get all the miners together once before," one miner offered shrewdly. "Story tells it that you took a hell of a beating for all your trouble. Some say that's why you limp like that, and why you got those scars on your face. Looks to me like you didn't do much good then. Not for the miners . . . hell, not for yourself either."

"I'm not trying to deny that," Simon admitted. He went on to tell them what had happened to him. "But I was young then, and dumb. I thought you could have justice just by standing up and saying your piece. I thought one man alone could make a change. Well, one man can't. It takes a united force. It takes men standing up together to get results."

"They'll shut the mines down."

"For how long? How long do you think the spoiled rich can go on without their money? You hit them in their pocketbooks and you'll see them change soon enough. Look, go to your homes. Look around at what you've got to show for all your labors. Then take a look at what the mine owners have. It's time they shared. It's time you had a living wage. It's time you had a chance to eat well and dress warm. It's time you had a chance to hold your head up and look the owners in the eye and see that you're equal to them. It's time to right what's been wrong and have a decent life of your own. Go home . . . and think about it."

There was silence, and then the men began to drift away in twos and threes. Simon prayed that he had them thinking. He sighed. God, with each group it was the same. It took so long to make these blind, defeated men see the truth. He walked toward the small three-room cabin he'd bought on his return to Aspen.

Inside, he sat down on his bed and lay back and closed his eyes. How often lately he wondered why he had to do what he was doing. Why didn't he just pick up and leave? Go back home to Georgetown. He'd written his parents often, but hadn't gone home.

He thought of Pete and Augustus. They were fighting the same battle in Boulder and Georgetown. But at least they had each other . . . and Doc . . . and April. What did *he* have? What light existed in *his* world? Much as he wanted to deny it, to push it away, Zoe's face came before him. Zoe . . . he hated and loved her in the same breath. He wanted her with a slow, burning passion that he knew would never die. She was within touch . . . and completely out of reach.

When he thought of Zoe, there was no doubt in his mind that he would stay, partly for the sake of the miners . . . but mostly for Zoe's sake. He couldn't be with her, and he couldn't leave her. Because down the road that Zoe walked, disaster waited, and he knew it as sure as he knew that he would do his best to stand between her and trouble if he could.

Finally he rose, feeling sluggish and thick-headed. He carried water in from an outside well, heated it on his wood stove, and took a bath in the steaming water after he shaved. Then he dressed in clean clothes. He would go to town. At the parlor houses and bars he would find plenty of miners to talk to. And if he came home drunk enough to sleep without dreams, so much the better.

On the way into town he decided he would go to Stelle's new parlor house. Business at Stelle's was always brisk. Simon had learned from Cara that when Stelle saw Zoe or her on the street, she made no attempt to speak to them. It was Simon who'd spoken to Stelle first, or she probably would have pretended not to know him either. Occasionally Simon found some kind of solace at Stelle's.

Now, as he walked into her establishment, Stelle was the first to see him. She poured two drinks and came to his table.

"Hello, Simon."

"Stelle."

"You're looking down."

"I'm just tired."

"Maybe," she said quietly, "it's your overtime hours that are wearing you out."

Simon looked at her closely. Just what did she know about what he was doing in his "overtime hours"?

"Don't look at me like that, all closed up" she said. "I'm a friend. It's just my way of warning you."

"Warning me?"

"Simon . . . stay out of other people's business."

"I just can't do that."

"Why?"

Simon laughed softly. "I don't know."

"You can get hurt."

"I've been hurt. It doesn't change anything."

"Why you?"

"Because it needs to be done and because no one else is doing it, and because I've damn well taken the one and only beating I intend to take."

"So it's some kind of revenge."

"You might say that's partly it. But it's more than that. I'm not the only one who's taking a beating. There are too many hungry kids and scared parents out there."

"I still think there's more to it."

"More? What more does it take?"

"Maybe . . . a mine owner like Stephen Dewitt, who has a son here in Aspen who just happened to get married a few weeks ago to a girl we both know."

"Stelle"—Simon grinned at her—"take your own advice and go mind your business."

"Even Cara's worried. She actually came here to talk to me about Zoe. Why did you let Zoe do it, Simon?"

"Let Zoe do it! That's a laugh. I tried . . ." He paused, then shook his head. "Like I said, Stelle, mind your own business. Zoe's life is in her own hands. Send that message to Cara too. I imagine she's driving Zoe crazy with good advice now that it's too late."

"I don't think so."

"Then you don't know Cara the way I do."

"Like I said, I don't think so. It seems Brent has convinced Zoe to give up her business. Cara has the house and the restaurant."

Simon inhaled a deep sigh. "I thought it would turn out that way. Zoe would want Cara to have as much as she could. Brent knew who Cara was, and he doesn't want the Dewitt name tarnished. Maybe I ought to drop around to see Cara."

"Yeah . . . during the day. She and Zoe worked hard to clean up their reputations. I'm staying away. You be careful too."

"Yeah, I'll do that."

Simon drank his drink slowly after Stelle left him. He felt defeated somehow. Zoe had just cut her last thread to the past. There was no one to help her now. She was alone.

Chapter Fourteen

When Brent received his father's letter he had been stunned. He would be disowned unless he rid himself of his bride and came home alone. His belongings followed soon after the letter, and Zoe watched him fall apart as their money ran out. He had few choices. At Zoe's insistence he took a job in the mine that one day he would have owned.

He was aware of the puzzled, distrustful looks of the miners, and he worked silently and never made a friend. Slowly he began to blame Laura.

Unwilling to share his father's damning words, Brent had never showed Zoe the letter, and she was not about to give up on the plans she had made so long ago. Wealth and the good life were almost within reach. She had only to convince Brent to see that pride was a useless commodity when one was starving. She was certain that if he wrote to his father, explaining their love and their dire circumstances, he would be forgiven.

But Brent knew that he could never take Laura to Denver . . . never. His father was a stubborn man; he would never accept the woman he referred to as "that gold-digging slut." The shame at home would be even greater than the shame in Aspen.

Almost a year had passed since their wedding, and Zoe wondered how they could have sunk so low in such a short time. She looked around the shack they rented. She had come from a place no better than this. Where were all her bright dreams now? She had given up so much to escape the past, only to find herself in the same circumstances again.

She had no idea where Brent was tonight, but she didn't plan on the situation staying this way. Brent's family was wealthy. There was no need for them to live like this. Some stiff-necked idea of Brent's was standing in the way of both their futures. It was time she convinced him to plead with his father. To go home . . . and take her with him, where they could live the way Zoe had always dreamed of living.

She made a decision. Tomorrow she would take what little money they had left and go to town to buy something good for supper and a bottle of wine. Then, when she had Brent in the right mood, she would tell him . . . no, suggest that they go back where they could be comfortable and happy.

When she went to her dresser to see how much money she had in her nearly empty jewel box, she saw the one piece of good jewelry she had tried to keep. The string of exquisite pearls Brent had given her as a wedding present.

It was no time for regrets or for dreams. She snatched up the pearls. She would take them to town and see what they were worth. At least then she and Brent could make the trip to Denver both in comfort and dressed well. She would not surrender her dreams because of Brent's failures.

Even as she was planning to sell the necklace, a subtle whispering voice gave her a sudden shivery feeling of dread. Brent grew edgy over the simplest of things, always making something out of nothing. She didn't know how he would take the two things in conjunction, selling the necklace and her insistence that it was time for them to go to Denver.

But she had been raised to know and face the facts. When you were hungry you sold anything you could get your hands on. It was as simple as that. And they were hungry now.

Simon had watched Brent's descent from arrogant, spoiled aristocrat to ragged, listless miner with a relish that at times made him feel guilty. But not guilty enough to smother the desire he had for Zoe.

In time, he thought, Zoe would see the truth for herself.

When she wakened from the dream she'd held so greedily for so long, she would see the truth. She would come to him.

As Brent's fortunes had declined, Simon's had risen. For the last year he had saved practically all his wages. With no family to support, he had put aside a nice little nest egg. During his spare time he had been working on his cabin, improving it for the time when Zoe would share it with him.

And he instinctively knew that time was near when a very distraught-looking Brent stumbled into the bar where Simon and a few of his friends were drinking and talking over future plans.

He watched Brent surreptitiously, and after the third and fourth drinks he was convinced Brent had reached the end of his rope.

If he felt a twinge of sympathy for the other man, he buried it beneath his anger and the desire he had for Zoe. All he could think of was the day when Brent walked away from a life of pain and toil his education and wealth had never prepared him for.

His marriage to Zoe had destroyed his comfortable world, and the shock had dealt a deadly blow to whatever emotions he had harbored for Zoe at the beginning.

Well after midnight Brent staggered out into the darkness. A light snow was falling, which soon coated his shoulders and bare head. Simon followed as far as the door and watched Brent disappear into the darkness. He smiled to himself. He certainly wouldn't want to face Zoe's temper in that condition . . . but then, he thought, he would never have gotten himself in that state if Zoe were waiting for him.

The thought of Zoe waiting for him brought visions that twisted within him. He'd held her once . . . only once. But that night was burned into his memory. If he closed his eyes he could still taste the sweetness of her, feel the soft texture of her skin against his heated flesh. The glow of her hair in the lamplight and the scent of it were poignant memories he could not rid himself of.

He had, for a moment, held her fire in his hands, and had made the mistake of letting her go. He hadn't really believed she would go through with the marriage, hadn't really known the depths of her dreams until then.

Now, deep inside, he knew, even if she did not, that a man like Brent Dewitt was not the answer. Zoe was a blazing meteor. Brent was a dying ember. Simon had only to wait for his flame to go out.

He knew what was coming might be painful for Zoe. But he also knew she had only to reach out and he would be there to make her dream more of a reality than she had thought it could be.

For one moment he was filled with the temptation to go to her, to offer a sympathetic shoulder. But he pushed it aside. He didn't want Zoe that way. He didn't want their reunion to be a shadowy, aldulterous thing in the darkness of night. No, he wanted Zoe in every other way but that. He couldn't take the chance that one day she would look at him with hatred.

No . . . he would wait. Brent would diminuish his own stature in Zoe's eyes, and when she was no longer blinded by her dreams she would see. He could wait. He could watch as this destructive affair burnt itself out. Until Zoe was free. It never entered his mind that just as time had changed him, it had changed Zoe as well.

Zoe clutched her cloak close about her in protection against the March chill. She gripped the pearls just as firmly. She moved through the bustle of town without noticing. Her feet crunched rhythmically in the crisp snow.

She stopped before the window of a jewelry store whose owner she knew well. She had met him several times and had seen him cast her sympathetic looks. She stared now at the trinkets in the window. Could she get fifty dollars for the pearls . . . sixty? She had to get enough to dress herself and Brent properly and get the precious tickets to Denver.

Suppose Henry was not interested in a pearl necklace today. A cold hand clamped around her heart.

"Afternoon, Mrs Dewitt." A sprightly male voice came from close to her elbow. "Looking to buy something pretty?"

Startled, she turned to find herself looking down at

Henry Wraith. He looked up at her with a calm smile.

"I don't want to buy anything," she replied with a smile. "I want to sell something."

"May I be of help to you?"

She looked at him thoughtfully. At least he could tell her what the necklace was worth. She went inside with him and drew the jewel case out from under her cape.

"I was wondering how much I could get for this." She pressed the snap, and the cover flew back, revealing the pearls lying on the black velvet.

"Hmm, very pretty . . . with your hair and coloring . . ." He tilted his head back to consider the pearls with her skin, the flame of her hair, and the unique color of her eyes.

"That's what my husband said when he gave them to me."

"Why do you want to sell them?"

"I . . . I have to. My husband is ill. Could I get you to tell me what they are worth? Please, Mr. Wraith."

He examined the pearls a little more closely, and then named an amount that made her gasp. "They are of good quality, worth every penny, but I'm afraid I can't help you right now. Money is a bit tight and it might be some time before I could resell them."

"Oh." Her shock at the worth of the necklace was profound. But she was just as crushed to realize, whatever its worth, she could not sell it.

"I truly am sorry. Maybe Mr. McIver on Johnson Street could help. But . . . I'm sure he won't pay you much. I don't know what else to suggest."

"Thank you anyway. You've been very kind."

"How ill is your husband?"

"Quite. He . . . he really needs to leave here and get to where the air . . . his lungs, you see. He's had pneumonia and he's never quite gotten over it."

"I see," he answered. And he did see. So much more than Zoe imagined he saw. Actually he felt a little sorry for both young people. He didn't think they belonged together. He had met Brent several times and thought him a weak-hearted snob. What he had ever done to win this straightforward, robust beauty was beyond him. Like most of the people who knew Brent, Henry Wraith felt more sorry for Laura than for him. "I'm sorry my dear . . . truly, I am."

"Thank you anyway," Zoe said hastily as she smiled and backed out the door. She hated the look of sympathy . . . of pity she saw in his eyes.

Zoe was tired as she moved along the streets with the flow of the crowd.

As always, the high wooden sidewalks were filled with miners, off shift, with their shawled wives; well-dressed ladies from the hillside, the wealthy side of town, daintily picking their way across the walks from carriage to shop; an occasional man of substance hurrying about his affairs; and countless men without substance, drifting from the mining exchange to faro tables.

She let the crowd carry her along for a while, then worked her way to a place where she could stop and catch her breath. She wanted to draw a clean breath again and wash away the recollection of the defeat she faced. Defeat was rare for her.

She brushed the back of her hand across her eyes in an oddly childish gesture of grief. It was always so. The situation she had just faced was only another justification of her firm beliefs. Money . . . wealth . . . position! They were the only protection. You could put your faith in nothing and no one else. It was her reality. If you did not have protection, you were open prey and the vultures did not hesitate to close in.

Then she moved on again. The walk home seemed much longer and colder than it had earlier.

She had gone only a few steps when she paused. Amid the unseeing throng she felt the eerie sensation that someone was watching her. She turned and let her eyes scan the crowd about her. No one seemed to be paying attention. But still the sensation persisted.

She looked across the street, letting her gaze drift slowly over the throng. Then she saw him.

He stood with one broad shoulder braced against a rough-cut wooden support. His arms were folded across his chest, and even from where she stood she could see the half smile that touched his lips.

Simon!

Her heart seemed to pause, then pick up a stronger thudding beat. She drew her cloak tighter about her as if it were some kind of protection.

He made no move to cross the street, or even to acknowledge that he saw her, yet his eyes never left her. She could feel them touch her with memories, and it drew a soft sound of protest from her.

His look was an invitation and she knew it, just as she knew he was aware of the deterioration of her marriage. She could cross the street and go to him ... but she wouldn't. She hadn't spoken to him since that night a year before.

Her head lifted and her chin jutted with the same stubborn pride that Simon had learned to love so long ago. Then she turned her head away and continued on.

Simon's smile faded, and worry and desire filled his eyes. At that moment he loved and wanted Zoe more than he ever had before.

There was no doubt in Simon's mind that Zoe was in trouble, just as there was no doubt who was the cause of it. He knew where she had come from; he had watched her walk from the jewelry store.

It puzzled him what Zoe was doing at a jewelry store when he knew for certain neither she nor her husband had the money to purchase anything.

Mr. Wraith was a kind old gentleman and a friend of Simon's. So Simon made a decision quickly. He watched Zoe as she approached another jewelry store. It was clear to him now. She was trying to sell something.

He walked across the street to Henry Wraith's shop and stepped inside. Henry looked up from his work and smiled.

"Simon, my boy, how are you? It's been some time since I've seen you."

"I'm fine, Henry."

"What are you doing here?" Henry's eyes twinkled. "Finally buying a ring for some pretty girl? Who is she?"

"No, Henry." Simon laughed. "You're wrong. I was across the street and I thought I saw a lady I know come out of your shop."

"Lady? Oh, young Mrs. Dewitt. Lovely thing she is . . . too bad."

"Too bad what?"

"I'm afraid those two are hard put to make ends meet. I for one don't know how she puts up with his ways. The man hasn't two dimes to rub together, but he persists in his arrogant snobbish manner."

Simon couldn't agree more, but he didn't voice his opinion. "Was she trying to sell something?"

"Yes, poor thing. I know the pearls she was trying to sell were a wedding present. It is a shame. I couldn't buy them now."

"What are they worth?"

He told Simon, explaining that he could probably sell the pearls for considerably more than the amount he'd quoted Zoe.

"That's a good profit," Simon said.

"Yes, if there's a buyer. Right now there isn't."

"Oh, but there is," Simon said softly.

Henry looked closely at Simon and knew what he was implying. He only worried about the motive behind Simon's words.

"You're suggesting . . . you . . . would buy them?" he said cautiously.

"I am."

"And?" Henry went on, his face becoming cold and a little grim. He hated to miscalculate a man, and he had thought Simon to be an honest one with a strong sense of honor. After all, he was becoming a leader among the miners. "You expect the lady to be . . . appropriately . . . grateful when she hears about your generosity?"

"On the contrary. I don't want you to breathe a word about me. I'll provide the money, but I want her to believe you've reconsidered your finances and decided to buy them. Then, I want you to sell them to me."

"I don't understand."

"The lady needs help. I want her to get it. But I doubt if she would understand if I offered her money for them." Simon grinned. "She might think what you were thinking . . . that there are strings attached."

"And there aren't?"

"Not a one. I've known Laura for a long time. I want to help, and she would refuse whatever I offered. This way she can get the help she needs and never know it was from me. No one would be the wiser if you kept it a secret."

Henry gave Simon a close scrutiny, then smiled. Of course Simon could be lying to him, but he doubted it. "What do you want with the pearls?"

"Someday I want to give them back to her," Simon said quietly. "A woman should not be forced to part with her last treasure to save a man's pride. Especially a man who would not do the same for her."

"I see," Henry said quickly. "Yes, I see. Laura Dewitt is a very fortunate woman to have . . . friends . . . who care for her so . . . so deeply. I'll do as you ask."

"Thank you. She went down to Mr. McIver's store. I'm sure he won't buy them. Not for the price you quoted. I'll go and get the money if you will catch up with her and tell her you've changed your mind."

"All right. Go along. I'll catch up to her."

"I'm grateful, Henry. You won't regret it. She needs help and this is the only way I can do it." Simon walked to the door.

"Simon?"

Simon turned to face Henry again, and Henry smiled at him.

"It's a pleasure knowing you, sir."

"Thanks," Simon smiled, then left the shop.

Henry left almost immediately after him, and walked briskly down the street. He arrived at McIver's just in time to see a rather dejected Zoe leaving the shop.

"Mrs. Dewitt! Mrs. Dewitt!"

Zoe turned in surprise to see Henry coming toward her.

"I'm so glad I caught up with you," he said. "You haven't sold the pearls yet?"

"No . . . no, I have them here." She withdrew the small flat box from beneath her cloak.

"I have changed my mind. I would like to purchase them if you are still inclined to sell."

He watched as a heavy weight seemed to lift from Zoe's

shoulders and she smiled a smile that belonged on the face of a young, beautiful woman.

"Come along," he said gently. "Come back to my shop and I'll get you the money."

An hour later Simon, who stood watching some distance away, saw Zoe leave. Only when she was out of sight did he go to Henry's and deliver the money. Then he carried the pearls to his house. One day . . . they would be Zoe's again.

Chapter Fifteen

When Zoe got home she found that Brent had returned from his all-night binge, but he would tell her nothing about where he had been or what he'd been doing. She would not have been surprised to hear that he had spent the night at a parlor house.

For several days after he came home and dropped into his bed, he was too miserable and sick to talk or to listen, and Zoe did not want to explain what she had done until he was over the worst.

It seemed now that Brent couldn't stand the sight of Laura or the house they lived in. It was as if both represented everything distasteful in his life . . . everything his nature could not bear.

She had begun to try and explain to him . . . approaching the situation cautiously. But his lack of response fueled her anger. She would have told him she now had enough money to buy train tickets . . . but his fury erupted before she could.

"It's time for us to go back to Denver," she said firmly. "I know you haven't told your family about our problems."

"I've no intention of writing to them again, and I've no intention of going home, now or ever."

"Brent!"

"You don't think my father would accept me back under these circumstances, do you? I'm a complete and total failure. In his eyes . . . even in yours."

"A failure!" Zoe's temper got the better of her common sense. "Of course you're a failure! You're so damn weak you wouldn't even defend our marriage to your father. What are we supposed to do, pretend our marriage was such a mistake that we have no right to live?"

"Yes! I was a fool to let you run my world. To let you shame me by being so aggressive. To allow you to get me a job in that hellhole. God, if I weren't spineless I'd . . ."

"You'd what?"

"Laura." He sighed deeply in profound resignation. "Let me alone. I'm ill, and facing your ugly temper is more than any sane man should be asked to bear." He turned his back to her.

She was so enraged that her first inclination was to strike him. Instead she grabbed up her coat and slammed from the house.

She walked briskly for a while in a furious release of emotions.

How could she make him see that his family was the answer to all their problems? His family had enough money to make them forget any failures he may have had. After all, she reasoned, what was wrong with his family making their lives comfortable and easy?

She decided to find out the exact cost of the tickets back to Denver and purchase them. Then she would do whatever needed to be done.

She decided to visit Cara first. She knew Brent was completely set against her having anything to do with Cara, but she continued to see her when she could. She felt she had to have someone to talk to who knew and understood her, someone who would agree with what she had done. She drew a deep breath. She always felt better once she had made up her mind about something. But it was a long walk between home and Cara's.

Then one of the miners' wagons rolled slowly to a stop beside her, and the driver asked her if she wanted a ride. Recognizing him, Zoe climbed into the wagon.

"Looks like the weather's breaking," he said conversationally as he slapped the reins against the horse's rump.

"Yes . . . it's about time. I don't mind winter all that much, but spring and summer are my favorites. I like to walk and be outside."

They chatted amiably the rest of the way. When the wagon pulled to a halt in front of the restaurant, Zoe got down and turned to thank him.

She swayed dizzily for a moment, putting out a hand to steady herself. Funny, she'd never been one to grow faint before. The miner was giving her a long, kindly, scrutinizing look. Then he tied the reins and got down from the buggy, coming to stand beside her.

"Are you all right?"

"Yes, I'm fine. Just dizzy for a minute. I got an early start this morning and didn't eat any breakfast."

"If I didn't have work to do, I'd wait and drive you home. You'd best be careful. On these icy sidewalks it's easy to slip and fall."

"Thank you for the ride."

"You're quite welcome. I just hate to see you taking that long walk home."

"I'll be fine. The dizziness is already gone. Please don't worry about me."

"Well, you take care of yourself."

"I will. Good-bye and thank you again."

She watched him ride away, still unable to understand why she had been so dizzy. Then, as she turned to walk into the restaurant, she paused. Once her mind was on the subject of herself, she began to recall subtle differences in her body lately. There had been many signals her troubled mind had missed. It had been over two months since she'd had her monthly flow. She'd been too caught up in all her other problems to give it much thought.

Since the beginning of her womanhood, her body had been erratic in its rhythms. The truth came to her in a brilliant flash. She had not given children any thought after the first few months of watching and hoping. She was pregnant. That truth was followed by another. She could not tell anyone, Cara included, and most of all Brent. Not until they were in the safety and comfort of his Denver home, where their child could be born in the luxury due a Dewitt.

Cara was more than delighted to see Zoe, but she was alarmed at her thinness and her pale face. She realized again that introducing Zoe to Brent Dewitt and urging their marriage had been a terrible mistake.

She couldn't understand what had happened. She knew

quite well Brent's family had more wealth than they could ever spend, and that they had always been more than free with Brent. He had spent money like water. But now . . .

Cara insisted Zoe join her for a meal, and while they ate, she broached the problem.

"What's wrong, Zoe?"

"It seems you've been asking me that question from the time I was a kid."

"What difference does that make? When I have a problem you're the first . . . no, the only one I can ask for help."

"Well . . . I don't have that much of a problem really. I . . ."

"Go ahead."

"I needed some money, Cara, and I sold the pearls Brent gave me when we got married. I'm going to buy Brent and me a ticket home."

"Home! You mean Brent's parents have finally come to their senses?"

"Not exactly. I'm going to buy the tickets. Then Brent will just have to face the fact that it's time for us to go home."

Cara wasn't too sure this was such a good idea. She knew Brent had a bit too much arrogant pride, but Zoe had just a bit too much disrespect for it.

"Do you think he'll accept that?"

"He has to. If he's made mistakes, he can just apologize to his father. I'm sure once he gets that over with, things will be different."

"Zoe, I would have loaned you the money and you would not have had to give up your pearls. I know how much you loved them."

"I'm grateful, Cara, but I owe you so much already. This is the best way."

"You owe me nothing. I just hope once you get back to Denver, you and Brent can be happy."

"We will be," Zoe said confidently. "We just have to get out of here. Brent will see. He'll be happier once he's in his own home again."

"I'm sure," Cara said, but she wasn't quite as sure as Zoe was. She could never say to Zoe that it had always been difficult to fit a square peg in a round hole. Brent did not fit in here . . . and she was scared that Brent already knew Zoe would not fit in Denver any better. She just prayed that for once things would work out the way Zoe planned them.

Laura is my wife, Brent thought, still searching for some kind of dignity. His father had come without notice and caught him unprepared and off balance. Besides, he hated to admit to himself how inviting his father's offer was. To come home to the pleasant, warm, and comfortable life . . . with no pressure to make his own way in the world.

Brent was staring fixedly down at his clenched fists. Something in his father's last words had decided the matter. Brent looked up with a bitter flash. There was a new edge of resolution in his voice when he spoke.

"You've convinced me," he said tersely. He turned to his father. "How soon can we get out of this hellhole? I don't want to take anything with me. I want to leave it all behind!"

His father exhaled a long breath and the pinched look left his face.

His father did not know his last words had broken Brent's resistance to dishonor and had made him realize he had failed again.

Over two hours later Zoe trudged wearily home with the two precious tickets to Denver in her pocket. As she neared the house she wondered vaguely why no smoke came from the chimney. Then she noted the wheel tracks in the snow.

How tired she was. Her arms ached. Her whole body ached. She had been so weary fighting battles day after day, but in a matter of days all her battles would be over. Now she was like an earnest child who sorely needed someone to assure her she had been a very good little girl.

As she went up the walk she heard the long, trailing whistle of a departing train. She stopped to listen, thinking it was the chill of the day and her exhaustion that made her shiver. Then she forced herself to go on. She, who had never been superstitious, could not dispel the sense of something portentous about that distant whistle.

She opened the front door. "Brent!" No one answered. The kitchen was empty. The front parlor was empty. Unwillingly she approached the bedroom. Empty. The bedcovers had been thrown back and there were signs of a hasty departure.

Still stunned with the silent emptiness of the house, she returned to the kitchen. It was then she saw the note. She slowly reached for the paper.

Your old friends in the parlor house should be willing to take you back, since you are no worse for wear.

My son is coming home with me. Surely now you admit that you have been bad for him. This chapter in his life is closed. I have been to the courthouse. You undoubtedly know you have no claim on him whatsoever.

I have legal counsel who will protect Brent from you should you try to contact him again. Brent knows the entire truth of your past and does not wish ever to see you again.

Stephen Dewitt

Pinned to the note was a check made out to Zoe Carrigan . . . *Zoe Carrigan!* And on the bottom was a cryptic note: "For services rendered."

At first she was too stunned to make sense of either the note or the check. And then she was too horrified. But slowly the words began to pound themselves into her brain. Her breath came with a harsh panting sound that was half a shriek of anger and half a moan of agony. She tore both note and check into little pieces.

She felt as if she had been betrayed in the most horrible, brutal way, and she wanted to lash out . . . to hurt him . . . someone . . . something.

She sobbed Brent's name aloud as she sank onto a chair. She had struggled to find them a way out of their dilemma. She had given up the one valuable and precious thing she owned to find a way to make their lives better . . . and Brent had destroyed all her efforts. He had left her.

He had left all his belongings but the suit he wore. Left them, like so much trash . . . as he had left her. There was something incredibly insulting about his leaving everything behind that had been part of their life together. What right did he have to go back to his wealth, his peace, his comfort, and leave her with nothing but these useless objects!

Her eyes hardened with obsessive determination. She would wipe him away as effectively as he had done her.

Quietly she picked everything up and carried it out to the backyard. Slowly and deliberately she poured kerosene on the pile. She stood gazing at it for several minutes as she gathered her hatred into a tight ball. Then she touched a match to it and watched the flames leap upward.

Only when the fire was nearly over did she go back into the house and shut the door firmly behind her.

The curtains on the neighbors' windows fell back in place, and even though they occasionally peeked out during the evening, no lights shone from the Dewitt house, no smoke came from the chimney, no sound emanated from the small dark cadaver of a house. Night hid the house for a while as if to give it and its occupant a moment's obscurity.

The sun was not up, only a pale streak of gray touched the sky, when Zoe crept from the house. She walked to the edge of the porch and sat down to survey the destruction. Only then did she give way to grief and weep. For a long time she cried. Then she rose, her face frigid, her heart still.

Three Weeks Later

Cara looked uncomfortable. Life had not trained her to mince words, and now she longed for diplomatic tact. She sat down at the table, avoiding Zoe's eyes. Cara sighed.

Since Brent's departure Zoe had seemed to lock every emotion away. She had begun to find excuses for Brent. She blamed his parents for everything. Now, to Cara's distress, she was waiting for him to come back so she could forgive him. Cara could hardly believe the self-delusion under which Zoe lived. She had no way of knowing it was the last barrier before total disintegration.

She sat down opposite Zoe, untied her bonnet, and laid it on the table. Then she brushed some stray locks from her eyes.

"The doctor wants you to eat better than you do, Zoe."

"I do eat, Cara," Zoe said calmly.

"Zoe, please do as the doctor says. You're not careful at all. You work hard . . . and you just don't take care of yourself."

" "I'll be careful, Cara. When Brent gets back . . ."

"Zoe!" Cara cried, half in anger and half in pain. Then she inhaled deeply. "I just came from the courthouse." Zoe looked at her, but deep in her eyes a shadowy fear lurked. "I didn't understand that note Brent's father left," Cara went on. "The part about you having no claim on Brent. So I went to find out. You aren't married to him at all."

Zoe's head went up. "I am too! You saw us get married. That old preacher . . ." Zoe paused uncertainly as the impact of her owns words struck her.

"That's just it, Zoe. He must have been some kind of a fake. I figure it was all my fault; I should have made sure. But I didn't have much experience, so I left it to Brent to hire the preacher. Now, I'm not accusing Brent of doing this deliberately. He was most likely fooled the way we were. This man probably was a preacher once. But he never did anything . . . official for you and Brent. He was supposed to register your marriage at the courthouse. But the man at the courthouse says there is no record of a Brent Dewitt marrying a Laura Champion. The preacher just never bothered to have your marriage recorded, you see."

Zoe stared lethargically at the small bowl of flowers that sat in the middle of the table. Cara eyed her uneasily. It was not natural for Zoe or any woman to act this way. It had been better when she screeched and smashed things. Perhaps it was her pregnancy that made her face things so calmly . . . and quietly.

"I don't care what you say, Cara. We were really married. He felt married . . . I know he did!"

Cara said nothing. She wished she thought so too.

"Write to him, Zoe. Tell him about the baby. It will make him come back if he is any kind of a man."

"I can't, Cara," Zoe said with a spark of her old fire. "I won't use this baby like a whip to drive him back to me. Don't you see . . . I can't. He must want to come back, not be compelled as if I were some wench that he accidentally got in a family way. He will want to come back. Wait and see."

But Cara couldn't see at all. Zoe didn't know that Brent, back home with his family, would be a different man.

"Zoe . . ."

"No, Cara. No. He'll come back for me. We'll both go back and live in that fine house. My baby will have everything! Everything! All the things I never had. You'll see."

For the first time Cara could remember, she was scared. Zoe was living a dream, and Cara was afraid of the day when the dream was finally replaced by reality.

Spring slowly pried loose the tight fisted grasp of winter. The days bled into weeks, and then into months. The river was high with muddy runoff water from the melting snow. The almost daily wet snowfalls, which at a lower altitude would have been spring showers, melted by noon.

Daily and devotedly, Zoe swept and scoured and dusted. She was a wife preparing for her husband's imminent return. But as spring gave way to summer, and then the warmth of September turned to cool, crisp October days, the money she'd gotten from the pearls dwindled. Zoe would not let Cara offer financial help, and Cara was frightened of the day when there would be no more money. She wondered if Zoe would really care. Her neighbors whispered together. Poor thing. Who did she think she was fooling? Still waiting, with no sign of the man who had left her nearly destitute. His folks had certainly put a stop to their wild affair in a hurry.

It was a quiet mid-afternoon when Zoe sat at her kitchen table. She sat for some time before she opened the newspaper Cara had brought on a visit the night before. Cara had tried everything to break Zoe's silent hopefulness. Zoe turned the page of the *Aspen Star* and stopped.

No, she thought, I must be reading wrong. My eyes are playing tricks on me. For a moment the sentences blurred together in the strangest way, but no matter how she read them, they remained the same.

Fashionable wedding unites prominent Denver families. Miss Barbara Crandell becomes the bride of Brent Dewitt. . . .

The paper fell from her numbed fingers. It was as if she had been struck. She picked up the paper again. Barbara Crandell. She sat very still for a long while, but the words hammered remorselessly through her brain. It couldn't be! Nobody else could be Brent's bride because he was married to *her*.

Her chaotic mind was beginning to function, was beginning to wind itself up like a tightening spring. But it was useless winding up.

For the first time she truly realized what Cara had been talking about. Tears she was not aware of ran down her cheeks. She rose slowly to her feet, holding on to the edge of the table, and paced back and forth across the kitchen.

She was only a . . . she thought of the short ugly word for herself. Her baby was . . . she thought of the other word used for a baby like hers.

Her shell of lethargy was shattered at last. She wanted to hurt somebody. She wanted to lash out, as she had always lashed out when she herself was hurt. But who was there to hurt? Brent was safe, far away in Denver, married to Barbara Crandell and living in an elegant new home on Sherman Avenue. Who was there to hurt? And then she knew. She could hurt all that was left of her and Brent. She could hurt herself.

Chapter Sixteen

Cara laid the newspaper down slowly. The cup of tea she had held in her other hand shook so badly as she tried to set it on the table that tea stained the white tablecloth.

She reread the article twice before she could actually believe she was really seeing those damning words. Her guilt and remorse welled up inside her.

"Oh, Zoe," she muttered. She rose quickly and reached for her wool shawl. Within minutes she was on the street, rushing toward Zoe's house.

Her heart pounded heavily. Zoe didn't deserve any more hurt than she had already had. When would life, for once, be fair to her?

She hated Brent at that moment, and a small part of her anger turned to Zoe. If only she'd had the sense to see that Simon Tremaine was by far the better man. But Zoe could only see the dream she had chased since she was a little girl.

Cara moved as fast as she could through the streets until in the distance she could see Zoe's house. The house was dark, and that scared Cara.

Maybe Zoe had read the paper and was there in the dark with her pain.

As Cara drew closer she could see that the door was swinging slowly back and forth in the cold wind. Fear was thick in her throat. She approached the house carefully, paused in the open doorway, then went inside.

The evidence lay on the table . . . the discarded newspaper. But . . . where was Zoe?

Cara was so afraid she could hardly think. The only thought that came into her head was that Zoe was in drastic need of help. The only person Cara could think of to turn to was Simon.

Simon could get people to search. Simon would care enough to make sure Zoe was found. She turned from the semi-dark house and ran out.

Simon had two lists—one of men he was certain were ready to follow him, one of miners who were not yet committed to the union. Over the last two years the former list had grown steadily as the latter shrank.

He was sitting alone, laboriously going over each name on the uncommitted list, picturing each man, his family, his problems, and preparing the best arguments to sway them.

Finally he laid his pencil aside and sat back in his chair to rub his tired eyes. He had stopped questioning himself about why he continued to battle against such high odds. He knew his answer was his own anger, Zoe . . . and most of all Brent and his greedy father.

He had it all perfectly planned. He would shake the foundation of wealth Stephen Dewitt stood on, and that in turn would put more and more pressure on Brent . . . until he broke.

He knew in his heart that Zoe still held on to the fantasy that Brent would take her back to Denver. That he would go on his knees to his father, that Stephen Dewitt would forgive and forget and take them into his magnanimous embrace. He knew that Zoe clung to that dream with a kind of desperation . . . and he knew he had to destroy it once and for all if Zoe was ever to turn her back on it and see what was real.

He knew almost everything that went on in Zoe's house, because Cara loved her as much as he did and told him what was happening almost daily.

He knew when Brent had left, and he had waited weeks for Zoe to face reality. But she hadn't. Instead she had retreated even deeper into her fantasy world.

He knew of the baby, and hated Brent even more for every day that Zoe had to do without the care and gentleness she needed.

Now he stretched his stiff muscles and returned to

checking his lists. Working the second shift at the mine
and carrying on his other work gave him little time for
rest. It was better this way, because idle hours only gave
him time to think . . . and to dream dreams of his own
that were better not dreamed . . . at least not now.

He wondered at himself. Any normal man would have
given up a long time ago. But he couldn't. His dreams had
the same hold on him as Zoe's had on her. Talons of desire
had dug themselves deeply and he could not extricate
them. He recognized his own weakness . . . it was Zoe and
the love he held for her. It was impossible to run . . . even
to walk away from it.

Unable to concentrate on arguments and lists and reasons for what he did, he folded the lists and put them
away. He didn't want them to fall into unfriendly hands.

He stood and looked about him. His house was small,
but comfortable. Simon had worked hard to make it that
way. It was five rooms now, heated by the two fireplaces
he had built. One in the bedroom and the other in the
sitting room.

He'd made nearly every piece of furniture by hand, and
was proud of the warmth and comfort around him.

A friendly woman who lived next door had agreed to
keep his house clean for a few coins to help her family.
And she had done so. She had also been the one to make
curtains and bedclothes.

Why he had worked so hard to improve his home was
a secret that he would admit to no one—one day he
wanted Zoe to live here with him.

He had a little time before he went to the mine. So he
decided to walk over to the small one-room school and
return the books he had borrowed from Caroline Dalton.
She had come to the mining town to teach school. She
and Simon had become friends, even though the school
at which she taught excluded the children of the miners.
Simon had always thought that if he could start a school
for the miners' children, he would ask Caroline to teach
there.

He admired Caroline. Every day their friendship grew
warmer, but never went beyond that.

She had appreciated his desire to extend his education

as far as he could, and had encouraged him with discussions and books. They had been able to talk, and that alone was a rare thing. He found himself telling her about his childhood and his plans . . . but even to her he never mentioned Zoe. Zoe was a part of his heart he could not reveal.

He gathered up the books and started toward the door. A loud knock brought him to an abrupt halt. It was a man's knock, he knew that, and a sudden fear filled him. Even when his mind refused to, his body remembered well. The memory of pain and fear very seldom went completely away.

The knock sounded again. He continued on to the door after he laid the books aside. He wanted his hands free.

He took hold of the latch and opened the door quickly, prepared for anything except the three people who stood before him. The last three he'd expected to see on his doorstep.

"Pete . . . Gus . . . what are you doing here . . . and April. I never expected to see you three this soon."

"There's four of us. Doc is on his way," Pete said.

Simon had stepped aside so they could enter, and Pete extended his hand to Simon.

"Something is wrong," Simon stated. Pete's face was not exactly filled with joy. He noticed then that April's face was . . . different. Her eyes seemed even more distant than usual.

"Yeah," Pete agreed, "there's a lot gone wrong since we saw you last."

At that moment another tread could be heard on the porch; then Paul Riley appeared in the doorway. Of all the changes, the one in Doc seemed to be the most drastic. He looked as if he carried bottled fury within him.

"What is it?" Simon was beginning to worry.

"It's a long story, Simon," Gus said. "Do you think you could put us up for a couple of days? Pete and I are tuckered out. As for Doc and April . . . well, that's another story. One that"—he cast a quick look at April, then back to Simon—"Doc can tell you about . . . later."

It was obvious he didn't want to say any more in front of April. Simon nodded his acknowledgment of Gus's warning. "Come on in and make yourselves comfortable. Are you hungry?"

"We've been travelin' since dawn," Pete said. "I'm both tired and hungry. I'm sure April needs to rest for a while."

"April, do you want to lie down for a bit?" Simon asked gently. "My bedroom's right over there. You go in and rest awhile. I'll rustle up some food. When it's ready I'll call you."

"Thank you, Simon," April said in a soft voice. "I am a little bit tired."

Simon led her to the door of his bedroom, opened the door, and pulled it closed behind her. Then he turned back to Gus, Pete, and Doc. "Now, suppose you fill me in on what is going on."

Gus inhaled tiredly and found a comfortable chair.

"Me and Pete have about three-fourths of the miners lined up . . . ready for whenever we say it's time to move. We'd have had them all, but . . . Doc needed us."

"Needed you?"

"Yeah." Pete's face was growing more grim, and Simon could tell that what was boiling inside him was very close to exploding. "Doc can tell you better than I can."

"Doc?"

"Check on April first, Simon. See if she's sleeping."

Simon was shaken by this, but he walked across the room and cracked the bedroom door open far enough to stick his head inside. April lay on his bed, sound asleep. He closed the door softly and came back to join the others.

"Now will someone tell me what's going on?"

"All right. I guess I'm the best one to tell you," Gus said. "There were a few rumors that ended up following you from Georgetown. I heard them, and I know they were started by mine owners. But I paid no mind. I figured they'd die away. But different kinds of rumors started growing. That Pete was involved in unionizing workers. It got worse and worse, coming back to me nursing you, and being sympathetic. Well, to make a long story short, some things got out of hand and a group of miners from the Stratton mine walked out on a kind of strike. They started to put some of the blame on Pete."

"And this is one time I wasn't guilty. We just weren't ready for a strike yet," Pete added.

"Right, but that didn't stop the owners from putting blame on him. They were mighty angry. They called in some strikebreakers . . . some really rough boys."

"Damn bastards! They ought to rot in hell," Pete snarled.

"I still don't know . . ." Simon said.

"I know," Doc said. "I'll finish the story. Pete got mixed up in a free-for-all and got himself shot."

"Shot!"

"He's all right. But he came to me. I patched him up and he went home. Only they didn't know that he'd left my place."

"Good God," Simon said. "You mean they . . ."

"Yes," Doc said heavily. "They sent three or four men to my house to finish the job with Pete. I was out on a call . . . April was home alone."

"They didn't . . ."

"No, but they terrorized her. After they tore my place apart they left. When I came home I found April huddled in a corner too scared to cry. I decided right then to get her out of Boulder."

"Wise move," Simon agreed. "She'll be safe here since there are four of us to protect her. We'll leave one of us home all the time."

"So we'll work from here from now on?" Gus asked.

"Sure," Simon said. "I need some help here anyhow. Paul, this town can use another doctor, and I'm sure I can get Pete a job with me. We'll just be working together from now on."

"Yes, we need to get organized into an official union and here is the best place to set up headquarters. Sooner or later, when we do begin to move, we'll need a center."

"Sounds like you've done some pretty good work here," Gus said.

"Not as good as I'd like. I'll explain everything I've done. Did you bring lists so we can get a count? We have to know how many we can call out on strike at one time. For a while, Pete, you and a couple of men I feel I can trust can travel from here."

"I've got lists," Pete said. "And I have a few men I'm sure we can trust completely. It looks to me like we're beginning to solidify into a real force. A little more time and we can call one big strike. That's the only thing that's going to make these mine owners sit up and take real notice . . . and deal honestly with us for a change."

"I hope so," Simon said. "One thing is certain. Violence is the worst way to go. Our men pick up guns and there could be a bloodbath. We have to use our heads, not force."

"Easier said than done. These miners have been trampled too long," Gus replied.

"Maybe easier said, but it has to be done. We're supposed to be the core of the movement, so it's up to us to keep our heads."

"You're right, Simon," Paul said. "But every time I think about April and those men . . . well, I guess violence is just below the surface with all of us."

"You're right, I guess," Simon said quietly. "There's a man . . . or two I'd like to use a little violence on."

None of them doubted from the look on his face that he meant every word he said.

After Simon had prepared them some food, they sat together to make plans. Satisfied that they were on the right course, Simon informed them he had to leave them for a while. "It's time for me to get to work."

"You keep some pretty hard hours, boy," Gus said.

"It's necessary. I have two jobs. Mining is a necessity . . . the union is the most important."

"What about some time for yourself?"

"Someday . . . maybe. Right now there's a job to do."

"Yes," Gus agreed. But he heard something in Simon's voice that made him worry.

"I'll see you sometime around midnight," Simon said. "In the meantime make yourselves as comfortable as you can."

"Be careful, Simon."

"I will."

Simon left his small house and walked to the mine with a lot of pressing thoughts on his mind.

He worked at a steady pace, making his body do the work while he detached his mind and let it drift. When he thought of the miners and their problems, he felt indignation . . . when he thought of April and what had happened, he felt anger . . . and then . . . then there was Zoe. And with the thought of Zoe there came the only respite he had. He could draw on her, and the one magical night they had shared, to ease his mind and his heart.

By the time his shift was over he was tired, dirty, and emotionally drained. He started home, trudging through the cold, empty streets. It had grown colder after the sun had gone down, and he pulled his heavy wool jacket tighter around him.

He was walking with his head down, bent against a raw wind, so he did not see Cara coming toward him until she cried out his name.

"Simon!" He looked up and abruptly stopped walking. He could feel a strange kind of shiver jolt through him.

"Oh, Simon, thank God. I tried to find you this afternoon, but you'd already left for work."

"What's the matter?"

"It's Zoe. You've got to help me find her!"

"Find her? Where's she gone?"

"I don't know! Simon, there's no time! I'm sure she's trying to kill herself and the baby. We've got to stop her!"

"Why should she want to kill herself? Cara, you're not making sense. Stop crying and tell me what's going on."

Between ragged sobs Cara explained about the newspaper article and how she had gone to Zoe's house, only to find her gone and the door standing open.

"Damn that bastard!" Simon shouted. "Damn him to hell. If Zoe dies, for sure I'll find him and kill him."

"Don't worry about him! We've got to find her before she harms herself."

"Who does she know that she might run to?"

"No one."

"There has to be someone!"

"Simon," Cara said bitterly, "Zoe had no friends but me."

He felt the blow as if she had reached out and struck

him. He struck back only in self-defense. "Then why did you come to me?"

"Because you love her, and you're the only one I know who will help me find her." Her voice was quieter and firmer, and he read her eyes and knew she was right.

"I'm sorry, Cara. I didn't mean to lash out at you. I guess I'm scared. Where have you looked?"

"I . . . I checked the bridge along the river." His fierce look almost stopped her. "I don't know where else to look!"

"Let's go."

He took her arm and they began a search of every possible place Zoe could be. But she was nowhere to be found. As the hours passed exhaustion claimed them, and a fear that when they found her . . . she might not be alive.

"Look, Cara," Simon said, "you go back to your place. If she gets through this, she might come to you. Stay there until daylight, then come to my place. If I haven't found her by then . . ."

"What?"

"I don't know. I guess I'll just keep on looking until I find her."

Reluctantly Cara did as Simon said.

Simon stood quietly for a minute, realizing that he really didn't know another place to look. He tried to clear his mind and think, but all he could envision was Zoe desperate . . . alone . . . afraid . . . or worse . . . dead.

The thought was too much. He started for Zoe's house. Maybe . . . just maybe, she might come home.

But the house was dark when he arrived. He saw the door slowly swinging back and forth, and he knew with a sinking heart that Zoe must have left in a state of anguish so complete that she had forgotten everything else.

Standing in the center of the room, he looked around him. Even in the dark he could see how little Zoe had. It hurt him to know she had been doing without. When Cara had told him that her husband had gone, he had been sure that Zoe would finally come to him. But she hadn't, and Cara had warned him away, telling him Zoe was in a strange state of mind and it was a bad time to see her. She'd told him to wait until the child was born. He'd waited. Now he wished that he hadn't.

A sound from outside made him spin about. Then she was in the doorway, and he could tell by the way she sagged against the frame that she was about to collapse.

He stepped toward her quickly, and knew she did not see or hear him. She did not see or hear anything. He moved forward quickly . . . just in time to catch her in his arms as she fell.

Pain tore at her like red-hot talons. She refused to cry out, certain that no one cared to hear her scream or beg for mercy.

Simon knelt by the bed and caught her clutching hand in his. He had lifted her up and carried her to her bed after she had collapsed. Then he had laid her gently against the pillow and turned to light the lamp.

When he'd looked at her again he had uttered an exclamation of shock. She was dirty, bedraggled, her clothes torn and wet, and her hair plastered against her head in wet tangles. Her pregnancy was far advanced and she looked . . . helpless. He would have gone for someone, a neighbor or someone to help, but she cried out and clutched the sheets. The cry was one of agony, and he knew whatever Zoe had done this night, she had done in an attempt to kill both herself and the baby.

He went to get some water and warmed it on the stove, in which he had started a fire. The house was cold and damp. Then he brought the basin of water and set it beside the bed. He found another sheet and tore pieces from it. Then he removed his jacket and sat down on the bed beside her.

Gently he washed the dirt and tears from her face, and cleaned the scratches and cuts on her arms and hands.

She moaned and writhed on the bed in fitful moments. One minute she lay quiet, her breath coming in soft panting sounds. But just when he thought she was going to lapse into a quiet sleep, she would moan again and begin to thrash about.

Wondering if Zoe was about to give birth, he decided to get her out of the wet, muddy, and torn clothes she wore. There was no doubt about it, he would have to go for help . . . only he was afraid to leave her alone.

He stripped the clothes off, bathed her carefully, then covered her with a sheet and a couple of warm blankets, hoping she could sleep for a while. She would need all of her strength.

He paced the floor, scared to leave her and just as scared not to. The dilemma had him at his wit's end. He returned to the bed and took her hand in his.

"Zoe . . . Zoe, can you hear me?"

Zoe swam in a dark sea of pain, and she could see no light, sense no help. From a distance too far away to reach, she could hear a warm and familiar voice. She could put no name to it; she knew only that it was an offer of peace and freedom . . . from what she didn't know. She knew only that she had to swim toward it or she was lost. The darkness beckoned from one end and that smooth, caressing voice from the other.

"Zoe," he begged, "please hear me, love. I have to get some help." Her hand clutched his, and clung. He had never felt so weak and useless in his life. "Zoe . . . darling, please. You have to hold on. I don't want to leave you but I have to. You need more help that I can give."

Her eyes fluttered open, and for a short time she seemed lucid.

"Simon." Her voice was hoarse and breathless, and he could see the dark shadow of pain in the depth of her eyes.

He breathed a deep sigh of relief. "God, Zoe. Stay with me, girl. Stay with me."

Zoe licked her dry lips. She felt disoriented and weak, and for a while she couldn't remember how she'd gotten where she was. "What . . . what are you doing here?"

"Cara and I have been looking for you for hours."

"Cara?" she repeated.

"Cara. She's still looking. Can you tell me where you were? Zoe . . . you haven't taken anything . . . done anything to hurt you or the baby?"

"The baby," she repeated again.

It was then he realized Zoe wasn't with him at all. Somehow he was a vague presence, but everything else was beyond reality for her. "Oh, Lord, Zoe," he whispered, half to himself and half to a God he hadn't prayed to for a long, long time.

"Simon." Her body tensed and she gave a soft moan. He could have wept in his frustration.

Cara picked that moment to burst into the house. She had come back with the same hope that he'd had. When she raced up on the porch and threw open the door, she called out, "Zoe, Zoe, are you home?"

Simon fairly leapt from the bed and went to meet her. "Cara, I'm here. Zoe's in a bad way. One of us is going to have to go and fetch her doctor."

Cara followed him back into the bedroom and ran to kneel by the bed. But Zoe had slipped back into her own personal agony. Cara turned to look up at Simon. His face was gray with fear. "Where was she? What happened?"

"I don't know. I came back here to check. She wasn't here. Then she came in and collapsed. She hasn't been really conscious since. Cara, I think the baby's coming."

"Do you think she did something to . . ."

"I don't know. One way or another, she's got to have a doctor."

"Do you want to go, or do you want me to?"

"I . . . I guess I . . ." He swallowed heavily.

"You don't want to leave her."

"No . . . I don't."

"I'll go. I'll be back as fast as I can."

"Thanks, Cara."

"Stay with her, Simon. I'd like her to know you're here when she wakes up. Maybe she'll finally come to her senses."

He nodded, and bent to kiss Cara's cheek. She smiled, reached up and patted his cheek, then turned and left.

Zoe was tossing and turning on the bed as if she were caught in a violent storm. Simon went to her and sat on the side of the bed. Gently he brushed hair from her dampened forehead.

"I love you," he whispered ". . . and you'd better not have done anything to hurt yourself. You can't die and leave me, Zoe. If I had a half a chance, I'd show you that life can be a sweeter thing if you love someone. You never loved him, Zoe, and he certainly doesn't deserve your suffering. He doesn't deserve one minute of your grief. I don't know if you can hear me, but I promise you I'll never let anything hurt you like this again."

He held her hand and listened to her ragged breathing. It grew worse, and he realized her hand was growing hot. He put his hand against her forehead. She was burning with fever. The touch of his cool hand on her seemed to unleash the delirium she held within, because she began to mumble. Her words were incoherent at first, but soon he began to pick out phrases.

"I will not fear what man shall do onto me." The Bible quote startled him. He wondered what torment was going on in her mind.

"Simon . . . Simon," she moaned.

"I'm here, Zoe . . . I'm here."

"I won't . . . I can't . . . don't . . . don't go . . . baby . . . baby . . ."

"It's all right, Zoe," he said, hoping she could hear him. "You don't need to be afraid."

She clung to his hand with a strength that surprised him. "Don't leave me . . . don't go."

"I won't leave you. I'll stay right here beside you. You don't have to be afraid, Zoe . . . you won't be alone."

He didn't know if it was what he said or simply that she was becoming weaker with each breath. But the words seemed to ease her. She grew quiet. He continued to sit beside her and hold her hand.

After a while he heard the clump of footsteps across the porch. Cara must have found the doctor. He laid Zoe's hand gently across her and rose. When he left the bedroom the doctor was already tossing aside his coat. He could read Simon's eyes well, so he said nothing, just started for the bedroom. Simon was right behind him.

"You'd best wait outside, Simon."

"No, I told Zoe I'd stay with her. That she wouldn't be alone."

"But she won't know . . ."

"I'll know. Besides . . . she's faced too many things in her life alone. She won't be alone with this."

The doctor remained silent for a moment, studying Simon's determined face. Then he nodded slowly, and Simon followed him silently into the bedroom. A very tired Cara sagged into a chair to wait.

Chapter Seventeen

For two days Zoe was desperately ill, and for the same two days Simon never left her side. The doctor fought for her survival. To Simon's surprise, the baby showed no signs of being born. But the doctor assured Simon it was not going to be long before it was.

"It's a matter of hours, Simon. I just hope I can get her stable before the baby decides to make its presence known in this topsy-turvy world."

"She's strong. She'll make it. They'll both make it . . . they have to."

"Simon . . ."

"I know what you're going to say. But this child's father is a spineless bastard who doesn't deserve either of them."

"What a man deserves is not always the same as what is his."

"I guess you're right. I don't really understand what happened between them. I only know he walked away as if he had no responsibility at all. Everyone must have seen the story in the paper. Cara has told me that there's no record of the marriage at all. Don't you think Zoe needs to be spared any more pain?"

"This child . . . the birth certificate . . . I . . ."

"I know," Simon said angrily. "You have to label it legally illegitimate. God. What's going to happen when he . . . or she finds that out?"

"Let's hope it's a 'he.' A girl has a terrible future with a start like this."

"And Zoe," Simon said quietly, "all her dreams are gone. I don't know what she's going to hold on to now."

"She'll find something. Women like Zoe are not the kind

197

to be held down for long. She'll find another dream to fight for."

"I hope you're right, Doc," Simon said. But he didn't believe it was going to be quite as simple as that.

Simon and the doctor stood in Zoe's parlor. The door to her bedroom was open a few inches so they could hear if she called out. But there was no sound. Zoe had fallen into a deep, heavy sleep.

"Simon, you ought to go home and get some sleep."

"I'm all right. I've taken a few catnaps. I've gone without sleep before. Besides, I have to be here when she wakes up." The doctor nodded.

There was a slight sound from the bedroom, and Simon moved swiftly.

The first thing Zoe saw when she opened her eyes was Simon's worried face bending above her. She felt weak and exhausted. He sat down beside her and took her hand.

"Zoe?"

"What . . . what happened?"

"That's what we all would like to know. Don't you re-member? We couldn't find you. Where did you go that night?"

"That night," she repeated. "I don't . . ." But suddenly, bitter and ugly memories returned with a vengeance. "My baby!"

"The baby is all right," the doctor said as he came to stand at the foot of the bed. "For a while there I couldn't say the same for you. But the fever has broken. In a few days you are going to be as right as rain."

"Thank you," Zoe said weakly. "I don't know how I can pay you."

"Don't worry about paying me. When you feel better we shall have to talk, you and I. There is a great deal to be said . . . and planned."

"Planned?"

The doctor looked a little taken aback. His face flushed. "Well . . . ah . . . I thought you might need . . . I mean, it's almost impossible for a woman to raise a child alone. There are means . . . I mean, you could have its care seen to . . ." He stopped, because the look in Zoe's eyes was so powerful he could go no further.

"This child is mine, and no one will see to its care but me," she declared.

"But it's . . ."

"Illegitimate! Say it! Illegitimate! I don't care what you or anyone says. The child is mine and the neighbors and the snobs of Aspen can go to hell!"

"Zoe, don't get excited," Simon said. "Nobody is going to touch the baby. Just don't get all wrought up; it will only make you sick again."

She sagged back against the pillow, and Simon turned to the doctor. "Maybe we ought to let her rest."

The doctor realized his presence was more hindrance than help to Simon right now. Maybe if he left, Simon could talk her into being sensible. She just couldn't raise a child by herself. Where would the money for food and clothes come from? And the stigma would follow the child forever. No, he would leave, and trust Simon to make her understand that it would be for the child's good.

"Yes, it would be better," the doctor said. "Call me if there's any change."

"I will," Simon said. Now he was anxious for the doctor to leave. He didn't like the pallor in Zoe's face or the shadowed, frightened look in her eyes.

He walked the doctor to the door. Before he left, the doctor spoke confidently to Simon. "See that you make her understand, Simon. It's really the best thing for her."

"I'll see that Zoe does exactly what's best for her," Simon replied.

The doctor wondered if there was a double meaning behind his words. He paused, then shrugged. If she wanted to be stubborn, he couldn't stop her. She would find out soon enough when she and the babe were starving.

Simon walked slowly back to the bedroom. He knew there was already a lot of gossip about his presence, but he also knew he would support Zoe in whatever she decided to do. He just couldn't see her giving up her baby. She had lost too much already.

When he walked back into the room, Zoe was braced up by pillows she had stuffed behind her. Half fainting, she lay there, feeling her heart pound until she thought it must be shaking the bed.

Suddenly the child within her kicked out with such force that it brought her sitting bolt upright.

She clenched her fists and lay back rigidly. She watched Simon approach and sit down beside her on the bed. For a few minutes both were silent.

"So, Zoe . . . what do you want to do?"

"There's no question, Simon. I won't give my baby away. Isn't it enough its father didn't want it? Do you think I could do that? I know it will be hard."

"Maybe if you wrote and told him . . ."

"No! Maybe . . . sometime, when the right time comes, I will tell him." Her voice had turned so cold that it stunned Simon into silence. "But it will be the right time, a time when I know it will hurt. He cannot see it, share it . . . or even know about it until I feel it's right."

"That sounds like some kind of revenge."

"And why shouldn't I have revenge? Don't you think he has a debt to pay?"

"A debt . . . of course. He owes the child . . ."

"And he owes me! He owes me all the time he's taken and all the years he'll spend with his *wife!* Yes, he owes me, and by heaven I will see him pay. When the time is right, I shall see him pay."

"Zoe, you don't know what you're saying."

"Yes, I do, Simon. I was sick. I'm not sick now. I'll be strong in a day or so. I'll have my baby, and I'll watch and wait. One day, I will find the means . . . and if I can"—her voice was brittle and her eyes frigid—"I will find a way to destroy his dreams and his life the way he has destroyed mine."

"Zoe, this has to be your illness talking. You have to be more sensible."

"Sensible . . . revenge is very sensible."

"No . . . it isn't. It will never work. You will only hurt yourself more than you have already been."

"And what is sensible?"

"I think," he said very slowly and very calmly, "that the most sensible thing you could do . . . would be to marry me."

"Simon! I—"

"No, hear me out. It would be for the baby's good too. It needs a name. You need someone to help you survive. Why not me?"

"You'd give your name to his baby?"

"No, I'd give my name to your baby . . . and to you."

"I don't know, Simon. All of me is filled with what I have to do."

"And what do you have to do?"

"I can't let it go," she said, desperate for him to understand. "I can't let him do this to me or to this child. I have to see that he pays. I will see that he pays!"

"What can you do? He has wealth, he has position . . . he has every means to stop anything you could try to do. Don't be a fool, Zoe. You let a dream blind you before; don't let revenge do it now. Look at what you can have, not what is out of your reach."

She looked at him unblinkingly for a moment. He didn't understand, he couldn't. But she knew that this time she had to exact an eye for an eye and a tooth for a tooth. She would bring the Dewitts down from their castle if she had to use fair means or foul. Even if she had to use the child, she would see them tumble.

"I'm . . . I'm so tired, Simon."

"I know. You've been through a lot. You need to get some healthy sleep." He stood up. He knew she hadn't been able to face what he'd offered. But in time she would. All the waiting was done. He would only have to make her forget, and that he could do in time. "I have a cot in the parlor. Cara has one there too. We've been sleeping there so we could keep watch on you."

"Where's Cara now?"

"She had to go to the restaurant to close up. She'll be back soon. If you need anything, call me." He bent to kiss her very lightly.

"You and Cara . . . I owe you both so much."

"Just get well, Zoe. That's all either of us want."

She watched Simon blow out the lamp and leave the room. She knew he cared . . . but she didn't dare let go of her need for revenge. If she did she would fall into a pit of despair and drown. No . . . she wouldn't let go, and no matter how hard it was, she wouldn't marry again. If she did, it would somehow be surrendering . . . admitting her first marriage was wrong . . . that she didn't belong with the cream of society. Well, she did, and one day she would prove it . . . no matter what the cost.

Simon too lay awake. He was shaken by a truth he didn't want to face. Zoe was still just as blind as ever. Only now she had replaced her dreams with a fierce need for vengeance.

He worried about the unborn child. It was innocent, but it just might pay the price for standing between Zoe and Brent. In their need to force their world to conform to their desires, they both might just blindly destroy anything, or anyone, who stood between them. He knew this, just as he knew he would stand between them as long as he could.

Three days later the doctor delivered Zoe of a healthy and beautiful seven-pound baby girl. The labor was relatively easy. The doctor chuckled as he brought the baby in and laid it beside her.

At the touch of that small child, a dam burst within Zoe. She surrendered to a flood of motherly love so fierce, so passionate, so protective, that it washed away a lot of her heartbreak . . . but not her bitterness. She put away the memory that once, in a fit of madness, she had tried to do away with this small part of herself.

Eleven days later Zoe was at the washtub. Not only doing the small washing of a tiny baby, but washing overalls and gray shirts and long grimy union suits for the men who lived in rooming houses on the flats. Cara had offered to let her work at the restaurant. But that would mean someone else would care for Emily, and Zoe wouldn't have that. She wanted to be with her daughter every day.

There was a quick, stern resolution in the way Zoe worked the pump handle up and down, filled the copper wash boiler, and measured out the bluing. Her arms were firm and strong; her young body was straight and healthy. And her heart had turned to stone.

* * *

The summer that followed Emily's birth was one of unrest among the miners. Simon and the men he worked with in the still-young union tried to restrain the atmosphere of violence that was growing.

It was not enough that the men worked a twelve-to-fifteen-hour day and for wages that were barely enough to keep their families alive. Now a message had been posted at every mine. Wages were being cut ten percent, but no shortening of hours would occur.

Simon was frightened by his sudden powerlessness. It was not the time, they were not strong enough! But his protests could not be heard over the growing roar of indignation, of anger, and of desperation.

But what Simon had envisioned as an organized strike became a bloody rout. It was as if someone had lit a match to a stick of dynamite. The air was charged with fear and anger. The mine authorities, sensing the gathering storm, issued a proclamation declaring that, since crowds, processions, and the like were dangerous with conditions as they were, they had ordered the police to break up such gatherings.

Still, the anger grew, dulling rational minds, destroying logic, and blinding the men to the pleading of the leaders who tried to raise their voices above it.

Deputies were sworn in, or brought in on trains. Hirelings of the Pinkertons were brought in and sent to guard the mines and the streets.

The tension reached its peak when a crowd of men stormed one of the mines to try to talk to the owner and supervisors. In a panic, the deputies reacted with violence. They killed nine and wounded many. The crowd, in fury, retaliated by burning the mine office and structures.

Now the men refused to go back to work, but Simon and his friends knew the action was too soon and too weak.

To break the wildcat strike, the companies advertised widely for strikebreakers.

Men were recruited from places as far away as New Orleans and sent to Colorado. But when they arrived, many declared they could not go to work and take the bread out of fellow workmen's mouths.

The crowds began to grow, taking over mine after mine. But once the workers had stormed a mine and blockaded it, they found they had not the food, water, and arms to maintain control.

They held out for two months in the face of terrible opposition, but ultimately the companies broke the blockade with strikebreakers and armed violence. Eventually the men were forced to return to work defeated. Then the punishment came. Most of the recognized strikers were refused their jobs, which had been given to strikebreakers.

It took Simon and the others the rest of the summer and all the long winter to try and repair the damage done. More than once Simon was faced with despair, wondering if it really was a possibility to help lead these people to a better life.

1885! Spring again. The early morning air was fresh as only mountain air is fresh. Zoe pushed a battered cart along the uneven wooden sidewalks of the flats, as she delivered neat little bundles of washing to the boardinghouses where the single men lived.

Emily was a year and a half old now, and Zoe was certain she was the most beautiful child ever to be seen in a mining town.

She was fair-skinned and delicate and finely made, Zoe thought. A calm sea . . . not like her mother. Zoe refused to think Emily looked more like Brent than like her. She took stiff pride in not mentioning Brent's name, even in her thoughts.

She paused to gaze about her. If you were young, and lived alone in a tiny shack on the wrong side of town, and had a child without a father, you were cautious of hungry miners. She always had to be on guard, locking the door the minute she got inside the house, never opening it after dark.

One of the worst offenders was Stu Collier. He was a property owner . . . not her property, thank God. She paid her rent to old Mr. Simpson, who never bothered her.

But Stu had his lascivious eyes on her, and always seemed to be amused at her aloofness, as if it were an act . . . one he could see through.

Zoe was far afield in her thoughts when suddenly she was jerked back to awareness by a presence beside her. She turned with a start. Collier! A futile anger filled her. Would she never be rid of him? He was much worse than the ones who tried to sneak down to her house after dark. Sometimes he reminded her of a wiry, clever, persistent little coyote circling around a lamb that it had marked for its kill.

He was smiling at her now, cynically and admiringly, as if he had all the time in the world. But she was no good at waiting games.

"What do you want?" she snapped.

"Why, nothing, nothing at all. I only thought you'd be interested to know that I've recently acquired some new property."

"Why should I care what property you've acquired?"

"Because it's yours. A three-room house, I believe. An owner has certain rights and obligations. So I'll be down this evening to have you tell me what repairs you need."

His voice was that of a perfect landlord.

She looked at him with loathing. So he had bought her house. And he must be thinking this would bring her to her knees. Why was she always in this box? Why could she not, just for once, climb to the top? Why did she always have to put up with men who wanted to take but never to give?

She gave Stu Collier a harassed glance. He only smiled in frank anticipation. He had several scores to settle with this savagely contemptuous beauty.

"I'll thank you to keep away from me and my house!" she told him belligerently. But even to her own ears her voice sounded strained and hollow.

She pushed past him, but he didn't try to follow. He did not need to, his manner said. He would be down tonight . . . an owner had rights.

She had been washing for the single miners. Scrimping and saving so that she could better herself. Her achievement in establishing a nest egg should have brought her satisfaction. But it didn't.

Zoe walked along through the jostling crowds. All about her was bustling activity, but she felt dead inside.

She was forced to halt because of a dense crowd in front of one of the mining exchanges. The blackboard, set up outside, was covered with chalked quotations. A man stood nearby informing the passersby of a new gold strike. A new promise of riches, Zoe thought with disgust.

Inured as Zoe was to wild talk and wilder expectations, her nerves vibrated to the tension in the air. Gold! She thought of her nest egg . . . and she thought of Stu Collier and his plans.

"Faint heart never won a fortune," said the persuasive voice. "Here's your opportunity, gentlemen. Step right up."

"It's the biggest gold strike since California."

The voice came from close beside her and she turned, recognizing the miner who stood beside her. She'd washed his clothes for the past ten months and knew he was far from striking it rich. Yet she knew he had a reputation for being honest and straight. Today he looked rather morose and withdrawn.

"Good morning." He smiled, his light eyes crinkling at the corners.

"Good morning, Grey," she replied. She always wanted to ask him where he had gotten a name like Grey . . . Grey Sinclair. But she had never done so because she was afraid to encourage any man to come too close. She was so unprotected. Of course part of it was her own fault. Simon was there . . . in fact he had asked her several times to marry him. But she hated both the idea that he felt sorry for her, and that he would try to put a stop to the revenge that was the mainstay of her life.

"Looks like they've got a good strike on their hands," Grey said.

"Yes . . . it's exciting. Makes me wish sometimes that I was a man."

"No," he said with a chuckle, "nature wouldn't be that ornery. To make a pretty thing like you into a man. It would be downright sinful."

"Thank you." She smiled, still unused to compliments. She cast him a quick, surreptitious look to see if he was preparing to be more aggressive. But he seemed to give no more thought to the matter.

"The assayer," he continued, "just told me that if a man had the means to grab himself a piece of this, he could be rich almost overnight."

"Why don't you go?"

"Because I don't have the means," he chuckled dryly. "I don't have one thin dime to rub against another one. Take my word for it, if I had it, I'd be out there in no time."

He continued to listen to the salesman's promises of extravagant riches. But Zoe watched him closely and slowly as if a new dawn were breaking. The words filled her mind. Rich . . . almost overnight . . . if one had the means. Well, she had the means. She just didn't have his strength and ability. But . . . if one were to put the two things together . . .

"Grey . . . what does it take to . . . well, to strike it rich?"

"First thing is it takes a lot of luck."

"I mean, what does it take in money?"

"Oh . . . well, let's see." He considered thoughtfully. "I guess two . . . maybe three hundred dollars."

"I see." Her heart began to pound heavily. It was a long and very slim chance. And she would be laying all her savings on the line. But if the gamble worked . . .

Zoe had never been one to beat about the bush, and she didn't plan on starting now. She turned to face Grey.

He was tall, and she had to look up into his light eyes. He was lean, but she could see the work-hard muscles and knew he was strong. A man could not work as a miner eight to ten hours a day and be weak.

"Grey, there's something important I want to talk to you about."

He returned his full attention to her, trying to keep his surprise from showing.

"Talk to me about?"

"Yes, it's important. It's a business deal."

"Business deal?" He seemed to be thrown off stride.

"Could you come to my house tonight?"

Now he was really surprised, and for a minute wasn't able to answer.

"Look, Grey. I don't want you to misunderstand. It really is business. I have a proposition to offer you that might be good for both of us."

"All right. When do you want me to come?"

"Well"—she smiled—"I'm sure, like all the other miners, you'd appreciate a good meal. I'll fix supper for you. I learned a long time ago that a man talks business better after a good, hot meal."

"I'll talk about anything for a good meal." He grinned. She liked the way he looked at her. There was none of the sly I-know-what-kind-of-woman-you-are kind of look. "I've been working here for over a year and there's been nary a flapjack or a cup of coffee or a decent piece of pie in the whole place," he said with mock mournfulness.

"Well, I'll soon fix that. I make one of the best pies around. Of course, you'll have to settle for apple. There's nothing else to make a pie from."

"I'll settle for anything."

Zoe was pleased. Among everything else she liked about Grey, he was a man who relished his victuals and who would never sulk and have spells or push his food around on his plate.

At that moment, to Zoe's intense chagrin, her perfect baby took it into her head to act in a distressingly human way. She fussed and whined and finally yelled.

"She's tired."

"I know," Grey said. He reached down and lifted Emily, who stopped yelling long enough to examine him closely. Obviously she liked what she saw.

"I had a wife and baby once," he said quietly. "Lost them both to cholera within a week."

"I'm sorry."

"It's past," he said, "but a man sure gets lonesome for the sight of a little one."

Zoe's spirits rose. Maybe fate had sent her a piece of good luck for a change.

"Well, I'd better get on," she said. "I still have a few bundles to deliver."

"What time do you want me to come?"

Get Four Books Totally FREE — A $21.96 Value!

"It would be better after Emily is in bed."

"No, ma'am," he said. "I don't mind the baby a bit."

"Then you come around six. At least she will have had her bath and be fed by then."

"Great." He handed Emily back to Zoe with what was obvious reluctance. "I'll be there."

Zoe smiled at him again, then replaced Emily in the buggy and trundled her off to deliver the last of her packages.

Zoe had finished her deliveries and rushed to Cara's to see if she could leave Emily with her until she was finished shopping.

After leaving Emily with Cara, she walked to the bank and to the shock of the banker, withdrew all the money she had.

"Miz Dewitt, are you sure you want to take all of this? It's a great deal of hard-earned money for you to lose . . . or for someone to steal."

"Yes, Mr. Brindle, I want to take all of it. All five hundred dollars. And I've no intention of losing it, or letting someone steal it from me."

"Might I ask what you intend to do with all that money? You're not becoming frivolous after all this time of saving, are you?" he asked imperiously, as if a woman could not quite be trusted to handle so much money.

"No, Mr. Brindle . . . I am not becoming frivolous." At least I hope not, she prayed. Then she smiled a dazzling smile at him. "And no, you may not ask." She picked up the money and left the bank, leaving the banker with a stunned expression on his face.

The aroma of freshly baked pie mingled with the succulent scent of roasting meat. Emily, well rested after a long afternoon nap, was her usual sunny self, but Zoe was as nervous as a cat. She was preparing speech after speech for the purpose of convincing Grey to do what she planned. She had forgotten entirely about Stu Collier.

She had put on a clean dress, with a crisp clean white apron over it, and had arranged her hair carefully atop her head. She looked neat; the house, poorly furnished as it was, was clean, and Emily was the treasure that brightened it. Zoe finally felt ready to persuade Grey to listen to her . . . ready for the knock that sounded on her door, just after six.

When she opened the door, the smile died on her lips. Stu stood before her, a knowing and pleased smile on his face.

"You didn't have to go to all this trouble to entertain me," he said with a chuckle. His gaze raked over her lewdly. "I would have settled just for your . . . ah . . . company for the evening."

"All the trouble, as you put it, is not for you, Mr. Collier. I would appreciate it if you would leave. I'm expecting someone important."

His already ruddy face flushed and his eyes grew cold with anger.

"Don't play sly games with me. You and I both know the position you're in. Now, you either come down off your high horse or I'll yank this house right out from under you. Where will you and your brat be then?" Before Zoe could answer, he pushed his way inside.

Zoe backed up a few steps, but she had no intention of running from this arrogant, evil-minded man.

"You can't 'yank this house out from under me.' My rent is paid for this month. I'll go to the authorities if you don't leave me alone."

"You may be paid up for this month, but the rent will be raised next month, and the month after, until you come to your senses. All you have to do"—he lowered his voice as he moved closer to her—"is to be a little nice to me. Who knows, if you're nice enough I might be persuaded to forget about your rent altogether."

"You really are a filthy man," Zoe said in as scathing a tone as she could manage. "I wouldn't let you touch me for the biggest mansion in the world. Please get out of my house."

"Damn you!" he grated. He reached out and took hold of her shoulders. Still, she was not really afraid. She had faced too much and learned too much about his kind of man.

She met his gaze eye to eye, never wavering. She was

not going to be bullied into submission . . . ever again.

"Take your hands off me."

"Think you're high and mighty, don't you?" he snarled, his equilibrium shaken by a woman who stood unbending before his will. "Well, maybe you ought to be taught a lesson or two about how to treat someone when they've got the upper hand."

"Just who has the upper hand?" came the mild-spoken question from behind Stu. He dropped his hands from Zoe's shoulders and glared at Grey, who seemed to fill the doorway.

"You're not welcome or needed here, Sinclair. So why don't you just leave?"

"Ah"—Grey chuckled—"but I've been invited for supper . . . and I don't think you were included. Now, why are you here, Stu? I think you ought to just run along."

Stu studied Grey carefully. He knew Grey was not a man to be played with. There was a lot of time to subdue Zoe; he had her where he wanted her. He would take care of her when Grey was not around. He turned to look down at Zoe, who was looking at Grey with an expression that made Stu grit his teeth.

So she was giving this man what he wanted. Well . . . the time would come when she would be more than anxious to give him what he wanted as well. After all, he and a lot of others knew what she was. Hadn't she pretended to be married to that rich mine owner's son? And hadn't he just walked away from her when he'd finished with her? He knew what she was, all right, and he would have his turn and make her pay for being so cold now.

"You're a fool, Grey. There's a lot of prettier parlor girls down on the flats. No one wants to fight for what he can get free."

Zoe gasped and Grey's face grew cold. But with these parting words Stu pushed past him and left, slamming the door behind him.

"I'm sorry," Grey said quietly.

"You don't have to be sorry, and don't worry about me. He'll never get in my house again. When he knocked, I thought it was you. Sit down, supper's nearly ready."

Grey smiled, but his eyes were drifting toward Emily,

who was contentedly playing on a blanket on the floor.

He walked to her and knelt down to smile into Emily's upturned face. Zoe continued to put supper on the table, still a bit surprised at the way Emily seemed to gravitate toward Grey . . . and how gentle he was with her.

When the meal was ready Grey ate with enthusiasm and a constant stream of praise. Zoe was both pleased and surprised at his appetite.

She was even more surprised when he insisted on helping her clean up. It was clear to Zoe that Grey was not born and bred a miner.

He lit the fireplace after Zoe insisted it was time to put Emily to bed. Once Emily was safely tucked in and already nodding off, Zoe returned to the kitchen and made two steaming cups of coffee. She carried them into the small parlor and handed one to Grey. Then she sat down on a chair opposite him.

"Don't you think it's time you told me what it is you want?" He smiled to soften the words. "I couldn't be in a better mood."

"Why, Grey Sinclair"—she smiled over the rim of her coffee cup—"I think I've picked exactly the right man."

"For what?"

"To make us both very, very rich."

Chapter Eighteen

For a few seconds Grey was totally stunned. Then, he found his voice.

"And just how do you intend to make us both rich?" he said with a touch of doubtful amusement.

"You were with me today. You heard about the new strike."

"Yes, I heard. I don't know what it has to do with us."

"It has a lot to do with us."

"Are you some kind of dreamer?"

"Not for a long time," Zoe said positively. "Wait right here." She went quickly into her bedroom, and returned with a wooden box. She stopped close beside him, opened the box, and spilled the contents on the table before him. He sat in silence watching. Then he looked up at her.

"And just what does this prove?"

"Look, Grey," she said as she sat down beside him. Her face was flushed with enthusiasm. "I have Emily . . . I'm a woman . . . and I don't have the strength or ability to go and dig for that gold. You have all the things I need. What you don't have is money. That's what I can supply. We could be partners in a way."

"So you supply the money and I supply the muscle."

"Right."

"Kind of trusting, aren't you?"

"How so?"

"I could take the money and leave."

"But you won't."

"Why won't I?"

"Because you're as much of a gambler as I am. Because you want to strike it rich as much as I do, and . . . you're the kind of a man who keeps a bargain when he makes it."

"You think you've thought of everything?"

"I think so. You said you'd need about three hundred dollars to get set up right. Well, I've got five hundred dollars there."

"What about you?"

"I've been earning enough to live on up to now. I can do it again . . . at least until you hit gold."

"What if I don't?"

"You can't think like that! This is an opportunity. We have to grab it, Grey. If we don't, we'll always wonder if we could have made it or not."

"What are you going to do about Stu Collier? You know he'll be back here."

"I'm not afraid of him."

"You should be. He's got a bad reputation and you're in a spot that gives him the upper hand. He'll take advantage of it. I heard what he said to you and he'll do just as he said, keep raising your rent until you do what he wants."

"I can take care of myself, Grey."

"Well, I've got an idea, if you'll listen."

"I'll listen," she said, smiling.

He grinned in return. "But it doesn't mean you'll do it."

"How do I know unless you tell me?"

"When I got here I bought a prime piece of land down by the river. I built my own cabin because I didn't want to owe anyone."

"I don't understand what—"

"Just let me get to it." He held up his hand to stop her. "If I'm going out to the gold field, my cabin is going to sit empty. All you have to do is tell Stu to go to hell and move into my cabin until I get back. I'll have a couple of friends keep an eye out for you. You'll be safe there and you won't have any rent to pay at all. That way what washings you take in will sort of put money back in your savings."

"And you were wondering why I would trust you," Zoe said chidingly. "I seem to know people better than you think I do."

He half smiled, but his eyes shifted from hers. She knew

what he was thinking. She knew . . . because Brent never left her mind. She longed to find gold so that one day she could face Brent with a daughter he could never have and enough money to make him regret . . . more than regret what he had done. She would use any weapon she could find, but one day she wanted to see Brent as broken as she had been when he left her.

She rose to her feet without answering, but Grey reached out to grasp her arm.

"I'm sorry, Laura, I didn't mean to hurt you."

She looked down into the honesty of his eyes. For the first time in a long time she wanted to erase all the lies of her past.

"I know, Grey. Most of the time I've been the one to hurt myself. I think you and I should begin this partnership with no lies between us. First of all . . . my name isn't Laura Champion. It's Zoe . . . Zoe Carrigan." Slowly she sat back down. "And maybe I ought to tell you the rest of Zoe Carrigan's life. I want you and the whole town to know who I am."

"You don't have to tell me anything."

"I know. But . . . I want our partnership to be special. Nothing special is built on lies." She went on talking, telling him of the past she had fled so desperately. She told about the pain and the misery and the squalor.

Grey remained silent, letting her get all the poison from her system. But she could see the gentleness in his eyes.

When she finished speaking they both were quiet. He held her hand, and neither wanted to break the momentary peace.

Finally it was Grey who spoke first.

"Zoe"—he smiled—"why did you ever change it? I think Zoe is really pretty."

"I didn't want to be Roger Carrigan's stepdaughter."

"But you were. Nothing could change that. He's a load you've been carrying around for a long time, Zoe. Maybe you ought to forget him."

"I can't."

"No . . . you'd have to forgive him first."

"Forgive him! For what he did? I'll never do that . . .

never. I'd like to see him die and roast in that Hell he was always shouting about."

"And you think your husband should be in the same place."

"No . . . there should be a special Hell for him. If I have my way, he'll wish over and over again that he was in it."

"Sometimes," Grey said gently, "when you wish hurt on somebody, it just comes back on your dish. It's hard to eat that meal."

"Grey . . . I know you mean well. But we are going to have a business partnership. I . . . I don't think that includes prying into each other's lives."

"You're right." He stood up. "I'll agree to take the money, to find the best spot I can, and dig like hell. Maybe we'll have good luck together, Zoe, but it's only with your agreement that you take my cabin until I come back."

"All right. It's agreed."

"Then let's gather up this money. Tomorrow it will be time for both of us to start packing."

Grey and Zoe gathered up the coins and bills that were on the table. Zoe never wondered why Grey hadn't put up any battle against her desire for revenge. But Grey had backed away because his own secrets made it nearly impossible for him to condemn or console. He just had to be what she needed . . . for now.

Simon dressed carefully. He was going to go see Zoe for the first time in several days. He felt elated. Zoe had to come to her senses pretty soon. She would have to see that a life alone, trying to raise a little girl by herself, was more than difficult.

And Emily . . . Lord, the child was a sweet, pretty thing. He would love nothing more than raising her as his own. He knew that Emily already took to him.

He thought of how he had used Emily as an argument for marrying him the last time he was with Zoe. He had tried to reach Zoe through Emily and had failed dismally.

"Zoe, Emily needs a real home," he'd begun, but he knew he'd struck the wrong chord the moment that he said it.

"This is home for her, Simon. It's a whole lot better than what I had."

"You know what I mean."

"I know . . . but you're not her father."

"I could be, for all she knows."

"Giving a baby your name is hardly a reason for marriage. Besides . . . marriage has not found a place at the top of my list."

"And what does find a place there, Zoe? Your damn hatred for your stepfather and that poor excuse you had for a husband?"

"I don't have time to think about marriage. I have other plans."

"You've never been close to a man who treated you fair, Zoe. You're afraid to take a chance."

She had turned on him then, those gold eyes flashing. "I'm not afraid of anything . . . or anyone, not anymore. I have my plans and when the right time comes to take a chance on something, I'll know it. In the meantime, I'm not putting my life in any man's hands . . . not again, maybe not ever. And Emily won't either. Not if I can help it."

"You're going to teach her your bitterness?"

"No, I'm going to teach her to be a lot smarter than I was."

"I said you've never been close to a man who treated you fair. I was right about that just as I'm right about you never being close to a man who knew how to love you. You need to be loved, Zoe . . . the way a woman should be."

"I don't want to love someone. There's no time. Simon . . . if . . . if you want more than to be my closest, dearest friend . . . then I don't think you should come back here again."

"Zoe! You don't mean that."

"Yes," she had said stoically, "I never meant anything more." Her eyes had held his. "Don't think that I don't remember, Simon," she'd added softly, "because I do. But . . . I can't afford ever to let that happen again."

He'd known then that she was both scared and vulnerable. But he had backed away because he also knew of the stubborn pride she had. Right now she thought she meant exactly what she said. But he had seen that one flicker of need, and he wasn't going to let her go easily.

Now he planned on a much more subtle approach. He would be Simon the friend again instead of Simon the would-be lover.

As he finished his preparations he heard a noise in the next room. How often had he forgotten that Doc and April were very nearly a permanent fixture in his home?

It was a complicated arrangement that he had explained to no one. Not even Zoe. Both Paul and April had been badly shaken by the attack on them in Boulder, and they seemed unwilling to leave a house that had a strong man's protection. Meanwhile, Pete and Gus had found work and had put up a rough shack not far from Simon's place.

Most people thought Paul a friend, so it kept the whispers down. April herself was nearly a recluse, going to the small room she slept in at the mere sound of anyone's approach and remaining there until whoever it was had gone. She was like a sweet little ghost that tore at Simon's heart.

He whistled lightly through his teeth as he left his house and started the long walk to Zoe's cabin. It was a crisp day . . . a good day to walk. Zoe's health had always been robust, and he knew she had all her strength back. He had only to get her out of that cabin and alone for once. Zoe was so possessive of Emily, it could hardly be healthy.

He walked slowly, stopping to talk to miners and their wives on the way, always with a word of encouragement and support. Their lot seemed to him to be worse than ever. He only wished he had Zoe beside him to share in the work he was doing. She would understand it: There was no doubt she knew the miners' lot better than anyone.

As he approached Zoe's house his steps slowed. Something seemed different somehow. There was no wisp of white smoke from the chimney . . . no signs of life about the cabin at all. It was unusual. What was even more odd was that the washtubs that were continually boiling in the side yard were hung on pegs against the porch wall. There had never been a day when Zoe wasn't washing clothes, and never a day when they didn't argue about it. But he'd never gotten anywhere with the arguments.

He continued up the steps and across the wooden porch to the door. Now he knew there was something amiss. By now he would have heard activity from inside. Voices, a child's laughter. But there was nothing.

What alarmed him even more was that when he lifted the latch the door swung open.

What met his eyes was chaos. Things were scattered about and wooden barrels sat in random places. Obviously Zoe was packing. For a moment, he was unable to think. That was when Zoe appeared, walking from the bedroom with a bundle of blankets in her arms. She stopped abruptly, then smiled.

"Hello, Simon."

"Zoe . . . what's going on here? It looks like you're leaving. Where's Emily?"

"I am leaving." She ignored his second question.

"Aspen?"

"No, just this house."

"For God's sake, why? And where are you going?"

"Why? Because I have a new landlord here, that's why."

"Who?"

"Stu Collier."

"So, a landlord's a landlord. He didn't raise your rent, did he?"

"Raise it!" She laughed coldly. "He put a price on this place that I have no intention of paying."

"You mean he—"

"He calmly informed me that if I was . . . nice . . . to him, he could be persuaded to forget my rent altogether."

"Son of a . . . I'll go have a little talk with him."

"That's not necessary. I have no intention of staying here."

"Zoe, you can't pick up and leave just like that. Besides, you could have told me. I'd . . ."

"You'd what? Take me in . . . take care of me and Emily?"

"You make it sound like it's something wrong. It isn't like I haven't asked you to marry me a couple of hundred times."

"Simon . . . you always seemed to try and understand me before. Try now. I can't marry you like this. Emily and I . . . we aren't charity cases."

"Charity cases! Zoe, where in hell's name do you get such ideas? You should know by now how I feel about you."

"I married once for money. My mother married for love. I don't see that either of us gained anything by it." She laid the blankets aside and turned away from him to remove objects from a small cupboard. "Well, the past taught me a lot. I learned that I was right all along. Money is the answer. With money I can—"

"You still have the same thing in mind, don't you? Some kind of revenge. You're a dreamer, Zoe. It will never happen. Come down off your cloud and face reality. He's out of your life and out of your reach. You can't touch him."

"Can't I now?" she replied angrily as she spun to face him. "You're the dreamer, Simon. I have the one thing he will want . . . and can never have! And as for being a dreamer . . . well, maybe. But just maybe I'll make all my dreams come true, and I'll do it my way."

"And just maybe, when you do, you'll turn around and look and there won't be anybody there who cares! Don't use Emily like a club. She's the one who'll get hurt. And . . . maybe there's still a lot about love that you don't understand."

"I understand all I need to know."

"You understand nothing but your blind obsession to see Brent Dewitt on his knees. It could be that the sight won't be pleasing when it does happen. Breaking a man is not a pleasurable thing."

"It will be for me. I want him to want what he so casually gave away . . . and Emily and I will walk away from him like he walked away from us."

"You're you," Simon said as he moved to stand close to her, "and Emily will be Emily when she's grown. Her plans for her life might not be the same as yours."

"She's my daughter!"

"Yes, I know. That's why I'm warning you not to try to make her conform to your plans. She's going to be her own person, Zoe. She gets that from you. Let her grow on her own. Reach out for something besides an old dream that got broken."

Suddenly he seemed too close, too potent for her nerves. She attempted to move back a step, but she'd forgotten she was so close to the cupboard. There was no room to retreat.

Her heart began a rapid hammering, and she could almost hear the blood roaring through her veins. She denied that she was hungry for the strength of a man's touch. But every fiber of her vivid healthy body leapt in response to a memory she had long since tried to bury. It had not been awakened since that stormy night Simon had touched her. There was a restlessness about his movements as he reached to put his hands on her shoulders. A slow, magnetic quality that was unbearably exciting to Zoe.

He drew her toward him until she was close enough to feel his warmth and power. Desperately she reached for resistance. But resistance seemed as elusive as snow beneath a summer sun. Her mind battled her body and her heart's response. Would Simon always be her weakness?

His mouth tasted hers in a slow, leisurely kiss that nearly drained her control. The kiss grew deeper, and she was conscious of the length of his hard body against hers.

Zoe had known that something always stood in the way of her responding wholly to Brent. But she had constantly denied it was the memory of Simon.

Her body cried out in hunger and self-enforced loneliness, and her mind was a whirling pinwheel of fireworks.

She wanted to push him away . . . then why did her hands rest weakly against his chest? Why did the heat she read in his eyes make her knees weak? Why did she want the taste and feel of his hard, seeking mouth against hers when all it could do was wreck her resolve?

"I'm not going to let you make another mistake, Zoe," Simon said softly. "You can lie about a lot of things, but not what I saw in your eyes that night and what I see now."

It took every ounce of control she had, but she gathered enough energy to move out of his arms to a safer distance.

"That night . . . it's past, Simon. I told you then and I'll tell you again! Love is a trap I can't afford." She looked at him with a direct gaze. "And I have Emily to think about."

He realized she was again in control and very deliberately keeping as much distance between them as she could.

"Where is Emily now?"

"Cara is watching her while I finish up here. We're just moving."

"Moving . . . where?"

"Into Grey Sinclair's cabin, down by the river."

For a moment Simon stood in stunned silence.

"Grey Sinclair," he repeated. He knew Grey, probably better than Zoe ever would. Grey was basically a good man who had been among the unfortunate few who had struck not even a glimmer of silver. Disappointment had altered his personality, making him into a shell of his former self. But Simon knew the boisterous, fun-loving, and often careless Grey who was hidden beneath the shell. He couldn't see Zoe and Grey . . . he wouldn't imagine it, nor would he let it happen. One man had taken Zoe from him with a promise of wealth and a better life. But for God's sake! He had much more to offer than Grey Sinclair ever would. "You're crazy. You've always been struggling to have a decent reputation. You move in there with Grey and you'll destroy everything you've built."

Zoe watched him closely. She could no more understand her own motives than she could fly. She only knew Simon was the only real danger to her plans. Plans she couldn't let go of. She had to push him away, to somehow force him to release the hold he had on her. If she let her heart rule her head, the kind of life she lived now would be the kind of life she would live forever. She could not do it, and she could not condemn Emily to that kind of life either.

Zoe never gave any thought to the fact that Emily might choose otherwise.

"What I do or do not do is none of your business, Simon. I know you've been a friend, and you did help."

"Friend!" Simon repeated angrily. "No, Zoe, you'll never get away with that!" He reached out and grasped her wrist, jerking her into his arms. "What we have been is much more than friends. If you won't take the blinders off, maybe I should take them off for you. You can't just live to get revenge! And you damn well are not going to go to another man. Not unless you can convince yourself and me that you don't feel anything for me at all. I don't think you can honestly do that."

He lifted both hands to tangle them in her hair on either side of her face; then he raised her face to his. He gazed down at her, and she returned his gaze. For a moment their wills clashed.

Unable to deny the power that drove him, he lowered his mouth to hers with slow sensual deliberation.

The ignited passion was more brilliant than before, as if it had been stored away, held at bay, until the moment they touched.

Zoe knew a long deep moment of panic. Simon was the only one who could reach past the barriers she had built between herself and the world. No one else could stir her senses or make her do the unforgivable . . . surrender.

It took every ounce of strength she had, both mental and physical, to break the kiss, and she made a soft sound, almost of anguish, as she did.

She tore herself from his arms and put the table between them. "Stop, Simon. This is not the answer to anything. This only makes things harder."

"Why harder, Zoe?" he challenged. "Unless you know it's the right thing for both of us and refuse to admit it."

"You make everything sound so simple. I guess from your point of view it is. But not from mine."

"My point of view?"

"Simon, why must we go on fighting this battle? You know how I feel. You just won't try to understand me."

"That's where you're wrong, Zoe. I understand you. Maybe more than you understand yourself. You're reaching for a dream, but I don't think you'd recognize what was right for you if it was standing in front of you."

"Oh, yes . . . yes, I'll know when I have what's right for Emily and me."

"How are you planning on building a dream for you and Emily by moving into Grey Sinclair's cabin? As far as this town is concerned, you'll just be a combination of wash-woman and whore."

She struck before she even thought, and the slap was like a rifle shot, stunning them both.

The only sound in the room was their ragged breathing. Both regretted the moment past, and neither could cross the gulf that was growing between them. Finally it was Zoe who spoke first.

"I'm sorry, Simon. There was no call for that. It's just that you and this town make me so damned angry! Why do they—and even you—think the worst of everything and everyone? Why do men sleep with women and scorn them for it? Why does everyone have the right answer for me and my child except me! Why, Simon? Why? Don't you trust me?"

"It's not a lack of trust, Zoe . . . it's . . . it's . . . damn it, I guess it's jealously. I don't want to fight another man and lose like I lost to Brent Dewitt. I've waited for your dreams to be fulfilled, and I'd wait again until you get this stupid idea of revenge out of your mind. But I'm not going to wait out another man. Not this time. This time I'll fight any way I can . . . any way."

"I'm not moving in with Grey," Zoe said quietly. In the face of his declaration of jealousy, some of the fire in her eyes had died. She didn't know why it was important that Simon knew the truth, but it was. "Grey is going away for a while and since my wonderfully generous landlord decided to make my home his, I felt the urgent need to move somewhere else. So you see, Simon, the conclusion you jumped to was wrong. I'll be living with Emily alone."

"Why didn't you tell me about Stu Collier?"

"Because I don't want your charity or anybody else's. What I have to do I will do."

"And there's no place in this dream of yours for me?"

"I didn't say that. Simon, you've always been a special part of my life. You were always there, but you want me to lean on you all the time. I . . . I don't want to lean on anybody. Not even you."

"So strong, Zoe . . . so self-sufficient . . . so determined. What's it going to take to batter those walls down?" He said the words almost as if he was talking to himself. "I hope it's not too late when you do need someone just to love and to share." He sighed and walked toward the door, then turned again to look at her. "Where's Grey going that he can turn over his house to you . . . or maybe he's not going to be gone all that long?"

"Don't, Simon. I didn't lie to you. I'd never lie to you."

"You sure as hell make it hard for me. I'd like to murder you and make love to you at the same time. You're the most exasperating, confusing, and exciting woman I've ever known. I'd like to walk away and forget I've ever seen you . . . but I can't do that either. I'll have to hope . . . well . . . Don't get hurt, Zoe." He opened the door and walked out.

"Simon!" She wanted to go after him, but she knew it meant surrendering just a little more than she could. When it was over, when she had paid the debts she had to pay, then she could think of other things.

She continued to pack slowly, unable to face the reason she felt so bereft . . . so alone.

Resolutely she straightened her shoulders. There was work to do and she had no one to help her. She would do what she knew had to be done. She placed the blankets she had been carrying from the bedroom when Simon came into a barrel, and returned to the bedroom for the last of her things.

Grey heaved the last barrel down from the wagon. He laughed. "Lord, woman, what did you pack in this barrel? Lead?"

"Nothing that a man with your strong muscles can't handle," Zoe joked in return. In the past few days she'd discovered how much fun laughing with a man was.

She'd been really pleased when Grey had made it clear he had no designs on her.

"I had a long talk with a few of my friends a couple of days ago," he said.

"Oh?" She was leary of "talks" among men.

"Don't look so suspicious. I wanted to make sure you will have no troubles here. They're going to keep an eye on the cabin. Anybody causes you any trouble, you call on James Murtree or Zeke Ellam. They'll make sure you're cared for."

"I'm grateful for all your concern, Grey, but you didn't need to trouble yourself. I can take care of myself."

"I know that." He chuckled. "It's my cabin I'm worried about. I don't like trespassers."

"Oh, Grey." She laughed in response to his blatant lie. "I have a feeling your cabin would be well guarded under any circumstances."

"Where's Emily, by the way?"

"She and Cara are at the store. We needed provisions. I don't want to go to town more often than I have to."

"That's a good idea. I don't know how long I'll be gone. You know it could take a long time."

"I know."

"Zoe . . . you don't believe . . . I mean there's still time to change your mind."

"And you'd have to lug all those barrels out again?"

"Be serious."

"I am serious. I've no second thoughts. You're taking a chance and so am I. I don't want to hear any more about it. The money's well invested. If we do strike it rich we'll name the mine 'The Future' because that's what it is. For Emily, for me, and I hope for you."

"I'll keep the name in mind."

"When do you leave, Grey?"

"Tomorrow morning."

"Then you may as well have your last supper here with me, Cara, and Emily. We'll make your favorite foods and give you a good send-off. Then you can spend the night and I'll fix your breakfast in the morning."

"I don't think so," Grey said gruffly as he laid down a second burden he'd carried in.

"You don't think so to what, the dinner, the sleep, or the breakfast?"

"I don't think so to all three."

"Why?"

"Because it would look as if both of us were lying. It would look—"

"I know. I know. I hadn't thought. I'm sorry, Grey, I didn't mean to cause a problem."

"This is not easy for you, Zoe. In fact I don't think too many things have been easy in your life. I guess a woman alone has a pretty hard row to hoe. I don't want to make it any harder. You're doing a real fine job of bringing up your little girl. If we strike it rich you can give her all the things you want."

"Yes," Zoe replied thoughtfully, "we'll both have all the things we want . . . no matter what anyone says."

"Anyone . . . who?"

"Oh, never mind. Let's just strike it rich, Grey. Let's have some good luck."

Chapter Nineteen

Emily had the usual independence of a two-year-old; she always seemed to insist on walking all by herself when Zoe was in a hurry to go somewhere.

The months that Zoe had kept to herself, cautiously saving her money . . . her immaculate house and sedate manners . . . her extraordinary devotion to Emily, all had eased much of the gossip surrounding her. To her immense pleasure, she had found some sort of acceptance.

Zoe savored her respectability. Only those who hunger and yearn for it can know its lingering sweetness. Because of her stepfather's constant preaching, she had always hated respectable people, but then Emily came into her life. Then the most important thing in the world became the safeguarding of her child.

She had almost stopped worrying lately. Grey had spoken the truth. She, Emily, and the house had been carefully guarded. She felt secure and successful. She did not admit that part of her complacency consisted of knowledge that, in spite of motherhood, hard work, and the fact that she was now twenty-eight, she was still desirable. She knew how Simon felt. It was small consolation for the hours of loneliness she would never admit to.

The mine she owned with Grey was some distance from town, too far for him to have the convenience of coming home often. Usually, he remained at the mine—first to keep close watch, and second, to make sure the work moved at a constant flow.

Emily, exuberant and anxious to explore the world and meet all the friends in it, scampered ahead of Zoe, who had to increase her speed to catch up with her. She turned a corner and all but collided with a small crowd. She did not hear the distinctive voice ringing out, so intent was she on retrieving her child.

Then the sound penetrated her consciousness. For a second she stood quite still. Roger Carrigan! She was overcome by a feeling of revulsion so great that she was almost sick there on the street. Then, white-faced, her lips gray, she forced herself to go on.

Zoe could hear the old familiar voice, and fought the urge to look at him. She continued to move as swiftly as she could, and finally caught Emily. Emily struggled, but Zoe managed to pick her up. Emily stiffened and let out a howl of rage.

The sound drew Roger's attention. He turned toward the sound. There was a moment of blankness; then his eyes gleamed in startled recognition. Zoe turned and ran. She could not, would not, label what she felt as fear. Yet she was shaking, and she could feel the perspiration on her entire body.

The misery of her childhood had too firm a grip on her mind to let her realize that all she had to do was stand up to Roger Carrigan and fight back.

She slowed to a walk and set Emily down. At the sound of running footsteps behind her, she turned.

"Zoe!" called out the boy who was racing toward her.

"Eli?" she asked incredulously. "Oh, Eli!" Her smile faded a little as he grew closer. Her brother did not look as if he had had a decent meal in weeks, and it made him look older than his seventeen years.

She caught Eli to her, kissing him unashamedly, the tears blinding her. He could only hug her ferociously.

"Oh, Eli, I've wondered about you. Come on, I have a friend who has a restaurant just down the street. Would you like something to eat?" Eli's eyes gleamed like those of a hungry stray dog.

Zoe took Eli's hand again, and this time propelled him firmly forward.

Cara was a bit startled when Zoe rushed in with Emily and Eli, but a quick explanation informed her of who the skinny young man was.

"Good Lord, sit down and let me get you something to

eat," Cara exclaimed. "And Zoe . . . you look as if you've seen a ghost."

"I have," Zoe said breathlessly. "He's here . . . Cara, my . . . Eli's father . . . he's here."

"Zoe! Get hold of yourself. He can't do you any harm."

"You don't really know him. He'll use his version of the truth like a weapon. He'll make everyone believe—"

"Let's get Eli something to eat; then we'll have to see what needs doing. You have too many friends, Zoe. We won't let him hurt you."

Zoe inhaled a deep breath as she reached for control. Then she placed Eli at a table near the kitchen so she could fill and refill his plate. She was shocked and touched by the amount he consumed. Later, she brought her own plate and sat down beside him.

"Eli, you don't look as if you get enough to eat."

He flashed her a quick look. "You know Pa."

"I used to worry about how you'd do in school after I left," she said.

"Not very good," he admitted. "But I'm all right in some things. I want to be something. If I could only stay in one place long enough to get some schooling, I could amount to something. I've got some books, and I try and study them all the time."

She sighed. What chance did he have with Roger Carrigan? If she could only help.

The restaurant was not as crowded as usual, but several men sat at random tables.

The door opened and Roger stood there, arms folded and face gleaming with a look of satisfaction. Zoe was stunned into momentary pity by his haggard look.

"So there you are!" He glared at Eli.

A half-dozen miners paused with forks in midair. Zoe put her arm across Eli's shoulders; she could feel him shaking. Zoe thought desperately, I must stand up to him now, for Eli's sake. He has no power over me, she told herself. But she wasn't so sure. Confidence, like her security, was slowly ebbing away.

"Won't you sit down, Pa? Let me get you some stew and a cup of coffee." Her own voice sounded strange and . . . broken to her.

"Is this your place?"

He seemed to waver; his nostrils dilated ever so slightly at the smell of food. Then he shook off his momentary weakness. "Where did you go that night you ran away? Who gave you aid?"

Zoe was silent, fighting the old terrifying spell that, in spite of all her efforts, threatened to overwhelm her again. Her hand shook as she walked to the stove, poured a cup of coffee, and went to him. He made no move to take it.

Emily, alarmed by the strained atmosphere, moved up close behind her mother.

Roger stared down at the child with a question in his eyes. "Yours?"

There was no need for her to answer as Emily frowned up at him from the shelter of Zoe's skirts.

"Who's the father?"

Zoe tried to answer, but the words stuck in her throat. She couldn't speak. What was the matter with her, she thought in desperation. But she knew. Old terrors were so hard to overcome.

"So! You have a child, and no husband. That's why you're silent! You have no husband to give you and your child a name."

The miners looked away and fidgeted. They wished they were anywhere but here, yet none knew how to break away.

Zoe stood, clenching her hands. She had only to hold her head high and refuse to answer, she told herself. But so great was the old domination that words come out against her will.

"I was married," she whispered.

"Oh, really, and did you flout his authority? Just as you thought you could flout your own father and run away and still come to some good end? But God's judgment overtook you, didn't it?"

Angry blood pounded in Zoe's temples. "You are not the hand of God's judgment!"

"Then where is your husband?"

Zoe shriveled.

"Perhaps it is not yet too late. Perhaps your soul can still be saved, even though you may have lived the life of a harlot. Let us pray for your soul," he said wearily. He was beginning to find satisfaction in having her again at his mercy.

A crimson fury filled her. She could kill him! She would kill him! She whirled and reached for something . . . anything that could be a lethal weapon in the hand of a violent woman. She found a heavy crockery bowl and snatched it up and swung it back. Before she could throw it, her arm was grasped in a strong hand.

Simon stood just behind her, his face a mask of cold anger. He held Zoe immobile, but his gaze was on Roger.

"Mr. Carrigan," Simon said, "Zoe's husband proved to be a weak man, but she was married. That doesn't make Zoe a sinner. She's done nothing to feel guilty about, and she certainly doesn't need your brand of redemption. I'm going to take her and Emily home. So please move out of my way." As Simon said the last words he bent and scooped Emily up in his arms and took Zoe's trembling hand.

"To your home," Roger sneered, "to live in sin. She is a condemned woman and I would wash her sins away."

"Take care of your own sins. Zoe and I don't live together. Zoe has a home of her own and I have mine," Simon replied coldly. "Zoe has no sins on her soul. If she wants to marry there is no difficulty. I will marry her and adopt Emily the moment she agrees. So take your penance and go. She's served penance enough."

She could feel the warmth of Simon's body beside her, could hear his heavy breathing. He reached out and drew her into the shielding circle of his arm. His left arm still held Emily.

At his words a vast and humble gratitude filled Zoe, for the tension in the room snapped like a too-taut bowstring. The men began to wipe off their mustaches, fumble in their pockets for change, and stand up to go. The whole atmosphere had altered within those few seconds. From sinister, the situation became only commonplace. Men like these were not overly fussy about youthful indiscretions. All they needed to know was that Zoe was safe. Again she could become the protected wife and mother. At that moment Simon could have been a god.

Roger did not easily relinquish his hold. He had known a moment of savage joy in finding Zoe again. But it was being snatched away from him. For when a young man who tops six feet and weighs two hundred pounds offers to make an honest woman out of a "soiled dove," there is little saving left to be done. He surveyed the situation dourly from under his lion's brows, and turned to go.

"Come, Eli," he said, and went out.

Eli didn't move. He sat staring after his father. There was abject appeal in the glance he turned on Zoe. She walked over and rested a hand on his thin shoulder.

"You can make your home with me, Eli. I'll be glad to have you."

"Can I, Zoe?" he asked with hopeful urgency. "I can work and help. I can get a job in the mines and . . ."

"No, you won't go in the mines," Zoe stated firmly. "Cara can find you something to do in the restaurant, and at least you'll get enough to eat. You'll have to eat steady just to get some meat back on your bones."

"I'll do anything you say, Zoe." She could hear his desperation in his voice.

"Then go on over to the house. It's the one set down close to the creek, with the black shutters. There's a storeroom in back. You clean it up and make it into your bedroom. You can look in Emily's and my room for blankets. I'll be home in time to make us a good supper."

"What if . . ."

"Don't think about him. You can walk away from him. You have every right. He never was a father to any of us. Go on, Eli. Get yourself settled. I have some business here I have to take care of."

Eli nodded, grabbed up the last of the bread, and bolted out the door. Zoe was certain he would run all the way to the house, just as she was sure it would be a long time until he felt safe from Roger Carrigan's reach.

She turned to look up at Simon; then wordlessly she took Emily from his arms and held her close. "Thanks, Simon." She half smiled. "It seems I'm always thanking you."

"I'm afraid, Zoe," Simon replied, "that just thanking me is not going to be enough this time."

"What are you talking about?"

"Your father."

"He's not my—"

"I know. I've heard you say it over a million times. But you don't think he's going away, do you? He'll stay right here to see you safely married, or he'll be right back bellowing recriminations at the top of his lungs. He's dying to save you from . . . whatever black ideas he carries, and he's going to stick around and make sure he does. Whether he's your father or not, he's going to shout loud enough for everyone to believe him."

"Oh God, I hate him," Zoe breathed bitterly. She turned defiant eyes on Simon. "And I won't be forced to do anything unless I want to."

Simon's smile was tight. "Going to pack up and run again, Zoe?"

"No, I'm not running, and I'm not going to allow you to play this game with me. I don't care what Roger Carrigan says. I'll just have to handle it."

"You didn't look like you were handling it too well a few minutes ago. Face facts, Zoe. It's the smartest thing to do. And I do love you and Emily. If you tell the truth, you care for me too. If Grey comes back, your father will be on a worse rampage. He'll pull this town down around your ears."

Zoe knew this was the truth. Roger would preach about her from every street corner in town until he ruined not only her life, but Emily's and Eli's and Grey's as well. She felt as if she were locked in a box. Why did the men in her life demand so much?

Yes, she cared for Simon. But to marry him meant giving up the force that had sustained her from the night Brent had left her.

It meant giving up any chance of revenge because Simon would stand between her and that satisfaction.

Yet if she didn't marry him, her life here would be a living hell . . . and she could not run again . . . not again.

"Simon, you're being unfair."

"It's a war, Zoe, and I have to fight with what weapons I've got. You need me, and I have a price."

"It will be a real marriage," she stated firmly. He could read the determination in her eyes.

"It will be one step. We'll let the rest of the steps take care of themselves."

"Don't do this, Simon."

"I can't let you go, Zoe," he replied in the same quiet tone.

The iron in her had to melt, but she found it more than painful. She opened her mouth to utter the words of surrender, but before she could speak, the door burst open. Both Zoe and Simon spun around in surprise. Grey stood before them, a broad smile on his flushed face and a look of intense excitement in his eyes.

For a minute it took both Zoe and Simon a while to digest the fact that he was there, and to guess the reason he had appeared so unexpectedly. Simon's heart sank as he felt Zoe slipping away from him, maybe for the last time. Zoe's eyes lit with pleasure and a bubbly excitement began to fill her.

"Grey?"

"We did it, girl! We did it! I struck a lode that will curl your hair! Look!" He reached into both pockets and drew out a handful of small glittering rocks. "It's rich, Zoe. Rich!"

Zoe could hardly breathe. She stood immobile for a minute; then she set Emily down and ran to Grey to embrace him. He caught her up in his arms and whirled her around.

Simon watched his dream die in the short minutes after Grey's arrival. If Zoe had money, there was no stopping her. She would walk down her well-planned road, and in the end she was going to be hurt more than she had ever known.

But he had nothing to fight with now. He had tried every avenue. He knew he had made her respond to him physically, and given the chance he could again. But he also knew that was not the way to get and hold Zoe. Love was something she would go on denying, because love had abandoned her so long ago.

He said nothing. He simply turned and walked out the back door. It was no use to stay; he couldn't share Zoe's happiness and he couldn't reach her with any kind of logic.

When Grey set Zoe back on her feet, she turned her smiling face toward Simon, but he was no longer there. She inhaled a deep breath, unsure of why she was filled with a kind of tearing feeling.

Zoe knew as well as Simon did that she truly cared for him. But it was not the right time for her to consider love. In time . . . when she'd finished what she had to do . . . then there would be time.

Still, she watched the closed back door for a long time, aware of a sense of loss. Surely Simon could have stayed to help her celebrate. She promised herself she would find him later.

"Zoe . . . Zoe." Grey had to repeat her name twice before she could tear her attention from the door.

"What?"

"What are you going to do first?"

"First?" She hadn't really believed enough to make plans.

"Sure. You're going to have all the money you can spend. Are you going to move out of Aspen?"

"Out of Aspen," she repeated thoughtfully. "No, no, I don't think I'll move just yet. Not just yet." She needed time to think, to plan, to remember all the slights and the painful things. She needed to bring Brent and his betrayal to mind again. Then she needed to figure the best way to do him the most harm.

The first thing Zoe did when Grey had begun to turn her gold to money was to approach the local banker. She smiled when Mr. Brindle looked up from his rolltop desk.

"They said I was to see you, Mr. Brindle. I'd like to start another bank account, if you please. I wonder if you can help me?"

Could he! His narrow chest expanded. He pulled a chair up for her close beside his desk. His eyes were bright behind his glasses as he looked across at her.

As he handed her her checkbook with the final instructions, he remarked. "You should thank your lucky stars you struck gold instead of silver. Gold is the only bright spot left in a nation on the verge of panic."

"Panic?" she repeated. She had been hearing the word over and over lately.

"It's something that happens when money gets tight and prices drop too far. The price of silver is down today. Crops have been bad and farmers are in debt. Naturally they want to pay back their debts with easy money, and naturally their creditors, the big-money interests, don't want them to."

Zoe listened carefully while he explained those cryptic words. Easy money, tight money, free silver, gold standard. It was not really so hard, she thought, if you had a head for figures and really listened. In fact, it was exhilarating, like learning to read, to have formerly meaningless symbols come alive.

This was the first of several discreet little talks between Zoe and her banker. Discreet, for Martin Brindle's reputation as a banker was quite as delicate as any woman's.

He vastly enjoyed his roll as tutor. He was sure that Zoe had a man's mind. But he was mistaken. She had the mind of an opportunist. Yet it was a good mind, quick to grasp anything that affected her. She was learning, to her surprise, that she could be savage and ruthless when it came to her world now.

"The whole trouble is," Martin explained one day, "that the country has never recovered from the crime of 1873."

Zoe smiled and wrinkled her brow prettily. He cleared his throat and settled back in his chair. Dispensing information to a pretty woman was almost as titillating as dispensing a piece of jewelry . . . and a good deal safer.

"Yes, crime," he repeated. "I'm a 'silver man' myself, even if I do make my living in gold. It was a black crime when Congress ordered the mint to stop making silver dollars back in '73. Why, do you realize this country had bimetalism—and prospered under it—since the days of Washington?"

Zoe had not realized anything; she was still a little vague about the significance of bimetalism. But she looked impressed.

"Oh, the East tried to offer the West a sop in the form of the Silver Purchasing Act of '78, but it wasn't enough. It's tight money, I tell you, that's responsible for this slump. Put the old populists in power and we'd cure the nation's headaches overnight by bringing back the coinage ratio of sixteen ounces of silver to one ounce of gold."

Slowly, Zoe began to realize effect these changes might have on her life.

Silver! Brent's family dealt exclusively in silver, and the federal government had made the value of silver drop. Gold was the commodity to own now, and she had a seemingly unending flow of it. It meant one important thing to her. She now had the tool with which she could reach the Dewitt family . . . a tool that could bring them to their knees.

Chapter Twenty

1893, Denver, Colorado

Brent Dewitt tilted back in his father's desk chair and stared out the window toward the peaks to the west. He had, as always, the feeling that the chair was a little too large for him, just as his father's office . . . and his father's shoes . . . were a little too large for him.

He had kept the office after his father's death of an obscure stomach ailment. Even after six years he was not used to being the only Dewitt left. It gave him a queer feeling to write finis to his line. A line that could trace its lineage back to Adam, he supposed ruefully. But he and Barbara had written it with their empty, sterile lives. He was almost ashamed of how badly he had wanted a child of his own. He had never confessed it to Barbara. He could imagine her look of pained disdain.

He also wished that "standards" were not such expensive things to maintain. Or that his father had picked a different time to die. For not even a financial wizard could have salvaged much from the Dewitt estate during the worst days of the panic.

His mother had passed away the year before his father, and now that the Dewitt financial empire was in dire straights, Brent was surviving on his wife's money and her father's largesse.

To the world it must seem a pleasant, easy life to be the husband of a rich wife or rather, the husband of a rich man's daughter. But the world did not know. It did not know that Barbara, so perfect on the outside, was just like her father on the inside. Just like Lester Crandell, the great railroad magnate and empire builder.

Brent thought he'd retch if he had to hear those laudatory phrases again.

He knew old Lester was on the top floor of his magnificent office building scheming up fresh humiliation for his son-in-law. Brent suspected it was his one real pleasure in life. It took all Brent's control to remain calm and not let the old man see his hatred.

He had never been able to put a cent of his own earnings away when the mines were producing. It was as if Barbara had wanted to see him penniless.

They had to belong to several country clubs. In fact, either they had to attend every social affair, or they had to be the ones to cater that social affair.

He had asked her once if she couldn't cut down somewhere, and she had turned on him with a viciousness that had stunned him into perpetual silence.

He gave a harassed sigh. His law practice was slim and never enough to keep up with her big house and clubs. Yet he dared not give up any of them, as that would be an admission of his ignominious circumstances. His only hope was to wait and pray for the death of Lester Crandell, who might live forever. Brent knew that if he displeased Barbara or her father in any way, the latter would cut him off without a cent, and take Barbara back into his home. Then all of Denver would know his failures.

He allowed his mind to drift back. Had it been nine years? Nine years since he had seen Laura? It was fruitless to think about her; she was gone forever. But lately he could not put her out of his mind. Her generosity, her rages, her rich and riotous beauty. She represented the one mad, uncalculating, glorious period in his life. And he had lost her through his own weakness. He tried to justify himself. He tried to remind himself that she had been unworthy of him. But all he could really remember about her now was that she had been beautiful and generous in her loving.

He flinched at the memory of his own conduct. Once more he marshaled all the old arguments, the old excuses, and they looked shabbier than ever before his eyes.

He blanched at the thought of Lester Crandell ever getting wind of the Aspen chapter of his life. Cara Jardeen. Stelle . . . and a beautiful girl from the row. Just thinking about it gave him the cold shakes.

Caught in his thoughts, he didn't hear his secretary speak to him until his name had been repeated for the third time.

"What?"

"There is an urgent message for you, sir. It's a police officer. He . . . he would only speak to you."

"What is it?"

"I don't know, sir, but it seems of the utmost urgency. I think you'd best come, sir. The man seems . . . distraught."

Brent rose at once and followed his secretary to the outer office, where he stopped in shock.

The man who stood before him wore a policeman's uniform. His heart began to pound heavily.

"What is it?" he asked, fear tinging his voice.

"I'm afraid there's been an accident, sir."

"Accident," he could only repeat inanely.

"Yes, sir. A carriage accident. I—" He looked about him, realizing that everyone had their attention on Brent. "I think it would be best, sir, if you came along with me. We can talk privately."

He took hold of Brent's arm, and numbly Brent moved with him. Outside, he urged Brent gently into a carriage and got in beside him. "Now, sir, I hate to break the news to you like this, but it's your wife, Mr. Dewitt. She's been taken to Mercy Hospital. . . . but I'm afraid it's pretty bad. We'll take you there at once."

"Thank you," Brent half whispered. He still could not grasp what was happening.

He sat immobile, his brain frozen, during the ride to the hospital. When he rushed down the hospital corridor, he still could not get his pounding heart and spinning brain to believe it was happening.

But he was minutes too late. Barbara lay still and white on the hospital bed. He had just walked into the room and had reached the bed to take Barbara's cold hand in his when a sound from the doorway made him turn.

Lester Crandell stood in the doorway, his eyes fixed on the bed. His face was ashen, and Brent could see that he was perspiring. His eyes were riveted on the bed, and there was stark pain in his eyes.

"I'm afraid we're both too late," Brent said quickly.

"What happened?" Lester said as he crossed the room to stand on the opposite side of the bed.

"I don't really know. The police said it was a carriage accident."

"My God," Lester Crandell's voice rasped thickly. "Barbara, my little girl." His voice broke on a heavy sob.

Brent came around the bed and put his arm about the old man's shoulders. He wished he could feel the same agony. It would assuage his guilt a bit. But he felt . . . nothing. Nothing, and he was ashamed and frightened at his lack of emotion.

He consoled Lester as best he could, and after a while tried to urge him away from the bed.

"Come . . . come with me. We . . . we have to make preparations."

"Preparations?" Lester turned his stunned gaze toward Brent. Whether Brent wanted him to or not, Lester could see his calmness, his lack of tears and emotion. Suddenly Lester's grief was supported by a kind of raw, despairing anger. Brent had never been able to give his daughter everything she deserved. For the past few years Lester had known they had not been happy together, and now his son-in-law did not even have the decency to grieve.

Something inside Lester grew hard and cold, like a fist grasping his heart and squeezing it. But his keen mind was active. There were many ways to revenge himself on this man . . . many ways. Brent Dewitt had been at his mercy for a long time, but because of Barbara he had held off.

"Yes, I suppose we must." Lester nodded his head. If Brent saw the gleam in his eyes, he accredited it to grief.

"We can do nothing here," Brent said. "Both of us grieve and we have lost our dearest one. We must do what we can for her now. At least we can support each other. You know I will always be here."

But of course you will, Lester thought with bitter anguish. You will be where my money is. The ultimate form of revenge occurred to him then. Let him believe, let him become more and more enslaved to the Crandell wealth There was still plenty of time to pull the strings, and make the puppet dance. Lester Crandell had lost the brightest thing in his life. Now, all he had was time and millions to make Brent pay for his daughter's short unhappy life.

"Yes, we have each other, and deservingly so," Lester answered. As they walked slowly from the room, Brent's arm was still about his shoulder.

At the funeral both Brent and Lester were in control, showing the world a unified front of support. But inside, Lester was seething.

It was after the funeral, when everyone had gone and they were left alone with only brandy for consolation, when Lester began to spin his web.

His father-in-law's machinations went unnoticed by Brent for a long, long time, for Brent had become a man obsessed. He no longer had the pressure of his parents, and he no longer had demoralizing obligations to his unloving, rich wife. He turned his thoughts to Laura . . . Laura, and the love he had tasted and left. He realized now the strength Laura had.

While he set about sending out feelers, searching for where Laura Champion had gone and what her circumstances were, Lester was drawing his net tighter and tighter. Brent did not notice that his clientele had changed. He never knew that most of his clients were Lester's friends.

Lester's largesse in helping him financially was an even bigger relief to Brent, who accepted help, disregarding the notes he signed—only to make everything proper for the bookeepers, Lester assured him.

He used a great deal of money in the search for Laura Champion. . . . never knowing that Laura Champion did not exist any longer. In her place was a wealthier and much wiser Zoe Carrigan.

When word was first brought to him that Laura Champion could not be found in Aspen, he was not surprised. It had been so many years, and Laura was probably gone. He knew he should leave it alone. He had left her under the worst circumstances. But . . . he couldn't. Something much stronger than he urged him on.

Maybe it was a need for some kind of redemption, some forgiveness. He didn't know. He only knew he had to find her.

All the men he had sent out to assorted cities in Colorado returned with the same word. There was no Laura Champion. Not in Georgetown or in Irontown. None of the other cities gave different results. Brent had begun to believe Laura had left the state entirely. But where would she go with no money?

It was late in the morning, and Brent was suddenly lethargic and extremely tired.

He sat at his desk, but realized now that he'd been doing absolutely nothing for the past two hours. Somehow it startled him. He called for his secretary.

"Yes, sir?"

"No client appointments this morning?"

"No, sir."

"That's strange, isn't it?"

"We've had four cancellations."

"And this afternoon?" Something stirred in Brent.

"No cancellations yet, sir."

"All right, thank you."

The secretary pulled the door closed between them, and Brent was left in a strange kind of silence. He allowed his mind to drift again. Laura . . . Laura. Nine long, very unhappy years. He had never realized what living in a vacuum, without love and without warmth, could be like.

He was thirty-nine. It was not too late to have all he had missed. He could still marry and beget children. He had money . . . or rather the man who thought of him as a son had money. And Crandell had not been stingy with it. Of course Brent owed him a monumental amount of money. But it was all in the family. Soon he would recoup the tremendous losses from the silver mines in Aspen.

He'd been very relieved when the pressure from Aspen was taken off him by a surprise investor. He'd received a letter from a Mr. Grey Sinclair, who had offered cold hard cash for a controlling stock in one of the mines. The offer had reached Brent when he was feeling a desperate need for money. He'd accepted at once.

But things had gone from bad to worse, and eventually the mine had failed. The cost had been almost debilitating. But he still had one producing mine left.

He'd heard the rumors of tremendous gold strikes, but he had very little cash to invest. Today he was going to face his father-in-law and ask for some money to make just such an investment.

An opportunity had finally come to reclaim his fortune. The same Mr. Sinclair had written to inform him that he had a small, possibly rich, gold mine and since Brent had been so generous in letting him invest in his mine, he would return the favor by letting Brent be the first to invest in *his.*

Brent hated to think of how overextended he was. But Lester would help; he always did.

He looked up when his secretary opened the door. "The two clients scheduled for this afternoon have canceled their appointments."

Still no tingle of alarm touched him. He stood up. He might just as well beard the old lion in his den instead of facing him across a dinner table. "All right, Miss Ramsey, I'm going out. I'll be at Mr. Crandell's office should anything come up."

"Yes, sir." She watched him leave, with something very close to pity in her eyes. If she'd liked Brent better she might have tried to tell him what he was too blind to see. But he had not been the kindest of employers, so she silently watched him close the door behind him.

Lester sat behind his desk in deep and very satisfying contemplation of the papers that lay before him. It was time to make his son-in-law begin to pay. He would make him twist and turn, but he would never set him free. He now knew all of Brent's weaknesses, and the most important one was his need to retain his gloss of wealth and civilized veneer.

Oh, yes, Brent Dewitt would continue with his life, just as it was, but he would no longer have control of it. No, Lester would.

He couldn't wait until dinner tonight to watch Brent's expression. His son-in-law was a weak man who survived by sapping strength from those around him.

Oh, he knew about the woman in Aspen. He knew that Brent had hired men to find her, and had paid them well . . . but Lester had paid them better. He knew the answers Brent had sought. The woman had become very wealthy, had built a fine home, and to Lester's supreme pleasure, now had a daughter that could quite well be Brent's.

Lester had made certain the information he'd obtained was kept from Brent. As for the child . . . He chuckled bitterly to himself. Brent Dewitt would have his child the day Lester's child was returned to him . . . in other words, never.

He had also taken the time to trace Zoe Carrigan's history. He even knew when she had struck gold and all that she had done since . . . even the temptation she had set before Brent. It was obvious to him that this Zoe Carrigan had some vengeful ideas toward the man she felt had deserted her. Well, she would wait her turn.

His reverie was broken when he was informed that Brent was in the outer office waiting to see him.

"Tell him to come in," Lester said with a smile. He opened his desk drawer and put the papers inside.

When Brent came in, Lester could see he had the same air of confidence he always had.

"What brings you here at midday, Brent?"

"I hope I'm not interrupting something important."

"No, of course not. Sit down."

Brent sat in the comfortable leather chair opposite Lester's desk. For a minute he contemplated the older man. There was some intangible difference about Lester . . . but Brent couldn't identify it so he ignored it.

"How have you been, Brent? I haven't seen you in nearly two weeks. Isabelle and I have been wondering why you haven't been over to dinner. When Barbara was alive you came over more often. We are beginning to feel a bit neglected."

If there was a hint of anger in his voice, it was subtle.

"I'm sorry. I've been awfully busy."

"Yes, I suppose you have."

Brent cast Lester a narrowed look. "What do you mean, you suppose I have? You know I have a practice that—"

"That's slowly dying."

Brent was silenced by the three gently said words, paralyzed by the underlying tone.

"Dying?" he said, his voice still thick with shock. "That's hardly the truth. Things have not really been going well, but . . . Actually, there was something I wanted to discuss with you. A . . . matter of business."

"A matter of money," Lester said. It was a statement, not a question.

"Well . . . ah . . . yes. As a matter of fact." He bent a little toward the desk, without realizing it was a movement of supplication. Lester smiled. "I have run across an investment of immense possibilities," Brent declared.

"I'm sure your father felt that way about sinking all his money into silver."

"Silver was very good to my family."

"Yes . . . it was. Tell me, how is the mine doing?"

"Not as well as it could. It's that damn union. The workers are giving most of the owners a hard time of it."

"Unions!" Lester scoffed. "There's one way to handle them. Get some . . . help, if you know what I mean."

"I leave that to my manager. Besides, silver mines are not what I came to ask you about."

"Oh? And what did you come to talk about?"

"A gold mine."

"A gold mine," Lester repeated.

"I've told you. I have an opportunity to invest in a great new project."

"And I'm to supply the money for this."

"I know. I am already indebted to you," Brent began, "but . . ."

"There is little room for buts. You are greatly indebted to me."

Brent flushed. His gentility could hardly accept Lester's brusque manner. It was not right . . . not gentlemanly to be so . . . almost aggressive. "I understand, but I have an opportunity to change all that."

"By going into deeper debt?"

"Only temporarily."

"Well . . . we can discuss it after dinner tonight." Lester smiled the same sharkish smile. "You can come, can't you?"

Brent knew well, if he wanted a dime from the old man, he had to agree. But deep inside he had a feeling . . . God, he had a feeling.

When Brent entered Lester's house that night, the feeling grew even stronger.

As usual he had dressed with meticulous care, something that set Lester's teeth on edge every time he saw his son-in-law.

"I'm afraid Isabelle won't be with us for dinner," the older man said. "She was called away earlier. Seems her sister is ill. We'll share dinner for two, then enjoy some brandies. I have a few things I want to talk to you about."

"You've considered my proposal?"

"Yes, I have. But we can talk about that later."

Brent knew Lester was deliberately dangling him on a thread, but the investment meant money and gold, and that meant freedom.

They ate a well-prepared meal, conversing about everything except what Brent wanted to hear. But he fought his impatience.

Finally, Lester suggested brandy in his library. Once they were settled comfortably, Lester began the conversation with words that shook Brent.

"Brent, I want you to come to work for me as my personal attorney. I need someone on staff to keep things going smoothly."

Brent had lived in Lester's shadow much longer than he intended. "I'm afraid I can't do that," he replied. "I have quite a clientele of my own."

"You don't seem to understand me." Lester's voice was gentle and his smile broad and cool. "It is not actually a question. It's more a . . . demand, you might say."

"A demand." Brent tried to smile. "I'm afraid I still must refuse."

"And I'm afraid you can't."

"I don't understand. I know I owe you money. But I earn enough—"

"Not nearly enough. In fact, as of tomorrow morning you will no longer have a client left. You will also, as of noon tomorrow, find that the bank is foreclosing on your home . . . and I will be calling in your notes."

Brent had been staring at him in shock. His face was pale, and his one hand held his brandy snifter halfway to his lips while his other hand gripped the chair arm until his knuckles were white. He could not speak.

Lester spoke instead. "You have not noticed that all of your clients are friends of mine or someone indebted to me? If you will recall, you had a day of cancellations to-day. Tomorrow will be the same."

"You . . . you can't do this!"

"Can I not?" Lester nodded his head. "Of course, you're right. By noon tomorrow you will have enough money to pay off your debts . . . and you will also have enough to survive until you acquire new clients . . . that is, if you think you can."

"You know I can't do that."

"Well, then, all you need do is accept the position I'm offering. It's really not a death sentence, you know. You will be paid well . . . and you will protect me and my firm. That way everyone will be happy."

Brent knew all the things that were left unsaid. He'd been under Lester's thumb all through his marriage, and Lester was going to make sure he remained so for the balance of his life.

Yet where would he go? Where could he go? If he left, he would not have a cent to his name. Independence, freedom, and his dreams of gold were fading.

Lester smiled. "Now it isn't that bad. I've named you in my will. I intend to leave you what you earn . . . what you deserve. What," he added softly, "you married my Barbara for. I would not want you to be cheated."

Brent's cheeks were gray as he sagged back down in his chair. He would be destitute . . . yet wealthy. He would have everything at his fingertips and be unable to touch it. He would have to live so until this man died, and even then he could not trust Lester not to reach out from the grave to destroy him.

But the alternative was just as bleak. He would be an

outcast of his own class. He would be forced to find employment on his own, and with Lester's extensive reach that prospect was negligible. He felt like a fly caught in the web of a huge spider.

"Why are you doing this to me?"

"What am I doing? I am securing your position. Making sure all the rest of your days are taken care of. You will not want for anything . . . as long as your work for me is satisfactory. And about your gold mine? I'm looking into that investment. I'm not sure of its quality yet."

"How did you . . ." Brent began. Then he shook his head as if to clear it. "Of course, you knew about the gold strike before anyone else."

"Of course."

"And you never had any intention of letting me invest in it. You were afraid I would acquire enough capital to free myself of you."

"Now, Brent, you are getting wrought up over nothing. Many men your age would leap at what I offer. You are nearly forty now, aren't you? Hardly an age to be starting over."

Brent could already imagine the laughter that would flow through Denver. He could hear the chiding, derisive remarks, and knew the gossip that would swirl behind his back.

He would be ostracized from all of the important social events. He would not be able to afford the fine tailor and the imported leather shoes he was accustomed to.

All the tasteful, expensive things he had long ago made an indelible part of his life would no longer be his.

He could not live without them. He knew it, just as he knew the man sitting before him knew it.

His defeat was written plainly on his face. His hand trembled as he drained his brandy in one heated gulp. Lester smiled. "Would you like time to think over my offer?"

"No," Brent said raggedly. "What is there to think over? I have no choice, do I?"

"Brent, my boy. A man always has choices."

"Damn you," Brent muttered.

"I shall expect you at work tomorrow. You can have the

office directly opposite mine. So I can be of help during your . . . adjustment period."

"You mean to spy on me, don't you. To watch every move I make, every person I talk to. To see I do not make friends that might interfere with you."

"I need not spy on you. I have others who mind the details. I have known every move you made from the day you left Denver eleven years ago. I know of your sordid liaison with that slut in Aspen. I don't understand why your father wanted to rescue you from that. But it seems he did."

"What do you know of Laura?" Brent snarled. "She was not a slut. I left because I was ill and weak, and my father persuaded me it was best for my health."

Lester chuckled deep in his throat. "How easy you foist your weakness off on others. No one could have 'persuaded' you to leave if you hadn't wanted to. What's the matter, Brent? Can't you face yourself?"

"I did what was best. I was a drain on Laura."

"Were you now? I guess your kind of man is always a drain."

"I knew Laura would survive better without me."

"You're right, she did. Much better."

"You know where Laura is?"

"Of course I do. But it's immaterial. As you said, she is much better off without you. My men had more success finding her than the ones you hired."

"She is still in Aspen?"

"Laura Champion?"

"Yes."

"No . . . Laura Champion is not in Aspen. But where she is, is something you will know . . . when I am ready to tell you."

"And that too depends on how well I perform?"

"Precisely. You will do as you have always done. You will present to the world your gentleman's face. You will wear fine clothes, eat in the best restaurants, dance at the finest parties—to which I will see you get invited. But . . . you will have nothing of your own, and you will want . . . yes, you will want. You will want until the day I die."

"What will you do if I refuse? I still have the one mine

my father left. I know it is not doing well, but I could survive with it if I were careful."

"You? Careful?" Lester laughed. "It might be a lark to watch that. But I'm afraid you don't even have that anymore."

"That's impossible."

"No. You had several notes against it with Aspen banks."

"And you bought them?"

"No, I wish I had, but I was too late. Someone else bought them. I have a feeling they will be called soon."

"I have a right to know who bought them."

"A young company, backed by quite a lot of gold. But I have not yet gotten hold of the name of the major stockholder. I only know it's a woman."

"Would you tell me if you knew?"

"Hardly."

"I can find out myself."

"Take my word for it. If I can't, you can't."

"You think you've won, don't you?"

"I have."

"How long have you hated me like this?"

"From the day my daughter first looked at you. You were not fit to wipe her shoes."

"She came after me," Brent taunted. He had to hurt him somehow.

"Her foolish mistake. She was my child and I loved her. You have never had a child." His eyes grew hard and cold. "And I intend to see that you never do. Because any woman of means who looks at you will soon be informed you are a destitute rake. No . . . as I will, you will have to live the rest of your life alone. Without love or family or the money you cherish so. And I do hope you live a very, very long time."

Brent set his brandy snifter down, rose from his chair, and turned to walk out of the room. He could hear Lester's malicious and satisfied laugh follow him.

He raged at himself as he walked toward home, denying the carriage he could have taken. He needed the cool air to clear his mind.

He knew there was no way out now. But time was on

his side. He would play Lester's game until some opportunity arose. He would know it when it did.

First he would write to Grey Sinclair and see if it were possible to invest very small amounts over time. Step by step, he would save small amounts of money and buy stock in the gold mine.

He was not going to be defeated by that wicked devil of a man with hatred in his heart.

He thought of what Lester had said. Laura was not in Aspen. Well, he would continue to search until he found where she had gone. She had loved him once. Maybe the spark was still there.

One way or another he had to defeat this man. But he could not sacrifice his breeding to do it. He knew it . . . and Lester knew it.

Chapter Twenty-one

Grey had never seen anyone enjoy the acquisition of money more than Zoe. She would stop by the bank almost daily for a conference with Brindle, who'd begun to admire her considerably.

For a woman who'd been born and raised poor, she had an uncanny grasp of investing.

Brindle's admiration made him talkative with her, and through him she found out that Brent's one remaining mine was on shaky legs. She had watched his other investments fail. She had known when his parents had died. And she had taken pleasure in watching the Dewitt empire begin to shrivel.

They had sunk everything into silver . . . and now gold was king and she seemed to have an unending supply of it.

Grey had given his house to Zoe when he'd seen how lovingly she cared for it, and had built himself a place only three miles away.

A strange kind of relationship had begun to develop between Zoe and the two men in her life. The catalyst that drew them together was Emily.

Emily was sunshine, and she drew Simon and Grey like a magnet, because deep within both men was the desire to make Emily and Zoe part of their lives.

Simon and Grey had a lot more in common than Zoe imagined. Grey knew the power Simon was slowly accumulating even if Zoe didn't. He knew the miners had developed a deep respect for Simon. He was always there—with the loan of a few coins when children were hungry, or providing medical help when they were sick, or a sympathetic ear when they were troubled. Grey knew Simon was their chosen leader . . . and that the day was coming when the miners would follow his lead. It meant trouble for Zoe, but Grey couldn't convince her of that. Zoe was sure that she and Simon were so close that he would not cause her or her mines any problems.

Grey also knew that Simon himself had tried time and time again to warn Zoe that hell was going to break loose one day. He'd even tried to elicit Eli's help, but Eli would find no fault with Zoe. His love, where Zoe was concerned, was totally blind.

Often one or the other of the two men would stop by Zoe's house in the evenings, to bring Emily trinket or story, but mostly to spend some time with the little girl.

Emily was a bubbling and entrancing child who worshipped Zoe, manipulated Cara, and had both Simon and Grey twined around her little finger.

She had learned to talk before she could walk, and would chatter happily with anyone. It made everyone laugh to see the fascination Emily had for a new word. When she heard one, no matter who said it, she would entreat them to repeat it over and over until she knew both the sound of the word and what it meant. After a while her vocabulary was astonishing.

Simon had not exactly proposed again, but he made sure that she knew of his desire to make Zoe and Emily his family.

To Zoe, Grey was more a quiet comfort than anything else. He never spoke of his feelings to Zoe or to anyone else. But he was always there, always doing the small things to make Zoe and Emily's life easier.

He resisted, at first, her campaign to bring down the Dewitts. But he knew Zoe's story better than anyone else except Simon and Cara. It was against his easygoing nature to do what Zoe wanted, yet he did it because he hoped that once she had the revenge out of her system, she might look inside herself and find the things she needed to complete her life. Grey hoped, if and when that day came, she might see that he belonged in it.

One evening they were sitting together in Zoe's parlor. Grey was sitting with Emily, helping her learn about a new game he'd brought. Grey was still unused to having a great deal of money. But Zoe had insisted that half of everything was his. He still lived in a small house, which seemed to be all he needed. There was no way he was going to tell Zoe what he had done with a great deal of his money. At this point he was pretty sure she wouldn't understand. He didn't want money ever to stand between them. He had helped Zoe renovate and add to his old house until it could hardly be recognized. What Grey spent, he spent mostly on Zoe and Emily.

"Grey . . . have you any further reports on Brent Dewitt?" Zoe asked him.

Grey looked up at her, reluctance in his eyes. "I know he's hired men to search for you."

"I don't want—"

"Don't worry, Zoe. From what I could gather, they were asking for Laura Champion, not Zoe Carrigan. I've been checking it out. I think there's a third party at work here. Much as Brent Dewitt seems to want to find you . . . someone else doesn't want him to."

"Probably that wealthy wife of his," Zoe said coldly.

Grey hated to see such bitterness and hatred Zoe's eyes. "Zoe, Barbara Dewitt is dead."

"What!"

"Some kind of accident. So you see, she's not the one behind it."

"Then who?"

"I don't know. But whoever it is has helped you in a roundabout way. Brent can't find Laura Champion and he doesn't know Zoe Carrigan at all."

"So what is the situation?"

"He's in pretty bad shape financially. In fact, Brindle told me the other day he's going to have to call several notes he has against Dewitt's one remaining mine."

"Buy them," Zoe said abruptly.

"Zoe—"

"Buy them. I want to own everything the Dewitts had here."

"All right. But once you own them, then what?"

"His purse strings will begin to choke him a bit."

"He's still part of a wealthy family. I've looked up Lester Crandell. He's a sly old fox."

Zoe stopped what she was doing and came to sit down opposite Grey. Emily, bored with the conversation of adults, and intrigued by the new book Grey had brought as well, went off to find a comfortable place to read.

"Grey, what do you mean? Just what kind of sly old fox is Lester Crandell?"

"The kind of sly old fox to make Brent work for him now."

"Brent? But why should he work for him?"

"Because he needs money, probably."

"And he'd bow and scrape to her father, wouldn't he," Zoe said ruthlessly. "He'd kiss the old man's shoes for money." Zoe suddenly smiled.

"Zoe . . . what's on your mind?"

"Did you write that letter to Brent?"

"Yes," Grey replied reluctantly.

"And is the paperwork drawn up to form the new company? We'll call it the Trident. We'll put your old mine and the two I got from Suttler in it."

"But they're damn near worthless. They only make enough to cover expenses."

"I know."

"He'll never invest in them."

"You don't know Brent like I do. If he is hungry, and I think he is, he'll jump at it."

"What is it you really want, Zoe?"

"I want him to come here. I want to be the one to tell him he's broken. I want to have him crawl to me. I want to watch his face when he realizes he has no wealth, no family, no friends, and best of all . . . I want him to know at last that he has a child he'll never know. You did say they were childless, didn't you?"

"Yes."

"Well, then . . . it's time to put an end to Brent Dewitt."

"Lord, Zoe . . ."

"I want to see his reply when you get it." Zoe bent forward and laid her hand on Grey's. "Don't be angry with me, Grey. It's not your fault, none of it. I have to do what

I have to do. It's asking a lot of you to help me, and I'll really understand if you don't want to do it."

He looked into her eyes and he knew she would understand. He knew that just as surely as he knew something between them would change. She would go on without him. Subtly she would close the door, perhaps not even knowing she was closing it. No. He'd decided to stand with her and he meant to do it until this demon she carried around was finally put to rest.

"I'm with you, Zoe. Don't worry about it. Besides, you have other things to worry about than this."

"Other things? Like what?"

"Like the kettle of trouble that's brewing in all the mines around here. Zoe, if you weren't so damn engrossed in you own private world, you'd see."

"I don't know what you're talking about. Except for the fact that the area is filled with more people, that a little more civilization has come, I don't think things have changed in this state since I was a little girl."

"And that is exactly not only what's wrong, but what's got to be changed. And the changes are going to take a lot of doing."

"Nothing changes, Grey. The rich get richer and the poor get poorer and work harder."

"There are a few men who've been working damn hard to make sure that isn't true."

"They're fighting a losing battle. Money always wins."

"Your philosophy is jaded, Zoe. There are some other things in the world that can make a difference."

"I've never seen them."

"I don't think you would recognize them if you did. Most of them you've already got. Sometimes . . ." He paused and sighed, knowing she would not even attempt to grasp anything he said. "Sometimes," he continued, "you have the power to scare the hell out of me." Then he grinned again. "And I suppose that's one of the million things about you that makes it impossible to do anything but swim in your wake and hope I don't drown."

"Grey," Zoe said with a laugh, "you're talking nonsense and I still don't understand you. But I love you anyway."

Grey was silent for a minute. He'd tried to laugh with

her, but it just didn't work. She'd said three words in jest that he wished with all his heart were true.

Zoe wasn't as insensitive as Grey thought. Those three casually spoken words had had an effect on her too. She suddenly realized it would not be hard to learn to love Grey. But love was something she did not want to have interfering in her plans. Sometime . . . but not now.

"Look . . . Zoe." Grey struggled to regain control. "I think you ought to really listen to what is going on. If you remember how bad it was, why can't you understand what these people are going through?"

"There's not much I can do about it. Are you suggesting I just turn over all the money my mine makes for us? It wouldn't do any good. But besides that"—she turned to look at him straight, and he saw the demon within her glow in her eyes again—"I worked my fingers to the bone for what I've got. I washed and ironed until I was so tired I couldn't stand up. I'm not going to hand my profit to someone who cries injustice and never does anything about it. Who got the money together to start our mine? Me! Who has the right to it? Me and mine! And that's who's going to enjoy it."

"I didn't say give it away. I only said do something with it that makes it all worthwhile."

"I plan to do just that."

"Get Brent Dewitt."

"That will make it all worthwhile to me."

Grey knew there was not much use in arguing this point with Zoe any further. She was a loving, intelligent person, but she had a blind spot.

"Grey?"

"Yeah?"

"Was part of what you're saying . . . was it Simon's idea?"

"No, Simon wouldn't ask me to talk to you. Whatever Simon has to say he'll say himself. In fact, I think he has more than once."

"You're talking about that . . . place they're trying to call a hospital?"

"Simon is doing a lot. That . . . place, as you called it, is a hell of a sight more than the miners had before, and he's got a little school going too. That nice Caroline Dalton teaches there. It took Simon a lot of coaxing to get her to teach the miners' children, but now she loves it. It's not much either. Still, it's better than nothing. Zoe . . . you don't have to give your money. That's not what anyone really wants."

"Then what?"

"You're a mine owner. For God's sake, open your ears and listen! There's a force building and if you and the others don't listen, it's going to wash over you like a tidal wave."

"Grey, nobody knows miners better than I. They won't work together. They're too scared of losing their livelihood. All the owners have to do is close down the mines. When they're hungry they'll come back to work."

Grey sighed deeply. This battle could go on for hours and he always lost. "I have to go over to Tucker's to check on supplies. Do you mind if I take Emily along? Mrs. Tucker really enjoys her."

"How long will you be gone?"

"The rest of the evening. We should be back before eleven."

Zoe felt secure entrusting Emily to Grey. He had won Emily's heart a long time ago, and he treated her as if she were his.

"All right." She turned to call Emily, who came at once to stand by Grey.

"Good enough." He put his arm about Emily's shoulder and she clung to him. "Give your mother a kiss and let's go for a ride."

Emily obediently bent toward Zoe with her rosebud lips puckered, but she still clung to Grey.

When they were gone and Zoe had waved to Emily until they were out of sight, she turned and walked back into the house.

Zoe spent the next three hours working her accounts. Gold had continued to increase in price, and her bank account had grown well beyond the comfortable stage. Still, some hard dark thing made her feel the urgent need for more . . . and more. Until the day when she no longer felt the fear that tugged on her in the middle of the night and made her wake in a cold sweat. Until she knew she was beyond the memories of poverty and degradation. Until she could wipe the past out of her mind once and for all.

She knew in her heart the real cause of her troubles. Her stepfather had never accosted her again, and she knew quite well Simon's influence stood between them. For some reason he seemed to respect Simon.

She knew quite well that Roger Carrigan was still a thorn in the side of the conscience of Aspen, and that the miners feared him. Yet now, it seemed they had begun to tolerate him as well. Zoe couldn't understand it.

But there were so many things Simon and Grey knew that Zoe didn't, for she would not allow her stepfather's name spoken in her presence.

He *was* a conscience, but he had become a force among the miners as well. As much as he chastised them for sinful ways, so also did he work among them. He had no money, but he begged food and carried it to the ill. He held the hands of the dying and promised them a better life. He went down into the mines and he listened . . . and eventually he realized Simon's way was the only way and that sometime soon the low rumble of anguish and discontent had to erupt. He only hoped, once Simon began it, that he could control it, for Roger Carrigan could see another voracious monster rising. The monster of death and violence.

But Zoe, who stood with one foot in each camp, knew nothing about Simon's involvement with her stepfather, nor did she know anything about Roger Carrigan's contribution to the unrest that was rising about her. Her head was filled with the dreams she held, while her feet were mired in the mud she had tried so desperately to leave behind.

Simon was tired, but then he realized he was tired most of the time. He worked a ten-hour shift in the mines, then gave another five or six hours to the miners themselves. The only times he was at peace were the few short hours he got to spend with Emily.

And every day Simon made love to Zoe in a million ways, none of which were physical. He kissed her with his understanding, caressed her with his consideration, stood between her and what might bring her harm, and eased her heart by being there when she became unsteady.

Desperately he searched for a way to change Zoe's course. Because he knew her so well, he knew that if he could just take her focus off Brent Dewitt and put that same energy into his work with the miners, it would have miraculous results.

Unfortunately, so far he had failed. The last thing he could do was tell her that he was in any way associated with Roger Carrigan. That would put an end to everything. He walked a nerve-jangling tightrope, and he loved Zoe too much to get off it.

Now it was just past dusk, and from his porch he could watch the lights of the town begin to glow. Brilliant light shone from the mine owners' houses and the houses of the foremen and other "well-to-do" residents of the city. Softer light flickered from the miners' ramshackle homes.

He was tired and he knew he needed sleep, but instead he had scrubbed the dirt away, changed his clothes, and prepared to walk to Zoe's house. He would use Emily as an excuse, but his need to see Zoe was the main reason for the trip. Besides, Zoe had to have at least one more warning. One more chance to stop being the kind of mine owner she had always hated. She had to open her eyes to people who were suffering even more than she had. He had to try one more time.

He walked down the porch steps and started toward Zoe's house. Zoe's house . . . he smiled a humorless smile to himself. It was not exactly a house anymore; it hovered somewhere near a mansion.

Like Cara and Grey, Simon had been certain that Zoe's memories would make her a different kind of mine owner than Colorado had ever seen. But she wasn't. She seemed to have built a wall between her and the workers' suffering.

But within the next three days things were going to happen that he hoped would breech that wall.

As he walked, Simon thought back to the days when

Zoe was a girl of thirteen. He'd begun to worry about her then, and all these years later he still worried about her. Their lives were entangled so completely that unthreading the tendrils of memories and emotions that held them together was nearly impossible.

As he neared the house he noticed that only one window glowed with light. This was unusual for Zoe. She seemed to need light around her, and had a deep aversion to coming home when no lamps had been left burning. Often half the rooms in the house glowed with light, even when no one occupied them.

He walked up on the porch, but before he knocked he walked a foot or two to the lighted window and looked inside. Through the haze of the sheer curtains he could see Zoe sitting. That she was just sitting with her hands folded in her lap was surprise enough, but she seemed . . . somewhere else. For a minute it angered him, because he had a reasonably good idea where she was. He hated Brent Dewitt with his whole heart . . . and wanted Zoe with the same degree of passion.

He pushed his feelings aside and went back to the door and knocked. When she opened the door he stood quietly for a moment. Zoe had the capacity to wrench something deep within him.

She was a strange paradox: a little girl who still wept for her lost childhood, and a magnificent woman who knew exactly what she wanted and how to get it. He wanted to cradle her in his arms and kiss her until she forgot everything and everyone but him.

"Simon? What are you doing here?"

"I . . . I was passing and I thought Emily might still be up."

"I'm afraid she's not even here."

"Oh?" He tried to sound disappointed.

"Grey has taken her visiting. They ought to be back before too long."

"Mind if I come in?"

Zoe wasn't too sure this was wise. In a group, among friends, with someone nearby, she could cope with Simon's magnetic appeal. But alone, he was not just appealing, he was dangerous. Reluctantly, she moved aside and let him enter. Then she closed the door and turned to face him.

"Can I get you something?"

He wanted to say yes . . . you. "No, not really."

She continued to watch him.

"You look tired, Simon." She said it quietly, as if she were looking at him in a new way.

"I am a little."

"Come and sit down." She moved past him, but he sensed that she was trying to keep her distance from him. Simon followed slowly, looking around the room as he did. He'd been in this room before, and never had it felt like Zoe. It didn't tonight.

"How many rooms do you have here now?"

"Nine." She smiled.

"For a little girl from the flats of Georgetown, this is sure some difference."

"What is it?"

"What?"

"What is it that really brought you here? There's something on your mind."

"You know me that well?"

"Shouldn't I?"

"I suppose, but lately I've begun to doubt it. I thought I knew you pretty well too."

"And now you're not too sure."

"No, I'm not."

"I haven't changed, Simon."

Simon walked to her, took hold of her shoulders, and turned her so that they faced the huge gilt-framed mirror that hung over the fireplace. Their eyes met in the reflection.

Zoe had matured into a woman of remarkable beauty. Her auburn hair was carelessly pinned up so that tendrils of it lay along her cheeks and neck. It gave her a rather seductive look. The scent of it was sweet and clean, and Simon enjoyed it for a moment without speaking, as he enjoyed the deep gold of her remarkable eyes. She was still slender, yet her body had become more softly feminine.

"Look at you, Zoe. If anything you are more beautiful

now than when you first came to Aspen. You have what you dreamed of having. Yet somewhere deep in those lovely eyes of yours, I still see an angry little girl. For some reason you think you have to fight your own private war. You have changed. Don't lose everything to get something that will, in the end, make you more unhappy than you ever were."

If Simon was aware of everything about Zoe, she was just as aware of him. From the large hands that rested on her shoulders to the cloud-gray of his eyes.

How easy it would be to fall into the trap of passion . . . a remembered passion, for no matter how Zoe denied him mentally and verbally, physically her body remembered well the only time it had been awakened. She was too close to what she had worked for to let Simon break down her resolve now. She could not let go when she had her satisfaction, her revenge, in the palm of her hand.

She moved out of his grasp and walked a few steps away. She needed space between them if she wanted to control the physical reaction that always threatened to overpower her.

"You have made one mistake, Simon."

"Oh?"

"Yes. You see, I haven't changed. And if you knew me as well as you say you do, you would know that I have fought all my life for one thing. I have never pretended otherwise. I have it now, and I don't intend to lose it . . . or not to use it to accomplish what I want."

"No matter what?"

"No matter what," she agreed. "Why do you look at me that way? You have a good memory. Do you deny I have a right to revenge? You of all people should agree with me."

"If I didn't love you, Zoe, I would. But the only one who is going to get hurt is you. Put away this ugly obsession with Brent Dewitt. It's eating you alive. He's beyond your reach."

"Is he now?" Zoe smiled a smile that was definitely cruel.

"I hate that look in your eyes," Simon said angrily.

"Don't you see he has more of a hold on you now than he did when you were—"

"Married?" Zoe said bitterly. "You mean when he was making a fool of me . . . when he was conceiving Emily, not caring about the name she would carry."

Simon turned her around so quickly she didn't have time to back away. He gripped her shoulders in a hold she could never hope to break and gave her a rough shake.

"Because he was a fool, why do you have to destroy your life and a lot of others as well? Zoe, listen to me! Just once don't close your ears to reason and listen to me! While you're playing some sort of game with Brent Dewitt, the world around you is disintegrating. You could have your very livelihood jerked out from beneath your feet if you don't wake up. People around you are suffering like you once suffered. You are one of the people who could help lead the way to change all that. Everything you have is in danger, and you're the only one who can prevent a disaster from happening!"

"A disaster of your making!" Zoe stormed. "You're the one who can prevent problems by staying out of other people's affairs. The world went on a long time before you came, Simon. It can go on if you leave it alone."

"You really are blind, aren't you? What's going to happen would eventually have happened with or without me. I'm only trying to keep it from being a bloodbath. All you need to do is come with me once. Come back to your origins and see for yourself what you now have the power to stop. Come down to the flats with me. Look at the children who are hungry . . . like you were hungry. Come to the hospital and see the pathetically sick that we hardly have enough medicine to help. Come to the school and see the few who have the courage to try."

Zoe's face had grown pale, and a fear Simon had never seen before danced in her gold eyes.

"No." It was a cry of panic. "I'm not going anywhere. Let them climb out of the dirt like I did. No one helped me."

"You don't realize that you're a survivor. You have a lot more strength than most people do. Please listen to me." His voice softened and he drew her to him. "I love you,

Zoe. God help me, I love you. But I'll do what has to be done."

"You're the fool, Simon. You don't have to do anything. You might convince them to do something, but if they start it, they're the ones who will suffer because they haven't the guts to stand up and fight. They'll go back to work."

"You're wrong this time. You're wrong."

"You believe what you want to believe. But I know them too. You'll lose. Didn't you pay the price for this once?"

"You really don't know how different things are this time. Zoe—"

"No! I don't want to hear any more. Simon . . . don't destroy what's between us. I value our friendship. But . . ."

"But you're too damned obsessed to see the handwriting on the wall. You're too obsessed to see a whole lot of things." Frustration was slowly overcoming Simon's control. He wanted to do something drastic to waken Zoe from the sleep of self-deception. "None of this can go on any longer." His voice was a deep angry growl. "We can't be friends, don't you know that yet? What's between us either makes us lovers or enemies, and I'm not going to become your enemy without a fight."

She struggled now as he drew her even closer to him. But hard muscle, used to the brutal work of the mines, held her effortlessly.

He held her against him with one arm, pinning hers to her side. His other hand tangled in her hair, loosening the few pins that held it, spilling the thick mass of hair about her shoulders.

Their eyes held, hers blazing with anger that shielded a more vulnerable emotion, and his filled with the virulent hunger only Zoe could create. But behind the hunger was something more volatile. She knew without doubt that he could destroy her defenses. What was worse, she knew he knew it too . . . and meant to do it.

She could not fight him physically. Even now, the walls she had built between them were crumbling like so much dry dust before the onslaught of a wave of heat that urged her to reach for what she wanted. But the small seed of obsessive anger that would not die made her reach in desperation for anything that would break the force forging them together.

His mouth lowered to hers and when they blended, Zoe knew this was not a momentary thing that she could argue away with the old words. Simon meant to finish what he was starting.

Some part of Zoe . . . a part buried so deep that the resurrection brought a groan of pain from her . . . began to come to life. It taunted her body with the knowledge that she wanted Simon, wanted him with every sense she had. She wanted to feel the touch of his hands against her skin, knowing they would burn and brand her if she did. Wanted to feel the hardness of his body . . . wanted him inside her, and wanted even more the cataclysmic pleasure she knew he could give her.

For a moment she was lost, drowning in the feel and the taste of him until her head swam, and her body felt as if it were on fire.

But surrender was something another part of Zoe could not tolerate. Forged by years of resistance, it rose to do battle now. Zoe did not know how to retreat . . . how to give up on an idea that had been her only life force for so long.

For a heart-stopping moment Simon felt her surrender. Her mouth parted to accept his and her body softened against him. He could feel her tremble, and sensed how agonizing it might be for her to have those barriers broken. But if he didn't break them now it would be too late.

He crushed her even closer, feeling the length of her fitted so perfectly to him. He wanted to hold her gently. He wanted to love her with sensitivity. But he was afraid to ease his hold or give her a moment to think. Zoe was made of soft warm flesh, sweet-tasting lips, and a passion to match his. But all of this covered a core afraid to love . . . a heart encased in protective iron.

Then Zoe tore her mouth from his, and both stood locked in an embrace that was as explosive as a volcano. Zoe reached for all the reserve strength she had. She looked up at him and when she spoke, her voice was quivering but the words were firm.

"Let me go, Simon . . . unless rape is what you intend. Obviously I am not strong enough to stop you . . . but I shall hate you for as long as there is a breath in my body."

"Zoe . . ."

"No. I don't want to hear any more of your threats. I don't want to fight you. Don't force me to."

"You can't win, Zoe. This time it's more than you can understand."

"I can . . . and I will."

Simon knew there was no point in trying to convince Zoe he was reaching out for her with love. He had no choice but to retreat.

"All right. Have it your way. But don't say you weren't warned. You can't understand anything else; maybe you'll understand a challenge."

"A challenge?"

"Yes. I'm asking you to come halfway. If you feel the same then . . . I'll stay away."

"What kind of challenge?"

"Tomorrow you go with me. Let me present my last argument. Let me show you what we've done and explain what we want to do. At least give that much."

"What good will it do?"

"I'm not asking you to stop your little vendetta. I'm asking you to look out for yourself. I suppose your hate will always be bigger than the love anybody can offer you. I'm sorry for that, Zoe, because I love you so much it's impossible to forget it. And I'm going to go on loving you. But that is not going to stop what I have to do. So I'm challenging you. Come down to the hospital tomorrow. Come and see for yourself where you should be putting your money and your energy. If you're not afraid . . . come tomorrow. I'll be waiting. I want to see if you really have let your heart turn to stone like your workers say."

Zoe was shaken by his words. But it was too hard to let go of her goal. She felt tears and refused to allow them.

"That's not fair."

"So what is fair?" he replied. "From now on rules don't apply. Are you coming?"

"Simon, why don't you try to understand?"

"Oh, but I do understand. That's part of the problem.

It's what hurts. I understand you . . . and I feel sorry for you. You've let this thing eat at you until compassion and the ability to love are gone, and only your little cause can fill your heart. Money is your means . . . and money is the only way to fight you. Are you going to come?"

Defiance lit her eyes, and anger made her cheeks flush. "All right, I'll come. But I don't see what good it will do."

"I guess . . . I guess it will define the relationship between us. I guess it will be a way to choose sides."

"We don't have to." Her eyes warmed. "You don't have to do this, Simon. When my problems are worked out, we could—"

"My self-respect and my responsibility to the miners are too high a price to pay, Zoe. I want too much for too many others to give it up because you can't see the truth. I love you. But I guess I can't meet your terms. And"—he sighed heavily—"I guess you will choose not to meet mine."

"You're considering everyone but me."

"No, I'm not. I'm considering all the other Zoes out there who might not be as lucky as you've been. I'm asking you to give up hate for something much bigger. I'm asking you to be the woman I know is buried somewhere inside. The woman that I love."

Zoe turned away from him, and Simon gazed at her rigid back with a sad look in his eyes.

"Zoe?"

"I'll come tomorrow. That will have to be enough for you, Simon. I . . . I can't let this go."

There was a long silence behind her. A few minutes later Zoe heard the door close. Only then did her rigid body relax. She sagged into a nearby chair. Zoe wouldn't cry. She had cried for no one since Brent. But it was a long while before she could control her shaking hands and the feeling that her heart had been torn in two.

Chapter Twenty-two

The hospital was located in one of the worst areas along the flats, and it was little more than a converted warehouse. Lanterns hung from the lower beams, and rows of beds lined both sides of the room, with a small space toward the back closed off for surgery and the delivery of babies.

Even Zoe, who was well used to unsanitary conditions, held her handkerchief to her nose to filter out some of the stench. The odor of unwashed bodies, of disease, blood, and death, was a combination that nauseated her. Paul Riley was struggling to help as best he could, but he was the first to admit the town needed a younger doctor. The old doctor had retired, quite unable to handle the long hours and harsh pressure any longer.

She would have turned away as soon as Simon opened the door if his firm hand had not been on her elbow. She glanced up at him, and knew he was expecting her to run. Grimly she pressed her lips together and forced away the threatening nausea.

They moved slowly down the aisles between the beds. Here and there a hand was reached out to Simon, or his name was called, and he would pause to speak to someone. Zoe remained rigid and withdrawn. It was going to take all she could just to keep her control until she could find some fresh air.

They neared the end of the first row of beds when the door to the small closed-off area opened. A woman stepped out and closed the door behind her. Then she sagged against the wall and wept raggedly. The once-white apron that she wore over a plain blue cotton dress was splashed with blood.

Simon went to her at once, and Zoe followed slowly, stopping some distance away, but close enough to hear Simon's gentle consolation.

"Anne," he said softly, "are you all right?"

"I lost them, Simon . . . I lost both of them. God, I wanted so badly for the baby to live and I lost them. I don't think I can take any more of this. We need another doctor. I don't know enough! We don't have anything to work with! I don't think I can go on watching helpless while so many die. We lost Marsh Thomas yesterday."

"Gangrene?"

"Yes, but the real reason was carelessness. He had no need to lose that arm. The mines are deadly hellholes."

"Anne, you couldn't have done more than you did."

"I know. And that's what destroys me. Do you realize how little money it would take to get a doctor here?"

"It's money we don't have, Anne. We have to make do with what we've got."

"I'm not enough, Simon," she said softly, "and I can't bear it anymore."

"You need some rest. Why don't you go home and get some sleep. Marcie and Tina and the others can take over for a while. I can't afford to lose my best nurse, now can I?"

The woman inhaled deeply, as if she were gathering what equilibrium she had. She laid her hand on Simon's chest and looked up at him.

She was a year or two older than Zoe. Her hair was an ebony coil atop her head. She was slender to the point of nearly being too thin. Her cheekbones were high and gave her face a sculpted look. She would be pretty, Zoe thought, if she didn't look so exhausted. Dark shadows rimmed deep blue eyes, and lines of tension drew her lips tight.

Zoe watched her respond to Simon's gentleness, and felt something unnameable . . . something close to envy . . . and something more she would never recognize.

"Go on, Anne, go home. For today we'll have to get along without you. Don't worry, we'll manage. Some of the boys are coming over after night shift and breakfast. They can clean up and hold the fort until you get some sleep. I don't want any arguments." He put his arm about her shoulder and turned to face Zoe.

"Zoe . . . this is Anne Chambers. Anne . . . this is Zoe Carrigan."

Anne started to smile. Then sudden recognition of the name burst through her exhaustion, and Zoe watched her eyes grow chilled.

"Zoe Carrigan . . . what are you doing here? Slumming?"

"Anne . . ." Simon protested. This was the last thing he'd planned on . . . something to drive Zoe away. Anne shook his arm away.

"You have no reason to be here," Anne said. "You've forgotten where you came from. Go back home. There's nothing for you down here."

"Stop it, Anne. Zoe is here because I asked her to come. Go on home now."

Zoe remained speechless. The attack was something she was totally unprepared for. When Anne had gone, Simon turned to Zoe.

"Anne is really a wonderful person. This place couldn't run without her. It breaks her heart when she loses a fight."

"Simon, why don't you do something about this place? It's horrible, and why don't you get a doctor?"

"Because when we buy the few medical supplies we can afford, we can't afford to pay a doctor anything. I've been looking around for some young and gallant doctor to try and entice here, but so far humanity and nobility are not a large enough price."

"What about that Dr. Wallace you spoke about from Boulder?"

"He's dedicated to Boulder. I've already written him. He did say that he knew an old doctor who had a young man who'd been apprenticed to him for a while. We're trying to get him."

"If you brought me here because you were harboring the dream that this would draw me back, you picked the wrong thing. This only makes me more thankful than ever that I had sense enough to get myself away from such poverty."

"I brought you here to meet someone."

"Who?"

"A friend. Her name is Chloe. Come on." Simon took her arm and guided her to a bed that sat in the farthest corner. White folding screens had been placed around the bed. It made Zoe pause. "Come on, you'll like Chloe."

Reluctantly Zoe let Simon guide her around the screen.

A girl of possibly twelve or so lay quietly in the bed. Her face was heart-shaped, small, pinched, and pale. Her dark brown hair was parted in the center, and plaited in two long braids that hung down over the sheet that was tucked about her. She looked so frail that Zoe was sure one touch would break her. The only thing about her that was radiantly alive was her huge green eyes. When she caught sight of Simon, they seemed to light up. She smiled up at him.

"Hello, Simon."

"Chloe." Simon grinned as he sat down beside her and took one of her hands in his. "How's my favorite girl today? Have you taken all your medicine?"

"Ugh." She made a face. "It tastes awful."

"I know. But you need it to get well."

"I . . . I don't want to get well."

"Don't say that, Chloe. You don't want to lie in this hospital bed much longer, do you?"

Chloe's eyes darkened and she nodded her head. "I don't want to go home. This bed is all mine . . . and it's clean here. Besides, I get to eat twice a day." She seemed awed by this.

Zoe felt as if a hand was squeezing her heart. Seeing this girl was like looking back through a long narrow tunnel of memory, at herself.

"Well, if you're good and take your medicine, tomorrow I'll bring you some of that peppermint candy you like so much."

"Okay." Her eyes glowed. "Two pieces?" she asked hopefully.

"You're a bandit," Simon said with a laugh, "but two

pieces it is. But that means all your medicine . . . no complaints."

"Okay."

Simon bent to kiss her cheek, and her small thin arms came up about his neck. Simon hugged her and she lay back in the bed, because even that seemed to drain what energy she had.

"See you later, Chloe."

"Will you come back?"

"Sure, don't I always?"

Chloe seemed satisfied with that. Up until then she had paid no attention to Zoe at all. Now she looked at her. Then she looked back at Simon. After a few seconds she returned her gaze to Zoe, and the closed cold look in her eyes startled Zoe.

Simon stood up and moved to stand by Zoe. "Chloe, this is another special friend of mine. Her name is Zoe."

"Hello." Chloe's face was closed to her and her attitude was far from welcoming.

Zoe knew at once that Chloe was both jealous and afraid. She was, or seemed to Chloe to be, a threat.

Simon seemed unperturbed that Chloe had closed Zoe out. He'd expected it. "I've got to go, Chloe. But I'll stop by tomorrow and if you've taken all your medicine all day, I'll be sure to bring the candy."

She nodded, and Simon took Zoe's arm and propelled her out before him. Zoe felt as if Chloe's eyes were boring into her back all the way out.

Outside, she turned to Simon, whose face was still and slightly grim.

"You brought me here for a reason," Zoe stated. "To see that little girl?"

"I brought you here . . . to the hospital, hoping maybe it would open your eyes."

"I've seen all this. I've seen worse than this. They are lucky to have a hospital. We didn't."

"Zoe . . . before a disaster happens, change the policies at your mines. Set an example for the others and maybe they'll follow suit. The Future is a rich mine. You can afford to be generous."

"Give my money away." She laughed brittlely. "I don't

think so. I pay what the others pay. If the miners want anything more they'll have to go elsewhere. I can always get men who want to work. I need what I make. And if I give it away I'll be right back in their boat, and I will never be there again."

"You don't want to see reason about this, do you? You just go on blindly as if you're untouchable."

"Look." Zoe turned to face him. "I'll compromise with you. I'll pay the price of your doctor. You send for him and I'll see he gets paid. In return . . . I don't want you to talk to me about mines . . . ever again."

Simon was defeated and he knew it. There was no way to prevent Zoe from a disaster of her own making. He felt helpless, and that made him angry.

"And Chloe," Zoe continued. "Why Chloe? Obviously she doesn't want anyone else in her world, and just as obviously she loves and needs you. You're you, Simon, and I'm me. Stop trying to make me into something else. I can't fit your pattern."

"I guess you're right, Zoe. I always regretted that I never tried to help you all those years ago. Maybe that's why Chloe got to me. She reminded me of you in a lot of ways. Except . . . she's not the fighter you were. Maybe that's one of the reasons I decided to fight for her."

"You couldn't have helped me then," Zoe said quietly, her gold eyes holding his. "Don't you see, it just proves I'm right. You can't help Chloe now. Because you don't have the money to do it."

"No. That I don't see. There has to be a way."

"Simon . . . what you're stirring up could lead to violence."

"If that's what it takes."

"Don't be a fool."

"I have my eyes wide open, Zoe. It's you that's blind."

"You're a dreamer, and the world is too hard a place for dreamers. I'm not a dreamer, not anymore. I know how to fight the world, and I have the only weapon it recognizes. I'll fight . . . even you," she added softly. Then she walked away.

Simon continued to watch her as she walked away from him. It was beyond him to understand how they could be worlds apart . . . and still that he loved her more every time they collided. He would have given his soul to rescue Zoe from what he knew was coming.

True to her word, Zoe arranged with Grey to have a portion of money sent monthly to Simon for a doctor for the hospital.

It surprised Simon, but he realized it shouldn't have. No matter how blind Zoe was to other things, she had not been able to ignore her visit to the hospital . . . and her meeting with Anne and Chloe.

"She's being generous," Simon said to Grey. "We ought to be able to get someone to come here, perhaps a young doctor beginning a practice."

"Anyone . . . even another nurse would be a blessing."

"Grey . . . I know you've tried, but . . ."

"Don't bother to say it. You've tried to warn her and I've tried too. It's no use."

"I'm calling the strike, you know that?"

"I know you don't have much of a choice."

"I feel like I'm betraying her somehow."

"Do you want to betray all the others who believe in you?"

"No, I can't."

"Then like I said, you don't have much of a choice. She's going to get roughed up in the fall, but Zoe is not the kind to stay down. She is a magnificent survivor. She's . . ." Grey paused, realizing he was revealing more to Simon than he wanted.

Simon knew this too, but replied evenly, "I'm going on over to the telegraph station and see about sending for the doctor."

Simon walked away from Grey. He had begun to realize how deep the relationship between Zoe and Grey had become. Yet Grey had become his friend as well, and he hated to lose a man as valuable as Grey had made himself. He could not help a sudden sense of . . . was it fear? He had fought Zoe in a hundred ways, had loved her in a million . . . and he didn't want Grey or someone else to be the one to take Zoe's hand when the real battles began. He was jealous . . . and he hated the emotion, because he and Grey had a unique kind of friendship.

There was no way of knowing what was going to happen, but Simon had put plans in motion that could no longer be stopped.

Two weeks later Zoe sat at her desk reading the letter that had been sent to every mine owner, present or absent.

She hadn't realized that Simon had unified the miners so well. But still she didn't worry. It was all a bluff . . . a threat. She refused to be blackmailed into giving up a dime. Besides, she thought, Simon really wouldn't do anything to harm her. She was safe.

She tossed the letter aside and rose from her desk to walk to the window. On the lawn below her, Emily sat on the grass with a book in her hand. Zoe smiled to herself. Her daughter would never know what she had known. She would never be hungry, or afraid if Zoe could help it. She would have all that money could buy.

Having no father would never cause her a problem because a large bank account, Zoe was certain, would take his place.

When her name was spoken, she dropped the curtains and turned around. Grey had been standing in the open doorway for some time. He enjoyed watching Zoe any time, but more so when she was watching Emily. Her face softened and the loving side of her, the side she refused to let the world see, was obvious. He wondered if it was possible to love anyone more than he loved her.

She was elegantly tall, and her glorious hair was elaborately coifed and glowed with life. She was slender as always from the days of work and a determination that would not let her slow her pace. She wore a dress of emerald green that made her skin glow, and Grey's heart beat a little faster.

"Grey?"

"I just got a message from Simon."

"Simon?"

"He wants to know if you can come down to the hospital right away. The note says he has a surprise for you."

"What kind of surprise could he have? Or is it another way to get attention?"

"I don't think so. If Simon says it's a surprise and he wants you to come quick, it must be something you'd appreciate."

"Simon's word has gotten to be pretty strong around Aspen, hasn't it? I do believe, Grey Sinclair, that you're a follower too."

"Not a follower . . . just convinced he has some damn good ideas."

"You like him?"

"Respect is more the word. He's been doing a lot more than you've taken the time to notice."

"Don't preach to me." Zoe laughed. "I get enough of that from Simon."

"Go down and see what he wants. Want me to come along?"

"Yes," she said quickly . . . then she shrugged. "Why not?"

Grey shrugged also, but left the question unanswered. When Emily came rushing into the house, cheeks flushed and eyes sparkling, Zoe asked her if she would mind a short visit to Cara. Always overjoyed to spend time with Cara, whom she loved dearly, Emily gave enthusiastic agreement.

The carriage ride to the flats was a good distance, and both Zoe and Grey were quiet during the ride.

As they reached the flats, Grey discovered the real reason Zoe wanted him along. He became aware of the cold and silent stares of the people. Zoe seemed unaware of them, and of the squalid conditions that surrounded them, but he knew her much too well not to know that she was shaken badly.

As soon as they stopped in front of the hospital, the door was opened and Simon stood framed in it. He waited for them to disembark, but it was with obvious impatience.

Before Zoe and Grey could reach the door, a woman came to stand beside Simon. Zoe paused for a minute, surprised. Then she continued on until she stood before Simon.

"You wanted to see me, Simon?"

"Thanks for coming so quickly, Zoe. Come on in. There's someone I want you to meet."

He took the strange woman by the arm and turned to walk back into the hospital. Zoe was somewhat shocked, and she and Grey paused only long enough to exchange a questioning look; then they followed the two inside.

Simon and the woman were quite a distance away from them, and Zoe could tell at once they were headed for the screened-in corner in which Chloe lay. As they passed behind the screen Zoe became a little impatient.

"Simon, in heaven's name, what is this all about? You're acting pretty mysterious." Zoe came around the screen and then stopped. Simon and the woman stood by Chloe's bed. Chloe's wrist was being held gently by a man whose back was still toward her.

"Zoe"—Simon grinned—"I want you to meet our new doctor and his beautiful wife, who, like an answer to a prayer just happens to be a nurse. I want you to meet Doctor and Mrs. Carrigan."

Zoe stood completely still, unsure if what she thought she'd heard was true. She stared at the young man, who was just laying Chloe's hand down gently and replacing his watch in his vest pocket. Then he stood slowly and turned to face Zoe.

Zoe was paralyzed with shock. This tall handsome man couldn't be . . . he wasn't . . . "Zach?"

She said his name in a disbelieving whisper. "Zach . . . you . . . oh, my God." Tears filled her eyes as Zach took a step toward her and held out his arms. With a cry of delight Zoe threw herself into Zach's arms.

"Zoe, Zoe," Zach said, "I thought I'd never see you again!"

Zoe was swung up in arms that were strong and full of life's vitality. She heard his deep, choked laugh as they hugged each other. Then he held her a little away from him. Both were laughing and crying at the same time.

"Lord, you're beautiful, Zoe."

"And you're so tall," she sobbed.

"I can't believe I could be this lucky."

"All those years, those terrible years!"

"I didn't know where you were. I hunted for you, but I could never find you!"

Grey, Simon, and Zach's wife stood by smiling as the two hugged each other again and again.

"I'll be a son of a gun." Grey grinned. "This is sure one hell of a surprise. From the name I'd be safe in saying that's Zoe's brother."

"Yes, they haven't seen each other since Zach was a kid."

Zoe and Zach finally turned to Simon, who seemed very pleased with himself. His arm about Zoe's waist, Zach extended his hand to his wife.

"Zoe, I want you to meet my wife, Amelia."

Amelia reached out her hand. "Hello, Zoe. I'm so pleased to meet you. You have no idea how much I've heard about you."

"And I'm pleased to meet you too," Zoe said. "You and Zach must come home and stay with me. We have so many years to catch up on."

"Well, Amelia and I will be more than pleased to go with you, but actually we have a place of our own just a short distance from here."

"Here?" Zoe said cautiously. "In the flats?"

"Well, Zoe," Zach said gently, "here's where our work is. This is what Simon hired us for."

"Well . . . there's a little something you should understand," Simon said, "I hired you . . . but Zoe pays your salaries."

"So that puts an end to the argument," Zoe said positively. "You'll come and live with me."

Zach and Amelia exchanged glances, and Zoe suspected resistance. She prepared for battle, and Zach was quick to recognize the old light in Zoe's eyes.

"Let's not go into it today. There's a lot of work we have to do here. Amelia and I will be glad to join you for dinner. I can't wait to get a chance to talk to you. But"—his voice was gentle, but firm—"Amelia and I will settle into our own house. We want to be near our work."

"Of course." Zoe accepted it as best she could, which surprised Simon and Grey.

Simon had a feeling Zoe was in for more than one surprise herself, once she and Zach had time to exchange stories of the past and views of the future.

"I'd really like to go on with my tour of the hospital," Zach said. "Zoe, why don't you take Amelia home with you now and I'll be along for dinner."

Amelia laughed a soft, musical laugh. "And who is going to drag you away from patients when dinnertime comes? You don't know him," Amelia said to Zoe. "He'll remember us somewhere around midnight."

"Now, Amelia." Zach laughed. "It's not as bad as that."

"Shall I tell them how we spent our first wedding anniversary?"

"No, I think not. I'll be fired before they find out what a great medical genius they have here."

There was no one among them who did not sense the love that seemed to emanate from Zach and Amelia every time they looked at each other.

Zoe tried to ignore the jab of envy that twisted within her, and she refused to meet Simon's eyes altogether.

"He is right, Amelia," Zoe said. "Why don't you come home with me now? We can talk. I can tell you enough stories to keep Zach under control for years."

"And I can fill you in on all the details Zach doesn't want you to know."

Zoe turned to her brother and laid a hand on his arm. "Oh, Zach," she said quietly, "it's like a miracle. I'm so glad you're here. All those years . . ." She brushed a tear away.

"I know, Zoe, I know. But somehow we'll try to make up for it."

"Oh, Lord, I should have told you. Eli is here too. He's living with me," Zoe said quickly, her eyes lighting with pleasure.

"This gets better and better."

"There are things that are not so wonderful," Zoe said. "*He's* here too."

"Pa . . . yes, I know. Simon told me about him being here."

"That doesn't bother you?"

"It's past, Zoe."

Zoe wanted to say so much more, but she was too

aware that this was not the time or place.

"We'll keep dinner for you," she said instead.

"Great." He kissed her cheek. Still keeping her eyes from Simon, Zoe left with Grey and Amelia.

In the carriage on the way home Zoe got a chance to assess Amelia more carefully. She seemed delicate at first glance. Very fair of complexion with flaxen hair, and eyes the color of spring lilacs. But Zoe could see also the capable hands that showed no signs of delicacy, and the firmness in her steady look. No, Amelia Carrigan was someone Zoe hoped to know a lot about before dinnertime came.

Simon and Zach stood together in silence for a few minutes after Zoe left. It was Zach who spoke first, and the words were said almost to himself.

"Zoe is certainly different."

"In some ways," Simon said softly, "and in some ways she's still the same little girl from the flats of Georgetown."

"How long have you been in love with her, Simon?" Zach asked quietly without looking at Simon, who took several moments before he answered, as if he were giving the question thought.

"I guess," he replied, "since I first saw her on that wagon train . . . from the time we first met."

"Why don't you ask her to marry you?"

"What makes you think I haven't . . . about a hundred times or so."

"I think there's a lot I'd better catch up on," Zach said thoughtfully.

"Yeah . . . I think there is." Simon looked at Zach and smiled. "Do you suppose you can hold off looking around here for a while? I have a place not too far from here and a bottle if you'd care to have a drink."

"Sounds like a good idea." Zach inhaled deeply. "It also sounds like there's more to this story than I thought."

"A lot more. Some of it you might not be too happy about."

Zach followed Simon from the hospital to the house where Simon lived. After Simon poured a drink for both of them, he set about explaining what had happened from the time Zoe had gone out of Zach's life. He left Brent out completely. Brent was Zoe's business to talk about or not.

Zach listened quietly, without interrupting or asking questions. When Simon finished the story, both men silently contemplated their drinks for a few minutes. Then Zach tossed down the last of his drink and set his glass aside.

"Zoe was always the strongest of us. She had to be. All the weight fell on her shoulders. When she ran away I hated Pa. I prayed for Zoe to come back until my knees were numb. Then I felt I would never see her again, and I turned my hate toward the circumstances that had robbed us of each other. There are things . . . things I can't even tell Zoe."

"It could only be . . ." Simon frowned at his own words.

"Martha. Martha is dead, Simon."

"Lord." Simon breathed raggedly. "It might be best if you told her so—"

"No. Then I would have to explain how . . . and where she died. You see Pa . . . Pa had held Martha too long . . . too hard. She broke. She ran to what Zoe dreaded the most. She needed love desperately, and searched for anyone who would give her even a shadow of it. She found men would ease her heart, even if it was only temporary. She . . . she was stabbed to death by a drunken, angry miner. You see . . . I can't tell Zoe that. She hates enough already."

"It will be a secret with me, Zach. I don't want to see Zoe hurt anymore. How easy it would be for you to retaliate now."

"What's the point?"

"You don't hate your father anymore?"

"I feel sorry for him. He was so caught up in fighting his own guilty soul that he didn't have the ability to love us. But I don't waste hate on him. I think he lives in his own torment, and that's hell enough. In so many ways I pity him. The rules he lived by were too rigid. The book he judges with was not meant to be interpreted with brute force, but with love. Besides that . . . I don't think he understood love . . . and I think he loved Zoe."

"He had a hell of a way of showing it."

"No," Zach said cautiously. Then he turned to look at Simon, and his face was filled with pain. "You don't understand. You see . . . I think he *loved* Zoe."

"Good Lord, that's . . ." Simon faltered in shock.

"That's a terrible thing that happens. Zoe was not his daughter. He wanted to be righteous on one hand; on the other . . . he had a demon riding him. For whatever he did to me, I've forgiven him a long time ago. You see . . . I learned about love . . . from Amelia. Now I have so much there isn't room to hate him anymore."

"I wish Zoe could learn about love. Maybe it would be a way to get rid of some of the ugliness she carries around inside her."

"Maybe I can help."

"I hope so."

"I think I'd better get back to the hospital, Simon. It looks to me like there's an awful lot of work to be done."

"Dr. Shoaf in Boulder has sung your praises, Zach. He says you're one of the best young doctors who ever worked with him."

"I'll have to write and thank him."

"So what are you doing here?"

"What?"

"I should think you would have had the opportunity to go into a big hospital somewhere, or to establish a lucrative private practice in some wealthy town. Why are you doing this for so little money?" Simon laughed. "What we're paying you will barely give you enough to live on."

Zach looked at Simon and smiled. "Why do I have the feeling I could ask you the same questions? We're needed, Simon . . . and I can't turn my back on people who need help so badly because of a little money. Besides, this is like coming home. I've found part of my family."

"A bigger part than you know."

"What's that mean?"

"You've found a sister . . . you also found a niece."

"Zoe has a child!" Zach's eyes lit with pleasure. "Why didn't she say so? That's wonderful!"

"I'm afraid there's a lot more to that story too. But it's

between Zoe and you." Simon smiled. "I can expound on Emily for hours."

"That's my niece's name?"

"Yes. Emily. And she is unique. Pretty and smart and . . ."

"And you're fond of her a bit?" Zach laughed.

"Just a bit."

"Look, Simon . . . I know I should dig in and get to work right now, but I've changed my mind. If you don't mind showing me where he is, I want to go and see my father."

"Of course I'll show you where he lives if you want me to. You're not going to like it, but the man is too stubborn to take any kind of help. I would have helped him if I could."

"You and he . . . talk?"

"Sometimes. He works like he's possessed . . . all for other folks. He goes to any miner's house when someone is sick. How he knows, I can't tell. He goes down in the mines and . . . listens. I can be called into some of the ugliest situations you can imagine, and suddenly he's there helping me dig a miner out of a slide, or burying someone who's died. Somehow he scrapes up food here and there, but he doesn't use much of it. He can be seen carrying sacks to houses at God knows what hours. I don't understand him or his God. I never have. But after what you said, I guess he's trying to atone for this personal sin he's been carrying around."

"I want to talk to him . . . make some kind of peace with him. We both have to live in the same town again, and it won't take long for the whole place to connect our names."

"No . . . I suppose not." Simon appeared hesitant.

"But?"

"I'm just thinking of Zoe."

"She never . . ."

"Zoe pretends he's not alive. She can't forgive or forget what he did to her. I'm surprised she brought him up to you. But I expect she thinks you are going to feel the same way."

"Poor Zoe. It must be pretty hard on her, him being in the same town."

"It's not safe to mention his name around her. I'd better warn you about that. As fanatical as he is, Zoe is just as fanatical about him, even though he can't do her any more harm. Maybe after all these years it's best to let the situation rest."

"You're probably right. I won't mention him to Zoe. But I still want to see him."

"All right. Let's go."

They left, and walked out onto the porch of Simon's house. It had been built on a shallow grade, and from the front porch the flats lay below them. Ramshackle homes lined dirt streets that meandered as if they had never been planned. There was no sign of brightness or color to break the grays and the blacks and the browns of the houses. In fact the absence of color made an onlooker feel the destitution of the place long before he entered it.

Simon pointed to the far edge of the flats, possibly two miles away. "He lives over there. We have to walk it; I don't have a carriage. Besides, folks can get a good look at their new doctor while you get a good look at them."

"I've seen the same faces since I was a little boy. They never change."

"Maybe they will soon."

"You and I know that's hardly possible."

Simon remained thoughtfully quiet. It was too soon to try to explain his plan to Zach. He wasn't sure yet if Zach would be sympathetic to an active form of revolt that might prove violent.

They started to walk. Two miles was little distance to strong men used to physical activity. Along the way Simon stopped to introduce Zach to the work-worn women in their cluttered yards. Their eyes widened in awe at the miracle of having a doctor among them. But Simon knew they would reserve their trust until they were sure he meant to stay. It was hard for any of them to believe a man with the opportunity to leave and find a better life wouldn't do it.

The shacks seemed to get poorer and poorer as they moved along, until they stopped before one that could be called nothing less than a hovel.

"Even our home back in Georgetown wasn't as bad as this," Zach muttered.

"He's too old, and not physically able to work the mines. The owners aren't too considerate of a man who can't give them ten hard hours a day. He does some odd jobs, but he can't make much. What he does make I really don't think he keeps."

"The mine owners ought to pay some kind of pension for men who can't work anymore," Zach said. "How do they expect them to go on living?"

"There's men to replace them. I don't think the owners really care all that much."

"Someone should."

"Yeah." Simon's voice was noncomittal.

Simon walked to the door with Zach close behind him. If Zach was nervous or bothered in any way by the visit to his father, he gave no sign of it.

Simon knocked. "Mr. Carrigan! It's Simon Tremaine."

There was no answer, so Simon knocked again. Still there was no sign of life.

"He could be anyplace."

"Simon . . . would you be offended if I said I'd like to see him alone first?"

"No. Of course not. But it could be hours before he comes back."

"I'd like to wait for a while."

"All right. Can you find your way back uptown?"

"Sure I can. I . . . I won't have any problem, will I?" He gestured toward the suit he wore with a gold watch chain across his breast.

"Not now. News is like a wildfire down here. By now everyone on the flats knows who and what you are. It won't be hard to get transportation once you get back to the hospital."

"Where does Zoe live?"

"Just tell the driver who you want. Everyone knows where Zoe's house is."

"Okay. I'll find my way."

"Then I'll see you sometime later."

"Fine. Don't worry, Simon." Zach smiled. "It's all right."

"All right. But you might be making a big mistake."

"I'll have to take that chance. It's time to close the circle, if you know what I mean. The past can't be carried around all your life. It can get to be too heavy a load."

"I guess you're right. I'll see you later."

Zach stood on the rotting porch for a while, looking about him with eyes that had already seen too much.

Finally, more out of curiosity than anything else, he tried the door . . . and found it unlocked.

He opened the door, stepped inside, and close it behind him. Since the shack had only one very dirty curtainless window, the light was muted to a soft shadowy haze.

The room contained an old wood stove, a table, a chair, one small cupboard, and a bed that had seen the last of its better days many years before. The floor was rough wood, and one lantern hung from the wall near the table.

He walked to the table, on which lay a well-used Bible. It was what he'd expected. He knew it was the only significant object in his father's life. He opened it to the section where records were kept, and saw the neat handwriting . . . his mother's handwriting. It listed the births and deaths in the family.

All this he expected. He didn't expect what he found when he turned the next page. He stood and gazed down at his find in temporary shock.

Zach was certain there had never been any pictures taken of any of them, but now he looked down at a four-by-four picture . . . of Zoe.

She stood gazing off into the distance, her hair loose and blowing about her. Her face was both young and old. She couldn't have been more than fifteen, and she wore a plain dress that she was obviously already growing out of. Zach didn't know exactly why he felt like crying . . . or whom he would cry for.

He closed the bible and slowly turned around to come face-to-face with his father, his stoop-shouldered, emaciated form framed in the doorway.

Zach was so shocked at first by his father's appearance that he could hardly speak. Then a surge of intense pity filled him. Roger Carrigan was paying a terrible price for the guilt that ate him, and Zach knew now there was only one person who had the key to redemption. Just as he knew Roger Carrigan was dying because he could not find forgiveness . . . and maybe never would. For Zach the past was washed clean in the breath of a moment. Whatever he had felt before, it was lost in his compassion for a man whose soul had died . . . to be replaced by fear. He took a step toward Roger and held out his hand.

"Hello, Pa."

Chapter Twenty-three

When Zach walked up the three steps to Zoe's front porch, he was more tired than his appearance revealed. He felt as if he had spent the longest few hours of his life. He carried his jacket over his arm, and his tie was loosened and his vest unbuttoned.

Zoe's brilliant coloring was muted in Zach. His thick hair was a deep wine color, matched by a mustache he'd grown for fun, then kept when Amelia decided he cut quite a dashing figure with it. His eyes were honey brown, deep, and compassionate.

He was about to knock when the door was opened, and he looked down in surprise at the girl who had opened it. She looked up at him with eyes that could only be a gift from one person. Eyes of molten amber gold.

"I'll bet you're Emily." He grinned.

"And you are Uncle Zach," she said with prim precision. "Mommy said I should watch for you. You were almost late for dinner."

If Zach was surprised at her precise and rather adult reply, he did his best not to show it.

"I'm sorry. Is Mommy upset with me?"

"No. She's with Aunt Amelia. They've been talking all day." Emily seemed rather put out about this.

"Do you think I should come in?" he said in a conspiratorial half whisper. "I'm not in trouble, am I?"

"No, Uncle Zach," Emily replied with a quick smile. "You can come in. If you want I'll hang up your coat for you and show you where Mommy and Aunt Amelia are."

"I'd like that. But you don't need to hang up my coat for me." Zach adjusted his tie, buttoned his vest, and put

291

his coat on, all the time aware that Emily had not taken her eyes from him. He laughed to himself, wondering if she was deciding if she liked him or not, and just as surprised at the fact that he really hoped she did.

"Okay, do I look ready?" He pretended to stand at attention while Emily, catching his humor quickly for a little girl nearing ten, pretended to study him intently.

"Yes," she finally announced, "I think you're quite handsome."

"Well, thank you. Pretty ladies don't often compliment me so charmingly. You wouldn't consider marrying me?"

Now she giggled in delight, "Oh, no, I'm too little yet."

"Well, what if I wait for you to grow up?"

"But I won't be grown up for a long time and you'll be old."

"Then, I guess we'll just have to be friends. What do you think?"

"I guess you can be my friend like Uncle Simon and Uncle Grey."

"I'd like that, Emily, I really would. Now that we have decided to be friends, how about taking me to see Aunt Amelia and Mommy."

"Okay." She slipped her small hand in his and led him toward the parlor.

Amelia rose from her seat and came to Zach to kiss him.

"You really did make it for dinner," she teased. "I am in a state of shock."

"How little faith you have, woman," he said with a chuckle as he put his arm about her waist and kissed her cheek. "I'm as hungry as a bear."

Zoe smiled at her brother from across the room. "Eli will be down soon, and I expect Grey to be here. Dinner will be ready in a little while. For now, come and sit down and talk with me."

Zach found a comfortable seat near Zoe, and Emily came to stand beside Zoe's chair.

"Does Eli know I'm here yet?"

"I'm afraid I was too excited not to tell him. He is simply stunned, Zach."

"Lord, he's twenty-six now, isn't he? A grown man."

"Yes," Zoe said softly. "We've lost so much time."

"Let's not think about it anymore, Zoe. It doesn't do any good. Water under the bridge can't be brought back. Whatever happened, we're together now. We can build on that."

"I guess you're right, Zach."

"By the way, your daughter is a real charmer. She talks like a young lady already and she's as pretty as her mother."

"Speaking of charmers," Zoe laughed, "what happened to shy, quiet Zach Carrigan?"

"He met charming and beautiful Amelia Hart and she made a new man out of him."

Before Zoe could respond, the sound of running feet was heard, and in seconds Eli appeared in the doorway, a broad grin on his face. The brothers approached each other with quick steps and wordlessly threw their arms about each other in a rough bear hug. Zoe watched with tears in her eyes. When she had run from Georgetown she had never expected to see either man again. Now her heart swelled with the first real joy she had felt in a long time. Still, she thought about Martha, and hoped that one day they could find out where she was and bring her safely back into what was becoming a whole new family . . . much larger and much stronger.

"You've certainly grown some since I saw you, Eli," Zach said.

"Yeah"—Eli grinned—"and Zoe told me you were a doctor. Boy, you must be rich by now."

"Hardly. I was apprenticed until a couple of years ago. Then I worked with a doctor up near Boulder. I feel pretty lucky to have found my way to Aspen. I'm getting rewarded with more than money."

"C'mon." Eli laughed. "There isn't a better reward than money."

Zach laughed, but it came to him that Zoe was Eli's prime influence and it seemed her desire for money was rubbing off on Eli.

"So what are you doing now?" Zach asked instead of continuing the discussion on money.

"I worked at Cara's restaurant for a while, until I got

apprenticed to Mr. Morgan. Now I'm second in line at the telegraph office."

"Well, congratulations. That sounds pretty good."

"Something smells good too." Grey's voice came from the doorway.

"Now that you're here it's time to eat," Zoe announced.

"Where's my girl first," Grey commanded.

Emily, who had remained unusually quiet, now laughed and ran to Grey, who caught her up in his arms. "Now," Grey said, "we can eat."

Dinner was a pleasant affair, with all of them putting forth every effort they could manage to make it so. Eli explained his work to an interested Zach, who in turn regaled them with stories of the assorted things he'd seen and done since he'd left Georgetown.

"By the way, Zoe," Zach said lightly, "I don't think I can pay you back yet."

"Pay me back, for what?"

"For the money you left me when you left Georgetown. Stelle made sure I got it. No one knew better than me how hard it was for you to earn it and that it was every dime you had in the world."

"Zach . . . I never left any money." Zoe smiled. "I guess Stelle was taking another Carrigan under her wing."

"But now you're paying my salary."

"That will be money well spent."

"Really? Are you so sure?"

"I am." She grinned. "Besides, it will keep Simon temporarily satisfied, and that I consider a very good investment."

"Simon? Satisfied?" Grey chuckled. "I think it's going to take more than a doctor. Simon has a lot of very big prospects in mind."

"Simon is going to have to learn he can't have everything he wants. He's also going to learn that no one is ever going to thank him for what he's doing. They won't thank him or care. He'll find out when the day comes when he needs them."

"I don't think Simon does it for that reason, Zoe," Grey said.

"Simon thinks he can save the world, and he doesn't even know that the world doesn't want to be saved. He thinks to build some kind of nobility into the poor and teach them to work together. It won't happen, first because they are as far from noble as they can get, and second because they won't work together. Simon doesn't know it . . . but I do."

There was a silence while everybody concentrated on his or her plate. Everyone except Emily, who was quite tired of grown-up talk anyway.

"Mommy?"

"What, Emily?"

"Now that we have company, do I have to go to bed early?"

"I'm sure we can let you stay up awhile longer. You don't get a new aunt and uncle every day." She looked from Emily to Amelia. "Are you sure I can't convince you and Zach to stay here?"

"I'm sorry, Zoe," Zach said, "but I've had our few belongings delivered and I hate to leave the house unoccupied all night with all our belongings there. Besides, our house is closer to the hospital and I want to get to work early in the morning."

"Well, I'd like to help as much as I can. Amelia, if you will make a list of what you need for your house, I'll see that you get it."

"Thank you, Zoe. I don't mean to sound ungrateful, but Zach and I really have everything we need."

"But you will come here often?" Zoe said quickly.

Grey said nothing. He felt the urgency in Zoe, and realized she had few women friends. At the same moment it registered on him that she was lonely.

"Of course, as often as I possibly can," Amelia replied. "But your brother's quite dedicated. When he gets into his work, time is something he doesn't understand."

"Zoe," Zach said, "you will let Emily come and stay with us off and on, won't you? I think we are on the road to being friends, and I'd like to know your daughter better. How would you like that, Emily?"

"Oh, yes." Emily was enthusiastic. Any new adventure was fine with her.

But Zoe's face had frozen in an aborted attempt to smile. Grey knew that she had shielded Emily carefully from the children who lived on the flats. She had built a protective wall around Emily, and the flats were a threat. Grey was certain the doors to Zoe's past would never be opened for Emily to see, and it worried him. Zoe, of all people, should know that no one could keep the world away, and especially with a girl as intelligent and curious as Emily. Zoe wanted Emily to see only the bright, shiny side of life. He knew this just as he knew Emily would not conform to her mother's will, that one day she would want to taste life on her own terms and make her own choices. Emily was more like Zoe than Zoe realized.

Reluctantly Zoe stood in the doorway and waved good-bye to Zach and Amelia as they left. Eli had gone out after the meal, and Grey had jokingly mentioned the fact that Eli was interested in a girl somewhere.

Once Zoe had seen that reluctant Emily was tucked safely in bed, she joined Grey while he sipped a drink before he left.

The living room was bathed in a mellow glow from the gaslights, but Grey was already in the process of extinguishing a number of them, leaving only one or two burning. He carried his glass in one hand and was dimming the lights with the other.

"It's a beautiful night," Grey said. "Let's go out on the back porch. I'd like to talk to you for a while before I leave."

"All right."

"Want me to pour you a glass of wine?"

"No. I don't want anything," Zoe replied. Grey watched her walk ahead of him as they went out on the shadowed back porch.

The porch, built to Zoe's plans, extended along the entire back of the house, and from it you could see only the mountains in the distance and the silvery sheen of moonlight across the water of the river.

Several steps led to a back garden. Grey had been surprised when Zoe first hired a worker to tend the garden. But he'd soon realized why. Zoe had lived too long where little grew and no beauty existed. The garden and the wide back porch were her places of escape . . . for, literally, she was turning her back on everything.

She walked to the steps and sat down on the top one, while Grey sank into one of the several comfortable chairs Zoe had placed randomly along the porch. Zoe sat in the beam of pale light where Grey could watch her, while he sat in enough shadow that she could not see him quite as clearly.

They had sat here together more than one night, and Grey valued these quiet times. He wished they could go from here to a room they shared and close the door. But he knew this time was short, so he savored it carefully.

Zoe was quiet for a long while, and at first Grey was content to leave her to her thoughts and watch her . . . but eventually he began to wonder just where her thoughts wandered.

"A penny for your thoughts," he said quietly.

"What . . . oh . . ." Zoe was brought out of her reverie abruptly at the sound of Grey's voice. "I was thinking that it really is some kind of miracle that the three of us have found each other. And I was wishing . . ."

"What, Zoe. What were you wishing?"

"I wish I knew if Martha was somewhere near. If I could find her, we could really be a family."

"Maybe it will happen. I could at least try and check to see if she's still in Georgetown."

Zoe turned to look at him. He was only a dark form in the shadows. She smiled. "You are so good to me, Grey. I don't know how I ever got along without you before or why I'm so lucky."

"I'm glad you appreciate my numerous fine qualities," he said lightly. He enjoyed the response of her soft laugh. "Your brother is a very fine man. Not too many men would do what he's doing."

"I just hate to see them living down there. It's like going back. I don't understand him."

No, Grey thought, you don't. I wish you did. "It's not so bad, Zoe. They'll get along better than you think. I have a feeling the people there are going to be so grateful that they'll see to his care and his safety."

"He could do so much more . . ." She paused.

"For himself you mean?"

"For himself . . . for his wife, for any children they might have."

"Amelia looks pretty happy to me."

"They haven't been married that long," Zoe said dryly.

"Zoe," Grey said, softening his words with a gentle voice, "they might be happy just because they have each other. Maybe . . . maybe that's enough for both of them."

Zoe didn't answer. Her thoughts had turned inward. She had felt she'd had control of the strange mood she'd been in all afternoon, but now something dark and angry seemed to pull at her.

She had a nice home, money to buy whatever she chose, a daughter whom she loved to distraction and who happily loved her in return. Besides that, she was slowly acquiring the power to bring down Brent Dewitt. Her world should have been bright. Yet a heavy depression held her.

She felt disorganized, as if there was something unfinished, something she needed tugging at her.

The night was balmy, and the sound of the river and call of the night creatures strummed her senses. The moon, high and full, did little to help her mood as it washed the scene before her with light. She felt intensely alone.

Grey could sense Zoe's withdrawal and her melancholy mood. He set his glass beside the chair and rose quietly. He sat down beside her on the steps, close enough that their shoulders touched and the scent of her perfume reached him on a breath of night air.

Zoe turned to look at him, feeling suddenly lost and desolate, and not knowing why.

Grey knew Zoe was wrong about so many things. He knew her stubbornness and her blind determination would not allow her to leave a road once she had started down it. He knew she could be brash, opinionated, and often hard. Yet he knew the gentle, loving Zoe as well. He knew that inside, Zoe bled now, and would always bleed from wounds inflicted so long ago. He knew that he wanted to protect her from any more hurt, no matter who was right and who was wrong.

Zoe could see the warmth in Grey's eyes and the compassion. On this lonely, beautiful night she needed consolation. She suddenly felt desperately unable to cope.

"About the letter, Zoe . . . I got an answer."

"Letter?" Zoe had momentarily forgotten.

"To Brent Dewitt."

"And?"

"He wants to know if he can invest in Trident in small pieces."

"What does he mean small pieces?"

"From what he says, a few hundred dollars at a time."

"I don't understand."

"Read between the lines. The man is running out of money. I've sent someone to look the situation over and find out just how bad off he is. If I'm right, then you don't really have to do anything. Brent Dewitt may have caused his own downfall. It would . . . sort of set you free, you might say." Silently Grey prayed that knowing Brent was penniless might be enough to satisfy Zoe. If he could get her away from this obsession, perhaps she would begin to concentrate on finding fulfillment in her own life.

"You think that's enough?"

"Zoe, the man lost his wife. If he's lost his wealth as well, there's not much more to do to him."

"There is a great deal more to do to him," she said in a half whisper. Grey hated the cold look on her face. He turned to her and took hold of her shoulders. He could see surprise in her eyes.

"Zoe . . . look," he began. "I know . . . and believe me I understand how you feel. But . . . try and trust me. You've brought him down. Don't destroy him. You're not going to enjoy it like you think. It's not going to change what you went through, and it's not going to make the hurt you felt any less. It's not going to erase one memory. It's time to let go. Can't you see that there is so much in your life that's more important? Can't you see"—his voice softened—"that there's so much love? You've got both your brothers back. You have Emily. You have enough money to live well. You don't need to do this."

Zoe was momentarily surprised. Grey had always kept

his opinions to himself. He had always kept control and never denied Zoe his help or support. Now he sounded much like Simon, and it jarred something within her. Something deep inside her recognized the truth, just as her pride denied it.

For the first time since Grey had met her, he saw something new in her eyes. Something he'd never believed he would see. Fear. At the same moment he realized what she was afraid of. She was scared to let go. Scared because it would leave a void she did not know how to fill. He realized Zoe had been living on this emotion for so long, she just didn't know how to let go of it.

"Zoe," he said softly, "don't you know yet that all you have to do is reach out?"

To Grey, Zoe was always beautiful. But she was more beautiful now when her vulnerability was reflected in her eyes. He saw beneath the surface of the cool woman who fought life like a gladiator, to the young girl who cried out for the love she had never tasted.

To Zoe, Grey was a dark shadow between her and the light. Unable to see his face, or read his eyes as she was usually able to do, she could only rely on senses, senses that felt the velvet of his voice, the gentleness of his words, and the comfort in his meaning.

Something within her vibrated to the touch of this new side of Grey. It was a moment when all the walls she had so carefully erected began to crack.

The combination of her own loneliness, the magic of a warm moonlit night, and Grey's masculine appeal set her equilibrium askew.

The strong willpower she always depended upon deserted her. Subconsciously she searched for comfort, for something stable . . . and on this moonlit night Grey seemed like stability itself.

Grey drew her to him. If he was momentarily surprised at the lack of resistance, he didn't question the pleasure he felt.

Their lips met gently, and Grey felt a surge of protective need. He'd waited and wanted Zoe for so long, yet he didn't know her mind. He didn't know what she truly wanted. He knew his own need, but he didn't want to be a temporary balm that would last for but one moment of weakness. He wasn't too sure Zoe knew her own mind either. He was not blind. He knew something powerful existed between Zoe and Simon. At least he knew Simon loved Zoe. But Simon was pushing Zoe away from him with every move he made.

Grey had decided long ago that there was nothing about Zoe he could change. Simon had never learned that lesson. Grey wanted to protect Zoe, to shield her from anything that could hurt her. Simon wanted to change her, make her see things the way he saw them. Grey was reasonably sure Zoe wouldn't conform to either of their expectations. Zoe was Zoe.

He felt Zoe stir in his arms, felt her mouth soften beneath his, and sensed a strong need . . . but a need for what?

"Zoe," he said softly against her hair as he broke the kiss but continued to hold her. She was warm and soft and vitally feminine in his arms. "You know I love you, don't you? By now you should, everyone else does."

He could feel her body tremble, and heard the intake of breath and a muffled sound that was almost a sob. "Oh, Grey, I need you."

They were words he'd wanted to hear for years, yet now the sound was hollow. Even the words "I love you" were too hard for Zoe to say. Yet, in a way he understood, and he hated the fact that he did. Zoe had never learned anything about love. She didn't know how to love anyone except Emily, Eli, and Zach, and that love did not make the kind of demands on her she couldn't face.

Momentarily frustrated, Grey released her shoulders and rose. He walked down the steps and stood with his back to her, inhaling a deep gulp of night air. "Jesus, Zoe . . ."

But Zoe was feeling a sudden sense of panic. If Grey rejected her, if he walked out of her life, she would have no one who cared, who understood. She too rose from the porch step and went to him. She came up behind him, and could hear his audible gasp as she put her arms about him and pressed her face against the breadth of his hard-muscled back.

"Oh, Grey, don't be angry at me. I don't know . . . I don't understand . . . Oh"—her voice grew choked—"I don't know how to love anyone, Grey . . . I'm so afraid."

As far as Grey knew, this was the first time in Zoe's life she had ever admitted to herself or to anyone else that she was afraid of anything. He turned to face her again. Tears glistened like silver in the pale light, and Grey could feel them tear at him. Of course she didn't know, of course she was afraid. Love had never given her anything but pain.

He also realized this was a rare moment for Zoe. To admit her vulnerability she must be tormented by her own fear.

He reached out with large callused hands and cupped her face gently. Could he give her enough love to fill her heart? Could he teach her that love was unselfish and did not have to be followed by pain?

He bent to kiss her cheeks, tasting the salt of her tears. Gently he drew her to him and cradled her against him.

His arms were a strong haven for Zoe, who had never clung to anyone else for strength. She wanted him to hold her until the terrible feeling of panic passed.

"I know, Zoe, I know," he whispered gently, "but you don't have to be afraid anymore." He held her a little away from him. "Zoe, I want to love you. I know you're afraid to trust anything or anyone, and that's all right. I can understand. I only want you to give me a chance to show you that love can be so much more. I'm not asking you to love me yet, Zoe. I know it's too soon. I'm only asking you to let me love you . . . let me love you." His voice died to a whisper as he bent to taste her lips again.

With a desperation born of a need she could not understand, Zoe surrendered to his kiss, returning it with the same will that had driven her all her life. Grey was a lifeline. Grey could wipe out all the bitterness. If a small angry voice deep within accused her of using Grey's love, she ignored it.

Grey gathered her close to him, crushing her against his chest, feeling the warmth of the soft curves of her body fit perfectly against his. The kiss deepened and Zoe's body, hungry for the touch of once-known passion, grew warm and responsive. She wanted . . . yes, she wanted.

When Grey released her lips he stepped back, her hand in his. She read his eyes, and did not have to speak to answer his question. They walked into the house together.

They stood in Zoe's bedroom in the mellow glow of one small lamp. He could not believe that his hands were shaking as he began to undress her.

Grey, having been married to a woman he had deeply loved, had learned long ago that the gentle hand and the considerate touch were important. This was something he had dreamed of for a long time, and he didn't want to spoil it in any way. Besides, the thread that held them together was as fragile as a spider's web.

Right now Zoe needed him, and he wanted to fulfill that need. He reached out and lifted her head gently by the chin, forcing her to look up at him. For a long moment they remained suspended, locked in each other's gaze. Then again he bent and took her mouth with his, but in a new, slightly more forceful way.

She became completely aware of the all-encompassing hunger that pulled at her, body and soul. It was as if he wanted to reach inside and wipe away thoughts of anyone but him.

His hands caressed the length of her body as he removed each article of clothing very carefully. There was a reverence and an intensity in his touch.

A thousand thoughts that tormented Grey's mind gave way to just one. His lips played across her shoulders as he drew her against him. Her arms slid up around his neck and her lips yielded to the intensity of his.

Then she was helping him undress, and he fought his own wild impatience. He would not rush this if it killed him.

They stood together, the heat of their bodies melding them as they kissed slowly. Grey's lips found every soft inch of her as they slowly moved to the bed.

Zoe felt as if she were away from her body, an onlooker, watching the scene with detached interest while the two on the bed continued to discover every tender spot, every exposed nerve.

But Grey was losing his fragile hold on control. His mouth parted hers in fierce, hungry kisses that left Zoe breathless.

On the wide bed Grey drew her so close she could feel the thunder of his heart. His hands moved over her now, taking possession without hesitation, yet they were gentle and her body responded. A soft, rather forlorn moan escaped her as she answered with all the vigor in her trembling body.

When he rose above her she looked up into his eyes, and he locked his gaze with hers, refusing to free her as slowly he slid deep within her.

Zoe's eyes fluttered closed and she reached for him with a low groan. He crushed her to him and they moved together. In this moment they took and gave until the surging passion swelled about them, lifting them from reality for this brief span. Zoe quivered beneath him, turning her face to his when her name escaped him with a quick sighing urgency. She answered his deep thrusts with all the vigor in her trembling body, and tried to answer the twisting currents that swept them away, thrusting them upward and upward until the height was dizzying and an explosive climax claimed them.

Grey rolled to his side, taking his weight from her, but he drew her against him and held her. He could feel tears against his shoulder, and he rose to look down into her eyes.

"You're crying . . . why?" he said gently.

"I don't know . . . I don't know," she sobbed, and clung to him.

"Shhh, Zoe . . . it's all right." He caught her face in one large hand and forced her to look at him. "It's all right," he said gently, understanding more than she. "Give us time. Contrary to popular belief, miracles don't happen overnight." His voice was soothing. "I couldn't love you more than I do right now. I love you enough for two people. I'll be here, Zoe." His voice was tender. "I promise."

"Teach me to love, Grey," she whispered.

"I will. I said miracles don't happen overnight, but they happen. For me, just holding you is a miracle. I'll give you all I have to give. We'll learn to trust together, and after that love will happen."

"I'll hold you to that promise, Grey Sinclair." She smiled through her tears.

"I want you to. You have to know deep in your heart that you only have to reach out no matter where or when, and I'll be there to take your hand. I want you to know you can trust me."

"And you have always trusted me, haven't you?" Her voice was thick with a kind of wonder. This kind of love was a revelation to her.

"I've loved you for so long it's hard now to remember a time when I didn't. When you didn't fill my life with everything I've ever wanted."

"Even with my sometimes willful ways and bad disposition?" She smiled.

"Even then." He chuckled in response. "Although there were a few times when my patience was stretched as far as it would go."

"Grey, do you think I'm wrong when—"

"Shhh." He bent to kiss her lightly. "I don't want to talk about right or wrong, or good and bad. Not tonight. Tonight we've closed the door on the rest of the world. You're here in my arms, Zoe." He looked at her seriously now, a small frown between his brows, "And there is not a damn thing I'll let touch you again. As long as there's a breath in my body, I won't let you be hurt again."

For the first time in her life, Zoe began to believe there was something and someone to stand between her and the problems that might come. She felt . . . relief . . . and pleasure and a new kind of happiness. But . . . she could not name any of her emotions love. She knew it . . . Grey knew it. But what she could give was all he would ask, for now. Eventually he would break down that last barrier of insecurity and fear . . . eventually she would be able to say she loved him too. He would teach her step by step that love was not a taking thing.

"Grey . . . I . . . I don't want to get married," she began hesitantly, hoping her words didn't hurt. But Grey had expected them.

"I know."

"Do you understand?"

"That you're afraid yet? You didn't think I was pushing you, did you?"

"No . . . but . . ."

"But"—he laughed softly—"you thought the honorable thing to do after compromising my honor was to make an honest man out of me."

"Don't joke with me."

"I'm not. But I don't believe it's just a gold band and some words spoken that make people married. As far as I'm concerned, all it takes to make you part of me is for you to feel that way. In the meantime, a ring and some words won't be enough for me either. I'll wait, until you're ready. You see . . . I love you and I want you on any terms you want to make."

"Is it enough for you?"

"I never said it was enough, but it's a step in the right direction."

"Grey . . ."

"No more talk about what we can't help yet," he said softly. Then he bent to kiss her. "Let's see about things we can do something about."

Both knew that their union and the emotions controlling it were fragile, but they both clung to it, because they were more afraid to let go.

A long time after Grey slept, Zoe slid from the bed quietly so she would not waken him. Wearing only her nightgown, she crossed the room and turned the lamp off, shrouding the room in darkness. Then she left the room and went out on the back porch.

She sat down on the top step, hugging her knees, and contemplated the huge silver moon that hung low in the night sky. Soon it would set and the dawn would come.

She had refused to face her questions until now.

Now she began to consider the questions as honestly as it was possible to do. She began to question herself . . . and she didn't like the answers.

She thought of Roger Carrigan and the accusations he had continually thrust at her from the time she could remember. She thought of the kinds of friends she had chosen over the years.

She thought of Simon and the powerful passion she had tasted in his arms. She had been afraid of it then. She was still afraid of it.

She wondered if Roger Carrigan had not been able to see to the depths of her soul. Was she the kind of woman he had always said she was? She had found physical pleasure in Simon's arms . . . and had found pleasure in Grey's too. What did that make her?

She hadn't given Grey the deepest part of her because she couldn't. She could not reach into that dark well and find that rare emotion called love.

She thought of Brent, and realized she had never given him love either. Was it impossible! Was she the kind of woman incapable of that emotion? Was it enough if her body found pleasure? The questions tore at her over and over again until she wanted to cry.

She wanted release from the terrible tormenting self-recriminations. She searched for a place to put the blame. Brent and his deception. All she needed was to complete his destruction and it would finally set her free. Then and only then could she find peace.

She felt the weight of an overwhelming depression, and could not stop the tears. She bent forward and rested her head on her knees and wept, never understanding why.

Behind her in the shadow of the doorway Grey stood listening for several long moments. Then he stepped out on the porch and went to Zoe, silently gathering her up in his arms.

He carried her back to the bed they shared, and wordlessly rocked her in his arms without talking. It was not the time for words . . . and not the time for questions he was afraid he already knew the answers to.

After a while, from sheer exhaustion, she slept. But it was dawn before Grey could find sleep again.

Chapter Twenty-four

The next day, to everyone's surprise, Zoe took her carriage and made a trip with Emily to Zach's house.

Zach was already at the hospital, and Amelia was putting the finishing touches on her morning's work before she joined him. Amelia was both surprised and delighted to see Zoe at her door, and more so when she saw Emily beside her.

"Zoe, what a nice surprise. Come in. Zach is gone, I'm afraid."

"That's all right, Amelia. It's you I wanted to talk to anyway."

When Amelia closed the door, she paused long enough to study Zoe's face closely. It was soon obvious to her that Zoe had slept little, and her face looked drawn and pale even though she tried to smile for Amelia's benefit.

"Then let's go to the kitchen after I show you the rest of the house. It will only take a minute to brew us some tea. I'm sorry the house is such a shambles, but I'm going to live from boxes until I have time to put everything away." She smiled over her shoulder as she led Zoe toward the kitchen. "At least we have the table and chairs, some of my dishes, and our bed in place. I guess everything else will just have to fall into place in time. For now Zach and the hospital are more important."

Zoe followed slowly, letting her eyes drift about. The house itself was only four rooms, one of which Zach intended to use as an office. It left the living room, one bedroom, and a kitchen. It was small. Rough wood framed the doorway, and the floor was bare, long ago worn smooth by the passage of many feet. The walls were dingy, and if they had ever seen a coat of paint, it was gone now. It reminded her much of Grey's house before she had acquired the money to change it.

Each room boasted only one window, and they were desperately in need of a cleaning. In the small living room a couch and chair had been placed with a braided oval rug between them. What caught Zoe's attention were the stacks and stacks of books that seemed to take up most of the available space.

"Zach is going to have to build a lot of shelves to take care of his books. There's plenty more in the other room. His reading habit is insatiable."

"He never seemed to like school when we were kids," Zoe said, half to herself.

Amelia looked at Zoe, whose eyes were still on the massive stacks of books, and the look was filled with a kind of pity she knew Zoe would never understand or tolerate. Zach had told her so much of Zoe's past, yet Amelia sensed there was even more hurt there than Zach knew. She wanted to know Zach's sister better . . . maybe to find a way to reach out to her.

Emily's eyes too were riveted on the books. Then she raised her eyes to Amelia. "Are there any books there I can read?"

"You like to read?" Amelia asked.

"I'm the best reader in my class at school," Emily said proudly. "Mrs. Thomas is a good teacher."

"Well, I brought all my books from home and I think among them there's . . . ummm, let me think. I think there's some Bible stories . . . and some fairy tales, and Zach has lots of adventure stories. Why don't you just sort out what you think you can read while your mother and I have some tea. Oh, by the way, there's some cookies if you like."

"Cookies and books." Zoe laughed. "You have found your way to Emily's heart."

"Come on, I'll get them for her. Then we can talk while she's occupied."

After settling Emily with a plate of cookies and a mountain of books, Amelia and Zoe left the girl to her choices.

Seated at the small wooden kitchen table, Zoe watched

Amelia prepare tea. Amelia was well aware of Zoe's intense scrutiny, and after she had put the kettle on to boil she turned to Zoe with a smile.

"I don't think you came all the way down here just for some tea. Did you, Zoe?"

"Actually . . . no." Zoe smiled. "I guess I thought I would have more chance convincing you to change your mind than I had with Zach."

"Change my mind? About what?"

"About coming to live with us . . . Eli, Em, and me."

Before Amelia answered she paused, then went to sit opposite Zoe at the table.

"Zoe . . . I don't think Zach will consider it, and there are a lot of reasons. One is that Zach is a man full of . . . compassion and humanity and love. He also remembers well."

"Remembers? I should think his memories alone would make him want to stay as far from here as possible."

"No one," Amelia said softly, "can change anything if they turn their back on it."

Zoe sighed deeply and clasped her hands before her on the table. "He sounds like Simon. Wanting to change things that can't be changed. Why are they such dreamers? Are you a dreamer too?"

"Zoe, I was born and raised in a place as terrible as this. In the coal-mine towns of Pennsylvania. I know hunger and hurt as well as anyone . . . as well as Zach. For a while Zach felt like you do, but you see, when he became a doctor he realized that someone had to try and do something. He felt he was given so much that he had to try to return some of it."

"But that doesn't mean you have to live here!"

"We discussed that. It's what we chose to do."

"But if you have children, do you want them to be raised here?"

"We won't have any," Amelia said quietly.

"You don't want children?"

"I didn't say that. I said we won't have any."

"I don't . . ."

"I can never have children. Zach knew that when he married me. It . . . it was something that happened a long time ago. You see, Zoe . . . you are luckier than you can imagine."

Zoe was momentarily silent as what Amelia said reverberated within her. She thought for just a moment what she would have done if she didn't have Emily to fill her life.

"I was a nurse in a very small town when Zach came along," Amelia continued. "Together we fought a lot of battles, both his and mine. I think we can say we've won."

"You've won? And you came to this?"

"Can you imagine how many lives we can touch, how much . . . thanks we can give for all we have? Can you imagine how many children we can have?"

"I don't think you can change anything. No one will thank you for your sacrifices," Zoe said defensively.

Amelia could see the battle Zoe fought, and there was no way to give Zoe the answers she seemed to be searching for. She rose and began to prepare the tea.

"I suppose," Amelia said thoughtfully, "we don't consider it like that. Zach loves what he does, and I love being with him, sharing his work and his life. I love seeing him enthusiastic and . . . committed, I guess. I really believe Zach would rather touch one life here than work in the wealthiest place in the world."

"I suppose," Zoe said as Amelia placed the cup of tea before her. "There is no use trying to convince Zach any differently."

"No, I think not." Amelia paused. "Zoe?"

"Yes?"

"I'm not prying into your affairs, and I never want to ask any questions you aren't prepared to answer. If I do, just tell me to mind my own business. But . . . I really want us to be friends. Zach loves you so much and . . . he does want to share Emily with you. Can you see your way clear to let Emily come to us once in a while? I know Zach would love it, and I would be grateful. It . . . it's as close to his own child as he will ever get."

Zoe wanted to shout no to this, but she couldn't. Her love for Zach and her deep desire to keep him close would brook no refusal.

"I never thought I would see Zach again," Zoe said. "If

Emily's coming here will make him happy, I don't see why she can't come once in a while. If you both promise to come to my house as often as you can."

"When I can pry Zach away from work, I'd be delighted."

Before Zoe could speak again, Emily came into the kitchen carrying a book.

"Look, Mommy . . . Peter Pan. The story you used to tell me." She showed Zoe the book she'd brought with her.

"You can take the book home if you like," Amelia said. "I'm sure Zach would want you to have it, Emily, if you enjoy it that much."

Emily looked quickly at her mother, who smiled and nodded. Then Emily turned her bright smile to Amelia. "Thank you. I shall be very careful with it. Will you tell Uncle Zach thank you too?"

"Of course I will." Amelia laughed. "Zoe, I cannot believe what a delightfully intelligent treasure you have here. What a wonderful job you have done."

"Don't talk too soon," Zoe said lightly. "She has her obstinate days as well." Zoe turned to Emily. "Aunt Amelia has asked you to come visit her and Uncle Zach sometime. Would you like that?"

"Oh, yes . . . I can read all your books."

"And we will have great fun together," Amelia promised Emily with a quick wink.

"For now we have to go. I promised Cara a visit too," Zoe said. "Amelia, I'm glad I came."

"So am I. Come again soon."

Amelia walked to the door and watched them leave. Only then did her smile fade. She went back into the house to get her shawl, and then walked to the hospital.

She went inside the hospital door and searched until she saw Zach bending over a patient. When she stopped at his side, he glanced up and gave her a quick smile and winked. "Be with you in a minute."

"Don't rush," Amelia answered as she moved away to hang up her shawl. She began at once to roll up her sleeves. Then she took an apron from behind the door and put it on. By that time Zach approached her, kissed her cheek, then grinned.

"I won't tolerate my nurses being late for work."

"Even when the nurse loves you something terrible?" she half whispered.

"Well, if that claim comes with some proof later, I might be enticed to forget your tardiness." He chuckled.

"Oh, doctor," she said, smothering her own laughter. "I fully intend to prove it to you just as soon as I can get my hands on you when there's nobody around whose temperature you have to take."

"What an impudent, forward creature you are."

"And you love it," she chided teasingly.

"You appeal to the wicked side of my nature."

"Is that all I appeal to?"

"That's another thing we'll have to discuss in private."

"Well, if we don't get to work, there won't be a moment of privacy until midnight. Oh, by the way, I was late because I had company."

"Company? Now don't tell me you're seeing someone behind my back."

"Don't push your luck, Doc. It was your sister."

"Zoe?"

"That surprises you?"

"I don't know . . . I guess it does a little," he said thoughtfully. "What did she want?"

"Zach . . . I don't know why, but Zoe seems to be so . . . so unhappy."

"Unhappy. She didn't seem to be that way at dinner last night. She was her old tough, determined—"

"Lonely," Amelia said quietly.

"Lonely? With Emily, Eli, and everyone else? How do you come to that conclusion?"

"I don't know. Just a woman's intuition, I guess."

"Amelia . . ."

"Let's talk about it later, Zach. Right now we'd better get busy."

"Right," Zach agreed. But Amelia was reasonably sure Zoe would be on her brother's mind all day.

Zoe and Emily rode slowly home after spending several hours with Cara. Emily's enthusiastic chatter made up for Zoe's introspective silence. But it lasted only for a short time before a very quick Emily noticed the change in her mother.

"Mommy . . . are you mad at me?"

"Mad! Good heavens, Emily, no, I'm not mad at you. Why should I be mad at you? You were very well behaved today."

"Do you like Aunt Amelia, Mommy?"

"Do you?"

"Oh, yes. I think she's really nice. And Uncle Zach is a lot of fun."

"Uncle Zach is special in a lot of ways."

"So's Uncle Eli."

Zoe laughed again. It seemed Emily loved everybody. It brought a thick lump to her throat. Amelia had told her she was lucky, and when she looked down into her daughter's trusting, upturned face, she knew what Amelia meant.

Still, she felt the same heaviness of spirit, as if something was pending. Something she had to finish. The thought of Emily's birth certificate, stamped as the law required—"Illegitimate, Father Unknown"—could still crush her and stir a wild fury deep inside her. It was Brent who was unfinished. It was Brent who still made her world dark. Brent whose memory ruined everything . . . whose memory she had to destroy once and for all.

When Emily and Zoe entered the house, it was a surprise to Zoe to find Grey there. He usually did not appear until supper time. And the look in his eyes was one of worry. Grey found it hard to handle things that would distress Zoe.

"Grey, what is it? What's wrong?"

"It's Eli."

"Eli! What . . ." Her face had gone pale. Past losses and past pain made every situation bigger than it was.

"They brought him home about an hour or so ago. No one knew where you went, so they called me."

"He's been hurt! How bad?"

"No, he's not been hurt. He's just sick . . . really sick."

Now she knew why Grey was so affected. He'd lost a wife and child to cholera and he was scared.

"I'll go up to him right now. Grey—"

"I've already sent for Zach."

"Thanks." Zoe started up the stairs, and Emily started up behind her, causing Zoe to whirl about, a new kind of fear dancing in her eyes. "No! Emily, you stay here with Uncle Grey." She turned her eyes to Grey, who understood completely.

"I'll take care of her . . . don't worry," he said.

Zoe nodded and raced up the steps. Emily watched her go, then turned to walk back to Grey. Within minutes a breathless Zach arrived.

"Grey, somebody sent for me. Is Zoe all right?"

"She's fine. I just brought Eli home. He's sick as a kid can be. I don't know what's wrong with him, but he can't seem to breathe and he's vomiting and running a pretty bad fever."

Zach said nothing more; he simply raced up the stairs Zoe had just taken.

Inside the bedroom Zach found Zoe bent over the bed. When he approached he could see Grey had not exaggerated. Eli was extremely sick.

Though Zoe had put a blanket over him, he was still shaking. His face was gray and his teeth chattered. His eyes seemed heavy-lidded and glazed. Zach sat down on the edge of the bed and took Eli's wrist. His pulse was racing.

"Eli, how long have you been this sick?"

"All . . . all day," Eli gasped.

"Why didn't you come home!" Zoe cried anxiously.

"I . . . thought," Eli groaned through gritted teeth as a convulsion gripped a stomach long emptied, "it would . . . uhh . . . go away. Maybe . . . it was . . . something I ate."

Zoe looked across the bed at Zach, who shook his head negatively. "This is not caused by something he ate. Zoe, go down and make a little tea."

"Zach, I don't—"

"Don't argue with the doctor." Zach tried to smile to ease her anxiety. "He's my brother too. Go on, Zoe."

"All right." Zoe was reluctant to leave, but she did.

Downstairs she found that Grey and Emily were just as anxious as she was.

"What is it, Zoe? What did Zach say?"

"He said make some tea."

Grey and Emily followed Zoe into the kitchen, and waited nervously as she began to make tea.

"What's really wrong with Eli?" Grey repeated. He didn't like the look in Zoe's eyes.

"I don't know. I think his doctor wanted to examine him in private."

"You think it's serious?"

"Eli really looks terrible and he's running a terrible fever. I'm no nurse, but I know he's a lot sicker than Zach wants to say . . . and a lot sicker than tea is going to help."

"What . . ."

"I don't know, Grey . . . I don't know."

Zach finished the most thorough examination he could manage while Eli continued to retch, then to shake with chills while his fever climbed higher.

"Zach . . ." Eli groaned. "What's the matter with me?"

"You had a cold lately, Eli?"

"I've been coughing and sneezing a couple of days, but it's nothing to put me down. God, I feel like every muscle is on fire and tied in knots. I hurt all over."

"Well, the cold got you bad. You have to stay in bed a couple of days."

"In bed! I can't do that. I got a job . . . I . . ."

"Eli, you're not going to be any good to your boss like that. I'll talk with him. You're too sick to go."

"Okay, Zach . . . God, I feel terrible."

"Try to relax, Eli. I'll have Zoe bring you some tea. See if you can hold it down . . . but don't eat. You'll only bring it back up, and trust me, that will only make you feel worse. You've got to have liquids, so I'll have Zoe keep feeding you tea. I'll be back tonight to see how you're doing. Try and rest, Eli."

Eli closed his eyes for a minute, but Zach was pretty sure he wasn't going to get much sleep. "I'm going downstairs, Eli. I'll be back tonight."

Zach left the room and closed the door behind him. For a moment a look of fear touched his eyes; then he fought for control.

He started down the stairs and met Zoe on her way up

with a tray in her hand. She paused and read his face with enough accuracy to send a chill of fear through her. "Zach?"

"Zoe, bring the tea in the living room. I have to talk to you."

"What is it, Zach? Please. What is it?"

"Come on," he said gently as he reached to take the tray from her hands. Wordlessly Zoe held on to the tray and followed him.

In the living room Grey stood up when they entered. One look at Zoe's face was enough to bring him to her side. When Zoe put the tray down she was struggling for control.

"Tell me, Zach. What's the matter with Eli?" Zoe asked.

"I think it's influenza," Zach said quietly.

"Influenza." Grey repeated the dreaded word as if he couldn't believe it. It was a word that could strike helpless fear in a strong man. It was a word that Grey understood, along with its implications.

"I hope to hell it's an isolated case. If it's not . . ."

"I don't understand . . ." Zoe began.

"Zoe," Grey said seriously. "I've seen epidemics of influenza wipe out a mining camp. I've seen it . . . God, Zach, are you sure?"

Emily had sat quietly just listening, but at Grey's words Zoe looked at her. "Emily! Zach, Emily won't . . ."

"I don't know. How close has she been to Eli?"

"You mean she can catch it if she's been with him?"

"Zoe, it's highly contagious. Eli's been carrying it around for a couple of days. I'm scared as hell we're going to see a lot of serious trouble if this gets a hold in town."

"She's been with him! Yesterday, last night, this morning . . . ohhh . . . she kissed him good-bye!"

"Lord . . ." Zach said. "You've got to keep her away from him now . . . and pray she's healthy enough that she won't catch it. I'm afraid we're not going to be so lucky if this thing gets a hold. Zoe, I've got to get back to the hospital. I don't know if we can prepare much, but we've got to try. In the meantime you'll have to nurse Eli . . . and you'll have to stay away from Emily."

"But who . . . I can't."

"Sure you can, Zoe," Grey said. "I'll take Emily home with me and take care of her until this is over."

Zoe didn't want to admit she was terrified, but she was, and both Grey and Zach knew it. Her face was pale.

"I'm going back to the hospital," Zach said. "You have to keep Eli drinking liquids, cool his fever as much as you can, and keep him clean. He's strong, Zoe, he'll make it."

"I'll try. What if . . . ?"

"I'll be back every chance I get. I'll keep checking on you, but if this thing gets hold I won't be able to come help you at all. Grey will take Emily home . . . but you'll be pretty much on your own. Keep strong, Zoe. You always have been. You can do it."

Zoe wasn't as sure as her brother was, but she gathered herself together.

"Emily, run to your room and get a couple of dresses and nightgowns, your robe, and whatever else you need. You'll have to go home with Grey for a while. Do you mind? You're going to be a big girl and not cry, aren't you?"

"No, Mommy, I'm not going to cry. I don't mind. But will Uncle Eli be all right?"

"I hope so, honey."

"I'll get Cara to come over and cook for Emily and give us a helping hand," Grey said. "She'll be all right. Zoe, you can count on it."

Emily ran upstairs and gathered what was needed. Zoe checked the bag when she came back down and found everything necessary. She hugged Emily fiercely, kissed her, and reluctantly watched her leave with Grey.

She was just as reluctant to see Zach leave, and when she closed the door behind him, she had to lean against it for a moment to gather her strength. Then she took the tray and walked upstairs.

Influenza swept the town like the Four Horsemen of the Apocalypse, cutting down young and old alike with no discrimination.

Zach was so inundated at the hospital that he, Amelia, and the other nurses worked twelve-to-fourteen-hour days and dropped into bed exhausted at night, only to be called before dawn. Paul too worked until he dropped every day.

Zoe nursed Eli in an agony of worry. He seemed to her to grow worse and worse every day. He groaned in pain and could barely keep down the unsweetened tea she continuously forced on him. After two days and two nearly sleepless nights she felt numb.

Simon had been on tenterhooks, finally prepared to call the strike that would bring all the mines in the area to a halt. But the epidemic struck with such force that he couldn't. Half the men working the mines were stricken, and he could not add more trouble to what they already had. He decided to wait.

When Zach sent a message for him to come to the hospital, he wasn't surprised. But he was surprised to hear that Eli was so sick.

"Why isn't he here, in the hospital?"

"Because, believe it or not, he's better off where he is. I've been looking in on him. Zoe's doing a fine job."

"Why the hell did you let Eli stay there with Emily and Zoe? What if they contract it?"

"Emily's not there. Grey took her home and Cara is keeping them going. She's a sturdy girl. Just laughs and says she's been through so much, a touch of this isn't going to do her any harm. So far she's all right."

"And Zoe . . . Zoe's alone there."

"I'm afraid it was necessary. There's a whole town to be taken care of, Simon, and . . . I'm one of only two doctors here. Do you think I should have forgotten the hospital and gone to take care of Eli when he had someone who could do it?"

"No, I guess you couldn't. How bad is it?"

"It's a disaster. People are dropping like flies. I wish medicine could find a way to combat this kind of thing."

"Well, we just have to do the best we can. How is the hospital fixed for supplies?"

"We'll be okay for a while."

"And Chloe?"

"She's the same. Quiet, still scared she's going to have to go home."

"I won't have her sent back to that hell. Just keep her until I find some way to take care of her."

"Where are you going now?"

"I want to go and see how Zoe is doing. Let me know if you need anything. This thing is beginning to scare me."

"It should. This is one of the biggest killers of the century, and the worst thing is that we can't do a thing to stop it. It just has to play itself out."

"Makes you feel kind of helpless, doesn't it?"

"I guess." Zach looked at Simon with understanding in his eyes. "About as much as the system you're trying to fight does."

"Yeah . . . I guess. Both problems are killers. I'm going to go up and see how Zoe is. Let me know how things go and please, keep a close eye on Chloe."

"I'll do that."

Simon left the hospital. He could not seem to fight a sudden feeling of urgency. He knew Zoe was a self-sufficient, strong woman . . . but she was alone . . . and most likely scared. Neither situation was tolerable to him.

Zoe passed the mirror in the hall on her way to Eli's room, and paused to look at herself. She'd had little time to care for herself for the past three days, and she'd begun to look it. Her face was pale and her eyes lusterless with exhaustion. Her hair, carelessly tied back with a piece of ribbon, had lost its shine, and she had barely eaten, living on sheer will.

She looked into the dulled gold of her own eyes and realized she was scared. More scared than she had ever been before.

Eli lay still in the bed, alive only because she had forced liquids between his lips. His body was wasted from the sheer force it took to fight the illness that had downed him.

He was thin and white, slipping in and out of consciousness. His breathing was a raspy harsh sound that filled the room, and Zoe was sure she would be able to hear that sound for the rest of her life.

She was also worried about Emily, even though Grey and Cara sent continual messages that she was doing just fine. Zoe had felt lonely many times, but never had she felt so alone.

She sighed deeply, then walked toward Eli's room, wondering if she could bear this strain one minute longer.

The room was quiet, and for several minutes she was too exhausted to realize it was much too quiet.

She set the tray down with hands that were shaking so badly the cups on the tray rattled. Slowly she walked toward Eli's bed.

The heavy raspy breathing had ceased in the few minutes it had taken her to take the soiled sheets down to the washtub, make tea, and carry it back upstairs.

She sat down on the edge of the bed, because her legs would no longer hold her, and took Eli's hand in hers.

Eli's young face was ravaged by the severity of his illness. Unable to eat, weakened by the raging fever, and retching when there was nothing left to retch, his body had been unable to fight any longer. Past deprivations had taken their toll on him too.

The reality of her brother's death had not yet penetrated Zoe's mind. She held his hand in both of hers, pressed it against her breast, and rocked back and forth.

Simon walked up the steps to Zoe's front door and knocked. He waited several minutes, then knocked again. There was no doubt Zoe was home. Eli was too sick for her to leave. He began to wonder if she was closed up in the sickroom nursing Eli and didn't hear his knock. He tried the door and found it unlocked, so he went in and closed it behind him. Then he stood and listened.

There was an ominous heavy silence. It felt to Simon as if some great hand had closed over the house, cutting off life and air.

The tick-tock of the grandfather clock echoed through the stillness, and every sense he had was brought to tense awareness.

"Zoe!" In the stillness his voice echoed hollowly. But there was no answer.

His first worried thought was that Zoe had become ill too. He knew Zach, Amelia, and Grey had been checking on her, but he couldn't think of another explanation for the utter silence of the house.

"Zoe!" he called again. Still no answer. He made a quick tour of the downstairs, checking every room. Then, taking the steps two at a time, he raced upstairs.

He knew where Eli's room was, so he went straight to it and opened the door. The scene that met him froze him momentarily in his tracks.

Zoe turned her head at the sound of the door opening, but the vagueness of her eyes alarmed Simon.

Then his eyes shifted to Eli, and he realized at once there was no need for help here. All of Eli's problems were over. At the same moment he realized that Zoe was unaware of much around her . . . and definitely refused to accept that Eli was no longer there.

Simon walked toward her, and she watched him come as if she was dazed. Somewhere deep inside, a part of her knew, but her mind would not accept Eli's passing as fact.

"Zoe?" Simon said with cautious gentleness. He could see the way she was gripping Eli's hand. "You're tired, Zoe, and you need some rest and something to eat. Come on. Come downstairs with me."

"No, I can't. I have to make sure he drinks this tea. Zach said he must. Simon, he's so sick." Her voice was plaintive and childlike.

"I know, I know," Simon said softly. He bent to release Eli's hand from Zoe's. Then he drew her up into his arms and held her close. "Zoe . . . Eli's gone. There's nothing more you can do for him."

Zoe's body jerked spasmodically and she tried to push Simon away, but he refused to release her. "He's gone, Zoe, and you have to let me take care of you before you are sick as well."

"No," Zoe gasped. Somehow she knew Simon was trying to comfort her, but he seemed a long way off. To take care of Eli was right, yet all the right things seemed wrong now. The awfulness went on and on as reality began to force its way into her mind. The grinding terror of Eli's illness had led to a kind of oblivion . . . then Simon had come and the terror had returned, only a thousand times worse because he brought the truth.

She could not speak or fight once the truth shattered

the barriers she had erected. She put her face against Simon's chest and let the weak, bitter tears flow.

He let her cry, feeling her weariness. Then, when she sagged in his embrace, he lifted her in his arms and carried her to her room.

Zoe had no idea she had slept around the clock. When she woke up, her mind was sluggish, and her body seemed a heavy weight she could not lift.

She turned her head on the pillow and saw Simon seated on a chair near the window. He was looking outside, his brow furrowed with worry.

"Simon." Her voice was so raspy she had to make two attempts to say his name before she succeeded.

Simon turned to face her, unsure whether she had said his name or not. Then, when he was sure she was awake, he rose, walked to the bed, and sat down beside her. He took her hand in his.

"How do you feel?"

"I . . . I don't know. My head aches."

"No wonder. I don't think you've eaten and I know you haven't slept." He put his hand on her forehead, and controlled his own quick reaction. She was hot, and her eyes had the same glassy look he had seen too often in the past week. "Look, Zoe, I'm going down to fix you something to eat. I want you to stay right where you are. Do you understand?"

"Eli . . ."

"Don't worry. I'm taking care of everything. Now rest, Zoe. You need it."

Zoe closed her eyes again, because her eyelids felt heavy and she felt strangely disoriented. Simon's voice seemed to come from a distance like a hollow echo from a deep cave.

Simon sat and looked at her for a minute; then he rose and went downstairs to see what he could scare up for her to eat.

When he returned, it was almost an hour later. "I'm not the greatest cook in the world, but this ought to help you get a little strength back," he said as he approached the bed. But Zoe didn't answer. Simon set the tray down and bent closer to Zoe with a sinking feeling. She was breathing deeply and perspiration was beaded on her skin.

He muttered a curse.

For the next three days Zoe struggled in a sea of pain. Weakened by her own fight for Eli, she fought a fierce battle just to keep breathing. And if possible, Simon fought even harder.

The second day Zoe was ill, Amelia came to check on Eli and Zoe's progress. Shocked to find the tragedy that had occurred, she remained with Zoe for several hours while Simon and Zach made the arrangements and took care of the funeral, which was unattended by the townspeople. It had to be quick and quiet. Too many people were burying their dead in the rapidly growing cemetery.

Zoe seemed to have shriveled up like a plant without water. When she opened her eyes again to reality, she felt so weak she could hardly raise her hand.

She had no way of knowing that Simon had sat for hours and listened to her delirious mutterings . . . listened to the ones who walked in her heart. Emily, Eli . . . and Grey.

When Zoe opened her eyes, Simon was there beside her bed.

"Well, it's about time." He smiled, but the smile was strained and she could see the tiredness in his eyes. "Want something to drink?"

She nodded, and he took a glass of water from the table, lifted her head, and helped her swallow a bit.

Slowly everything came back to Zach, and she looked up at Simon. "Eli?"

"Zach and I . . . we took care of everything," Simon replied. It hurt him to see the silvered crystals of tears form in her eyes. "He and I were . . . carrying Eli up to . . . well, anyway, I thought the two of us had to do it alone, but then someone fell into step beside me."

Her throat constricted. She knew. "Who?"

"Your pa. He carried a shovel. Zach and I both forgot to bring a shovel. He never said a word. It was really strange for him not to say a word during all that long walk to the cemetery. When we got there, he dug the hole. He was the one who filled in the grave too. Then, he stood there and said a prayer. He called it a prayer for a young soul. He said, 'It's only here that folks are punished. Later, God meets young souls and carries them on . . . special.' He was grieving too. Zoe. . . . he wept too."

Zoe couldn't handle any more. She turned her face away from Simon, closed her eyes, and wept in bitter silence.

Chapter Twenty-five

Grey walked up on his own porch, reluctant to see Emily for the first time since he'd met her and Zoe. He had been told that Eli Carrigan had been buried just the day before, and now he had to tell her first before he went to Zoe.

He knew how close Eli and his niece had become since he and Zoe had been reunited. The child had given her love to Eli unreservedly.

Now, when he opened the door and walked in, he found her as he usually did, curled up at the end of the couch with a book in her hand. He was grateful for Amelia's constant but short visits, because she always brought new reading material for an insatiable Emily.

She looked up when he closed the door, and as he so often was, Grey was aware of the intense depth of her gaze and the mature intelligence behind her eyes.

This sweet child had, over the short years he had known her, become so much a part of him. If she had been his own daughter, he couldn't have loved her more than he did.

"Uncle Grey, you're home early."

"Yes, I wanted to talk to you."

She was silent for a moment, her gold eyes so like her mother's searching his. He walked to the couch and sat down beside her, taking one of her hands in his.

"Is my mother all right, Uncle Grey? She didn't get sick, did she?" Her brow furrowed in worry.

"It's not your mother I have to talk about. As far as I know she's tired, but she's all right."

"Then why do you look so unhappy?"

"It's . . . it's your Uncle Eli, honey. I'm afraid . . ."

"He's not worse!"

"I . . . I'm afraid he just couldn't fight the sickness away. He died, Emily."

Emily's eyes pooled with tears and her lips trembled. Her hand clutched his, and she made a soft sound that was half disbelief and half misery. Grey lifted her onto his lap and held her close. He felt her slender young body tremble, then heard the sobs muffled against his shoulder.

The young, he thought, can ease their pain with tears. Why was it nearly impossible for some adults to do that? Even he fought the tears, and Zoe had always done the same.

Emily's grief was deep and poignant, and Grey could only ease her by telling her they could go out to the fields, pick some wildflowers, and put them on Eli's grave and pray for him.

"Mommy says God never hears prayers anyway. That bad things always happen no matter how hard you pray for them not to."

For the first time in all their time together Grey had to fight a sudden burst of anger toward Zoe, who had consciously or unconsciously taken her daughter's faith away.

"That's not true, Emily."

She raised her head and looked up at him, her cheeks wet with tears and her eyes wanting to believe.

"Do you think God will hear me if I pray for Uncle Eli?"

"I'm sure he will."

"Uncle Grey?"

"What?"

"Uncle Eli was so nice. He smiled and laughed and he was nice to everyone."

"I know . . . I know."

"Then why did God make him die when there are so many mean people? Why couldn't he have taken one of them?"

"You can't think like that, Emily. Maybe, because Uncle Eli was so nice, God wanted him in heaven."

"But . . . I loved him too. That's not fair."

"I know, but things are meant to be, and we just have

to learn to accept them. Life is not always fair. God takes things away, but if you look around you'll see he gives you a lot of things too. We have to learn to thank him for what we do have and not be angry when he does something we don't like. I'm sure there are a lot of people in Aspen today who could question God. But they're trying to understand. You'll have to try to understand too. Much as we want to, we can't always change things."

Emily nodded as if she were trying to understand, but he knew she couldn't quite cope with it yet. She just needed to be surrounded by love.

"Come on, let's go pick those flowers." He stood her on her feet and took her hand, and they left the house.

As they walked to the newly dug grave with an armful of wildflowers, Emily gave voice to her thoughts.

"I want to go home, Uncle Grey," she said softly.

"We'll see. As soon as we get back to my house I'll go check on your mother. If everything is all right I'll take you home. I promise."

She nodded.

At the grave he watched her place the flowers carefully and stand quietly. But he wasn't sure her quietness meant she was praying. It was just a barrier of silence that, for a moment, he couldn't cross.

They walked back to his house in the same contemplative silence. As they approached the house Grey pointed out the small carriage that sat before it. "Aunt Cara's here."

"Let's hurry," Emily answered. They increased their pace, and Emily ran up the steps and into the house when they arrived.

"Aunt Cara!" Emily ran to Cara, who opened her arms and embraced Emily in silence. She looked over Emily's head at Grey.

"She knows?"

He nodded. "We just came back from the cemetery. She . . . she put some flowers on his grave."

Cara looked down at Emily, and when she raised her eyes to Grey again he was puzzled. Something more was going on.

"I want to go home, Aunt Cara. I want to go home, please."

"I . . . I'm afraid, Emily, you're going to have to wait a few days. Your . . . your mother needs a little more time. I've got you a present, though. Why don't you run out to my carriage and get it."

It was obvious to Grey that whatever was bothering Cara, she didn't want Emily to hear about it now.

When Emily closed the door behind her, Grey looked at Cara.

"What more can go wrong, Cara?"

"It's Zoe."

Grey felt as if he had been struck a physical blow.

"She's not . . . God, she's not . . ."

"No. She's just terribly sick. Has been for the past three days. Things have gone from bad to worse, and I was running between the hospital and here, so I didn't get a chance to go up there until today."

"And Emily wants to go home. She's terrified."

"You and I both know she can't. She'll be more than terrified if she sees Zoe sick or if—"

"Don't say that! Don't even think it!"

"I don't think I've ever been so scared in my life."

"I'm going up there."

"Grey . . ."

"Who's taking care of her? Zach? He's needed more at the hospital. I'll go."

"Grey . . ."

Grey paused. It was obvious Cara had more to tell him.

"Grey, Simon is there. He's been there for the past three days. He and Zach are the ones that took Eli up to the cemetery. He's been taking care of Zoe."

It took a moment for Grey's resistant mind to accept what she had said. Then his mouth tightened into a grim line.

"Thanks, Cara," he said quickly, and before she could reply or say anything to stop him, he turned and started for the door. "Take care of Emily, I'll see you later," were the words tossed back over his shoulder as he left.

Cara expelled a half a breath. She wondered just how far the relationship between Zoe and Grey had gone. Grey had loved her for a long time, but she was afraid of commitment, of giving any man power over her emotions, and of marriage.

"I don't know how long this can go on before something . . . or someone explodes," Cara muttered as she started out to meet Emily, who was just coming up the porch. In her arms she carried the small white kitten Cara had retrieved from the streets and cleaned up. A blue ribbon was tied around its neck in a bow that the kitten was energetically trying to remove at the same time it was just as energetically trying to get out of Emily's arms. Emily's eyes were shining.

"Can I take the kitten with me when I go home?"

"I told you, Emily, it will be a little while yet before you can go home. Your mother is exhausted, and you want her to get some rest, don't you?"

Emily paused, her hand absently stroking the kitten, which had calmed under her gentle ministrations. Her eyes were wide and unblinking. "Aunt Cara . . . is my mother sick . . . sick like Uncle Eli?"

Cara was somewhat taken aback, and she wondered whether Emily had overheard her conversation with Grey. She went to Emily's side and put her arm around her shoulder. "Emily, come and sit down. I think it's time you and I had a long talk."

Simon had slept for the first time in more hours than he cared to remember. Then he'd risen early to prepare what breakfast he could. All Zoe needed now was to regain her strength, and he knew he had to make her eat.

He'd sat with her until she slept. He knew her grief for Eli had finally made an exhausted sleep possible. But he knew Zoe's resilience. She would want to be up. She would want to see her daughter and she would want to see Eli's grave.

He might be able to keep her down today because her vitality was drained. If he could, he wanted to leave her to rest and go see how Zach was faring at the hospital. It had been a horrible time, but he hoped the worst would soon be over.

He carried the tray of food upstairs. He didn't knock,

for if he found Zoe still asleep, he meant to leave her that way.

It shocked him when he quietly opened the door to find Zoe standing before the window looking out. She turned when the door opened and gave Simon a tentative smile. Her face was pale and she seemed so much thinner to him.

"What are you doing out of bed? You've been through enough to put a strong man in bed for a week."

"I'm a little weak, but I'm fine, Simon. And I'm not used to being pampered."

"Well," he said with a grin, "maybe you should get used to it. I'd like to pamper you for the next hundred years or so."

Zoe turned back to the window, and Simon cautioned himself to be more careful. This was not the time or the place for such declarations.

"Look, my dear lady, I want you to get back in bed and eat this breakfast. Then I want you to stay put while I go on over to the hospital and check on Chloe and your brother and sister-in-law. I promise I'll bring all the latest gossip and news back."

Zoe obediently returned to the bed, which made Simon suspicious that she was not quite as well as she pretended. He could see the lingering sadness in her eyes. He came to the side of the bed and set the tray down. Then he sat down beside her.

"I know how you feel, Zoe, believe me. But you have to look out for yourself now. For Emily, Zach, and all the rest of us. We need you."

"Simon, as soon as I can I want—"

"I know, and I'll take you there as soon as you're able."

"Thank you."

"Simon . . . Emily . . . ?"

"She couldn't be better. None of this has touched her, at least not physically. I'm sure she misses you."

"Not as much as I miss her."

"Well, you'll be together . . . but not until you're on your feet. Understand?"

"Yes." She smiled. "That's taking unfair advantage, you know."

"What is?"

"Bullying a defenseless woman when she's in no position to fight back."

"You? Defenseless?" Simon laughed. "That will be the day." He paused, looking at her closely.

"What is it?"

"It's the first time I've seen you smile for a long time. I'd like to hear you laugh," he added gently.

"Oh, Simon, I wonder if I'll ever laugh again."

"You will. I promise you, you will. Life has to go on, Zoe, whether we like it or not. We all have obligations, people who love and depend on us. I guess that's the only thing sometimes that can keep you going." He smiled again. "Enough talk. Eat before I begin to think you don't appreciate my cooking."

"These things with the lacy brown edges wouldn't be eggs by any chance?"

"Hmm, the lady is getting well, isn't she? Just eat, don't criticize."

"I've eaten worse, Simon . . . honest . . . I just don't remember when."

"Then I'll just leave you to suffer through them. But when I come back I expect to find that tray empty."

He rose and stood looking down into Zoe's upturned face. None of the memories of the past days had left his mind. He remembered her long-limbed body as he cooled her fever. The touch of her skin beneath his hands. But as he remembered those things, he also remembered the words that had told him of Grey's part in her life. He did not deceive himself that Grey did not have a tenuous hold on Zoe . . . but he did not mean to let her go, even if he had to fight a man who had become a friend.

It was not going to be an easy situation, but Simon had never run from trouble in his life, and he didn't mean to do it now.

It had been a long time since Zoe had mentioned Brent Dewitt, and he prayed that maybe she had given up her idea of revenge. He didn't want to open the door by mentioning it. Time, he prayed, would heal all her wounds.

He bent and rested a hand on each side of her, and before she could react he kissed her lightly. "I'll be back."

Zoe watched him go. She wanted to feel something besides this heavy lethargy that claimed her. Something told her that all her life was a half-finished proposition. And she wasn't sure now how to finish it so she could begin to live.

Simon and Grey missed each other by minutes. Zoe had barely begun to eat what she could of Simon's meal when she heard footsteps on the stairs.

She looked at the door expectantly, and smiled when Grey walked in, a worried frown on his face that turned to a smile when he saw her sitting up in bed.

"Lord, when Cara said you were sick it scared me out of a year's growth," he said.

"I'm really feeling all right now. A little weak in the knees maybe, and I couldn't manage one washtub of clothes, but I have a feeling I'll be fine."

"I wouldn't doubt it." He smiled as he came to sit beside her. "You're too obstinate to do anything else. Zoe . . . I'm sorry as hell about Eli. I wish I'd been here for you." He took her hands in his and kissed her fingers gently, warming her with the heat of his gaze.

"In a way you were with me. You were taking good care of the most precious thing I have."

"Emily is fine. She wants to come home."

"And I want her here."

"Not yet. Not until you're really better."

"Grey . . . did you tell Emily about Eli?"

"I did my best. It's hard for her to understand. Hell, it's hard for *us* to understand."

He watched Zoe's smile waver and her eyes fill with tears. He gathered her into his arms. "I came here to make you smile, not to make you cry," he whispered against her hair. "Oh, Zoe . . . I love you so much. I thought part of me was going to curl up and die when Cara said you were sick. All I could think of was holding you . . . somehow taking some of the pain away."

Zoe rested in his arms for a minute, letting his hard strength surround her.

"Simon was here?" he asked softly.

Zoe leaned back and looked up into his eyes. He knew she wouldn't lie to him.

"Yes . . . he came just as . . . as Eli . . . anyway, he and Zach took care of everything. I'm grateful, Grey."

"Sure, and you should be. I guess I should be too, but all I can do is wish I'd been here when you needed me."

"You're here now, Grey," Zoe said softly, "you're here now."

Yes, Grey thought, and I intend to stay.

When Simon arrived at the hospital, he was pleased to find that the overcrowding had eased. Most of the beds were full, but over half the patients were recuperating.

He found Amelia first, and she smiled when she saw him approaching, but the smile was wan.

"How are you holding up, Amelia?"

"Pretty good. Say, your doctor friend, Paul, was a real help. I'm glad his daughter is going to be all right. She was pretty sick, but he found a little time for us."

"Yeah, Doc and April. They're pretty special." He looked around. "Where's Zach?"

"He's here somewhere. I think he's lived here. Simon . . . he was going to send someone for you . . . he . . ."

"What are you trying to tell me? Who . . ." He studied her face, then groaned softly. "No. Oh, no. Not . . ."

"Simon, she was too . . . too fragile, too little and weak. Zach said . . . well, he said he thought she didn't fight. That she died of desperation, loneliness, and poverty more than anything else. She never wanted to go home."

"I know. I took her out of that home. But I hoped one day to adopt . . . to make her part of a family she could find some happiness with. She reminded me so much of . . . of someone."

"Of Zoe?"

"Yes. Chloe was so like her that I . . ."

"He feels terrible that he lost her."

"I guess . . . I guess we never had Chloe. She was lost to us at birth. I think I'd better talk to Zach."

He found Zach seated on the small cot behind the screen where Chloe had been before. He sat with his elbows on his knees and his hands dangling. His head was bowed and he looked totally beaten. Simon sat down beside him.

"It's all over, Zach."

"One death too many. I'm sorry, Simon."

"It's not your fault. It's the system's fault."

"We have to stop it."

"You sound as militant as I do."

"What are you going to do?"

"Right now . . . nothing. There's no fight left in these people. We have to recoup. It will take a while. There are not enough families that are not suffering losses. We have to give the men time. We've waited all this time, I don't think a few more months are going to make a difference."

"I guess you're right." Zach stood up stiffly. "I'm going home for a few hours before I fall down. Things can run here without me for a while."

Simon stayed beside Zach while he talked with Amelia for a minute, and she insisted Zach go home too.

"You're exhausted, Zach. Go home and sleep. I'll be home a little later."

Zach nodded his head. "I don't think I'm useful right now. I think I'm more in the way."

Simon left with him and walked as far as his house with him, and they hardly spoke. When Simon left Zach at his front porch, he continued on toward Zoe's.

He walked slowly, deep in thought. He wondered if there were any in Aspen right now who hadn't been touched by the epidemic and how long it was going to take to pick up the pieces and begin to move on.

The town had a strange kind of quietness about it, and he longed to see again the bustle of a busy, healthy place.

He knew the planned strike would be too much of a burden for the families in the flats to bear, and he would have to call a meeting after a while and lay out a new strategy. But not today. Today and for a few more days, he needed rest just as the town did. He needed to spend some time with Zoe and Emily and his friends. He needed the sweetness of Emily to ease the bitterness. He needed laughter like a drowning man needed something to cling to. He needed to see life around him to wash away the death he had seen.

He walked on until he came to Zoe's house. When he went inside he could feel the quiet coolness about him. He inhaled a deep breath and expelled it, feeling his body relax.

He walked to the stairs and began to climb slowly. Maybe because he walked slowly, or maybe because Grey and Zoe were not expecting any intrusion, they did not hear Simon until he swung the door open.

Grey was still seated on the bed next to Zoe, and was holding one of her hands in both of his. They were in the midst of a conversation . . . or more like a minor argument about whether Zoe should be getting up and getting dressed or not. Grey was insisting she stay in bed a day or two more, and she was just as insistent that she was tired of this sickroom and wanted to be in the sun again. Simon picked up Zoe's last few words.

". . . I just need some sunlight and some activity to get me back in order. And I need to see Emily before she really begins to worry."

"You're not strong enough—" Grey began.

"Grey's right, Zoe," Simon interrupted. Both looked up at him in surprise. "Getting up and doing too much will only put you back in that bed sicker than you were."

"You two are ganging up on me."

"It takes two of us." Simon chuckled. But Grey was much too smart not to see that the humor did not reach his eyes.

"And if you're not careful," Grey added with a grin, "we'll call Zach and Amelia and Cara, not to mention Emily. Then you'll be so outnumbered you'll just have to give up."

"All right, all right. I'll stay in bed and rest today. If you'll promise to bring Emily here tomorrow."

"The lady drives a hard bargain. But I promise," Grey said. "Now try to rest for a while. Simon and I have some business to discuss anyway . . . about the miners." He looked at Simon, who nodded.

"This is ridiculous," she said. "I've been in bed for days. What I need is to get up and get moving."

"Zoe," Simon said warningly.

With a disgusted sigh Zoe slid down in the bed and pulled the covers up to her chin.

"Now stay there," Grey added. He and Simon stepped out into the hallway, and Simon pulled the door shut. They walked down the hall . . . down the stairs, in silence.

It was a difficult situation at best. Simon and Grey had enormous respect for one another. It might have been better if they had been enemies. At least they would have been able to fight each other.

Each was well aware of the always tenuous hold the other had over Zoe. It was a fragile thread that could snap with the least pressure.

"How are things going at Zoe's mine, Grey?"

"Pretty good. It's still coming in with high color."

"So . . . Zoe hasn't changed her mind about anything, has she?"

"Did you expect her to, Simon? Zoe knows miners as well as, or better than, we do. She's never seen them stand together and fight back, and she doesn't believe they're going to do it now."

"Zoe has forgotten too much."

"Or," Grey added softly, "she's remembered too much."

"If you want me to be honest with you, Grey, I'm scared for her. She's got a lot of unpleasant surprises coming."

"I don't think anyone—you, me, or anyone—can change Zoe. I, for one, have accepted that. I wish I could make her see. But either way she chooses to go, I'll stand with her."

"And you think I'll give up . . . just like that?"

"Not for a minute. You're not the giving-up type either. But I have an advantage. I'll stand with her. You want her to make changes I don't think she'll make. I love her, Simon, and I know you do too. But much as I know what you're fighting for, and respect it, I'm not going to lose Zoe over it. Eventually, if she doesn't change, you'll have to become enemies."

"I won't let that happen."

"You can't stop it unless one of you changes, and you're both too stubborn to do that."

"You're supporting her obsession with revenge and her need for wealth. She thinks it can protect her. You and I know she's wrong on both counts."

"As far as revenge is concerned . . . maybe she has to face him one day and find out it doesn't matter anymore. As far as wealth is concerned . . . if it makes her happy . . ." Grey shrugged.

"Has it made her happy?" Simon asked quietly.

"I don't think you understand—"

"No, Grey," Simon interrupted, "there are a lot of things you don't know . . . that you never shared. I knew Zoe a long time ago and I know her now. She'll never be happy, really happy, until she finds out that revenge will never satisfy her . . . until she knows in her heart that she wants and needs something or someone more than she wants money. Only then will she really be free."

There was a heavy silence; then Grey spoke softly.

"Something or someone more . . ."

"Think about it, Grey. She's obsessed with hatred and money. If that's all there ever is . . . Zoe will never know what it is to truly love and be loved. You see . . . there's just no room."

Simon's voice died to a whisper. Then he turned and left the room, leaving Grey standing silent, caught in his thoughts.

After Cara had explained Zoe's illness to Emily, they sat for a moment without speaking. Then Cara smiled down at Emily.

"That kitten needs some milk. And I think a glass of milk and something to eat would do you some good too. What do you say?"

"I'd like that."

"Then bring him in the kitchen. Oh, by the way, what are you going to name him?"

"I don't know," Emily seemed to be giving this some serious thought. "Maybe I'll call him Charlemagne. He was a king. Uncle Simon read me a story about him."

"That's a mouthful of a name for a little thing like him."

"We can call him Charlie for now . . . until he grows up, I mean."

"Charlie . . . I like that better."

"Aunt Cara?"

"What, honey?"

"Is . . . is Simon really my daddy?"

Cara was so shaken by the question she didn't answer for a minute. "What makes you ask that?"

"Is he?"

"No . . . he's not."

"Is Grey my daddy?"

"No, Emily. Why don't you tell me what's on your mind?"

"I thought maybe that was why Grey was so mad."

"Mad? He wasn't mad. He was just worried about your mother."

"No . . . he was mad. Grey hardly ever gets mad, but when he does his mouth gets all scrunched up and tight and his eyes get all cold and funny."

"Well, I don't know what he could be mad at."

"I do."

"Emily."

"He was mad because Uncle Simon was taking care of Mommy. I heard you tell him that. Is Mommy going to marry Uncle Grey?"

"I don't know, Emily. Goodness, you have a lot of funny ideas for a little girl. Simon and Grey were . . . are friends."

"I know."

"Then where are you getting these crazy ideas?"

She watched Emily pour some milk in a saucer and set the dish and kitten down. Then Emily looked up at her. "Aunt, Cara"—her voice was soft and her mouth tremulous—"Mommy won't die like Uncle Eli, will she?"

"Oh, Emily," Cara said softly as she went and knelt before Emily. "I'm sure everything will be fine. Grey will come back soon and he'll tell you . . ."

"I want to go home."

"I know you do. I know you do. It won't be much longer, Emily, I'm sure. You've been so patient and good."

Cara did what she could to take Emily's thoughts from the tumultuous events that must be churning in her too bright mind. The child was confused, and Cara knew it. But she knew also it had to be Zoe's place to explain what she felt should be explained.

She made sure Emily ate, and was pleased when her

attention turned to the kitten. But she knew the questions were just lying in wait. She also knew Emily was becoming curious both about who her father was and, though she loved them, what place Grey and Simon held in her and Zoe's life.

Cara was more than relieved when she heard Grey coming. Emily was at the door before Cara and flinging her arms around Grey, who hugged her fiercely.

"Grey?" Cara began.

"It's okay, Cara," Grey said gently. He looked down into Emily's face and smiled. "Your mother is fine, just fine, and you are going home tomorrow . . . you and me. I'm going to stay and take care of you for a while. What do you think about that?"

"I'm glad," Emily said enthusiastically. "Uncle Grey, do you want to see the kitten Aunt Cara brought me?"

"I sure do."

Emily ran to gather up a thoroughly confused kitten, and then carried it to Grey, who examined it very seriously. "Well, he looks like he's really going to be a handsome cat when he grows up."

"You like him?"

"Yep. He's fine."

"Then"—Emily smiled with a delicious mischievousness—"you can tell Mommy you think we ought to keep him."

"Well, you little imp." Grey laughed. "I guess I walked into that one. Okay, I know when I've been had. I'll see what I can do."

"Am I really going home tomorrow, Uncle Grey?"

"You are."

"I'll give you a basket to carry Charlie in," Cara said.

"Charlie?" Grey questioned.

"His name is Charlemagne, Uncle Grey . . . Charlie for short."

"Oh . . . I see."

"Emily, why don't you take Charlie outside for a while. I'm sure he'd like to play."

"Okay." Emily smiled. She walked to the door with the kitten in her arms, and had only stepped out on the porch when Grey and Cara heard the beginning of her whispered conversation with the kitten. "I know you don't want to play right now, Charlie . . . but grown-ups don't want to talk in front of us kids." The door closed behind her, and Grey and Cara exchanged glances.

"When that kid grows up I'll have a lot of pity for the young men around here," Grey said with a laugh.

"She's going to be something," Cara agreed.

"I'm starved. I've got to find something to eat."

"You sound like you're feeling all right."

"I am."

"I take it Zoe really is well."

"She's a little weak, but you know her. I'd be safe in saying she'll be out of bed tomorrow."

"Lord, Grey, I hope this thing is finally over. I've never seen such a terrible time," Cara said as she walked to the kitchen with Grey a few steps behind her.

"I don't think this whole town has ever seen anything like this," Grey answered. He found a seat at the table, and Cara began to prepare a sandwich.

"Grey . . . what's going to happen now?"

"What do you mean?"

"Don't joke around with me. You know darn well what I mean."

"Simon . . . he'll wait awhile. Give the miners and their families a chance to get over this. If I was to guess, I'd say sometime early next year he'll start things rolling."

"Zoe won't easily forgive him if he really calls a strike against her mine. She doesn't believe he'll do it."

"He'll do it, Cara. He has to. There are too many who depend on him. He's convinced them. Now he has to stand behind his own words."

"Those two, buckin' head to head, both too stubborn to realize they're only hurting themselves, but too blind to see what they're doing. If Zoe would only bend a little bit, none of the men in her mine would consider going against her."

"But she won't, and we both know why."

"Grey, if you could convince her to go easy, maybe Simon . . ." She paused, looking at Grey's face intently. "You won't talk to her now, will you?"

"Nope."

"Grey."

"Simon is right about what the miners need, but as far as Zoe is concerned, I'm not pushing her anymore. When this happens, she's going to need all the friends she can get."

Cara sat down opposite Grey and was quiet for a moment, but she was aware that his eyes didn't meet hers.

"I know how much you love her, Grey," she said softly. "That's no secret."

"And you know how much Simon loves her too."

"That's not much of a secret either," he stated firmly.

"And you're not going to do a thing to try to stop them from colliding, are you?"

"No, I'm not." Grey rose to his feet, and Cara thought absently that Emily was right: When Grey was angry his eyes did go cold and his mouth did get hard. "I'm going to keep Zoe safe! Come hell or high water, I'm going to make sure she doesn't get hurt again, and especially not by Simon Tremaine. Look, Cara, I admire the man, believe me. I have a great deal of respect for what he's trying to do . . . but I'm not giving up Zoe for anything or anyone, and that includes Simon."

"Maybe giving Zoe up won't be your choice."

"It will be the damnedest fight he's ever been in, I can promise you that. He wasn't enough for Zoe before. He can't give her what she needs."

"And you can?"

"Yes, I can! I can make her happy, and she needs to be happy for once in her life."

Grey strode from the room, and Cara sat alone at the table for some time. The people she loved were tangled in a web, and she was scared about the outcome.

But Zoe was her first priority. She had been with Zoe from the time she was a child, and no one knew any better than she how Zoe had struggled for an unreachable dream.

At that moment she hated Brent Dewitt and his kind with an unbelievable passion. Brent and Zoe's desire for money had drawn Zoe into a dream that was not real and never could be.

Zoe had all the love in the world at her fingertips and

she couldn't see it. Two strong, wonderful men loved and wanted her, would have protected her from anything, and she couldn't see them. Obscuring them was a mist of memories Zoe could not seem to put behind her.

A sudden apprehensive shiver made Cara wrap her arms about herself. She wanted to do something desperately . . . and she didn't know what to do.

Chapter Twenty-six

The whole town seemed to breathe an almost audible sigh of relief when the worst of the disastrous epidemic seemed to pass. One week followed another, and almost daily the hospital sent patients home.

Zach found the time to help Amelia put their house in order and to catch up on the nights of lost sleep.

Now he walked briskly toward home at the end of a busy day, but not one that could be compared to the long days of the siege.

People stopped to talk to him on the way, or waved and called out to him as he passed. Zach was considered one of them, and their respect for him as a doctor was no greater than their love for him as one of their own.

As he started across the street he heard his name called out, and turned to see the pastor of the largest church in town approaching.

"Good evening, Reverend McBride. How are you this lovely evening?"

"It is a nice day, isn't it? I'm fine, Doctor, and you and your lovely wife?"

"We couldn't be better."

"Might I walk along with you a way? I would like to talk to you."

"Of course," Zach replied. They walked slowly along side by side. "You said you wanted to talk to me."

"Yes. I don't know if anyone else has taken the time to do it, but I, for one, would like to take this opportunity to thank you for all you've done for us. And your wife. What an angel of mercy she has been."

"Well, we're both glad we were here when you needed us."

"Between you and Simon Tremaine, we have made our little hospital quite a successful endeavor."

"I think so. But you've forgotten someone else who's responsible for a lot of things."

"Oh?"

"Zoe Carrigan?"

"Ah . . . yes . . . she's your sister, I've been told."

"I'm proud to say she is. But she's a little more than that."

"I don't understand."

"She's my employer also." Zach smiled pleasantly. "She is the one who paid for a great deal of the supplies I've been using the past weeks, and paid for the time my wife and I spent helping the town to survive."

"Ahem . . . ah . . . yes, of course. I'm sure she has been quite generous with you, sir. Since you are her brother, one would expect that."

Zach gave a slight negative shake of his head and smiled as they continued down the street. "Did you say you had something special to talk to me about, Reverend?"

"Yes, I did. It has been only a short time since our town has been freed from this terrible, terrible plague. But I feel as if the people need to be uplifted."

"Uplifted?" Zach repeated. "I won't deny that. The whole town's spirits need to be raised. What did you have in mind?"

"A . . . celebration, you might say . . . of life . . . for the living. Do you understand?"

"Yes, I do. And I think you might just have a good idea. There have been too many tears. The town needs to laugh again."

"I'm glad you agree with me. I intend to talk to the pastors of the other churches." He chuckled. "I think it might shock a few to see we can all work together."

"It might." Zach smiled. "But it will be worth it."

"Thank you, my friend. I shall begin to spread the idea today." He turned to Zach and extended his hand. "And again . . . let me thank you for the incredible dedication with which you and your wife worked. Please extend my thanks to her as well."

"I shall do that, Reverend." Zach shook his hand, and stood for a minute watching him as he walked away.

Zach continued his walk to his house, and took the front porch steps in two bounds. When he opened the front door, the delicious aroma of food came to him.

"Amelia!"

"Here in the kitchen," she called back.

When he pushed open the kitchen door he was met with a quick smile from Amelia, who was intent on several kettles that were bubbling energetically.

He came up behind her and slid his arms about her waist; then he kissed the soft curve of her neck. "Ummm . . . you smell good."

"Don't you kid me. I know what you're sniffing around for, and you're not tasting until dinner."

"You are a hard woman."

"And you're a hungry man, I take it?"

He tightened his arms and kissed her again.

"I'm hungry all right," he murmured. "But I could be persuaded to take care of other things first."

"You? Forsake your stomach?" She laughed as she laid her spoon down and turned in his arms. "I should call your bluff."

"Do you accuse me of selfishness? I'd be delighted to sacrifice my satisfaction for yours."

"Oh, would you now? How gallant." She looped her arms about his neck and stood on tiptoe to kiss him. "Don't polish your armor yet, Sir Galahad. Dinner is ready and you are not going to eat another cold, leftover meal. Get cleaned up."

"Only if you promise to let me sparkle up my armor at a more convenient moment."

"That's a bargain."

He helped her set the table, and they ate conversing casually. It was then Zach mentioned his conversation with the reverend.

"What kind of celebration?"

"I guess the churches would unite and throw one big to-do."

"Well, I'm sure it would be the right thing. Maybe I'll stop around and ask the reverend if I can be of any help."

"Yes," Zach said casually, "you might ask Zoe to go along with you."

Amelia regarded him in silence for a long enough moment to make him chuckle to himself. She saw the reflection of laughter in his eyes, and smiled herself.

"I'll do my best, Zach, but I can't make any promises. You, Simon, and Grey have a regular campaign going, don't you?"

"Yep. As long as we can get Zoe not to upset the applecart. Simon and Grey are working at it. Trying to get her to ease up at the mine and forget about her ideas of revenge."

"Is it working?"

"I don't know. Simon is in an impossible position. He has to call that strike before long or lose all the momentum he's built. That is going to cause quite a rift between him and Zoe. Grey is trying to get her to ease up at the mine . . . bend a little and forget that"—he inhaled deeply—"man she has her heart set on destroying. And—"

"And maybe one of you can get Zoe to forget all the 'religious' lessons of her unique childhood and her hatred of your father and all the churches. Maybe you can get her to forget all the terrible things she's been through, the struggles and battles she's fought. Maybe you can get her to shake off the ugliness that she carries around and her belief in money and money only. Maybe."

"I know. So few people know Zoe like I do . . . or like Simon and Grey do. Amelia, inside she's a kind and loving woman."

"I know that, Zach."

"She . . . she deserves so much more than she's getting."

"Zach." Amelia put her hand over his. "She has Emily, Simon, Grey, you, and me. That's a lot in my book. If anything can pull Zoe out of this, we can. As the book says . . . love begets love. We'll just love her and keep working until she realizes it."

Zach, locking his gaze with hers, raised her hand to his lips and kissed it. "God, I'm glad I married you."

"I'm kind of glad you did too." She smiled. "So let's concentrate on having that celebration. You and I have not laughed and danced in a long, long time. I'm interested in finding out if you still can."

He laughed, stood up, his hand still holding hers, and drew her to her feet and into his arms in one fluid movement. Then they danced to silent music, and only Amelia's soft laughter could be heard.

Zoe and Cara were sitting on the back porch of Zoe's house, sharing tea and watching Emily as she sat beneath a nearby tree with the kitten curled in her lap. She was concentrating on dangling a ribbon just out of the kitten's reach and watching it paw the air to get to it.

Cara could read Zoe's face well, and she did not misinterpret her deep introspective silence.

"Emily is growing into quite a lady," Cara remarked.

"Yes." Zoe's one-syllable answer left Cara sure of Zoe's feelings.

"Then why are you worried about her?"

This drew Zoe's quick attention. "What makes you think I'm worried?"

"Come on, Zoe," Cara said gently. "You're talking to me, not the rest of Aspen."

Zoe sighed and returned her gaze to Emily. "I suppose I am. I . . . I want her to have so much, Cara . . . so much I didn't have."

"But she does have everything. Pretty clothes, a nice place to live, people who love her. I don't understand what you're saying."

"She . . . she has so few friends," Zoe said softly. In her voice Cara could hear the cry of a girl who had never known giggling, girlish friendships. Neither time nor money could wipe away some kinds of pain.

"Maybe," Cara said gently, "it's because she isn't quite sure what friends you would agree to. From what I hear from Amelia, the couple of times you let Emily stay with her, she had a great time with the Summers kids, and the O'Neil kids as well." She accepted Zoe's look of surprise for what it was. "She never told you about them?"

"No."

"Figures. I guess she thought you wouldn't like them, and Emily would turn herself inside out before she would go against you."

Zoe listened in the same introspective silence. If the words hurt or angered her, she showed no sign of it.

"Zoe," Cara continued cautiously, "I'm gonna say something and you can listen or throw me out, whatever. But it needs saying." Zoe didn't answer, but her lips tightened in a forced half smile. "You got to let that kid pick her own friends. You got to let go a little bit and trust her judgment. She's a good, sweet kid, but you just won't let her grow up. Pretty soon she'll get a little scared about her judgment and begin to think she's not capable of choosing. One thing will lead to another, and after a while she'll be scared to think or decide on anything if you don't give the word first. That's not fair, Zoe."

"I don't want her to run with that crowd from the flats. I want her to be something, to amount to something. I want her to be . . . accepted. To go to school and get a good education."

"Knowing or associating with girls from the flats—nice girls, I might add—is never going to change Emily. You look at her, but a lot of times you don't really see. Emily has a lot of intelligence and she has a lot of good common sense. She has a pretty good idea where you want her to go with her life, and I'm sure she'll go along with that. But you have to give a little too . . . and start trusting her."

"It's not a matter of trust."

"No? What then?"

Zoe considered the answer to this for several seconds. Then she answered quietly. "Fear maybe."

"What kind of fear?"

"That somehow it will all fail, that Emily will be dragged down to that place and those people. I couldn't live if Emily had to face the things I did. I couldn't bear seeing her struggle . . . or having her feel that ugliness . . . that emptiness."

"I guess maybe I understand," Cara said gently. "But Zoe . . . you can't stand between Emily and everything she has to face. It will only hurt her."

Zoe gulped. "I know . . . I just can't . . ." She shook her head. "I can't take chances."

"What are you taking chances on now?" The question came from the doorway behind them, and both women turned to see Grey.

"I'm not taking chances on anything." Zoe smiled up at him. "And what are you doing here so early in the afternoon?"

"I had to go over to the bank, and there are some papers for you to sign. So I thought I'd bring them on over."

"I have to get going anyway," Cara said. "The restaurant gets real busy this time of day, and if you don't get right behind those people nothing gets done." Cara rose from her seat as she spoke. "I'll see you both later."

"Before you go, Cara, I was told to let you know," Grey said. "Reverend McBride and the other ministers have gotten together and they're tossing a big hoopla. You and all your employees are invited and their families as well. Should be quite a to-do."

"A celebration?" Cara seemed puzzled, and Grey answered her unspoken thoughts.

"The whole town needs it. Everyone seems drained. We have to put a little life back in. Maybe help folks keep goin'."

"I guess you're right. It is a good idea. When?"

"Next week." Grey grinned. "Gives every lady a chance to get a new dress."

"I'll go spread the word. Thanks, Grey. See you later, Zoe."

Zoe smiled. It had occurred to her, if not to Cara, that most likely she herself had not been invited. After Cara left, Zoe remained silent. Grey came to sit down beside her.

"And what about you?" Grey said. "I'm sure you have something spectacular to wear, and Emily as well. I will have the privilege of escorting the two prettiest girls in town."

"I . . . I'm invited?"

"You and Emily. Reverend McBride came to me personally and asked if I would make sure you came."

Zoe found this a little hard to believe. Yet Grey had

never lied to her, and besides, why would he lie about something like this if there was a chance Emily might be hurt too?

"Reverend McBride." Zoe laughed. "I'll bet he choked on every word."

"Now, Zoe," Grey said lightly, "be nice. Emily hasn't ever gone to a party. It would be fun. It's time she began to get out. You too. You haven't had a chance to dance—"

"In years," Zoe finished for him. "But I would go even if I never danced a step. Just to see some faces."

"I wish you'd stop doing that."

"What?"

"Feeling sorry for yourself and slapping at every hand that reaches out to you. Maybe Georgetown didn't give you much of a chance, Zoe, but I think Aspen would if you could bend a little."

"Was I feeling sorry for myself?"

"Weren't you? Sometimes you don't see what you've got because you've to busy looking for something else."

"So you want me to give them the benefit of the doubt and go to the celebration."

"Yep. I want you to leave all other thoughts behind except laughing, dancing, and having fun."

"All right, I'll go."

"Great. You'll have fun and Emily will be ecstatic."

"Hmmm. I'm not sure if you're as pleased I'm going as you are that Emily is."

"I'm pleased about you both."

"Grey?"

"What?"

"You could have told me this tonight. You didn't make a special trip here just to tell me about that party, did you?"

"Well . . . not exactly."

"You have something else to tell me."

"Yeah." He withdrew a letter from his pocket and handed it to Zoe, who unfolded it and read the name at the bottom of the page before she read the contents. "Brent." She said his name softly. Grey waited while she finished the letter.

The look in her gold eyes made Grey press his lips together to restrain his thoughts.

"I've got him," Zoe whispered.

"Zoe."

"All I need do is pull the rug out from under his nice, shiny expensive shoes."

"Damn it, Zoe!"

"It's taken long enough." She raised the letter and waved it slightly. "It's nice to hear him beg."

"Look, Zoe, all you need to do is tear up the notes you hold on his mine and let him go. You don't need this."

"I could. I could help him . . . let him have the mine again. I could give him back his life . . . if I wanted to."

"If you wanted to?"

Zoe was silent for a thoughtful moment; then she turned and smiled at Grey. "Send for him, Grey. It's time he came here, and it's time he met Zoe Carrigan." She paused to look at Grey's face closely. Then she added the next words quietly but firmly. "I can send for him myself."

"And I could tell him who you are."

"But you won't. Besides, it wouldn't do you much good."

"If I send for him, what are you going to do when he comes?"

"Will he come?"

"You know he will. You have his life in your hands. One word and he's bankrupt. You know the situation he's in. Old Lester Crandell will make the rest of his life a Hell on earth."

"I need to see him, Grey. Before I decide just how far I'll go."

"What good does seeing him do? Just let it go."

"You want to be so fair with Brent. What about me? What about Emily?"

"Emily's as happy as a child can be. She doesn't need him. She doesn't need any kind of vengeance."

"And me?"

"If you don't see it, how can I convince you? You don't need to do this, Zoe."

Zoe rose from her chair and crumpled the letter in her hand. Then she dropped it on the table. "Send for him,

Grey," she said softly. "I want to look in his eyes. I want him to know who and what I am . . . at least I want that much. I think I deserve it."

She walked into the house, and Grey sat motionless for a minute. "I hope that's enough to satisfy you, Zoe. . . . I don't want to see you hurt anymore."

Grey had thought the invitation to the celebration would have made a difference to Zoe. It was why he'd told her about it before he gave her the letter. It was also why he would have died before he told Zoe that it had taken the combined efforts of Simon, Zach, and himself to secure the invitation in the first place.

Actually, it was more Simon and Zach than it was him . . . but he damn well didn't intend for Zoe to know that either. After all, Simon was the most real and deadly threat to everything he wanted.

He remembered quite well the almost amusing clandestine meeting of the three of them. They had met in a tavern at a back table, and when Simon and Zach stopped beside the table, Grey smiled up at them. "This is a bit on the ridiculous side."

"I agree." Simon smiled. "Three men . . . afraid of one woman."

"It's not fear, gentlemen." Grey grinned. "It's caution."

"Uh-huh." Zach laughed. "I believe Shakespeare once said, 'A rose by any other name . . . '"

"You two wanted to talk about something special, I take it?" Grey said.

"Sure," Simon said agreeably. "How you are going to tell Zoe about this celebration . . . after we twist Reverend McBride's arm and a few others' to get them to extend her an invitation."

"Me? Why me? Zach, you're her brother."

"And I'm obvious. She'd know I did something to get that invitation. And Simon is too close to the ministers. No . . . you're the chosen one, Grey."

"We're doing this for Zoe's good, Grey, you know that as well as I do," Simon said urgently. "It would only take a step or two to make people see her in a different light."

"You're still trying to call a strike?"

"We can't yet. There's been too much suffering. For

now, what we need is a celebration . . . and Zoe needs it too."

"Yeah, I suppose you're right. Okay, I'll try to convince her it's a unanimous invitation."

"Good luck," Simon had said quietly, and Grey had not been too sure exactly how he meant it.

Grey knew that Simon went to see Zoe as often as he could, just as he knew Simon's intent was to remove Grey from her life. Still . . . it was unique and strange. They knew each other, trusted each other . . . and were friends.

He rose now and walked back into the house, quite unaware that a silent and immobile Emily, still sitting close to the tree, had heard every word and was watching intently.

Zoe sat before her mirror immobile, hardly seeing the extraordinary beauty reflected there. Her mind was on another place, another time . . . another gathering to which she'd been unexpectedly invited . . . and a night when shame and humiliation changed her life as she ran half-naked through the streets of Georgetown. She remembered a dress of deep, deep blue. Maybe that was why the dress she had chosen to wear tonight was a striking, midnight-blue silk.

Her thick mass of auburn hair was coiled atop her head. Gold eyes reflected the light, and her skin looked like ivory.

She wondered now if she wasn't a little afraid. An old memory was very hard to destroy. If Emily hadn't been so excited about the prospect of the huge celebration, Zoe might have changed her mind and not gone.

At that moment Emily burst into her room, and came to an abrupt halt when Zoe turned to look at her.

"Oh, Mommy . . . you're so pretty."

"And you, my pet, are beautiful." Zoe laughed. She caught both of Emily's hands in hers and held them out from her sides so she could examine her carefully.

Pink lace, with a matching pink bow in her dark hair, made Emily look suddenly so grown up. It made Zoe's breath catch. She was going to be a beauty . . . but was she going to be happy?

"Mommy, is Uncle Grey going to take us?"

"Yes. He should be here with the carriage soon."

"If Uncle Grey is supposed to take us, then why is Uncle Simon downstairs?"

"Uncle Simon is here now?"

"He's downstairs, and he wants to see you for a minute."

"All right. Now you run to your room and get your cloak. Be sure to put out the lamp and close your door. I don't want that kitten on your bed."

"Mommy." Emily giggled. "You know he'll want to sleep with me. He always cries . . . and you always let him."

"Well, just close your door, miss, and get ready to go. I'm sure Grey will be here soon."

"Okay."

Zoe walked down the stairs slowly, wishing she could control the effect Simon always had on her. Fight it as she might, he could still make her nerves sing.

When she stood framed in the doorway, Simon slowly rose to his feet, his eyes telling her more than words ever could.

"Zoe," he said softly, "you look absolutely wonderful."

"Thank you." She walked toward him and when she was close, the subtle scent of her perfume reached him. "I didn't expect to see you here tonight."

"I wanted to stop by . . . to give you something."

"Give me something?"

"Yes. Now that I look at you I'm sure I'm right. This is the time to return something you lost along the way. It was yours and I couldn't see it belonging to anyone else."

"I don't understand."

Simon moved to stand behind Zoe, and to her surprise he took hold of her shoulders to keep her from turning with him. So she stood quietly, feeling without seeing him move.

Slowly Simon took the pearls he had kept for the right time from his pocket. Gently he placed them around her throat and hooked the clasp.

Zoe was so stunned when she looked down that for a moment she was speechless. She touched the pearls gently, and unbidden tears came to her eyes.

"Simon . . . how . . . ?"

"Don't be angry, Zoe. I . . . I knew you loved them and I knew you were forced to sell them. I didn't want you to lose them. I had to . . ." He took hold of her shoulders and drew her back against him. Zoe was held in a strange kind of lethargic stillness. Suddenly Simon's hold seemed a comfort, a protective shield. This, coupled with her gratitude at the return of her pearls, made her remain resting against him.

"Mr. Wraith didn't buy my pearls. You did!"

"Yes."

Confusion tore at her. She should be furious . . . but other emotions were getting in the way. "Simon, why do you do this to me!" she cried softly.

"It's simple, Zoe. I love you. I've told you that before. One day you might begin to realize it's true."

She spun around to face him, wanting to fight his words and the brilliant desire that Simon stirred within her.

"You've become a very powerful man, Simon . . . but it doesn't change me, what I want, or what I have to do."

"No." He sighed deeply. "I don't suppose it does. The only person who can change you . . . is you." He laughed a brittle kind of laugh. "I just wanted you to know that I haven't changed either . . . I still want you more than I've ever wanted anything or anyone."

"Except your beloved union and those ungrateful people on the flats. You're going to be disappointed one day when you find out this is all for nothing."

"No, Zoe, I couldn't want anything as much as I want you to be a part of my life. You know, I think you're lying to yourself more than to me. You think I don't know how you've given those same people medicine and food and care through Zach." His voice softened. "You're the same little girl from Georgetown, afraid to be hurt again. Don't be afraid anymore. There's a lot of us that would be there for you if you'd let us."

"I'm not a little girl anymore, Simon. I'm not going to be in that position again. I have what it takes to protect myself. I'm not afraid . . . and I don't need anyone." Her stubborn chin came up defiantly.

Simon knew her defenses were in place again, and battling against them was nearly useless. There had to be another way to reach Zoe, and he meant to find it come hell or high water.

"I suppose Grey is taking you to the celebration."

"Yes, he should be along soon."

"Emily is really excited."

"More than I've ever seen her." Zoe seemed to relax. "It's her first party."

"She looks like a young lady," Simon said. He smiled. He was about to speak again when the sound of footsteps on the stairs made them both turn. Emily, her usual self, already bubbling with excitement, rushed to Simon.

"Uncle Simon, look! Isn't my dress pretty?" Before Simon could say any words of approval, she continued. "Mommy had Mrs. Tucker make it for me, and she let me pick out the material . . . and Mommy says I can stay up for the whole celebration!" She inhaled a deep breath as if she was preparing for a long speech, but Simon took the opportunity of the momentary pause.

"You sure are a sight, Emily. Why, I'll bet you're the prettiest girl in the prettiest dress at the party."

"Oh no, Uncle Simon." Emily laughed chidingly. "You know Mommy is much prettier than me. Remember, you told me Mommy was the prettiest lady in the whole world?"

Simon didn't look at Zoe . . . who was watching him. Instead he went to Emily. "You'll remember that you have to save a dance for me."

At this Emily's face suddenly grew serious. "I don't know how to dance."

"Well, don't let that worry you. I'm right good at it despite my limp, and I wouldn't mind teaching you."

Again the sunshine of her smile reappeared. Nothing clouded Emily's life for very long.

"I have to go along," Simon said. "I have a couple of committees to check up on and Reverend McBride is frantic by now. He just doesn't know that if you put the responsibility in the hands of the ladies, you won't have a problem with organization. I'll see you two there."

"You won't forget you have to teach me to dance?" Emily said quickly.

"Not for a minute." Simon bent and kissed her cheek;

then he turned to look at Zoe. Her lips were slightly parted and one hand rested gently on the strand of pearls. They seemed, to Simon, to pick up the warmth and the glow of her skin. "And Mommy has to remember to save a dance for me too," he said.

Zoe said nothing as their eyes held for a long moment. Her breath seemed caught in her chest, and she could actually feel Simon mentally reach to touch her. Then she shook off the sensation. "I'm afraid Mommy doesn't dance very well either. It takes practice, and I've had very little opportunity."

"That's all right. It should be fun to teach you both."

"I don't—"

"I'd better get going," Simon said, interrupting what he knew was a refusal. "I'll see you both there."

Zoe watched him go, her hand still resting on the pearls. They felt warm to her touch, as if they pulsed with life.

Grey's arrival broke her reverie, and in a short while they were on their way. What misgivings and tensions Zoe had, she kept well hidden for Emily's sake as well as her own. And Grey kept his recognition of it to himself as well.

Zach and Amelia made a point of arriving at the party first. Zach was more than established with the people of Aspen, and he wanted to make it clear that Zoe was his sister and he expected her to be accepted as he was. He had had more than one opportunity to make pointed remarks already.

Amelia smiled up at him. There was no doubt in her mind that Zoe would have no problem tonight. Her sister-in-law would never know the real reason she was so well accepted.

Simon arrived before Grey and Zoe, and sought out Zach almost at once.

"Amelia," Simon said with a smile, "how beautiful you look."

"Thank you. Are Zoe and Emily on their way?"

"Yes, I don't think they'll be too far behind me."

Zach raised an inquisitive brow, and Simon laughed. "I

stopped by on my way here. Wait until you see Emily. I don't know how that child could get more excited. She looks absolutely charming."

Amelia was the first to spot Zoe, Grey, and Emily's arrival. She and Zach stood on the opposite side of the room. Amelia realized that even in this crowd Zoe somehow stood apart. She was a vibrant force, gold and amber, radiating a beauty and vitality that could never go unnoticed.

Most male heads turned toward her with rather avid looks. Clearly, the men were wishing silently that this brilliant creature had arrived on their arms. Most women turned toward her with a touch of awe, mingled with an envy they could camouflage but never deny.

"Zach, Zoe's here," Amelia said.

Zach turned to follow her gaze, and a feeling of deep pride filled him. He, more than any other except Simon, knew the things Zoe had survived. A woman of lesser strength would have submitted to that battering long before.

But Zoe stood, her head erect and her beauty undimmed. It was as if she challenged the world and was completely unafraid of it. There were very few who knew how really terrified Zoe was.

Grey stood beside her with Emily, whose eyes were wide with wonder.

"Go to her, Zach," Amelia said softly, and received his look of gratitude for her understanding. He nodded, and began to rush through the crowd.

No one there missed the fact that Zach had moved to stand beside Zoe, symbolically supporting her . . . even Zoe knew it. She smiled at Zach as he approached, took her hands in his, and bent to kiss her cheek.

"My God, Zoe, you look great." He smiled down at Emily. "And who is this beautiful young lady you've brought along? Surely it's not my tomboy niece?"

Emily smiled up into the eyes that were filled with teasing laughter. "It's me, Uncle Zach."

"Well, you do look pretty. Ready to have some fun?"

"Yes! Uncle Simon said he'd teach me to dance."

Grey reacted imperceptibly to the news that Simon had

been to Zoe's . . . but Zoe sensed it. She said nothing.
There was nothing to say.

"How about something to eat first, Emily?" Zach asked.
"The dancing will start soon."

They all agreed to this, and were ready to walk to the
area where well-laden tables were set up when Zoe
paused. She was somewhat startled by the fact that Reverend McBride and his wife were headed in her direction.

Chapter Twenty-seven

When Reverend McBride and his wife were introduced to Zoe, Mrs. McBride smiled pleasantly. "I shall be glad to relieve you of that dish and find a place for it on the table," she said, "although it's already laden with goodies. I think there will be quite a feast tonight."

"Thank you." Zoe forced a smile as she handed Mrs. McBride the dish of baked sweet potatoes and ham she'd brought.

Mrs. McBride carried it away, and Zoe's attention was again drawn back to the reverend.

Zoe's early exposure to religious fanaticism had left her suspicious of all religion. She stiffened, but for the sake of the others she controlled herself. It might have surprised her to know that there were none in her group who were not well aware of her feelings . . . and all were watching the way she handled the situation.

"Good evening, Grey . . . Doctor." The reverend paused. "Miss Carrigan."

"Reverend McBride," Zoe murmured politely.

"It . . . ah . . . is nice to see you at this gathering, Miss Carrigan. From what I'm told, the town has you to thank for acquiring for us this fine doctor."

"My brother is an excellent doctor who most likely would have come to help whether I paid him or not. I just happen to think a good physician should be rewarded. No matter who he's forced to treat."

Zoe's unwavering gaze held the minister's, and even Grey was tempted to say something to get the reverend out of a very uncomfortable situation. Neither the town, the reverend . . . nor the other church dignitaries were yet prepared to accept Zoe ... but Grey knew Reverend McBride was trying, and Zoe wasn't.

"Well, I'm glad I came," Zach interjected, "and I'm ready to celebrate."

"Excellent." The reverend was more than relieved. He had a feeling Zoe was more than he could handle. "Go and taste the food," he suggested quickly. "You'll find some of Aspen's finest cooks have outdone themselves. And be prepared to dance and enjoy yourself."

"We'll do just that, Reverend," Grey said, and as the reverend moved away he could no longer control his deep chuckle.

"What's so funny?" Zoe inquired as he guided her and Emily toward the well-filled tables.

"Zoe, you've given the poor man indigestion. I think you scared him to death."

"Don't be silly, Grey. His kind is just used to people bowing and scraping, and I've no intention of doing any such thing."

"Zoe ... now you promised to try."

"Yes, I did ... and I will." Zoe finally smiled. "So stop worrying. I want Emily to have fun. I won't spoil it."

"Then let's eat," Grey suggested.

At last Zoe laughed too, and the group began to move toward the dishes and down the line to fill their plates.

The food, as the reverend had said, was excellent. Every woman in town had brought her best dish.

In trying to make Zach feel their warmth and affection, the people began to warm toward Zoe. They already felt a genuine affection for Grey, and were enchanted by Emily. At first Zoe was stiff and somewhat reluctant ... until one mother began to ask questions about Emily, a subject Zoe found easy to warm to.

Simon, Grey, Cara, Zach, and Amelia watched with pleasure as the people began to discover that maybe Zoe was not the ogre they'd imagined, and she began to discover that she was not facing a battle ... not tonight.

By the time the dancing started, Zoe had begun to unbend and enjoy herself. Once her reluctance was breached, she joined in the laughter she heard around her, the laughter she'd sought for so long.

Grey watched her, as did Simon, and both felt as if a small battle had been won.

The music was provided by a group of local musicians who handled any social occasion, including weddings and birthdays. It was not exactly a symphonic orchestra, but what it lacked in finesse it made up for in enthusiasm.

Grey was the first one to lure Zoe to the dance floor, and he complimented her at once on how quickly she picked up the steps.

"For a lady who told me before she didn't know how to dance, you have sure learned fast."

"I have a good teacher."

"Having fun, Zoe?"

"More than I expected to," she admitted.

"I told you, didn't I? All you have to do is reach out."

"This is tonight, Grey. Everyone's having fun. Tomorrow . . ." She shrugged.

"You don't know about tomorrow. Things can be changed, Zoe . . . believe me."

Zoe went from Grey's arms to Zach's. Then she found herself dancing with several other single men who'd realized for the first time that Zoe was not the cold woman they had thought her to be.

Simon stood some distance away, but close enough to watch Zoe. He watched her unfold like a flower to the rising sun. This was the Zoe he had always wanted her to be. This was the way he wanted to see her, laughing, her cheeks flushed, and her eyes aglow. Happy.

He watched her for as long as he could, then made his way toward her. Her back was to him, and she was laughing at something when Simon came up behind her. He thought how much he liked to hear her laugh.

"Zoe?"

She turned to look up at him, and he could feel himself tremble like an expectant boy with his first girl.

"Simon," she said softly.

"I asked you to save me a dance. Is this it?"

"Yes, if you like."

"I'd like." He smiled as he extended his hand to her. She responded to his smile and put her hand in his.

They began to dance, and for a while they did not talk. It was Simon who spoke first.

"Having a good time, aren't you?"

"Yes, I am."

"Have any idea why?"

"What?"

"I said—"

"I know what you said. I just don't understand why you said it."

"Think about it. Do you have a real idea why you're enjoying yourself? After all, three fourths of these people are from the flats, miners and their wives and families, and not only are you enjoying yourself, but Emily couldn't be having more fun."

"It's your question and you seem to have the answer."

"Because you've made a discovery. You've found out that all people don't fit your mold. You've found out they're just people . . . like you, and that all the money in the world wouldn't make it any different. They're kind, Zoe . . . and so are you."

"Zach and Emily could be part of the reason."

"They could be. Part of it, but not all of it. You came halfway. That's all it takes. They're more than willing to come the other half."

"You're such a stubborn man."

He laughed. "I think I've mentioned your stubborness a few times."

"A few times?"

"Well, maybe more than a few."

"I'm not going to be angry or argue with you tonight, Simon. I'm enjoying myself too much."

"That's one thing I don't want to argue about."

"So did you give Emily a dancing lesson?"

"You trying to change the subject?"

"Yes," she responded with a quick laugh.

"All right. I tried to give her a dancing lesson, but she's having so much fun with a group of friends that I felt a bit unwelcome, so I went off looking for her mother."

"She actually . . ." Zoe began.

"She looked at me with those big gold eyes and told me

in a roundabout way that she didn't need my services, thank you, sir. I suddenly felt very old."

Now Zoe laughed aloud at Simon's pretended distress. "You sound downright fatherly."

"That's my plan," he said quietly.

"I'm not looking for a father for my child. She had a father."

"He let go of you, Zoe. Why can't you let go of him?"

"That's not fair. I deserve—"

"I know what you deserve. I've been around a long time . . . remember?"

Zoe had been so intent on their conversation that she had hardly noticed that they were moving toward the door until they reached it and Simon suddenly stopped, took her hand in his, and drew her outside before she could protest.

Outside, the night was cool. The area behind the large hall in which the party was being held was an expanse of green lawn, studded here and there with large trees.

Simon tucked Zoe's hand through his arm and they walked for a while, until they stopped beneath a large tree whose branches created a shadowy area. She rested against the trunk of the tree and Simon stood beside her, leaning one shoulder against the tree as well.

"I haven't seen such a night in a while," Simon breathed softly. "That's quite a moon."

"It's a harvest moon when it's big and yellow like that," Zoe replied. She looked up at Simon. "And you didn't bring me out here to talk about the moon."

"Why not?" His smile was white in the dim moonlight. "A man who can get a beautiful girl out in the moonlight . . . all alone . . . can develop a lot of ideas in his head."

"Simon," she said with a laugh, "I thought we were past the young courtship stage."

"Where have I been? I didn't know we'd gotten to it." His smile faded, and he reached to lift the strand of pearls and held them gently between his fingers. "I'd give anything to be able to court you, Zoe . . . to show you how to have fun . . . to . . ."

Zoe looked up into Simon's eyes and felt his warmth envelop her.

"We can't go back, Simon, nobody can and I, for one, wouldn't. I couldn't live through my life again."

"Maybe, knowing what I know now," he said gently, "I could have made it easier on you."

Zoe laughed a soft laugh, but tears glistened in her eyes. "Maybe . . . maybe one of the reasons you are so dear to me, Simon, is because you are a dreamer still. You want to right everything for everyone. I lost my dreams so long ago."

"Then let me share mine with you. Dreaming is not wrong, Zoe. Sometimes it takes courage, and I know you have that." Simon braced one hand beside her and held the pearls with the other. "You are the most courageous woman I know." His voice softened as he bent his head and kissed her. The kiss was gentle and lingering, and for a moment Zoe was caught in what might have been.

She could sense the desire building in both of them, and for the first time felt a real fear. Simon was her weakness . . . a weakness she couldn't afford. Maybe sometime . . . but not now. She would have to surrender too much of herself.

She put her hand over his and gently withdrew the pearls. Without a word she moved away from him.

"Maybe," she said quietly, "there was a time when you could have made me happy." She turned to face him. "I'm not a girl any longer, Simon, and you're not a boy. Maybe, once, the girl and boy we were could have . . . but . . . don't you see, we can't reclaim what's past or change it to be the way we want it to be. You can't go back and smooth all of life's rough spots, not for you and certainly not for me. I can't undo anything, and maybe I don't want to."

"What is it going to take to make you want something more than you want your revenge? Whatever it is, one day you will run across it. One day you will come face-to-face with a choice. I hope, for your sake, you make the right one."

"Whatever choice I make," Zoe said in a controlled voice, "I'll have to live with it as I've lived with all my choices." She turned and walked away from him, back toward the hall. After a few minutes Simon followed.

With a fierce determination Zoe threw herself into

having fun for the rest of the evening. She might have impressed the townspeople, who laughed with her and enjoyed her almost furious gaiety, but those closest to her sensed that something had gone drastically wrong. It was only Grey who guessed the truth . . . and it worried him.

Grey took a sleepy but contented Emily and a very quiet Zoe home. He wanted nothing more than to question Zoe about what had happened, but she left him no opening to do so.

He might not know the particulars, but he was sure Simon was to blame. He cursed himself for admiring and respecting a man who had more ability to hurt him than any other. He just wished he could learn to hate Simon Tremaine.

Zoe tried her best to accept the fact that Emily made friends as easily as breathing, and that she had to learn to accept her daughter's friends. Still, she did not care to accompany Emily on her occasional visits to her aunt and uncle. She knew that Amelia's house was open to many young girls and Emily was happy with them. Somehow that knowledge hurt Zoe as much as it frightened her. Emily was all she had, and these were the people she had tried to protect her from.

She was considering this aggravating situation two weeks later when Grey arrived. It was late morning, and she was surprised to see him.

"Grey? What are you doing here this time of day?"

"I thought it best to bring the news I have in person."

"News, what news?"

"On the morning train," Grey said quietly, "you have a long-awaited visitor."

Zoe looked at him for so long that Grey began to wonder if it had registered in her mind whom he was talking about. Then she spoke in a whisper.

"Brent?"

"Yes, he's here, and most anxious to meet Zoe Carrigan."

"Where?"

"Down at the hotel," Grey replied. "Zoe . . . I could go see him. I could just read the papers, let him go back home. Let it go, Zoe." It was a last desperate pleading.

"You've seen him?"

"Yes."

"What . . . what does he look like . . . I mean . . ."

"I know what you mean. It's easy for me to read him. I know how desperate he is." Her look made him pause. "He's older, of course. What the hell do you want me to say? He's a desperate man. He'll be totally bankrupt if you do what you plan. Zoe, for God's sake . . ."

"Tell him to come here this afternoon around three. That I'll see him then."

Zoe walked to a window to look out and Grey, frustration on his face, took a step toward her. But he knew any words he had would fall on deaf ears. Her revenge would be complete this afternoon, and everyone but Zoe knew that it was not going to change her life in any way.

"All right," Grey said with a ragged sigh, "I'll tell him. I'll bring all the papers and—"

"Grey."

"What?"

"I want to see him alone."

"He's a man who's about to be ruined. He might not be able to control himself. Zoe, it's a dangerous proposition."

She turned to face him. "Brent was always a weak man who needed someone else to fight his battles. He won't do me any harm. He's not man enough."

"A cornered rat goes for the throat."

"I want to see him alone, Grey. I have to."

Grey fought a crowd of emotions. "You want this so bad?"

"Yes, I do."

"You're a fool," Grey said finally. "You want this because you're blind. When you open your eyes you may find there was something you wanted more and you've lost it."

"Funny, Simon said the same thing to me once. Both of you refuse to understand."

"Maybe we understand more than you think."

"I'm going to see him," she said firmly, her voice suddenly cold. "Don't get in my way now. When this is over . . ."

Grey looked shaken, as if she had struck him. "I didn't know I was in the way," he said quietly, "but I guess I am. Just like Simon, Cara, everyone is in your way. All right, Zoe, I'll tell him to come here. Then I'm going up to the mine. After that . . . maybe it would be best if I leave Aspen for a while. I'd like you to care, but I suppose that's a useless dream too."

"Grey!"

"I can't stand to watch your hate at work anymore. I love you, but when you balance love against your damn vendetta, I guess love is the loser. I'll go see him, tell him to come here at three. Then I'll go to the mine and get the crews moving and find a new manager. I wish . . . I wish I'd been enough to come between you and this . . . but then, I don't think any man is. I'm sorry."

He turned and walked out, and Zoe stood in stunned silence for a moment. She couldn't believe it, wouldn't believe it. Grey would come to his senses. When this was over she would concentrate on Grey and his part in her life . . . when this was over. She turned back to the window. At that moment she heard the door close, and suddenly it made her shiver. It had a frighteningly final sound. She pushed the thought away and began to consider what she was about to do, and to wonder what Brent was feeling.

Brent had opened Grey's last letter with trepidation at first, read it, and immediately made plans for his trip to Aspen.

The one last thing he'd done was to face Lester Crandell and tell him that he was no longer his puppet . . . his slave. The past months had been a particular kind of hell, and Lester had taken glee in making them so.

On the train ride to Aspen he thought of his last confrontation with Lester. He had made his position clear. He'd acquired a wealthy mine and he was resigning as Lester's lawyer. Lester had been taken by surprise at first. He was clearly annoyed that Brent seemed to be slipping from his grasp long before he was finished with him.

"And where did you acquire all this newfound prosperity?"

"Aspen. I've been investing slowly and regularly in a mine up there. Everything I could borrow, save, or sell is there . . . and now I've been invited to supervise what I now own most of. I'm afraid I'm saying good-bye to Denver . . . and to you."

"Who is your benefactor?"

"A man named Grey Sinclair."

"Grey Sinclair . . . the name is vaguely familiar. Is he the owner of the mine?"

"No, just the manager."

"Ah . . . and the owner?"

"Is a lady who wants to travel and is about to let me become sole owner. It's a rich mine . . . a very rich mine. One that will make me independent from you for the rest of my life. You have tried to drain the lifeblood from me and failed. Now sit here and rot for all I care. I'm leaving tomorrow."

"This . . . ah . . . lady, does she know you for what you are?"

"I have never met her. Everything has been done through her manager and by mail. But now I'm going to meet her, and thank her for my deliverance."

"Who is this woman who is so foolish as to trust you to deal honestly with her or anyone else?"

"Her name is Carrigan, Zoe Carrigan, and she has given me all the wealth I need, so don't try to interfere in my life again."

"Zoe Carrigan," Lester repeated. The brilliant truth was almost too much for Lester to bear. It was as if all his misery, anger, and hatred of Brent had been gathered in one force . . . a force that he knew was not planning on Brent's salvation at all . . . but on his complete destruction.

He wanted to shout out his knowledge. But that would have let Brent see the truth before its time. No, let him cut away his lifeline, let him go to Aspen with no road to return on. Let him face Zoe Carrigan and know the truth then, when there was no way back.

"Well . . . I see I have failed. May I wish that you get exactly what you deserve." Lester's smile made him look like a sly Buddha. Brent was surprised, but felt this diplomacy was Lester's only way out of the situation. His father-in-law was clever, Brent thought; he would keep things level enough so Brent would return and perhaps reinvest his wealth with Lester.

"I'm sure I will." Brent's old arrogance was back.

"Give my regards to Zoe Carrigan. Who knows, we might do business one day."

"I doubt it. I told you she has plans to travel, but"— Brent's look was gloating—"if you contact me I might consider it."

"I'll do that, Brent," Lester said softly. "I'll do that."

Brent walked out of Lester's office without a glance back at the man who sat at his huge desk contemplating the door that had closed between them. A low chuckle was born deep within Lester, and built to a rumbling laugh.

Now Brent stood alone in his hotel room, impatiently waiting for news of when he could meet with Zoe Carrigan. He had found it difficult to glean much information from Grey Sinclair, except that Miss Carrigan had no husband. This alone excited Brent. Who knows what might happen? They just might hit it off. He knew quite well how charming he could be, and he planned on using every ounce of charm he had.

The rap on the door shook him from his thoughts, and when he opened it to find Grey there, an excitement he hadn't felt in a long time coursed through him.

"Mr. Sinclair, come in, please."

"I'm afraid I've no time right now," Grey said. He didn't want to have to face Brent's enthusiasm. "I have to get up to the mine and settle some last-minute details. I've only come to tell you that Miss Carrigan will see you today, at three at her home." Grey went on to explain exactly how he was to get there. "She'll be waiting for you in her . . . library. You're to go right in."

"Thank you, sir. You're sure I can't interest you in letting me buy you lunch? You have been a strong instrument in the success of this venture, and I feel—"

"You owe me nothing, Mr. Dewitt. I follow Miss Carrigan's orders, that's all."

"Then how about the three of us celebrating over dinner tonight?"

"I'm afraid I'll be tied up at the mine until very late tonight. It's best you see Miss Carrigan before you make decisive plans."

Brent was puzzled at first; then he shrugged it off as Grey's discomfort at sharing dinner with his employers. After all, he was entirely out of his element, wasn't he?

When Brent had groomed himself carefully, he bolted down two shots of whiskey for support while he watched the time creep toward three. Finally, Brent found himself on his way.

When he arrived at the house, he was impressed. It was most likely the biggest and most elaborate place in Aspen. He began to feel that he and Zoe Carrigan had a great deal in common. Both appreciated the finer things in life.

He walked up on the porch, opened the door without hesitation, and stepped inside.

The inside of the house was cool and carried the clean scent of polished wood and soft breezes through the open windows.

He stood for a moment looking about, and discerned quickly where the library was. Its door was half open and from where he was standing, a floor-to-ceiling bookshelf could be seen. She would be there, the woman who had offered him redemption.

He took a step toward the room, but he suddenly sensed they were not alone. He looked about him and saw no one. Then he looked up at the carpeted steps and saw her. A little girl sat on the top step, a kitten in her lap and her intent gaze on him.

Some premonition seemed to drag its fingers through his senses, but he dismissed it as nerves.

"Hello."

"Hello," Emily replied in a soft voice. She'd been instructed by her mother to remain in her room until her guest left, but Emily's curiosity had gotten the better of her. She regarded him with serious eyes.

"And who might you be?"

"Emily."

"You're Miss Carrigan's little girl?"

"Yes."

"Would you like to come down?"

"Uh-uh." Emily shook her head. She rose and, carrying the kitten with her, disappeared down the upstairs hall.

Brent shook his head and smiled at her timidity. Maybe he would have a chance to meet her later. He started again toward the library.

Within the library Zoe stood at the window, her back to the door. She heard the footsteps approach, heard the door swing open. For a moment she could only close her eyes and inhale a deep breath.

Brent looked at the tall slender woman who stood with her back to him, and again felt a sudden feeling of familiarity. It was a strange thing, as if his senses seemed to know this woman he had never met. He spoke her name softly, and Zoe felt it brush against her spirit with wings of memory.

"Miss Carrigan. . . . Zoe Carrigan?"

Slowly the woman turned about to face him. The sunlight of the window haloed her, picking up the live flame of her hair but casting her face in shadow. But shadow or not, he knew her! He knew her! It was . . .

"Hello, Brent." Her voice was like velvet. "It's been a long time."

He felt as if the force of a tidal wave was swelling up within him, drowning every thought. He stood welded to the spot, unable to move, unable to breathe, feeling his life and strength vanish before the power of his emotions.

"Laura?" He gasped her name in disbelief.

"No. It was never Laura. It was always Zoe . . . Zoe Carrigan. Daughter of an itinerant preacher. A girl from the flats."

"I don't understand . . . I . . . Laura . . ." He gasped the words out, feeling the walls of his life tumbling about him.

"Maybe I can help you understand, Brent. After all, it's so very simple. Being the businessman you are, surely you can understand when it's time to call in debts."

Shame followed a tumultuous flood of guilt. He tried to think clearly, but he'd been given a mortal blow and the realization of it was just beginning to reach his mind.

"It was you? All the time it was you? The mine . . ."

"The mine you own . . . is worthless, and the debts you owe are all in my possession. In fact, Brent, I own you."

She watched his face go gray, saw the trembling hand that reached for the back of a nearby chair and grasped it until his knuckles grew white.

"What . . . what are you doing to me?"

"I'm doing to you what you did to me. That's only fair, isn't it? You left me with nothing and I'm leaving you the same way."

Zoe watched Brent sag into the chair as the full reality of what was happening swept over him.

"The mine I have is worthless?" His voice broke in disbelief.

"Yes . . . and you owe me more money than you will be able to accumulate in the rest of your life."

Brent was so utterly defeated that he no longer seemed to be able to feel. He sat, looking at her with eyes dulled by defeat. He had lost his bravado, his arrogance, his gentility, and just about all that made him Brent Dewitt.

Zoe waited for the flow of expected satisfaction to flood her being with the pleasure she had thought this day would bring . . . but it didn't.

It was minutes before Brent's sluggish mind began to stir. Zoe Carrigan . . . Zoe Carrigan . . . the child had said . . . He looked closely at Zoe and he knew. The pain of the knowledge made him groan and bury his face in his hands. Then he looked up at her.

"The child I saw when I came in . . . Emily, she said her name was. She's . . . ?"

Zoe was shaken that he had seen Emily, but only for a moment. Maybe it was better for him to see what he would never have.

"Yes, Brent, she was yours. When you left me so coldly, so alone, you left your child as well."

"Ah, God . . . Laura . . ." His voice broke on a little sob.

"No!" Zoe said sharply. "Zoe Carriggan. And the child's name is Emily Carrigan . . . the certificate of birth says father unknown . . . illegitimate. This is why I will see you fall. You didn't even have the decency to marry me and give Emily a name. I have damned you for so long."

"Zoe." He almost sobbed her name as he extended a helpless hand toward her. "It's not true. What you think is not true. We were married."

"That is the biggest lie of all. We checked the courthouse. Our marriage was never registered. We were not married!"

"No! That's not true. The . . . preacher who married us was a drunk. He wandered around for several days after the wedding in a drunken spree before he discovered the fact that in his drunkeness he'd not registered the marriage. He did it then . . . in Connellsville. It's registered in Connellsville. My father found it and"—he bent his head as a new shame and desperation washed through him—"he managed a divorce proceeding, hoping you would not find out and fight the divorce before it was accomplished. You didn't . . . the divorce became final."

Zoe was almost overcome by a mass of conflicting emotions. Relief that she could make her daughter legitimate, and pity, an emotion she didn't want to recognize, pity for this man who was too weak to control his own life.

Brent could read the scorn in her eyes, and he crumbled before it.

Zoe wanted to go on hating him, to lash out and destroy him. She wanted to leave him bloody and broken. "You knew this and you still let your father—"

"Zoe, it was a mistake, a terrible, tragic mistake. But I've changed. I have!" Brent was desperate. He could not go back and face Lester as a broken man. The rest of his life would be hell. "Zoe, you never married again?" His voice was full of his old conceited hope, and Zoe recognized it for what it was.

"No."

"You loved me once. The child, that beautiful child, is mine. There is so much wealth. You have so much money. We could . . . we could try again. With all that money we could . . ." He stopped before her icy gaze.

Zoe felt something akin to horror go through her. Money! That was all he wanted. He did not ask about his daughter, he did not ask about the years that they had been separated, all she had gone through. He felt money was the bridge that would connect them.

At the same time the truth came to her as clear as crystal. He had not left her with nothing; he had left her with everything. He had left her with Emily, the best thing in her life, and he had left her with love . . . Simon. She had more than Brent had ever known, or ever would know.

Suddenly the hatred and the need for revenge were washed away before the brilliance of truth. The need for revenge died a silent death. She looked at him in a new light, and wondered how she had let this poisonous need for money blind her to Brent and his kind.

"Emily is not yours . . . she's mine," she said with finality.

Brent was fighting for his life and he knew it. He would fight like a cornered animal.

"I have our marriage certificate. I can prove you were my wife then . . . and that is enough to go to court." He sucked in a ragged breath. "I will take Emily."

Zoe regarded him coldly, and it shook him to see that she showed no sign of fear. She was remembering Simon's words. Someday, he had said, you will have to make a choice, and someday you will discover something or someone you want and love more than you love money. That day had come, and she accepted it like a flow of healing water.

She understood everything Simon and Grey had tried so hard to make her see. She loved Emily with her entire being. She loved Grey with the warmth of deepest friendship . . . and she loved Simon with a passion she knew now would never be extinguished.

"You would take Emily from me?" she said softly.

"If you forced me to it." He tried to sound firm and brave, but was struck by her sudden derisive laughter.

"Brent . . . I will make you a bargain."

"A bargain?" He was suspicious of this quick-minded, seemingly heartless woman. This was not the Laura he had known. In fact, he knew now he had never known her at all. "What kind of bargain?"

"I will return your notes marked paid. I will sign over some of the profits of my mine to you, which should keep you comfortable the rest of your life." She was well aware of the sudden light of hope in his eyes. "But you will get the money in yearly payments. That way you will hold no power, for you will not hold a percentage in the mine itself."

"What is it you want from me?"

"First, my marriage certificate, and then the divorce papers. I want proof that you are no longer a part of my life or Emily's. Then a signed paper that relinquishes all claim on Emily and states the fact that you will never be seen in Aspen again. Nor will you ever try to see Emily again. You will have the money you need to survive . . . but nothing else."

She knew in her heart that the money was all he was really after. She could read the relief in his eyes even though he tried to bluster.

"Emily is my daughter," he said.

"Is she really? Where were you when she was born? When she was ill? While she was growing? You were married to your wealth. Well, now, take your wealth and leave us alone." She bent toward him, and he read finality in her eyes. "Or . . . I will destroy you, and that is a promise. You see, I know what money can do . . . and without me you have nothing."

He was defeated. Brent could not survive going back and facing Lester again. He knew as well as Zoe that he could not survive being penniless. She had won . . . yet she still felt pity, because Brent would never know love . . . never.

"I agree."

"I'll have the papers drawn up at once. I want to finish this business once and for all. It is time Emily and I put you behind us and began to live our lives. I have so many plans you will never understand. Remain at your hotel. I will see the papers are brought to you. Good-bye, Brent . . . and for what it's worth . . . good luck."

Brent looked in her eyes and knew there was nothing more he could say. He had won what he'd come for . . . but he was defeated, and the years ahead looked blank and empty. Without another word he walked from the room.

Zoe stood, hardly breathing, for some time. It was over.

She had faced her past and wiped away the pain and misery with a sigh of relief.

She walked to the window again and stood looking out. Yes, Simon, she thought, I have made my choices. I have found the things that mean more to me than all the wealth in the world. Friends . . . Cara. Family . . . Zach and Amelia and Emily. Security . . . Grey. And love . . . Simon.

A sound from outside finally penetrated her consciousness. It must have been filling the air for several minutes before she realized what it was. An ancient sound that belonged to the mines . . . a sound that could make her heart squeeze into a hard knot. It was a sound that screamed like one of Dante's dying souls.

The high-pitched scream of the siren at one of the mines. It jolted through her like a silver-bladed knife, cutting all thoughts of Brent and the past away. It meant only one thing . . . *disaster!*

With a low sound of pure fear deep in her throat, she turned and ran from the room.

Chapter Twenty-eight

By the time Zoe reached her front porch, she could see that the town was swarming with people, drawn from their houses and businesses by the siren.

There was no way of telling which of the five mines surrounding the town was facing the problem that had prompted the call for help. But something deep inside her rose up like a fist shutting off her air. She raced back inside the house and up the stairs to Emily's room.

"Emily, get your cloak. You must go to Aunt Cara's restaurant right away."

"What's wrong, Mommy?"

"I don't have time to explain now, darling. Please, you must hurry."

"Can I take Charlie?"

"Of course. Just hurry. Tell Aunt Cara I'll explain everything to her later. I know she won't leave the restaurant. I'll come as soon as I can."

Emily's eyes regarded her intently. She had never seen her mother in such a state. She knew this was not the time for questions.

By the time Zoe flew down her porch steps again and ran to the end of the walk, a number of carriages were already racing by. A feeling of fear seemed to fill the town like a silent cry, a moan of anger and fear that could only be heard in the hearts of those who had loved ones and friends in the dark pits.

The distance to her mine was much too far for her to attempt on foot. Gathering her nerve, she stepped out in front of the next carriage she saw racing toward her.

With an angry curse the man holding the reins drew

the horses to a skidding, hoof-pounding stop.

"What the hell! Lady, are you crazy? I could have killed you!"

"Please," Zoe begged, "do you know what happened, which mine?"

His face lost its anger. He could see the live terror in Zoe's eyes.

"Yes, ma'am. It's the Future."

"Oh, God," Zoe cried. "Please, please can you take me there? I'll pay you! I've got to get there!"

"No need to pay me." His eyes narrowed. "You're Zoe Carrigan, aren't you? You're the owner of the Future?"

"Yes. I've got to know what happened . . . if anyone is hurt."

"Climb in. We'll be up there right quick."

Without any hesitation Zoe climbed in beside him, and he slapped the reins, goading the horses into a run.

"Do you know what happened?" Zoe shouted over the confusion surrounding them.

"I ain't sure. But if I was to guess, I'd say either an explosion . . . or a collapse. Either one, there's sure to be men in trouble. The siren don't blow like that unless there's something real serious."

Zoe could only think of Grey. Grey had planned to go up to the mine right after he talked to Brent. Was he still there? Had something happened to him? Terror made her heart pound furiously. She said nothing more, merely clung to the carriage as it careened along its way.

When they arrived at the mine pandemonium reigned. Clusters of people milled around the entrance, where a cloud of grey-brown dust, debris, and smoke obscured visibility.

As Zoe climbed down from the carriage, she searched the milling crowd.

It surprised her that Simon was nowhere about. She located the friends who shared his house, Paul and April, and shortly after she spotted Zach.

She could see he was already caring for men who'd been injured and Amelia was nearby. Forcing her way through the crowd to Zach's side, she grasped his arm.

"Zach! Zach, what happened?"

"I'm not sure. Timbers collapsed, some kind of an explosion. But I don't know what." He was moving as he talked, and Zoe moved with him. "You'll have to ask one of the men who are conscious."

"Where are you going?"

"With the rescue teams."

She stopped dead in her tracks for a moment, then raced to catch up with Zach's long-legged stride. She caught his arm and spun him around to face her.

"Zoe, I can't stop to talk now."

"What rescue teams? What do you mean rescue teams?"

He looked at her in momentary surprise. "You don't know . . . Lord . . . Zoe, there are still five men down there."

She tried to read his face, but her heart refused to believe what her mind already knew.

"Grey," she whispered.

"Grey," he said, "Pa . . . and Simon, plus two others."

For a second she couldn't think; then it exploded in her mind. "It can't be . . . it can't. What's Pa doing here?"

"He came to see if he could go and talk to the men. You know how he is." Zach was tense. "Zoe, there's no time. I have to go. Go on back with Amelia and see what you can do to help," he said roughly as he moved away from her.

She could tell the depth of his worry by the strain in his voice. Slowly she stumbled back toward Amelia.

Grey . . . Simon, both of them, down in the dark bowels of the earth . . . maybe dead already. No! Her mind would not accept that. They couldn't be dead, they couldn't! Blinded by worry Zoe staggered toward the hurriedly set-up rescue camp where Pete, Gus, Paul, and April worked to help Amelia with the injured.

Amelia watched her approaching, staggering beneath the weight of her fear. She felt a surge of understanding pity. If it had been Zach down there she knew how she would feel.

"Zoe."

"Amelia, I can't believe . . ."

"It was an accident. It seems Simon got several men out, but he and Grey, and your father, went back for the last men, and then it felt as if the whole mountain had collapsed."

Zoe's face filled with misery. "They can't be dead, Amelia," she sobbed, "they just can't. I never had a chance to tell them . . . I have to tell them . . ." She couldn't speak. She merely hugged herself as if she were shattering.

"Zoe, you have to get hold of yourself. This is no time to collapse. You need all your strength, and there are others who need your help."

Zoe raised her head and looked at Amelia as if she could not quite grasp what she was saying. Amelia knew a shock had immobilized her. Perhaps another shock would snap her out of it.

"If you can't be of any help, Zoe," she said firmly, "then get out of the way and let us do our job."

Zoe gasped as if she'd been struck. Then the old resilient Zoe reappeared. "It's my mine . . . they're my men. I can do whatever needs to be done."

"Good girl." Amelia smiled and her voice was soft enough for Zoe to realize what she had meant to accomplish with her harsh words. Zoe smiled. "I'm sorry."

"I know . . . and they'll know too. We'll get them out, Zoe."

Zoe could only nod, then follow Amelia to a place where several men were lying on blankets. As she walked she rolled up her sleeves. Work was better than waiting helplessly. As she worked she realized the eyes of the women were on her. The word of this would spread as quickly as word of the disaster did.

Pale light flickered against the dark cavern. Simon remained very still until the last rumbling sounds of the collapse slowly faded away. For a minute he was afraid to move. Afraid that more rocks would come.

"Grey?"

A low cough followed by a raspy voice was a welcome sound.

"Yeah."

"You all right?"

"I think so." His laugh was shaky. "I'll have to check as soon as I get enough guts to move."

"Mr. Carrigan? Mr. Carrigan?"

A low groan was his answer as Simon struggled to sit up and look around. The dust-filled light was so pale that he could only make out shadowy forms.

The little light there was came from one lantern that had miraculously escaped the destruction that had destroyed the others.

Simon crawled to it, testing his arms and legs at the same time. He lifted it and examined it closely. There was enough oil in it to create light for some time yet. Then they would be left in utter blackness. He wondered if the air they were breathing, bad as it was, would last that long.

He tried standing, and lifted the lantern with him to survey the area better. Grey had just struggled to a sitting position. But Roger Carrigan lay some distance away and from the way he was lying, Simon knew he was not going to get up so easily. Lantern in hand, Simon went and knelt by his side.

While he checked Roger, Grey moved to the other men, who were groaning and stirring.

"Mr. Carrigan?" Simon said softly.

Roger opened his eyes again and looked up at Simon. "Did we get them all out?"

"We came close. There's a couple here to share this cozy little place."

"Simon . . . how bad is it?"

"I haven't had time to look around. How are you?"

"It really doesn't matter, does it?"

"You're not giving up hope, are you? That's not exactly in your line of business."

"Being dishonest with myself is not my line of business either." Roger's voice was so controlled that it confirmed Simon's earlier suspicion.

He used both his hands to examine Roger gently, but even the most sensitive touch brought a ragged sound of pain. Roger's chest was nearly crushed; he would not be able to move or to be moved.

Simon had no words of consolation, and Roger didn't seem to expect them. "See to the others and see if there is a way to get them out of here," Roger said.

"I'm sorry," Simon said with quiet sadness, and he meant it.

Simon moved away from Roger and went to Grey, who looked at him questioningly. Simon gave a slight shake of his head. "How are the other two?" he asked.

"Bruised and shaken, but all right. Are we going to run out of air or light first?" Grey asked.

"It's going to be a close race, unless we find a way out. Talk to Roger, Grey. I'll scout around and see how we stand."

"Okay. Damn . . . this is a hell of a place for him to end up."

"Yeah . . . well, it's not a nice place for any of us to end up. So let's not think that way."

"I'll look after him. What . . ."

"His chest, it's pretty smashed up. I have a feeling the lungs are not going to hold up much longer."

"I could tear up my shirt and bind him."

"It's useless. Don't make him suffer by moving him around. Besides, binding might do more harm than good."

"Okay. I'll talk to him."

"Keep him calm."

"I'll do my best. Simon?"

"Yeah?"

"Find us a hole."

"I'll do my best. They'll be digging for us."

"If they think we're alive."

"Miners don't give up on each other like that."

"Maybe we should start digging from this side."

"We should, but I want to look around first."

Grey nodded. There was much unsaid between him and Simon, but now, and in the face of death, was not the time to confront one another. Grey wondered if they were going to be allowed the time.

He could have told Simon that Brent Dewitt was in town, most likely talking to Zoe at this very moment. He could have told Simon Zoe's revenge would be complete. He wondered what Simon would have done if this had not happened. It was too late to worry about that now. He went to try to comfort Roger.

*   *   *

The sun was nearing the horizon, and lanterns and small fires were being used so the digging could continue. Amelia and Zoe, exhausted but too frightened and much too nervous to find any rest, waited for word from the rescuers.

Zach came to them a time or two to tell of their progress, and each time he did, they could read growing worry in his eyes.

"They're going to run out of air, aren't they, Zach . . . if they're not already dead," Zoe said.

"They're not dead, Zoe! We won't believe that until we know for sure."

"But they will run out of air soon." Zoe was pleading for him to assure her that it wasn't true.

Zach didn't answer. He merely turned and walked away. There was no need to answer. All of them knew that time was no longer on their side.

To Zoe every minute seemed like hours. She lived in a valley of torment. It seemed to her self-accusing mind that she had thrown away every opportunity for happiness with her own hands.

The hours gave her time to recount every past day . . . every past hour. She was beyond tears, and felt as if she were being drained of life.

What would the rest of her life be like if she lost . . . she could not bring herself to think of Simon and Grey being dead.

For a long time she forced that thought away by thinking of Roger, and all the times that Simon and Grey had told her she would never be satisfied until she could bring herself to face him and realize he could not bring any more harm into her life.

Simon and Grey . . . the two men who had made her life worth living. She knew and understood them both so much better now. It was as if a curtain had been drawn aside and she was allowed to see the panorama of her life.

She began, as all those filled with desperation did, to bargain with God. In mental prayer she made her offer. If He would let Simon and Grey come out of this alive, she would promise to forgive. If He gave her Simon and

Grey, she would give Him herself. She would learn to forgive if only He rewarded her by fulfilling her needs. If He gave . . . she would give. If He answered, she would answer. She held on to this self-deception like a drowning person.

Surely, if God was benevolent, He would hear and answer. She could not let go of these thoughts or she would sink in the black waves of despair.

Amelia, her face pale and her body weary, came to sit near Zoe.

"It's been so long, Amelia."

"I know."

"They're not dead, they can't be!"

"I pray not, Zoe." She turned to look at Zoe and saw that her eyes were filled with tears and that the salty tears were escaping to trace down her cheeks.

"There are so many things I never said to him, so many times I could have told him and never did. Oh, Amelia, it's not fair."

"I guess, because life is not fair, that we have to take every opportunity to express our love. You don't know when the opportunity might be gone."

Zoe struggled for a new kind of understanding that had been totally alien to her. She had never considered total surrender before. She was too vulnerable to be able to bear it. She looked at Amelia, who seemed to have this calm confidence.

She questioned Amelia's depth of faith . . . a faith that had no qualifications. "I made God a bargain," she told Amelia, explaining her silent prayers.

"You can't bargain with God, Zoe," Amelia said gently. "You have to have faith in His will."

Zoe was silent, afraid to let go of that last restraint, afraid of giving something or someone else that control.

Amelia could only reach out and lay her hand over Zoe's, and the look in her eyes was one of understanding and sympathy.

Twenty-four hours later, within the mine the lantern burned low, and the air was thin. The men were still now, trying to conserve what air they could. There was no other way out. If they were not reached in time, this dark and dismal place would be their grave.

"Simon?" Grey whispered.

"Yeah?"

"I was planning on leaving Aspen . . . for a spell at least."

Simon was surprised, but he said nothing. When the specter of death loomed, it was difficult to bring the petty jealousies and angers to life.

"Why? I can't see you being at home anyplace else. Besides . . . Zoe . . ."

"Zoe." Grey inhaled deeply. "I guess I couldn't watch her tear a man down, even if he deserved it. It was she I was worried about."

"I think"—Simon laughed a soft bitter laugh—"I've been worried about Zoe since she was a kid. But I think she's stronger than the both of us."

"She would have broken a long time ago if she hadn't been. He's . . . he's in town, you know."

"Brent?"

"Yeah."

"I guess it had to be, Grey. There just was no turning Zoe away. Who knows, maybe if she gets it out of her system once and for all, she'll find a way to be happy."

"You believe that?"

"Whether I do or not, there's not much either of us can do about it. The walls were built for Zoe a long time ago. We both love her and that just wasn't enough. So, I guess she'll have to tear her walls down by herself. Sometimes things are taken out of our hands by something a whole lot more powerful than we are."

Roger heard their words and knew his own guilt, just as he knew he was going to die with the unforgiven sin on his soul. He wished there was a way he could right that wrong done so long ago.

Grey, Simon, and the men with them had dug until their hands were bloody and their strength exhausted. They knew they had made little progress against the barrier between them and the outside. Now they sat quietly, trying to conserve what hope they had left.

"Have any idea how long we've been here?" Grey asked.

"I don't know," Simon answered. "It's hard to tell . . . except"—he chuckled mirthlessly—"I'm hungry as hell and I sure could use a drink. I wonder if it's day or night up there . . . an Aspen night."

"Yeah. One of those nights when you can reach up and touch the stars," Grey said softly.

Both men were caught in memories for a long, quiet moment . . . memories and dreams seemed to be all they had left.

The lack of air made them unable to do more than just stay still, trying to cling to what little remained . . . for as long as it remained.

Outside, hope was waning as well. No one knew better than the crowd gathered there just how slim the possibility was that they would ever see the trapped men alive again.

But Zach, watching Zoe's face grow more and more defeated, would not let the effort to dig them out slacken in any way. Zoe watched both him and Amelia and realized, for the first time in her life, that they possessed something intangible, something she couldn't grasp.

Amelia's words came back to her: You don't bargain with God, Zoe.

Well, if you couldn't bargain with Him, what did you do? Zoe, who had never had the occasion to receive anything without a very high cost, could not quite believe that one could ask without making some kind of deal for payment.

But hope now was a very slim thread to which she clung.

She sat alone, forcing herself not to pace at the entrance of the mine. Huddled with her shawl tight about her, she felt the pain and misery of the loss of Grey and Simon begin to batter the remnants of her pride. She had allowed the only love she had known to slip through her fingers.

Weak, despairing, all hope slowly draining away, Zoe finally turned herself to the final power. This time she opened the doors of her heart.

This time there were no promises, because Zoe knew

she had nothing left to give. This time she was reaching with her very soul toward the final hope.

"Please . . . please don't let them die. Let me make amends for my blindness. Give me one chance to make up for all I've taken. I'm sorry," she whispered as tears blinded her eyes. "I'm so sorry. I cannot stand any more. I need help . . . I need help . . . help me." Her inner cry tore at her.

She had her arms wrapped tightly about herself and was rocking back and forth. To her the time seemed to move with unbearable slowness. The sun was hovering over the mountains. Soon night would be on them again; already they were preparing lanterns and torches to be lit.

Zoe knew that another night, another day would mean the last of the air that they hoped was present where the men were . . . if they were not buried beneath a ton of stone from the avenging mountain itself.

Zoe closed her eyes and prayed over and over again until time had no meaning. Only her reaching for God filled her mind, her heart, and her soul.

Oblivious now to anything but her reaching out, she didn't hear Zach's approach, did not know when he stopped before her and spoke her name. She was not conscious of him until he reached down and took hold of her arms, drawing her to her feet.

She looked up at him through a haze of tears.

"They're dead," she said.

"No. We've just broken an air hole through. They're alive!"

"Oh, God." Zoe almost sagged in a heap as her legs grew weak. "Simon?"

"He's all right, Zoe. So is Grey."

She looked at him more closely and knew. She could feel it twist in the pit of her stomach.

"It's Pa, Zoe. They're bringing him out first. He's dying . . . and he wants to talk to you. He's dying, Zoe . . . there's very little time left. Will you come?"

At any other time Zoe would have felt a wave of delight that the man who had plagued her life was dying. But now, to her surprise, she felt a wave of pity. She had been given the chance she'd prayed for. Now it was up to her to give the same compassion in return. She nodded and followed Zach to the entrance of the mine, where Roger was being very carefully laid on a blanket. She went to his side to kneel beside him.

She had not really believed it was possible that he could die. She had thought him invulnerable, destined forever to haunt her and castigate her. So this great frowning crag of a man was mortal after all. She felt a brief surprise, followed by a shocked awareness of the terrible, haphazard, casual ease with which human life could be snuffed out.

She saw that he was trying to tell her something, groping for her with a wavering hand. She took his hand in both of hers, and his eyes opened and fastened on hers. He was not commanding now, or berating, or even judging. He was pleading and uncertain.

"Zoe . . . Zoe . . ."

"I'm here . . . Pa."

"You . . . you . . . before I die . . . forgive me. If . . . if you can't forgive me . . . how can He . . ."

She could not believe her ears. Could he be wavering in his faith now, here, at the very end of his life? She could not contemplate a world where he could doubt.

"I was too hard on you," he gasped, "because I could not fight the blackness inside me. I have been wrong . . . and I cannot face Him . . . forgive me, Zoe . . . forgive me."

She saw now that it wasn't his faith in his God that had wavered, but his faith in himself, his own worthiness. What a hell he must have lived in all his life, she thought, maybe even a worse hell than the one I lived in.

She knew now that no one could bring him that final comfort but herself, and she had spent her whole life trying to forget what he believed, trying to forget the words he found comfort in.

"I forgive you, Pa. I understand and I forgive you." She sought more words to help. "The Lord is of tender mercy . . ." She recited the words she had heard and never understood.

"Mercy . . ." he gasped between graying lips.

She went on with the words, wondering if you could bring peace with words you had tried to forget. But as they filled Roger, they filled her as well.

"He will not forsake you, Pa," she said gently.

Her voice broke, because she saw that those words would be the last Roger Carrigan would ever hear. She had eased his burden . . . and she had eased hers as well.

She saw a swift tightening of his features, and then a gradual letting go. The thing that had lashed him and driven him was quiet at last. His hand slipped from hers.

Zoe rose from Roger's side, and for a moment brother and sister faced each other. Then Zach took her in his arms and held her.

The two injured miners were the next to be drawn out through the rough hole. Zoe watched closely, and then Grey appeared.

She went to him at once and took his hand in hers.

"Oh, Grey, I'm so glad you are safe. You are all right, aren't you?"

"I'm fine, Zoe. A little bruised, that's all. I'll heal just fine. Your father . . . ?"

"He's gone," she said quietly. Her eyes lifted to his. "You were right, Grey. To forgive him was easier than I thought . . . and I'm free."

"I'm glad for you, Zoe." He could see in her eyes that Zoe had been changed in many ways. He looked into their amber depths and sensed that Zoe had found more than one answer for herself. He gave a mirthless laugh and pulled Zoe into his arms. He wanted to hold her, because he had the shaky feeling it might be for the last time.

She went into his arms willingly, sliding her arms about him and holding him close. She loved Grey in a unique way, and he would always be a source of strength and peace for her.

But Grey, when he held her, knew the embrace was one of shared joy, of contentment and of peace . . . but not the embrace of a woman in love.

He crushed her to him for a long moment, then held her away from him to look down into her eyes. He struggled for a smile. "Simon?" he asked gently.

"I . . . I guess maybe I've always loved him, Grey."

"And I think maybe I always knew it. I just loved you too much to give up easy. You have to follow your heart, Zoe . . . and in a lot of ways I'm happy for you."

This brought new tears, but she smiled through them. "I love you too, Grey. In a very special way."

"I know, Zoe . . . I know." He bent to kiss her good-bye.

Simon had stepped out of the mine at the moment Zoe stepped into Grey's arms. For an instant he felt as if the weight of the heavy rocks in the mine had truly crushed the life from him.

He saw them embrace, and stood frozen. Then he saw their conversation and Grey bending to kiss her. He closed his eyes to gather his strength.

But when he opened them, he saw something it took him a moment to understand. Grey had seen Simon before Zoe. After he kissed her he took her by the shoulders and turned her to face the mine entrance. Then he gave her a light shove toward the man who stood immobile in the darkened hollow of the Future.

He could not believe the reality of what he saw. Zoe moving toward him. Zoe, her face breaking into a joyous smile. Zoe, her eyes alight, running toward him.

He could only speak her name in a ragged whisper and open his arms to her. Crying his name, Zoe threw herself into his arms, saying his name over and over until his mouth silenced hers.

They kissed each other, laughing between kisses. Zoe reached up to touch his face, sobbing out her love.

Simon rocked her in his arms, a joy filling him such as he'd never known. Zoe was his! She was his and he would never let her go again.

Epilogue

Three Months Later

Simon stood at the window, gazing out at the brilliance of a full moon that lit the surrounding area. The past three months since his miraculous escape from the grave had been like a whirlwind.

Because of the harsh reality of disaster, a new kind of concord seemed suddenly possible. Even the mine owners had been affected by the strange malady of new vision. Simon wondered how long it was going to last. At least for now, they were beginning to deal with him and the angry men he represented.

It was fear, he supposed. For one minute the veil had been lifted and they had seen both the near tragedy and the near revolution it could bring. He just wondered how much he could accomplish before greed again overcame the owners.

He thought of all the people whose lives touched his, whose lives had been affected by the cave-in.

Zach and Amelia had endeared themselves to the people of the town with a bonding that would never break.

Emily was the belle of the entire town. She was the daughter of Zoe Carrigan, who had supported the hospital, paid for their doctor, and now, since the near disaster, had made changes in her mines that the people could hardly believe.

Zoe blossomed in warmth of the town's gratitude. She was accepted as she had never been before.

Simon smiled to himself. He had a feeling it was his and Zoe's wedding that had completed Aspen's change of heart toward her. She had married one of their own.

Pete and Gus worked feverishly to keep the miners unified to fight future problems. Cara had enlisted April's help at the restaurant to give her more time with others outside the house that April had almost made a prison. Paul had begun to work with Zach instead of keeping a separate practice, and both men were enjoying their teamwork.

Simon breathed a deep sigh of relief and turned from the window. He had thought Zoe asleep, but he realized when he turned to face her that she had been lying very still, watching him.

Zoe . . . he looked at her now as if he were seeing her for the first time. All the old barriers had been broken, and her gold eyes were often filled with laughter and warmth now. He could actually feel the love that emanated from them. It reached with gentle fingers to wrap itself about him and draw him back to her. He crossed the room and sat down on the bed beside her.

"I didn't mean to wake you," he said quietly, reaching out to thread his fingers through her hair.

"You didn't. What were you thinking?"

"Oh, a lot of things. Mostly what a fortunate man I am." He bent to brush her lips with a gentle kiss. "I guess I was counting my blessings."

Zoe sat up and looped her arms about his neck, drawing him to her to kiss him so deeply that it sent his senses spinning. He gathered her to him and returned the kiss with enthusiasm. Then he laughed a boyishly exuberant laugh.

"What do I owe this reward to? Not that I'm questioning it. I'll accept any you want to throw my way."

"Oh, just being you, I guess. For not giving up on me when I was being so blind . . . for loving me . . . maybe for teaching me to love."

"Zoe." Simon laughed again, hugging her for a minute. "You've had love bottled up in you for years and never a chance to release it. I'm grateful that it was me . . . I thought, for a while . . ."

"That I loved Grey? I do, in a way. I never knew there could be so many ways to love someone. Maybe that's why my life is so full now. I know I don't have to be afraid. I know love can't be selfish, so I'm going to spend every bit of it that I possess before I die."

"Great idea," he said softly, "but it's my turn to be selfish. I'd prefer you to spend as much of it one me as you can spare."

"I can spare a lot, because somehow . . . I always seem to get a new supply every time we're together."

"Zoe, I love you so much. I want everything in your life to be good from now on. I'll do everything in my power to make it that way."

"I suppose I've learned that you must accept the pain as well as the pleasure. But from now on I'll be able to handle anything. You see . . . I have you, and that is enough to make the rest of my world complete."

Simon knew more happiness in that moment than he'd ever known before. As he began to make love to Zoe with gentle hands and sensitive kisses, he vowed that he was going to devote the rest of his life to keeping it this way.

The moonlit room was the only witness to their blending, to the joy that filled it, and the promise that formed within it. This would be forever.

THE LADY'S HAND
BOBBI SMITH
Author of *Lady Deception*

Cool-headed and ravishingly beautiful, Brandy O'Neal knows how to hold her own with the riverboat gamblers on *The Pride of New Orleans*. But she meets her match in Rafe Morgan when she bets everything she has on three queens and discovers that the wealthy plantation owner has a far from gentlemanly notion of how she shall make good on her wager.

Disillusioned with romance, Rafe wants a child of his own to care for, without the complications of a woman to break his heart. Now a full house has given him just the opportunity he is looking for—he will force the lovely cardsharp to marry him and give him a child before he sets her free. But a firecracker-hot wedding night and a glimpse into Brandy's tender heart soon make Rafe realize he's luckier than he ever imagined when he wins the lady's hand.

_4116-2 $5.99 US/$6.99 CAN

WINTER LOVE

NORAH HESS

"Norah Hess overwhelms you with characters who seem to be breathing right next to you!"
—*Romantic Times*

Winter Love. As fresh and enchanting as a new snowfall, Laura has always adored Fletcher Thomas. Yet she fears she will never win the trapper's heart—until one passion-filled night in his father's barn. Lost in his heated caresses, the innocent beauty succumbs to a desire as strong and unpredictable as a Michigan blizzard. But Laura barely clears her head of Fletch's musky scent and the sweet smell of hay before circumstances separate them and threaten to end their winter love.

_3864-1 $5.99 US/$7.99 CAN